– A NOVEL –

HOLY CRUSADE

THE FIRST
ADDISON J. FREEMAN
STORY

– A NOVEL –

HOLY CRUSADE

THE FIRST ADDISON J. FREEMAN STORY

J. J. ZERR

PRIMIX
PUBLISHING
THE WRITE CHOICE

Primix Publishing
11620 Wilshire Blvd
Suite 900, West Wilshire Center, Los Angeles, CA, 90025
www.primixpublishing.com
Phone: 1-800-538-5788

Published by Primix Publishing   02/16/2024

ISBN: 978-1-955177-52-8(sc)
ISBN: 978-1-955177-53-5(hc)
ISBN: 978-1-955177-54-2(e)

Library of Congress Control Number: 2021921661

For my One and Only Squeeze

Thank you, God, for editors,
and for the lavish spenders of red ink in
my Coffee and Critique group.

Note: a list of crusaders is provided in the end matter.

O n a Sunday in March 1858, Addison J. Freeman, the deacon's son,
changed his middle name to Job. Until that Sunday morning,
John had suited that J just fine.

Except for two or three times in his life, during bouts of illness
marked by significant intestinal distress, he'd never had trouble falling
asleep. He spent this entire night, however, rolling from one side to the
other, trying on his stomach, then his back, searching for the elusive
position, the portal into easy darkness and peaceful slumber. This night,
he sank into hopelessness. Sleep would not come. He'd wrestled with
his sheet and quilt and pillow so long he thought it had to be time for
his mother to light the lamps and start breakfast. But no light peeked
around the edges of the blanket strung over his bedroom doorway. Nor
any sound from the kitchen. Ma was quiet in the morning. How she
could fire up the iron woodstove and get coffee going without making
a sound was a mystery, but that's how she did it. For sure, she was out
there.

I'm blind!

The thought hacked through last night's misery. He listened hard.
Still no noises. Except for the wall clock. Tick. Tock. Tick. Tock. He
had to know. Untangling his legs from the sheets, he pushed himself
to his feet and reached for the wall, and then found the blanket and
moved it aside. The curtains over the kitchen windows glowed.

I can see!

Joy flared, then snuffed, like a one-blink lightning bug. He felt his way to the bed and flopped onto it again. It had been too dark to read the clock face. He rolled onto his stomach, pulled his pillow over his head, and pressed it tight against his ears. Tick. Tock.

Without having been aware he had been fighting, he surrendered. He rolled onto his back, and his pillow fell to the floor. It didn't matter.

His anguish, as if angry that mere blindness had held it at bay, re-bloomed with a new intensity. He felt it in his head, in his teeth, in his chest and stomach, and strength drained out of his arms and legs, and he lay there inert and powerless.

Let me die, Lord.

Job. The quintessential sufferer asked for death, too. God denied the prayer. He knew at that moment, The Almighty refused his plea, too. A denial from The Father to heap atop the one from his earthly parent. As with Job, the Lord wanted Addison J. to bear it.

That's when he baptized his middle initial with a new name as old as the Bible.

His mind dredged up last night's supper table.

Since last Sunday, he'd tried to work up the gumption to ask. Being Saturday meant he was out of days that week. Ma was dishing up dessert. A rivulet of sweat trickled down his ribs from his left armpit. He'd glanced across the table and swallowed a big dry mouthful of nothing. "I'm eighteen, marrying age, Pa? Wouldn't that Lizbeth Waverly make a good wife?"

His father looked up from stirring his coffee. Addison could never tell what he'd say by his face. That stony visage hid any emotions simmering in the man, if any did.

"You are not getting married now. When you do, it won't be to any Lizbeth Waverly. Plain girls make the best wives."

It hit him like a slap he didn't see coming. Pa had denied Lizbeth to him as the Lord denied Moses entry into the promised land.

Lying in the pitch blackness, he recalled Moses had lost faith and struck the rock twice.

What did I do, Lord?

No answer.

Then he remembered that time, a few years ago, Preacher Larrimer had spoken about Job. The point of that book in the Bible, he'd said, is not that when you suffer, if you persevere and pray, things will get better. "Not the point at all!" The preacher flat rattled the windows when he told what the point was or was not. "Affliction is an opportunity to repay The Father for the almighty suffering the Son endured for our salvation."

Affliction, suffering, anguish: Those were opportunities and blessings? Addison had not accepted that as gospel. In the years of Sundays and funerals and weddings, he'd listened to Larrimer preach countless words; this was the only lesson he rejected. It worried him. Did disagreeing with a man of God mean disagreeing with the Supreme Being also? He sure couldn't ask Pa or Ma about it, so he'd worried it by himself until time eased it behind him.

He'd forgotten he ever had that worry. Maybe denial of Lizbeth was punishment for disagreeing with Preacher Larrimer. Maybe it had been denying God.

My own dad-burned fault!

Will this ... night ever end?

Light from the kitchen seeped around the edges of the blanket over his doorway. He had just enough strength to lift an arm and drape it over his eyes. Ma was in the kitchen lighting the lamps. The long night had ended. Realization dawned, and he groaned. Job's nights were terrible. His days were worse.

Sunday. He'd hoped; he'd dreamed how it would happen. After services, before dinner, somewhere on the grounds around church, he was with Lizbeth, and he was telling her his father gave his blessing. He dropped to a knee. In the dirt. In his Sunday suit. He took her hands in his. Her blue eyes locked onto his and froze him, and pushed something half physical, half spiritual inside him. What entered him passed through his head and down and melted his insides from his Adam's apple to his belly button. He wanted to ask, but he couldn't speak. Until he gathered himself. And, buoyed on a wave of confidence, he asked her. *Yes,* gloried over her face and in her voice, "Oh, yes, Addison John Freeman."

"Addison John Freeman. Are you in there?"

Coming back to earth took a moment.

"Are you sick?"

His mother shoved the blanket aside. "Why aren't you up?"

He didn't want to answer, but she'd stay until she got one. "I don't want to get up." He rolled on his side, away from her.

In the next instant, his bare butt was sitting on the cold wood floor. He jumped up and hiked his nightshirt down.

"Do I have to dress you too?"

"No, Ma. I'm all right now."

"You are not, but you won't get over Lizbeth moping in bed. Get dressed, do your business, and eat breakfast. Come on."

"What happened last night? After Pa said—"

"Pa ate his pie. You ate one bite of yours. Pa ate the rest. You took a bath and went to bed."

"Wait. Pa let me take the first bath?"

She smiled and for the first time that morning, she looked like his mother. He remembered then. He'd just sat in the shallow tub, and, through the blanket strung across one end of the big room, Pa said, "Don't dawdle. You let that water get cold before I get in, I'll take a willow switch to you." If he'd gotten a switching, he figured he'd remember that.

Ma held up her index finger and left. That finger repeated the "Get dressed." He pulled on his clothes and socks and boots and stepped into the smell of bacon and coffee perking.

On an ordinary day, those aromas triggered a gush of the juice of anticipation over his taste buds. That morning, however, a vinegary and sulfurous dew settled onto his tongue.

Ma stood in front of the stove. She had on her sleep cap, her summer robe over her nightgown, and an apron over that. A spatula in her hand hovered over the black skillet. She looked over her shoulder at him, and his eyes and hers held onto each other for a moment.

Then she returned to the sizzling popping skillet and the eggs frying there. He took a lantern with him to the outhouse.

As he completed his morning business, he thought about Job. No question, bad things happened to the man. He loaded his prayers with complaint and even bitterness. Still, God considered him a good guy and put him in the Bible as an example for how a man should bear adversity. And despite Preacher Larrimer's cut on things, Job had persevered with prayer, and in the end, things got better for him. Better even than they had been at the start of his troubles.

That morning, he hadn't been able to get out of bed by himself because there was no hope the agony he felt would ever go away.

He cleaned the razor and replaced it on the shelf next to the mirror at the good weather wash up and shaving place on the porch. Then he remembered God and Satan and the deal they made. The devil must have worked hard to take away Job's large family and his herds and his riches. To bring down Addison J. Freeman, however, the Evil One wouldn't have had to raise a sweat. All he'd had to take away was Lizbeth, and that before he even had her.

Bed no longer appealed. His stomach wanted nothing to do with food. His eyes did not want his mother looking into them again as they had.

He crossed the lot to the barn, saddled the horse, and returned the lantern to the porch. As he prepared to mount, the door opened, and his mother stepped onto the porch. Backlighted from the kitchen, he could not see facial features. Nor eyes. She held something out to him. He walked over, knowing she wouldn't place her house slippers onto the dirt. He took from her a sandwich wrapped in a flour sack dishtowel.

"Son. Thank God. Even on your worst day ever. Thank Him. Look, and you'll find a reason to."

She went inside. He stood, holding the sandwich and staring at the door. For days on end, she was Ma. Just Ma. Then she'd say something like that, and no matter what filled his head, her words busted through and sat there in his mind, an eleventh commandment fresh chiseled on a flat rock. Her sayings endured. For a long time afterward, he'd recall what she said, consider it, and wind up agreeing with it and taking it in as an idea he owned.

He stuck the bundle in the saddlebag pocket atop the tools and mounted. When he'd been little and Pa'd brought the little horse to the farm, he'd named it Percy the Pony. Addison made a noise that was part cluck, part click, part tsk, and the horse set off, its head bobbing as much as its legs walked. He gigged his heels into the animal's belly, and Percy kicked it up to a canter.

"If walking would do, I'd have left you in the barn."

The dirt road ran straight as a line drawn with a ruler through three other farms all the way to Found Church.

"Thank you, God," he said and appended, "for Percy." So it'd be thanks for something specific and from him, not just words he said because Ma told him to say them.

After a moment, his legs and butt adjusted to the gait. Above, stars, millions of them. No brightening in the east yet. Pastures and hayfields appeared as lakes of silver gray. A cornfield was a dark rectangular box of shadow with sharp sliced sides. Facades of Reedley's house and barn. A whiff of Reedley's sty. *Clippety, cloppety, clippety, cloppety.*

The horse knew where it was going.

Addison drifted back to supper.

Ma was about to serve a slice of cherry pie to his father as Addison posed his question. The response hit him hard, and now he remembered his mother standing there as if she'd been slapped, too. Besides denying Lizbeth to him, Pa's words had insulted his wife in her own kitchen.

Either Ma was pretty and a poor wife or a good wife and plain.

Was she pretty? He'd never thought about that before. Sure as shooting, she was not ugly. Even plain seemed a harsh tag to stick to her, though.

A motion high and to his right pulled his gaze. A falling star.

It hit him, then. Not the star, but the realization that when his mother had peered at him over her shoulder that morning, she was looking for something from him.

And he'd let her down. Last night Pa had not only ruined Addison's life, but he'd also insulted Ma, and he'd failed to stand up for her. That morning, she wanted affirmation from him, and he'd been too stuck on his own woes, too busy wallowing in a sty of oh-woe-is-me-ism.

He was wrong. You're beautiful, Ma.

Stupid. How could a boy say such a stupid thing to his mother?

Then he knew. *No boy is smart enough to pray for a ma like you, and when Pa lets me marry, I hope it's to someone half as good a wife as you and half as beautiful. That will make of me a very blessed husband.*

Why couldn't I think to say that when it'd do some good?

A black ghost shape rushed from the side of the road and lunged at the horse with a ferocious growling and barking. Percy reared. Addison grabbed the saddle horn and stayed on as the horse bolted into a full-out run.

His hat blew off and hung on the string around his neck.

They'd passed the O'Riley brothers' farm. Usually, they kept their wolfhound chained.

As Percy thundered over the road, he tugged on the reins. "Whoa there, Percy. Whoa. Fearsome beast, that dog. Scared the liver right out of me too! Whoa now."

The animal coasted down to a walk. He patted the horse's neck as his own heartbeat slowed from hammering to don't-know-it's-there.

He thought of his friend Maurice Reedley. Folks called him Maurice the wiseacre. He had a story he liked to tell about O'Riley's wolf hound.

> "One day, a traveling salesman and pot mender pulled his wagon into the O'Riley's yard. He knocked on the front door. No answer, so he started walking around the house. He saw the dog lying on the ground but thought it was a discarded muddy rug made of rags. Now the dog was chained to a steel peg in the ground, and it seemed to know its chain was exactly seven yards long. When the stranger stepped within twenty-one feet away, the scraggly matted hair that looked like a rag-rug parted to reveal an eyeball peering out. The man took one more step and that hound exploded like a streak of snarling, snapping black lightning. The salesman jumped back and the dog hit the end of the chain going full out and jerked around from meat-eater teeth first to tail first. That salesman walked to his wagon like a two-year-old

who just gave himself a lesson that potty training might not be too much trouble after all."

Maurice the wiseacre and his stories.

Addison's stomach growled, and he pulled out the sandwich, unwrapped it, and bit off a chunk.

"Bacon and hard fried eggs," he said with his mouthful. "Good as any nosebag of mash you ever ate, Percy."

He swallowed. "Thank you, God, for Ma." Talking to God with his mouth full, that wouldn't have been right at all.

2.

In the meeting house, Addison removed the ashes and laid in kindling and started fires in the oven and wood stoves in the kitchen addition to the meeting house. Next he primed the pump at the sink and filled four buckets with water and set them atop the stove. He lit lanterns and placed them inside the house of worship, then he set about the specific task his father assigned. "Replace the cross."

He climbed the ladder leaned against the front of the building. The cross had the arm busted off. It took but a feather touch to pull the vertical free. The wood at the foot of the cross rotted to sawdust.

Behind him, the sun had gotten around to rising. On the dirt roads cutting through the congregation's farms, a wagon and two buggies headed toward the church. He cocked his head and heard hooves clopping a canter rhythm. From the east, a wagon and a buggy headed toward him. He'd never appreciated it before, but the roads leading to the center of worship were like spokes of a wagon wheel. A circle of scoured-of-grass, packed dirt made the hub on which sat the house of worship and the meeting house.

Atop his ladder, Addison thought his view of Found Church must be akin to the one the angels in heaven had. Well, close enough to get him to wonder what the angels thought of all the wagons and buggies heading down those spokes carrying the half of the women in the congregation with cooking and cleaning duties this morning. Would the angels be pleased that so many women, and the deacon's son, would work hard to prepare for the worship service and the gathering afterward? Or would they tsk disapproval that all this fuss and commotion, by that passel of women and the deacon's son, desecrated the Lord's day rather than preserved its sanctity?

At times, the Bible confused Addison. What it said one place contradicted what it said in another. It never confused Pa nor Preacher Larrimer. He wondered if others of the congregation were ever confused. Perhaps that was the point of Sunday, and the reason to keep it holy. Ordinary people needed a Man of God to keep them straight.

It occurred that half the females worked so the other half could observe Sunday as a day of rest, aside from cooking, tending children, gathering eggs, milking cows. All the men observed it. Half the women did by not washing clothes and cleaning the house. Only the deacon's son did not. Ever and in any way.

He stopped working for a moment, and there was Job again, plopped square in the middle of his head. Job. And Lizbeth. Forbidden, denied, untouchable Lizbeth. But desired as desperately as air to breathe.

Several times during the morning, as he moved around doing his chores, he forgot about her, as if in moving, he ran away from her faster than she could keep up. Then he'd stop, and she'd run in to him, not in to him, but into, inside him, and he'd become aware all over again that she'd melted a hole in his soul.

He sighed around the nails clamped between his lips and looked down. The ground was fifteen feet below, and the rickety ladder was old as the cross he was to replace.

"Daydreaming is the devil's innocent-sounding term for sloth," Pa liked to say as he ripped a green sprig from a tree and slashed it across his son's shoulders. Addison's upper arms were still purple from last week's switching.

After he finished nailing up the new cross, he stowed the ladder and carried two buckets of warm water into the church.

As they did every Sunday, the cleaning ladies swept and dusted and twittered away like a tree full of sparrows bust-a-gut happy that winter was over, and spring was here at long last.   Most of the women didn't notice him, but two married and three younger women thanked him for carrying the water. He wasn't obligated to do that. The women were capable of carrying a bucket of water. But half the time, it got him a few minutes to stare at Lizbeth and to drink in her eyes washing over him. She wasn't there today, though she should have been.

Addison needed to see her, to speak with her, to see for sure if she felt for him what he did for her. If she did, he would ask her to run away with him that night. Lizbeth.

Running away from Found Church community seemed like the earth being flat and running off the end of it. Not running away, being on earth and not having Lizbeth, and her with—

That was worse than falling into oblivion. Worse than hell. It was being Job without his forbearance.

He responded to the married ones who'd thanked him and smiled, and to unmarried ones who'd thanked him and blushed, and he saw it for the first time. The Sunday morning cleaning and cooking were not chores but an opportunity to enjoy female talk. In their labor, they found joy. Addison found the surety he would never know such. Lizbeth was not there. Only illness or betrothal excused a young woman from Duty Sunday.

He closed the outside door and leaned against it.

People came to church on Sunday to find salvation. Grace. All he'd found so far were two of the deadly sins. Sloth on the ladder and envy, coveting another man's wife before they were even married, and these sins committed in the house of God.

As he left to chop more firewood into kindling, he pushed his mind back to the view he'd had from the ladder. Found Church sat in the hub of a wagon wheel and the angels of the Lord looked down on wagons and buggies full of worshipers traveling toward the center for their weekly renewal of their grip on God's grace. Addison had lost his grip. Could he Find it again?

The rest of the morning, he went through his chores, determined to stay clear of the other five deadlies. It worked until a half hour before services when his father parked the buggy, and his mother handed him his suit, and he entered the room at the back of church where brides put on their gowns of purity. There, with one of his legs in one pants leg, it hit him. Not being able to have Lizbeth wasn't the worst of it. She would use that room. She would march down the aisle on the arm of her father, and he would give her to another man. And she would give her purity to that *other*.

Despair, which, last night, had seemed as dark and deep as it could get, found a new bottom. And it petrified him for a moment, until rage burst, sudden and full-blown. The picture of Lizbeth's husband had no face, but it had arms. That those arms could embrace her purity infuriated Addison with the strength of Goliath. He would rip that man's arms from his shoulders. The intention to do that got his pants on and buttoned. An instant later, his wrath sputtered out with the realization his vengeance had no real target. Ebbed wrath left him filled with profound weariness.

Ma's instructions from that morning: *Get dressed. Do your business.* Those instructions put his strength-less puppet limbs into motion. His business amounted to walking down the aisle to the first pew on the right.

Fifteen rows of benches with backs, sliced by an aisle down the center, took up most of the floor. In front of the pews, a raised platform two steps high, accommodated two podiums and two chairs, one each for the deacon and the preacher, and a table between the podiums. The table hosted The Remembrance, the breaking of the bread.

Larrimer was in his chair. Once he sat there, whether it be prior to Sunday services, or a Saturday wedding, or a funeral for a congregant who died from an illness, from difficulties during childbirth, or from being kicked in the head by a horse, silence reigned in the house of the Lord until the preacher booted it out.

Addison and his mother occupied the first pew on the side facing the preacher's podium. Mrs. Larrimer occupied the first pew on the side facing the deacon's furniture. Ma was not there yet. The only other worshipers in place were the Reedley family, who always arrived first.

He sat, closed his eyes, and willed the reverent silence to seep into him and fill his head with its blessed emptiness. And it did. Until Ma's hand on his shoulder startled him, and he found Pa's eyes skewering him.

That meant a switching for falling asleep in church. But today, that didn't matter much.

Behind him, boots, some big and heavy, some small and light, clumped on the wooden floor. Clothing rustled. A pew squeaked. A baby fussed. The mother shushed. Little lips slurped. Mother had given the baby a finger to suck.

Beside him, Ma looked up at Preacher Larrimer. Pa also looked at him, as did Addison. The preacher sat statue still, and stillness, like that between a tick and a tock, filled the church. Then Larrimer stood, raised his arms and face to heaven, and cut loose.

"Almighty Father God in Heaven, we have come together on Your Holy Day, to join our prayer of thanks for your greatest of blessings, grace. Thank You for this gift. Thank You for guiding us to it. Thank You for opening our hearts to let it in. We, together, lift our humble thanks, All Powerful Lord of heaven and earth." He lowered his arms and bowed. "It is what we have to offer."

Pa nodded to Ma. She raised her pitch pipe, blew the note, and the women and girls in the pews launched into the opening hymn.

In Found Church, only females sang. Neither curse words, liquor, nor tobacco had corrupted their voices—according to the preacher—and thus, their voices were as pure as angels'.

As the heavenly choir sang, Larrimer closed his eyes, and his face, not known to smile except on Sundays, transformed into a mien of holy delight. Pa closed his eyes, too.

That's when Addison could turn for a glance of Lizbeth Waverly across the aisle and two rows behind. The last several Sundays, she glanced back and smiled, just for him, as she lifted her distinct, clean, clear, pure soprano gently above the altos and more timid in her range. Her **voice** rode on the shoulders of the choir all the way to heaven because of its sweetness. As the preacher's deep rumble did because of the volume.

Today her voice was pure and sweet as always, but she didn't smile or sneak a look at him.

Addison faced forward. His chin sank to his chest and stayed there until the song ended.

Rake-handle thin, tall, and straight, Larrimer stood behind his podium and gripped the sides. His chin-strap whiskers framed a stern visage of sharp-cut jaw, a nose just long enough to hold up his spectacles, bushy black eyebrows over dark eyes, that, when they settled on Addison, made him squirm.

"We. Have found. Grace!"

Each Sunday, the preacher surprised Addison. How could such a booming voice issue from a mere stick of a man?

"But does blessed grace long abide in the heart of a man unless he works to keep it there? No!"

Addison winced at the *no.*

"Retaining God's gift of grace takes a committed daily, hourly, and even a minute-by-minute effort to fight Satan working ceaselessly to drag *you*—"

The preacher's fierce gaze ceased sweeping over the congregation and settled on Addison, as if there, he had found a soul besmirched with the very sins his hard voice condemned.

"—and make no mistake, Satan does work tirelessly to drag *you* into complacency and then, indifference. With indifference, Grace, which once was yours, will depart, and you will be lost. Again. And maybe forever."

The preacher shifted his gaze to Ma and nodded. Addison inhaled, as if he'd just popped up after swimming under water for a long time. Ma piped a note, and the women and girls in the pews behind him sang "Amazing Grace."

When the song ended, Pa moved to his deacon podium and read from the Good Book. Addison paid no attention. He'd read and heard all the words before, but the word "abomination," after it had been repeated a couple of times, cut through his wide-awake dream of loss and longing and living in a place worse than hell.

Pa was reading every passage that listed something as an abomination. He'd marked the pages with slips of paper. The list of that type of sin, especially loathsome to the Lord God Almighty, droned on in the deacon's put-a-man-to-sleep monotone. When his father snapped the

Bible shut, it startled Addison. And it announced what came next—a righteous indignation sermon.

His father moved as slow as an arthritic hound back to his chair, and the preacher inched toward his podium. Silence returned to fill every corner of Found Church. Larrimer stood still for a long moment. Then he blew the silence to smithereens.

"Abomination!"

Addison's friend, Maurice Reedley, sat three pews behind him. He imagined the wiseacre saying, "Clear across the state of Illinois, somebody on a paddle-wheeler on the Mississippi just looked up and said, 'Abomination? Who said abomination?'"

That morning, slavery was an abomination, even though, in the deacon's reading the litany of especially despicable sins, slavery had not been mentioned.

"But as surely as the sun rises in the east, slavery is now, in our nation, in our time, the greatest *abomination*," the preacher thundered, then softened, "If that is so, why doesn't the Holy Bible list it as such?"

Addison had no answer to the question. He was sure no one else in the congregation did either, even Maurice, the wiseacre.

The preacher spelled it out for his flock: "When Jesus walked the earth and said such things as, 'The meek shall inherit the earth,' and, 'Why do we deal treacherously, each against his brother?' Men and women of that time had no experience behaving the way the Son of God intended. Now though, for almost two thousand years, there have always been some of us who strive to live according to the teachings He gave us.

"And, those of us blessed, who have found grace and opened our hearts to it, we are obliged to serve as an example to our brothers and sisters less enlightened than we.

"Accordingly, as God Almighty gives me the power to discern it, the path of righteousness for Found Church leads to—"

Addison's hands moved from his lap to grip the edge of the bench.

"*Kansas!*"

The preacher's booming voice had filled the church, ruled it. Now, profound silence ruled.

Kansas? Was he suggesting the congregation move to Kansas?

First, one had to cross the state of Illinois, with a goodly number of rivers to ford or ferry over. Then there was the mighty Mississippi. Addison knew the geography from the schooling provided by his mother and Mrs. Larrimer in the meeting house. The mightiest of rivers was deep and wide and ferries operated in only a few spots. But the real challenge for Christian people traveling west came after they crossed and headed away from the Mississippi: The farther west you traveled, the farther you entered into a heathen land populated by savages, murderers, thieves, and immoral women. Why would the preacher want to take them into that? Where temptation to leave the state of grace abounded?

"Kansas is not yet a state." Larrimer's voice flat jerked a man out of a daydream and plopped him hard on the pew and into here and now. "But soon it will be. Its citizens will vote to enter the Union as a free state, or a state promoting and sanctioning and harboring the *abomination of slavery.* Tomorrow, some of us will load furniture and tools on wagons. Tuesday morning, we strike out west on a holy pilgrimage.

"A holy crusade."

Pull out on Tuesday?

"Half of us will travel to Kansas, and there we will build New Found Grace Church. Half of us will stay behind and sell our property. Once that is done, they will rejoin us, and we will all become citizens of Kansas, and we will vote against the *Abomination!*"

He named the families to go and those to remain. Addison and his parents were going to Kansas. Lizbeth and hers would not. Then, Larrimer was done talking. He stood behind the podium, a towering thunderstorm, one moment full of flashing fire and explosions. Now, still towering and black and full of threat, but all out of thunder and lightning.

The preacher, with the deacon close behind, walked down the aisle and out.

The look on Ma's face said she hadn't known Kansas was their future. Addison turned around. Stunned looks sat on all the faces. Did the preacher's wife know? Did Pa? Then he noticed Lizbeth's father. He knew. When Sylvan Waverly looked into Addison's eyes, it was certainty. The man knew. And Lizbeth, beside her father, stared straight ahead. She knew, too.

Addison had never been farther than thirty miles from home, and that only once, and never thought about leaving, except that morning when he thought about leaving with Lizbeth.

No final song that day. Other Sundays, services ended with the choir singing "The Happy Land of Canaan."

Found Church had been the promised land. The preacher said Addison had to leave it. Without Lizbeth, there wouldn't have been anything to be happy about staying. There was nothing to be happy about leaving either.

Glory Hallelujah! thought Addison Job Freeman.

"Son."

Ma stood in the aisle. With her lacey white Sunday bonnet, there was something little girl about her. "We have work to do," she said and walked out.

After-services dinner would go on, apparently, just as if it were any other Sunday.

There was work to do, and he should have gone with Ma to help. But he stayed. Lizbeth would be there in the gathering hall. Maybe Mister Waverly had already promised her to someone else.

Addison left the building, skirted it on the side away from where the congregation gathered, and walked home. He didn't want to wade through the people to get Percy. Pa would tie the pony to the back of the buggy. If he didn't, it didn't matter.

3.

The list of Kansas-bound crusaders included twelve families, plus wives and children, plus the bachelor O'Riley brothers. A couple of the families included young men who would be of voting age if the vote wouldn't be held for a couple of years. In all, thirteen wagons, plus a few cows, plus a couple of dogs, including the O'Riley's wolfhound.

That Tuesday morning, Preacher Larrimer scheduled a 7 a.m. service in the church and departure on the journey an hour later.

Pa'd left early because of his deacon duties, leaving Addison and Ma to finish loading the wagon. Which turned out to be a bigger job than it had looked to be the night before. It was ten to seven when Addison trundled the Freeman wagon into the lot around the church.

The way Larrimer had said to park, the stay-behind families were to park with their teams headed east while the departing crusaders were to park their wagons with the tongues pointing west. Then, at the conclusion of the service, the travelers would exit the church, climb onto their transport, snap the reins, and be on their way.

A quick count of the wagons pointing east told Addison all the stay-behind families were represented.

Lizbeth. Maybe he'd get a last look at her.

Only three wagons pointed west. None of them had a team hitched to it. Maurice Reedley rode his saddle bronc around the meeting house, up to the Freeman wagon, and tipped his hat to Ma.

"Ma'am," he said. "Pa says he bets it's noon time before we get underway. He told my brother Robert and me to meet the wagons as they came in and take the teams and animals to graze on Fishboch's meadow." He hooked a thumb back in the direction from which he'd come. "Paw says on this journey, any chance you get to feed the animals, you best take it."

"What time did your paw really say?" Ma said.

"Uh, well, ten. He said ten."

"You probably wonder why folks call you Wiseacre, don't you?"

"Yessum. It's a right puzzlement why they stick that brand on me."

As Addison swung the team around, three more wagons entered the lot all rattling and with trace chains jangling. Otto Vogelsang, Royal Howard, and Gallant Argyl.

"I'll help with the teams, Maurice," Addison said.

"Go on inside. If I need help, Otto's boys will give it."

Otto's two oldest were in the close-to-voting-age bunch.

Ma started walking toward the church.

Maurice, with a big grin smeared all over his face, waved to Addison. To the wiseacre, the Holy Crusade was a great adventure. Addison wasn't sure what lay ahead, but what he could imagine of it filled him with trepidation.

Inside, Addison found Lizbeth's father sitting in the Waverly pew by himself. Then he noted none of the stay-behind women and children were there.

Addison settled onto his spot in the front pew and, as they always did, his eyes went to Preacher Larrimer, seated in his chair. Today the preacher stared at the opposite wall of the church as if he was mad at that wall.

Behind him, the last three arrival families clumped in and settled on their pews. Seven of the twelve families, he figured. Then, it seemed like forever before anyone else made that entry racket. When a family finally did, the temptation to check his watch and turn around and identify the late comer was as insistent as his longing for Lizbeth. If he did either, Pa would see, and either would earn him a switching.

"In church," Pa liked to say, "time don't matter. Time is in the hands of the preacher."

Time passed, but not by ticks of a clock, rather by palpable anger mounting drip by drip like rain through a leak in the roof. He had counted the families straggling in. One more to go. He was sure.

Larrimer sat in his chair, unmoving, except for his jaw as he ground his teeth.

Joshua Reedley, in the pew behind Addison, left the church and returned a few minutes later.

Finally, the door opened. Boots and shoes pecked at the wood floor. Petty coats rustled. Then silence filled the church, so thick and heavy it seemed to push the air out.

A red-faced Larrimer rose, and Addison sucked in a deep breath as the preacher moved to the podium. In one simple sentence, he thanked the Lord for grace. Pa, Deacon Freeman, read about the Israelites departing Egypt. Then the preacher named Sylvan Waverly Second Deacon and placed him in spiritual and physical charge of the stay-behinds. Larrimer asked the Lord to bless their holy crusade, said, "Amen," and walked down the aisle and out the door.

Was that it? Was it over? Addison had never witnessed such an abbreviated service in Found Church before. And this one to launch a holy crusade? He turned around. Most of the congregation gawked at his father in his deacon chair. His father, it was clear, didn't know what to do either.

Joshua Reedley and his wife filed out. "Josh Reedley," folks said, "Had an uncommon amount of common sense."

The rest of the congregation sat there, struggling, Addison thought, to believe what their eyes had seen. The sound of a wagon rattling out of the churchyard entered the church. Giant Otto Vogelsang stood and herded his wife and sons and daughters out of their pew. That spurred the other crusaders into motion.

Addison followed his father and mother. He was the last crusader to walk out, and as he passed the second pew, Second Deacon Sylvan Waverly, Lizbeth's father, stared at him. Sneered more like it. *What did that mean?* It didn't matter. Not like Lizbeth's absence mattered. He'd wanted to say goodbye to her. But hours of sitting on the hard pew, waiting for the tardy travelers to show up, had dulled the ache over her not being there.

In the lot outside, the Freemans found their team hitched. Addison's father rode his saddle horse. Addison drove the team with his mother beside him on the bench and Percy tied behind. As they left the churchyard, he turned and found Second Deacon Waverly standing in the doorway watching them depart. None of the stay-behind men had left. Was Waverly watching to make sure the crusaders were all leaving before addressing the men? The men of *his congregation*. Well, Second Deacon wasn't his concern. Eating dust as the tail-end wagon was. He had to do some talking to get Ma to tie his bandana over her nose.

They made two hours before Mort Nielson wanted to stop. The last arriver and his family had not had breakfast. They were starving. Larrimer halted the train and got it moving again three and a half hours later.

Late that afternoon, the wagon train came to a grassy meadow next to a stream. "Overnight here," rolled down the line. Ahead, wagons turned left and found places. Pa told Addison to park next to the preacher. Which he did.

As he unhitched the team, Addison heard Solomon Adler complain to the preacher. "Nielson got us off late and stopped early. Make an example of him. Send him back."

"We will need his vote when we get to Kansas."

"With him slowing us down, it'll be 1870 before we get there," Adler said.

"We'll make more miles tomorrow."

"For that to be so, you have to talk to him, Preacher."

"If you feel so strongly about it, Solomon, you talk to him."

Addison unhitched the team and led them to the stream. As the horses bent their necks and their noses rippled the smooth surface, a commotion arose from among the wagons.

Mort Nielson and Solomon Adler had gotten into a fistfight. Joshua Reedley broke it up, and Larrimer called the traveling half of his congregation to assemble for prayers. His message rolled like thunder: "On our Holy Crusade, we will be faced with many difficulties before we reach Kansas. In this blessed enterprise, we are brothers and sisters, and we'll help each other through these difficulties. Tomorrow the wagons roll out early and travel until late."

The women sang a hymn, and the preacher dismissed his flock to prepare their suppers as the bottom of the sun kissed the horizon.

In the twilight, the children found a patch of raspberries and gorged on them, after which, the squirts afflicted a good number. The next morning, many of the women had clothing to scrub, and the train did not get underway until midmorning. During the second day on the road, the crusade made more miles than on the first. But not many more.

Thursday morning, as they were about to set out, with the sun fully up, Albert Fishboch discovered a cracked wheel spoke. Still, on their third day of travel, they made more miles than on the second. But not many more.

The responsibility for waking the crusaders and inspiring timely readiness to move rested with Addison's father, First Deacon Freeman.

On Thursday evening, Addison and Maurice Reedley walked to the out no-house house, as the wiseacre called it, before dusk gave way to dark. His friend looked around to see if anyone was within earshot. "Nobody listens to your pa. He goes to a wagon, tells them to get a move on, and when he goes to the next one, those at the first do whatever they please. Without livestock or crops to concern them, they are like a houseful of kids getting ready for school without a ma to prod them."

Addison knew it for truth. He'd seen it too. It took a wiseacre to put it into words, though.

Friday morning, things changed.

On Friday morning, still pitch dark in the east, two horseshoes clanging together rousted the Holy Crusaders from sleep. Between *whang, whang, whangs,* Joshua Reedley hollered, "Get dressed and come to the preacher's wagon. Hurry." *Whang, whang, whang!*

As men and boys and women and girls headed off to the bushes, Preacher Larrimer and First Deacon Freeman intercepted them. The women were allowed to take the children for their morning business. The men, young and old, including Addison, were herded together, and the preacher climbed up onto the driver's box of his covered wagon.

"Men, we are not a holy crusade. We are a disorganized rabble wandering aimlessly in the desert. We do not have forty years to get to Kansas if we are to make a difference in the battle against the abomination of slavery. I have appointed Joshua Reedley as wagon master. He will deliver us to our destination. All of us will listen to him, and all of us, including me, will obey his orders. Brother Joshua, climb up."

The wagon master was black-haired, broad-shouldered, clean-shaven, and a handful of inches shorter than the preacher. He stepped onto the front wheel axle hub, and up and into the driver's box, turned, and spoke at the upturned faces.

"Look east."

Sullen mumbling rose above the shuffling of feet.

"East, I said!" His bellow mowed through the still half-asleep morning like an angel's flaming sword. "Half of you don't even know where the sun is coming up. Preacher Larrimer was dead wrong."

Addison's mouth dropped open. From his spot near the rear of the wagon, he couldn't see the preacher. *Why was he allowing Reedley to spout … heresy?*

"No," Reedley thundered. "The people of this wagon train are not a disorganized rabble. Each one of us is *Judas!* We have erected an altar to worship the deadly sin of sloth, and we are stabbing Preacher Larrimer and this Holy Crusade in the back."

Reedley let that one stew for a moment. After a disastrous first day, on the second and third, the crusaders had milled about just like Maurice said.

"At this time of morning, there is plenty of light to travel. Instead of traveling, we waste a big chunk of daylight before we roll." Reedley announced that the wagon train would pull out in one hour. Breakfast would be ham and biscuits to be eaten once the wheels were turning. "Mrs. Larrimer has coffee brewing. Bring your own cup if you want some. Don't dawdle over it, and do not go back for a second. In one hour, I'll holler, 'On to Kansas!' You do *not* want to be the man whose wagon is not ready to roll. And it'll be the same from now on. From get up to giddy up, all of us, women, children, all of us hustle. And you men are responsible to get your families hustling, not Deacon Freeman or me. From now on, first light will see us on the road."

Men hustled off to the bushes and hustled back. The wagon master was everywhere hollering at anyone moving too slowly or doing unimportant tasks. Reedley directed his oldest son, Robert, to help Larrimer, and Mrs. Reedley aided the preacher's wife putting out the fire and stowing the coffee pot. Maurice prepared the family wagon and tied the two cows behind.

When the train was almost ready, Joshua told Maurice and Addison to stick close to him. Then he ordered his oldest son Robert and Oscar Wilson, nineteen and twenty, to pick out the two best saddle horses and ride back to the Found Church settlement with the list of provisions he'd drawn up. He didn't say the preacher had put too much faith in "The Lord will provide," but Addison thought his list said it. Two wagons with teams and four extra teams as well, and four saddle horses, and each animal sound and sturdy. Cured meat. Canned vegetables packed in straw. Axle grease. Powder and shot and a dozen handguns.

Oscar and Robert both wore holstered pistols, as did Joshua Reedley. He told the two to push their broncs hard. They should be back to Found Church settlement by noon. "Get the second deacon to help. Fill the list. Get two more twenty-year-olds to come back with you, like the Niedlinger boy. One other who'll be old enough to vote next year. Orson Seiling, maybe. Don't dawdle. Coming back, push the horses, but not so hard they won't be good for anything but eating." He gave Oscar a hand-drawn map of the route he would follow. "Skedaddle."

The two men galloped toward dawn.

Addison frowned at Maurice. "You Reedleys eat horse?"

"Sure," said Maurice with so much earnestness and so much *as God is my witness* slathered on his face it practically dripped off him. "All the time."

"We all might before this trip is over." The wagon master handed Addison a musket. "Tie a cord to it and hang it across your back like Maurice has his."

"No!"

The three of them stood in the road by the preacher's wagon. All turned.

The first deacon strode toward them. "You're teaching these young men that wearing a gun is no different than wearing a hat or a coat. That's a sin against God and this Holy Crusade!"

"Deacon Freeman." Reedley's voice was reasonable, pacifying.

"First Deacon!" Larrimer's voice blasted argument to smithereens. "You do not want to be the man." The preacher kept charging forward and the deacon stepped back. "Whose wagon is not ready to roll. Is your wagon ready?"

Addison winced to see his father slink away, shrunken by shame.

When the teams were hitched, and wagons lined up, Reedley asked the preacher to say the morning prayer. "You got one minute."

Larrimer stood in the driver's box of his wagon in the center of the train. He raised his face and arms to the sky, now almost wiped of stars. "Father God in heaven," the preacher's voice filled the wilderness, but not, Addison thought, like he filled Found Church back—well, it wasn't home anymore. "Look down on Your servants here below, bless our poor efforts so that we may serve Your holy purp—"

Reedley stood in his stirrups and cut him off with, "On to Kansas!"

Addison didn't look at his watch, but he was sure the train pulled out pretty close to Reedley's sixty minutes.

Mrs. Reedley snapped the reins to her lead-wagon team, and it stepped out. "Heyups!" sounded down the line, as did a *Moo* from a cow unhappy to be jerked into walking at the ungodly hour. Startled cooped chickens squawked.

The wagon master posted Addison and Maurice astride saddle horses beside the road. As the teams clop, clopped past them, they were to note wheels squeaking a need for axle grease.

His ma drove the last wagon. As it rumbled past, she smiled at her son. Pa's job was to ensure no one straggled. He walked his saddle horse on the other side of the road next to Ma's team. He wouldn't look at his son.

As the wagons pulled away from them, Reedley rode up to the boys. "How many wagons need axle grease?"

Maurice answered, "Six."

"Which six?"

Addison ticked off family names on his fingers.

Reedley humph-ed and reined his mount around to trot after the wagons.

"Did I get them wrong?" Addison asked.

"Nope," Maurice said. "You got them all just right. My pa, you got to learn to read his humphs. That one meant we done good."

Addison tried a humph of his own and decided his needed practice.

Maurice, with Addison a length behind, set off to catch up with his father.

The train rattled and jangled along a well-used dirt road lined with woods and occasional cleared fields, fenced pastures, and lonely farmhouses with barns to keep them company.

They caught up to the wagon master and trotted alongside him. The sun was up some and laid a whispered promise on Addison's shoulders under his dark shirt: *It's gonna' be a hot one today.*

They passed a farm, and dogs set up a ferocious barking and howling. The breeze carried a whiff of a just manured field to them.

The road entered a tree-walled canyon.

"Listen," Reedley said. "What do you hear?"

Addison glanced at Maurice, but it didn't look like he would respond.

"Listen," Reedley repeated.

Behind them, the dogs had gone quiet. They were far enough ahead of the wagons they couldn't hear them. There was the *clop, clop, clop.* That was too obvious.

"Listen."

Addison cocked his head. He frowned. "The bugs and birds?"

The wagon master humph-ed and reined up.

"You boys are our scouts. Keep your mounts to a trot. Ride down the road for forty-five minutes. Then find us a place with grass and water. We'll stop there and grease axles. Maurice," he handed his son an ax, "cut us a pole to hoist a wagon bed."

Reedley reined around to rejoin the train.

Maurice checked his watch and stuck it in his pocket. Both boys turned to check the sun. Then they set off, side-by-side.

"What did that humph mean?"

"Why that meant, most of the time you are exactly as dumb as you look. But not always."

Addison ripped his hat off and swatted Maurice across the shoulder.

Maurice laughed out loud, and then rode on with a smile on his face.

Addison cocked his head and listened.

The bugs and birds had gone silent.

Humph.

4.

Maurice and Addison walked their horses over a three-yard wide, stone-bottomed ford in foot-deep water. Sunlight sparkled in the ripples. The clear stream gurgled, and the sound reminded him of a time Ma had sent him to check on his baby sister. He'd eased open the door to her room. She was awake, unaware of him, and seemed like she had just discovered she had hands and fingers. She cooed and gurgled. Happy.

That's the way he remembered her. Happy.

But as always happened, thinking of his sister, Allison, released dammed up other memories and thoughts.

Ma must have been fond of "A" names ended with "ison." What would she have called a third child?

He was happy for Allison that she'd had a moment so rich with simple joy in her short life.

He wondered if he'd ever experienced a time, or times, like that.

Ma had. He'd seen her with Allison.

Pa had not. That was a sure thing.

And how could a string of memories begin on such a happy note and always smash to pieces on Pa?

Allison had been such a happy, healthy baby. Then, that morning when she was three months old, Ma woke Addison with her screaming. Ma found Allison in her cradle, dead.

"God's will," Pa'd said, and he wrapped Allison in her blanket. He told Ma to fix breakfast, Addison to take the cradle out to the shed, and he buried the little girl behind the barn.

Maurice's, "This'll do," jerked Addison back to here and now.

"What?"

Maurice nodded to the swath of knee-high grass alongside the stream. "Graze for the animals while they grease the wheels. Just what Paw ordered."

"So, we just wait here until they catch up?"

"We'll wait, but we won't *just* wait."

The wagon master's son stripped the saddle and rubbed his horse down with the saddle blanket and spread it on the grass to dry. The deacon's son followed suit. He stood up after hobbling his mount and found his friend with a hand cupped behind an ear.

From across the stream squirrels chattered. Taking their muskets, they followed the noise to a big old hickory with a passel of the "tree rats," his friend called them, up in the top branches. Addison unslung his musket and fired, as did Maurice. *Boom, boom.* Two furry bodies crashed down through the branches. Some skittered away. A few froze hunkered flat against a limb. Maurice fired a second time while he was still reloading. Another hit. A moment later, b*oom, boom.* Maurice killed three with three shots. Addison killed two, one shot for each.

"Five," Maurice said. "Enough for supper for my family. The critters will come back. Then we'll get your family fed."

"You sure reloaded fast," Addison said.

"Pa had all of us practice loading fast Sunday and Monday and again each night since we left. 'Liable to come in handy,' he said."

On the way back to the clearing, Maurice picked out a wagon-bed-hoisting sapling. After they returned to the horses, Addison set to work gutting the squirrels and Maurice took the ax to chop down the lever pole. After removing the innards from each animal, Addison wrapped the carcasses in the ground cloth he'd had rolled and tied behind his saddle; then he helped Maurice carry the hoisting lever to the clearing.

After dropping the sapling next to the pile of intestines, Maurice took the axe and loosened the dirt and Addison used his belt knife to scrape out a guts-burial trench.

As he scraped, Addison asked Maurice if he knew why the preacher had appointed his father the wagon master that morning.

"Sure. Mrs. Larrimer told him to." Maurice dropped a handful of squirrel guts in the hole. "Guts attract flies. You don't close your mouth, you'll have a bug lunch." The wiseacre laughed. Then he explained it was women who came up with the idea.

"Your own ma talked to mine, and together they went to Mrs. Larrimer about the Holy Crusade's lack of progress."

Maurice laughed. "Your mouth's hangin' open again."

Addison closed his mouth.

Maurice said, "Honest to God truth. I heard my maw tell Paw. Your ma and mine went to Mrs. Larrimer and told her that at the rate they were traveling, they'd never get to Kansas in time to make a difference with their votes—the men's votes. They talked about things and settled on a solution.

"Then Mrs. Larrimer laid into the preacher something fierce. She told him if Moses had had any sense at all, he'd have appointed the right man as leader, and the Israelites would have found the promised land in forty days, rather than forty years. She told him to appoint Joshua Reedley as the leader on the trail."

"It's obvious your pa knows what he's doing and the rest of us don't." Addison used the side of his boot to move dirt over the entrails. "Why didn't he say something before we left?"

"Pa don't put himself forward." Maurice stood and scooted more dirt into the trench.

Addison watched the wagon master's son walk toward the stream. Then he followed, knelt beside him in the mud, and washed the slime and gore from his hands.

"Sounds like your ma is more master than your pa."

"Ask him. That's what he'd say. Or he'd say your own ma should be boss. She's the one started it all."

You just didn't get the last word on the wiseacre.

*****

The scouts stood beside the road, short of the ford, their mounts saddled. Joshua Reedley dismounted next to them. Maurice traded horses with his father. The wagon master pulled a notebook from a shirt pocket, handed it to Addison, and directed him to list the grown men in the crusade with a separate page for each. Under the man's name, he was to write the names of the man's wife and children.

"By the time we get across Illinois, I need to know what I can count on from each person."

Addison sat cross-legged in the grass and penciled names. Royal Howard rode up and dismounted. He directed the wagons needing axle grease to one side of the road and the rest to the other with room in the middle for traffic to pass.

The wagon master sat his horse with his back to the ford and watched Royal.

As the last wagons pulled into their stations, Mort Nielson and Solomon Adler set off into the woods with shovels. They'd been assigned latrine duty for fighting the day before, and their job was to dig holes for Maurice's "house-less-outhouses."

The first order of business: water the thirteen teams, the eight cows, and the twenty saddle horses and then tether them to graze. Between the men and women, married and unwed, and the older boys and girls, there was plenty of labor to see to the animals. Royal strode down the line of wagons, urging haste and efficiency.

Addison finished his task, stuck the notebook in a pocket, and went to help the preacher with his team, but Larrimer waved him away. The shepherd would be an example to his flock. From where he stood, he could see his parent's wagon. Pa, instead of unhitching his team, wagged a finger in Ma's face. Addison ran to them.

Pa hollered, "You will never sneak behind my back to Mrs. Larrimer again. Ever. You hear me, woman?"

"Pa, we have to water the team."

"Boy. You best remember your place in this family and in this congregation."

"Deacon!" Joshua Reedley stood in the road, hands on his hips, and glaring at Freeman, all slicked up in his go-to-church suit. Even Preacher Larrimer wore work clothes that morning.

"Addison," the wagon master said. "Help your ma unhitch and tend the team. Freeman, you come with me."

"I will not!"

Reedley moved fast, grabbed Pa's upper arm, and shoved him up the road. The wagon master was a couple of inches above the deacon's five-eight. Reedley also outweighed the other by a good forty pounds. Pa looked like a misbehaving boy in the grip of an out-of-patience parent.

Addison started down the road to help Pa. His mother stopped him.

"We will do as the wagon master said."

They unhitched the team. Addison, with a hand on the cheek strap of each horse, walked them toward the stream. Ma trailed, leading the saddle horse by the reins. The team sensed they were moving toward water. They pulled against Addison's restraint.

"*Hoooo*," he cooed. "We're going to water. *Hoooo*, Wally. But we will walk. *Hooo,* Willy."

Pa always lit into him when he talked to the horses. "Dumb animals, same as boys, need whipping more than talking to." Pa said that, but not when Ma could hear.

As they passed the rear of Larrimer's wagon, Addison saw Pa and the preacher facing each other.

Pa said, "We were a holy crusade yesterday. We had prayer three times a day. Today we are a heathen enterprise. Today, you're not even dressed like a man of the cloth. All because you," Pa aimed accusation with a finger, "listened to the women."

"Turn around!" the preacher commanded.

Pa jerked as if he'd been slapped. Larrimer grabbed his arm and forced him to face the wagon.

"Keep walking," Ma said.

Addison did, and he continued to soothe Wally and Willy against the harsh words flying from close by. He looked across Wally.

Larrimer sliced his pocketknife blade up, ripping Pa's black coat apart. Then he tore the halves of the coat off his father.

"Keep walking," Ma said again.

"Adolph Freeman, this is, in part, my fault. I meant to talk to you this morning about your suit, but there didn't seem to be time. Fogive me, Father God in heaven. I should have made the time. You, Adolph Freeman. You have clasped the deadly sin of pride to your bosom. It has corrupted your soul with decay. You will strip off your white shirt and take it, and your black coat, to the men greasing axles. You will give them as rags to them to clean their hands."

They passed the preacher's wagon, Addison between the team and Ma between Willy and the saddle horse.

"You all right?" Ma said.

They walked on. Addison didn't answer right away. Then, "The sins of fathers are visited upon sons. I knew that. I didn't know the shames of my father would be visited on me too."

They got the horses to the creek. The animals bent to their drinking.

"I hated seeing Pa shamed," Addison said. "I wanted to help him. In the end of it, though, maybe I was being selfish. Maybe what I really hated was his shame sliding onto me."

"Thank You, Father God in Heaven, for blessing my son with a good heart," Ma prayed.

Behind Addison, Wally spurted a vigorous yellow stream onto the ground.

Ma turned to look, shook her head, and laughed. "You see how it is, Son? God doesn't want us to get too serious about things. Or ourselves."

Addison noted Wally's growing puddle, and to avoid it, he stepped out into the creek and passed in front of Willy's nose. With his feet squishing in his soaked boots, he stepped onto the bank by Ma.

"Do mothers ever commit sins that visit on their sons or daughters?"

"Why, Addison." She caressed his cheek and looked into his eyes.

He felt the calluses on her fingers rough on his skin.

"Any father-sins that visit a son, have abided with his mother first, foremost, and for longer, and if she could, the mother would absorb all her husband's sin so there'd be none left to push onto her son." She patted his cheek. "Mothers don't commit sins. That's why the saying only mentions father-sins."

"Addison Freeman!" It was Reedley who bellowed.

"Go," Ma said. "I'll take the horses to grass."

She took the lead ropes for the team from him and shooed her son on his way. As he *squish*ed down the road, he looked back.

Thank You, God. He took a handful of steps. *For Ma. You knew that right?*

Pa's embarrassing behavior, Addison saw, did not embarrass her, not like it embarrassed him.

At the preacher's wagon, Reedley waited for him. "Maurice is saddling your broncs. The train moves out in forty minutes. I want them to roll for four hours. You scouts find us a place, like this one, with water and grass. Go."

As Addison started *squishing* across the road, Reedley stopped him and made him sit on the tongue of the preacher's wagon to wring out his socks.

As Addison unlaced the strings of a boot, the wagon master said, "Boy, a scout is almighty important to a wagon train. To do his job, a scout has to understand priorities. First, take care of your horse and your gun. Take care of yourself, especially your feet and your teeth. Every other thing in your head ought to be worries about the wagon train. Understand?"

He wriggled his foot into a damp sock. "I'll have to think on what you said before I answer. I'll do that, um, while riding. And listening. I'll let you know in four hours."

Reedley walked away.

Addison was disappointed he didn't get a *humph.*

A team of men worked on the wagon across from the preacher's. Six-foot-five, barrel-chested Otto Vogelsang and a-foot-shorter Sean O'Riley carried the hoisting pole around from the far side. Sean placed the thick end of the pole on the ground at mid-wagon as Otto squatted behind the tailgate with the pole on his shoulder. Then Sean got in front of him. "Up," Otto said, and the two strained and straightened their legs. The rear wheel lifted clear of the ground. Preacher Larrimer undid the axle nut, and holding it, stepped back. The other O'Riley brother and Gallant Argyl grabbed the wheel and pulled it off the axle. Pa smeared on grease as Royal Howard banged a hammer on the axle-nut wrench on the front wheel, busting the nut loose. The rear wheel went back on. Larrimer hand-tightened the nut. Royal moved to the rear axle, and with the men holding the wheel, he tightened the nut with the wrench. "Down," Royal said. The wagon bed lowered, and they moved the lever pole to the front wheel as Royal used the hammer on the wrench to bang the rear axle nut tight.

The crew greased four wheels almost as fast as Addison wrung out two socks. He stood as Mr. Vogelsang and Mr. O'Riley grunted and lifted the front of the wagon.

Maurice walked his horse down the road leading another and handed over the reins to his partner. "Scouts shouldn't dawdle so."

Addison mounted, and they rode side-by-side to the ford and splashed through.

Maurice said, "Folks are saying the only Judas in this wagon train is the first deacon."

"The way I figure it, Maurice, is two scouts riding side-by-side equals about half a scout. Two scouts with distance between them, why that equals as much as three scouts."

Addison kicked his mount into a canter. As he pulled away, he was pleased with himself. For a moment. Then it occurred his family already had one sinner guilty of pride, and he did not want to be the Judas Scout.

5.

A ddison crested a gentle rise, reined up, and checked the position of the sun. Not time to stop yet. Maurice trailed him by fifty yards.

Ahead, the road fell away, and, at the base of the hill, forest surrendered to cleared land stretching in all directions. About a mile ahead, the road they followed cut through a town. He could make out three streets, one being the road. Reedley's crude map didn't show this town, nor most of the others. His map only showed a line heading west to the city of Urbana, then one south to Broughton, and another southwest to wind up at Alton on the Mississippi River. Each day of their travel, they'd passed through such towns, villages, and townships. One had only been a road crossing with buildings in the corners of the intersection: a blacksmith shop, a saloon, a general store, and a freight hauling business. Not all these places posted a sign telling the name, but if one of these civilized spots didn't act hostile and you talked to a resident, you found out the places did have names. The crossing was named Kapfer's Corner. Kapfer owned all four businesses.

The wagon master said Urbana and Broughton were railroad towns. Addison had seen pictures and drawings of trains but had never observed one. The size of a train engine was hard to imagine. One drawing he remembered showed a man leaning out a window of the engine. It appeared to be a sizeable monster, all shiny black metal and belching smoke and towing a long line of what were called cars behind it.

Well, he would see it, perhaps soon.

Maurice clopped up next to him.

"Why'd you stop?"

"The town there," Addison said. "Remember how the people eyed us as we passed through that place this morning? It wasn't friendly looks they gave us."

"Pa wanted to make four hours. We ought to push on, find a place to stop on the other side of it."

"I know what he wanted, but he also made us scouts. He expects us to study things he can't see and figure out the best way to handle them. I think he will want to rest the teams before we meet those people living down there. That grassed over field of stumps just behind us. That'll do."

Maurice shook his head. "There's no water there."

"Right. And ahead, there's none far as I can see. We crossed three streams this morning. Your pa would have let the animals drink."

"Pa said four hours and find a place with water and grass. I'm pushing on."

"We should stick together."

"I agree with that one. Come on then."

"I'm waiting at the stump field."

Maurice gigged his mount and cantered down the hill.

Addison sat atop Percy, watched his partner ride away, and wondered what the wagon master would say about what he'd done.

Call me a Judas scout, maybe.

*****

Addison sat on a stump next to the road. His tethered horse grazed behind him. When he saw the lead wagon, he saddled and was waiting by the time Joshua Reedley pulled up.

"Where's Maurice?"

Addison explained what lay ahead, why he stopped, and why the wagon master's son pushed on.

"I wish you'd have stayed together." Reedley took his hat off and mopped his brow with his shirt sleeve. "If I'd appointed Maurice boss scout, would you have done what he ordered?"

"I thought stopping here was the thing to do."

"No water," the wagon master said.

He gave the man his water argument.

Reedley studied his scout. Addison didn't turn away from the look-right-through-you blue-gray eyes. After a moment, the wagon master put his hat back on, humph-ed, dismounted, and turned over his horse to his scout.

Royal Howard lined the wagons up alongside the road in two rows, leaving a clear lane in the middle. Two of them still needed axle grease. Otto Vogelsang and his crew sprang into action. Women, boys, and girls unhitched teams and led the livestock into the grassy stump field to graze. Men checked their wagons. Two young men with shovels hustled into the trees to dig latrines. Seeing the organization and energy, there was a mighty difference from the days before and even that morning.

Addison, a few paces from the edge of the road and abreast the lead wagon, rubbed down Reedley's mount. The sound of a galloping horse came from the direction of the town. A lone rider. Coming hard. Addison unslung his musket.

The man jerked on the reins and hauled his chestnut to a stop between the lead wagons. "Who's in charge?" The man tried to sound tough, Addison thought. And hadn't pulled it off.

Those tending the teams and cows, the axle grease crew, the parade to and from the latrines, all halted and stared at the intruder.

A cloud of thin dust sifted over the rider and onto the lead wagons.

"Who the hell's in charge, I said?"

Addison, standing slightly behind the mounted man, held the musket in a slant across his chest. "Joshua Reedley's the wagon master."

The man jerked his horse around.

Addison was close enough to see his eyes grow big.

"Drop that gun!" The mounted man grabbed at the butt of a large pistol in a holster on his right hip and struggled to jerk the weapon clear.

Indecision froze Addison. He held his weapon. He didn't think he should drop it. He didn't want to point it at the man either.

"Stop!"

Joshua Reedley stood by the lead wagon driver box on the right side of the road. He had his pistol out and pointed at the rider. "Leave that gun in the holster. Raise your hands."

The rider jerked his horse around again to face Reedley, then lifted his hands. "You … you're interfering with the law."

Reedley directed Addison to hold the reins of the man's horse and Royal Howard to take the man's pistol.

"We'll see about the law without guns in our hands." The wagon master holstered his in his shoulder rig.

Mr. Howard took the man's handgun and ordered him to climb down. He did and immediately raised his hands again.

Next to Royal, the lawman stood a head shorter. Bushy whiskers covered his face. Dark, darting eyes peered out from under a flop-brim hat. Maurice would describe him as a beer keg with fat stubby arms and walking around on chicken legs. Beer Keg wore a belt and suspenders as if his pants needed twice the normal support to keep them up. There was a tin star pinned to the left suspender strap.

"Put your hands down," Reedley said. "Who are you?"

The man's barrel chest puffed out a bit. "I'm the sheriff of Thompson Township, and you all are under arrest."

For a moment, nothing moved. There was no sound. Addison had the sensation he was in a picture, but he was alive and not a glop of paint. Besides being in it, he also viewed the picture and the sky, wagons, and the people, and animals arrayed around the stump field and frozen in neck lowered to graze poses.

The sheriff's horse swished its tail. A crow cawed.

"What are we under arrest for?" Reedley said.

"You're … you're blocking the road. And you're trespassing on private property with that livestock out there."

Reedley didn't reply.

"I'm going to fine you five dollars for each wagon. And five for each and ever one a those animals. Plus twenty for interfering with an officer of the law."

Preacher Larrimer strode up beside the wagon master.

From Reedley: "Altogether, how much is this fine?"

The lawman sputtered, then blurted, "A hundred dollars."

The wagon master smiled. "We Are Found Church, and the church is charging you two hundred dollars for fertilizing your stump field there. That about right, Preacher?"

Larrimer scratched his chinstrap chin whiskers. "Our manure is worth more than that. But, as people of God, we should be generous. Two hundred will do."

"Abolitionists!" The lawman ripped his hat off and smacked it against his leg. "You're crazy. Two hundred dollars for horse biscuits and cow plops! Only a lunatic abolitionist would think his animals poop gold."

"Abolitionists?" Reedley started across the road. "Who said we were Abolitionists?"

"The chicken thief I got in my jail."

Reedley stepped up to the sheriff. "Chicken thief?" The lawman tried to back away from him, but Royal held his arm. "What's this thief's name?"

"I ... I didn't get his name, but he said he was from a wagon train, and you all was headed to Kansas to vote to keep the state free. According to my brother Wes, that makes you Abolitionists."

The wagon master held his hand up. "Whoa. This chicken thief, what's he look like? Describe his horse."

The sheriff pointed at Addison. "His age, his height." Then he detailed the key features of Maurice's brindled saddle bronc.

To Addison, it was as if the wagon master grew in stature as he questioned the lawman about the theft of a chicken, while the sheriff continued to try to back away but was prevented from doing so by Mr. Howard.

"So, you caught the man in your jail stealing chickens?" Reedley said.

"No, didn't really catch him in the act. But we all knew he done it.

"Early this morning, a shotgun blast woke the whole town up. Turned out Jurgen Hult heard a racket from his chickencoop just before sunup and thought a fox was trying to get through the wire. He fired his shotgun. Then Jurgen saw it was a thief, and the man ran and left the cage open. It wasn't clear if he stole a chicken or not as half Jurgen's flock escaped. But the thief left a trail we followed easy with the sun being up by this time. The tracks led north for a bit, then cut east. But the sign petered out. Me and my posse just got back to town when this young feller moseys down Main Street coming from the east. Straight off, I knowed he was the thief. I grabbed him and questioned him. That's when I figgered out he was an Abolistionist, and that cinched it. He was the one tried to steal Jurgen's chickens."

Reedley humphed. "You take chicken rustling seriously, in, what did you say, Thompson Township?"

"We take any kind of thievin' seriously."

Preacher Larrimer had been standing there quiet and listening to the story.

"Sheriff," he cut loose with his preaching voice, "at sunup, we were all twenty miles from here. Including the young man locked up in your jail. That boy did *not* steal a chicken from any of your town-people." The last sentence boomed out.

Joshua questioned the lawman further. His name was Chester Thompson. His brother was Wesley Thompson. He was the mayor and owned the bank, the general store, the saloon, and the land office. Wes had ordered his brother to turn the wagon train back. Abolitionists, he said, were the same as the Mormons twenty years ago. They'll steal anything not tied down. "Like chickens."

It had been Chester's own idea to try to squeeze money out of them before making them turn around. The sheriff puffed up like a bantam rooster in courting mode and said, "Brother Wes is sure to be waiting with a half-dozen armed men at the entrance to town."

Reedley told Addison to tie the lawman's hands. "In front of him." Then the wagon master summoned the men and married women to a conference. He explained how they were going to pass through the place up ahead, which took three minutes. Then the wagon master hollered, "Hitch the teams!"

Boys and girls swarmed the stump field to collect the animals. Mrs. Larrimer herded up the two best seamstresses and Mrs. Reedley,

Eunice Carlson, and Addison's ma. Two men with shovels ran to fill in the latrines.

Addison stood next to the bound lawman, held the reins to the sheriff's horse, and watched boys and girls scurry like ants from a kicked-apart ant hill. In the next moment, though, the youngsters and horses and cows on lead ropes all moved with haste and purpose.

"Boy," the sheriff whispered, "You know what's good for you you'll give me my horse and let me go."

Addison turned and noticed the horse's bloody mouth. "Sheriff, you say one more word to me, one more, and I'll put the bit in your mouth and jerk on it till you bleed."

Reedley walked up and told Addison to ride the sheriff's horse. The lawman started to protest. "You should have shot him," the wagon master said. "He was pulling a gun on you. And he was dangerous because he's stupid and scared plumb through. You should have shot him."

Reedley said he had hoped he could use the transit of Illinois to train his scouts, but Thompson Township wasn't going to give them the opportunity for leisurely learning. He also hoped they wouldn't have to shoot their way through the town. "But if it does come to shooting, you cannot hesitate."

The wagon master ripped the star off the man's suspenders and threw it out into the field of stumps.

It didn't take long for the teams to be hitched to wagons, and Addison anticipated an "On to Kansas," any second.

Before that happened, mumbled, indistinct voices rose from the wagons.

Mrs. Reedley, and Eunice, Delbert Carlson's daughter, walked between the wagons leading horses by the reins. Sixteen-year-old Eunice was a head taller than Mrs. Reedley. Addison had no trouble thinking *she* was plain. Folks, though, called her, "Big-boned."

Then Addison noticed their skirts, and his face heated up some.

He'd seen women and girls wear pants. It was not seemly to do so, but sometimes, on rare occasions, pants on a woman made sense. But Mrs. Reedley and Eunice wore skirts that had been split up the middle right up to …. It wasn't right to say up to what. And the material had been sewed so it was almost like pants with very baggy legs. But it wasn't pants. It was a split-up-the-middle skirt.

"Addison," Reedley called. "Bring that so-called sheriff over here."

Reedley and Otto Vogelsang hoisted the squatty sheriff onto the near draft horse of the lead team; then Otto hustled back to his wagon.

The wagon master mounted and hollered, "Let's go!"

Larrimer, wearing his preacher suit, mounted. Eunice and Mrs. Reedley, wearing those split skirts, climbed up onto their saddles without assistance. Reedley handed a single barrel shotgun—a sixteen gauge—to his wife, and a ten-gauge double barrel to Eunice. Most of the women knew how to shoot. Eunice sure did. Last winter, she'd killed two wolves trying to get at calves. When that story went around, it squashed the jokes about her looks. For a week or so.

To that point, everything the wagon master had done had been right and proper. That morning they'd already made as many miles as they had during an entire Wednesday or Thursday on the road. And Friday was only half spent. But taking a sheriff captive and putting women astride saddle broncs *like a man wearing a split-up-the-middle dress* and giving them shotguns; then having them up in front with the preacher to lead the wagon train into a town where a hostile reception was expected?

Larrimer led off. Eunice and Mrs. Reedley trailed him by a length, and behind them, the wagon master and his scout.

Reedley sidled over next to Addison and eyed the harness on the sheriff's horse. "Maybe you should have left the bit in."

"We talked it over." Addison patted the sheriff's horse on the neck. "Outlaw and me. We don't need it."

"Outlaw? *Humph.*"

When Addison looked back up at the wagon master, he saw the time for joshing was finished.

6.

The train trundled down the hill. Traces jangled, brakes ground against wheels, drivers said "Whoa," and "Ho," in voices suitable for a lullaby to a cranky baby. The road leveled, and although Addison kept his eyes ahead, the way Reedley told him to. Behind him, he felt tension wane as the drivers' voices lightened up some.

The edge of town lay about two hundred yards ahead. Five or six men had clustered on the boardwalk in front of the first building to the right. Four men peeled away, lined up across the road, and assumed spread-leg stances. They carried sidearms in holsters and had long guns angled across their chests.

One man had stayed on the boardwalk. He stood with his thumbs hooked in the waist of his trousers. He was dressed in a tan suit, fancier than what those in the street wore. Addison couldn't see a gun. But that didn't mean he didn't have one.

Addison had rested his musket across his saddle behind the horn. He plodded along beside Reedley.

"Now," Reedley said, and the line of wagons pulled itself apart, from a single file to two. The McTavish family led one line, the O'Riley brothers the other. Sean O'Riley drove the team. His brother Timothy held a musket in his hands. The barrels of other muskets and shotguns leaned against the front of the bed between the brothers.

Women, or girls, drove the other wagons. At least one male in each wagon held a shotgun or a musket.

Preacher Larrimer, sitting his saddle ramrod straight, walked his horse down the middle of the road. With his black stovepipe hat, he looked to be ten feet tall. Nose-to-tail behind him and to the sides rode the women wearing bonnets, those split skirts, and shotguns.

The wagon master stayed abreast the McTavish team, and Addison, with his long rifle resting on the saddle, paced Outlaw to the O'Riley's.

A pitch pipe whispered above the wagon rattle and jangle of trace chains.

The females, aided by the tenor voices of the O'Rileys, raised "Amazing Grace" to high heaven.

The four in the street looked over at the one still standing on the boardwalk. He watched the wagons approach and tilted his head back as if he wanted to avoid some stink rising from the ground. Tan Suit gestured. His message was clear: *You stay right there!*

The first stanza cut off without the drawn-out last note.

"We come in peace." Larrimer extended his arms, showing his palms to those in the street. "We mean no harm to anyone." He reined his mount three paces from a blocker. "But we will pass through this town."

Mrs. Reedley pulled up in front of another of them. The wagon train halted. Addison stopped. So did the wagon master. Eunice Carlson did not pause. She rode up to Tan Suit. Then she stopped and pointed the shotgun at his face.

Tan Suit spluttered. "See here—"

"Shut up!" Eunice said those words hard as a man would.

"No one needs to get hurt here. Step aside." Larrimer delivered the words with righteous indignation.

For a moment, nothing moved. It was quiet.

Until Eunice cocked the hammers of her gun one at a time. "Tell them to put their guns down in the street and step aside." Her voice was barely audible. "Tell them!" Addison heard that.

Tan Suit backed up against the wall of a hardware store. He raised his hands. "Boys." He licked his lips. "Put your guns down and step aside."

The wagon master: "Drop the handguns, too."

Eunice: "Say it."

Tan Suit: "The handguns, too."

"Addison!"

The wagon master's voice snapped like a whip. Heat bloomed on Addison's cheeks. Under his shirt, beads of sweat broke out. He'd done just what he'd been warned not to do: let his attention wander from the armed men right in front of him.

The one in front of Mrs. Reedley had placed his weapons on the ground and was moving to the side, to join the others in front of Tan Suit. One still held his musket slanted across his chest and glared at Addison. A visceral internal scream, *Do something,* sought to bust him free from indecision.

"Do I want to die?" Mrs. Reedley had her shotgun pointed at the holdout. "Ask yourself that question."

The holdout turned and looked up at the mounted woman. He wasn't afraid of her, Addison was sure. Mrs. Reedley cocked the hammer. The man's eyes grew big. The sides of his droopy mustache covered half his open mouth. She nodded toward the ground. He released the stock and raised his right hand, holding the barrel in his left and off to his side. Droopy Moustache knelt and laid the long rifle on the ground, stood, and looked up at her again. Again, he wasn't afraid of her. During his genuflection, reckless courage returned to the man's face. Reedley had told Addison the sheriff had been dangerous because he was scared. Droopy was dangerous because he wouldn't stay scared. He intended to pull his pistol. Addison was sure.

Addison aimed his musket and cocked it. "Don't even twitch, Mister." He swung his left leg over the horn and hopped down off the right side of the horse, keeping his rifle on the man. Once on the ground, he ordered Droopy Moustache to raise his hands and turn around. Taller than him. Broader across the shoulders. The man glared at him.

He thinks I won't shoot.

Anger flashed in Addison like lightning from a nighttime thunderstorm. He strode across the ten feet separating them and jammed his musket barrel hard into the man's belly. Droopy stepped back, but Addison kept the muzzle pressed against him. The man raised his hands.

*****

When the wagon train passed the first buildings, none of the town people were about on the boardwalks, but a few of them peered out the windows of the general store, a dress shop, and the bank. All of them built with roofs over the boardwalks. A single story snugged against the bank sported a "Sheriff" sign. Reedley dragged the lawman off the horse and marched him into his office. Addison looked around. It unsettled him, being stopped in the middle of a town that, so far, had shown them nothing but hostility.

Most of the buildings along the street through town were two-story. Some had second-story windows open, and the tails of curtains riffled in the breeze. He shifted in the saddle. More open windows behind them. A few rifles and shotguns up there and the whole wagon train would be fish in a barrel. He pointed the windows out to the O'Riley brothers.

"You see a gun barrel poke out, you shoot." After he said it, Addison felt strange bossing older men.

"Reedley said don't shoot unless we have to," Sean O'Riley said.

"Gun barrel poking out a window is a *have-to-shoot.*"

Sean O'Riley glared at Addison for a moment; then he wound the reins around the brake handle and picked up a shotgun.

The wagon master stepped out of the sheriff's office with his son a pace behind. Addison intended to resume scanning windows when he caught sight of Maurice's swollen lip and black eye.

Eunice screeched his name and ran across the street. "Who did this to you?"

Maurice nodded at Droopy Moustache.

Eunice took two strides to the man and stomped a boot heel on his foot. He bellowed and hopped on his good one. She shot a left jab to his mouth, which choked off the howl and snapped his head back. She stepped toward him again and planted a roundhouse right on the side of his jaw. He spun around and plopped face-down on the dirt and raised a puff of dust. She stood over him. "Don't look like he's gonna be getting up for a spell." She turned and looked at Maurice.

Addison caught a glimpse of the face she must have used on

Maurice's assailant. It lasted a second. Then a warm, pleasant smile flash-flooded the scowl away.

"Oh, Maurice!" She grabbed him by the arm and led him toward the rear of the line of wagons. He winced and held a hand over his ribs on the right side.

"Thompson, stop right there!" Reedley pointed at the mayor, who was about to enter the dress shop. "Addison. Grab him and march him to the jail."

Addison dismounted, pulled the pistol he'd taken from Droopy Moustache, and hustled across the street. By the time he got Tan Suit moving, Reedley and his wife had herded the other three blockers into the sheriff's office. Otto Vogelsang's fifteen-year-old son Hermann, and Eunice's next younger brother, Alphonse each grabbed one of the fallen man's arms and started to lift him when Droopy snatched Alphonse's long gun. Hermann swung his musket butt against Droopy's face, and he plopped back onto the dirt. He moaned, and the toes of his boots dug tiny furrows in the street.

Addison pushed Tan Suit into the sheriff's office.

Inside, a single large cell occupied most of the floor, leaving room for a desk, two chairs, and a round stove. The only person in the cell was the badge-less sheriff. Reedley opened the cell, shoved the mayor and his three henchmen in, and locked it again.

"Abbie," the wagon master said to his wife. "Find Royal Howard. Tell him to get the wagons moving. There's not a minute to lose. And tell him to keep his head on a swivel. There's bound to be others want to do us harm." Addison admired what he saw on Mrs. Reedley's face. She listened to the wagon master, weighed what he said, and saw rightness in the words. Compared to her face, he was sure his own would disappoint her husband. "Go."

She hustled out the open door, and Reedley took the pistol from Addison.

"You never handled one of these before."

"No, sir." He answered as if it had been a question.

The wagon master sat on the chair behind the desk and jerked open a drawer. He pulled out a handgun, checked it, and laid it beside the other one. "Loaded." He jerked open another drawer and took out another weapon. "Colt Pocket Pistol." He smiled. "Unloaded."

Royal Howard's voice boomed in from the street. "Move out! Watch them upper story windows."

Reedley moved to the door and motioned Addison to follow him.

Across the street, and opposite the sheriff's office, four women stood on the balcony above the "Saloon" sign. Addison's jaw dropped. One of them wore bloomers!

"Judas, boy! There's people out here want to kill us. And you're staring at the saloon girls. Take this." Reedley handed a pistol to Addison. "Cock it."

He pulled the hammer back until it clicked.

"That's half-cock. It's a double-action weapon. It ain't full cocked until you hear two clicks."

Addison thumbed the hammer back until it clicked again.

"Now. Aim it at the sheriff. It's not loaded. Pull the trigger."

The mayor protested. The sheriff backed away from the bars. The other three watched.

He pulled the trigger.

"Do it again. Watch what happens to the barrel this time."

The sheriff had backed to the rear wall.

This time when he pulled the trigger, the barrel moved left and up. If he had been shooting a bullet, he wouldn't have hit any of the five men locked in a cell three paces from him. His bullet would have sailed over the heads of all of them.

"When you learned to shoot a long rifle, you had to learn to squeeze your whole hand, not just pull the trigger. Squeezing the trigger, not pulling it, it's even more important with a handgun."

The last two wagons rumbled past. From next to the saloon, Preacher Larrimer crossed the street with a short, skinny man in a black suit and chinstrap whiskers and a black stovepipe hat. It was like the preacher had found a half-size replica of himself.

Larrimer stopped next to the boardwalk. "This is Reverend Redmond. He's invited us to stay with him for a day."

Reedley shook his head. "We're making good time, and the people here don't like us. We need to move on."

The reverend took off his hat and craned his neck back. "Mr. Reedley. You are the wagon master. What you say goes. But maybe you will agree to my proposition. First, you have nothing to fear from anyone in town except for the men you have locked up. And the gambler and the manager of the saloon. Aside from them, the rest of us are quite fond of you and your wagon train. Mayor Thompson had this town, and us, in his pocket. You set us free, Mr. Reedley.

"Now the gambler and the saloon man, both of them live up there, with those women. If you don't lock them up, they will release Wes Thompson and his cronies, and they will come after you."

Addison, though tempted by the conversation, turned to watch the men in the cell. He thought somebody ought to. Behind him, Reedley wanted to know about the proposition.

The little reverend talked up a pile of big arguments. The arguments convinced Addison. The wagon master bought them, too.

7.

Found Church Crusade was stopping in Thompson Township. Reedley's earlier decision to push on had worried Addison. They'd taken Maurice to see the town doctor. Maurice had busted ribs and shouldn't travel. Leaving him in that hostile place hadn't seemed like a good idea.

The crusaders rumbled their wagons onto the lot around Christ Redeemer Church on Second Street and parked. Now, though, members of Christ the Redeemer, with property adjoining the church, made their meadows and pastures available to graze the wagon train's horses and cows.

While some tended the animals, Reedley assembled the other men, women, and children, twelve and older, for training with handguns. Everyone would learn to shoot and load a pistol. Larrimer went first. He dry-fired one taken from the sheriff's desk. Then he fired his two allocated rounds at the tree five paces away. He didn't hit it.

The wagon master ordered First Deacon Freeman to fire next. He refused.

"You will fire the gun." Reedley grabbed the deacon's hand and slapped the dry fire weapon into it. "If you refuse another order of mine, you will be expelled from the crusade."

Addison turned away.

"Face this way," the wagon master ordered. "We do not have much time, and we don't have powder and shot to waste. We learn by shooting and watching others."

Addison did as he was told.

Preacher Larrimer grabbed Pa's upper arm. "Adolph. We are not in our sheltered community back home. There we were off the beaten path, and the world let us alone. To get to Kansas, we will have to fight with sinners of every stripe. We will have to do hard things. Afterward, I will have to figure out how we keep those hard things from changing our hearts. I will need your help with that. But right now, do what the wagon master says."

Larrimer walked away from his congregation toward the church as town people's wagons and buggies trundled into the lot and wedged into spaces. Reverend Redmond's white clapboard house of worship was larger than Found Church building. It had four windows to a side versus two. And a bell tower. Redmond had called a meeting. It looked like the whole town was attending. Except for those in jail.

Reedley demonstrated a two-handed pistol grip to Pa.

Addison was next. After dry firing, he shot one round two-handed and the other with a one-hand grip. Then the wagon master sent him to the sheriff's office where Royal Howard, Eunice Carlson, and the O'Rileys guarded the prisoners and watched for interference from the saloon.

The O'Riley brothers stood at the corners of the Sheriff's building with shotguns. Mr. Howard and Eunice occupied chairs on the boardwalk with the door open between them. After tying his horse, or the sheriff's, to the rail, Addison stepped behind the other two hitched there. And stopped. And looked away from Eunice. Down the street to the east.

"Miss Eunice," Mr. Howard said, "it appears young Addison finds your ... posture disturbing. And unladylike."

She had the chair back leaned against the building, her legs spread and draped over the sides of the chair. Her split-up-the-middle skirt, and her posture, laid heat on his face.

"He can think what he wants."

"Ah, Miss Eunice. It's not Addison should worry you. It's what Maurice would think."

Her chair legs clunked onto the boardwalk. She blushed, stood, spun on her heel, and entered the sheriff's office. Only to exclaim, "Saints preserve us!" and come back out. "Smells like someone tossed a week-old dead skunk in the window."

The prisoners clamored for help. Their chamber pot needed emptying.

"Miss Eunice," Addison said, "the wagon master wants you at the church for pistol practice."

"I know how to fire a handgun."

"Mr. Reedley needs to see how well," Mr. Howard said. "You either shoot or empty the chamber pot."

She untied her horse, grabbed the horn, swung up onto the saddle, reined her animal around, and gigged it with her heels. Addison watched her canter her mount toward the sound of a pistol pop. And thought about Lizbeth. For the first time that day.

The prisoners kept hollering for help, which drew Addison's attention away from Eunice. The sheriff gripped the bars of the cell door and rattled it against the lock. The rest of the prisoners yammered for relief from the stink.

Mr. Howard stood in the doorway. "We best tend to that." He told the O'Rileys to keep a sharp watch on the saloon, upstairs and down; then he entered. Addison followed him. And grimaced. He felt the stink settle onto his tongue.

The sheriff, Chester Thompson, gripped the cell door bars. "Ya hafta empty the chamber pot."

His brother, the mayor, Wesley, stood behind the sheriff. The two didn't look alike. Wesley was tall, thin, and sported clothes and a face which proclaimed, "I am a man to reckon with." Short, squatty Chester wore a ratty working man outfit, and his eyes darted about continuously, as if he knew something was coming to hurt him. He just didn't know where it would come from.

Mr. Howard ordered the prisoners away from the cell door and Chester Thompson to pick up the chamber pot. The mayor moved against the rear wall with a henchman to either side. The other fellow sat on the cot.

"Addison. Draw and cock your gun. You have five rounds. There's five of them. Any of 'em makes a move toward the door when I open it, you shoot them. Shoot them all."

Addison pulled the hammer back. The *click, click* cut through and stopped the yammering.

Mr. Howard stopped in front of the cell door with the key in his right hand, his Colt in the holster on his hip. He glanced back, and Addison nodded and then aimed his weapon into the cell, using the two-handed grip.

Royal unlocked the cell. "The rest of you stay real still. Sheriff. Come out." He swung the door open enough for him to make it through.

As Chester Thompson, carrying the pot with his arms extended and his head averted to the side, stepped one foot out of the cell, his brother yelled, "Now!" and the two men to the mayor's sides jumped forward. Addison fired and knocked the man to the mayor's right against the wall. He collapsed to the floor. The left man slammed into Chester's back and rammed the door into Royal. He fell onto his back and dropped his pistol, which had just cleared the holster. The sheriff lay sprawled on his belly. The chamber pot had spewed its contents.

Mr. Howard and the man who'd shoved the sheriff wrestled just outside the cell. Inside the cell, the man on the cot stared big-eyed and raised his hands. Wesley Thompson stood still, his eyes on the men fighting for the gun. Addison aimed at the mayor and shot him. Cot Sitter, hands still raised, eyes still big, shook his head side to side.

Addison switched his aim to the man on top of Royal and moved, so there was no danger to Mr. Howard, and shot the man in the side of his head. Then he aimed at the sheriff. Chester looked up. His mouth opened, and he raised a hand as if to ward off the next bullet.

Gun smoke filled Addison's nose. Ringing filled his ears. *Shoot them all!* He heard that like an echo that took a while to bounce back to him. The pistol felt hard in his hand as he started squeezing the handle and trigger. At the end of his barrel, the sheriff squinted his eyes tight shut. Addison lifted his finger from the trigger.

The stench of the spilled chamber pot wrinkled his nose. His pistol hand started to shake. He grabbed the gun by the warm barrel in his left hand and took it away from his right.

Royal Howard shrugged the body off him, jumped to his feet, and grabbed the younger man's pistol. Addison thought about it, then let him take it, then sank to his knees. "Oh, Judas!" came out of him along with a gurgling, choking half sob, half laugh.

"Oh, Jesus. Goddamn. Son of a bitch it hurts." Wes Thompson sat on the cell floor, his hands on his belly. A dark red stain spread over his tan waistcoat and into his tan pants.

Addison staggered to his feet as his stomach lurched. He clamped a hand over his mouth, stumbled out the door, stopped at the edge of the boardwalk, and spewed vomit onto the dirt. Between the legs of a horse. Joshua Reedley's. Reedley tugged the reins pulling his mount sideways to in front of the hitching rail and stepped down.

"What happened?"

Addison shook his head, hacked, and spat a mouthful of chewable vinegar into the street. The wagon master stepped behind him and into the sheriff's office and came right back out.

"Judas!" Reedley waved his hat in front of his nose.

Royal Howard walked onto the boardwalk dragging Chester Thompson by the arm. Royal grinned at Joshua. "You get used to it."

"Even a maggot couldn't stand that stench." The wagon master peered in the door. "Judas."

From in the jail: "Ooooh. It hurts!"

"Royal, you shoot those three?" Reedley said.

Mr. Howard shook his head and pointed.

"All three?"

Another nod. Addison waited for the wagon master's eyes to impale him with *Thou shalt not,* but Reedley turned away and looked down the street. Toward Kansas. After a moment, Reedley faced Mr. Howard. "Get that imitation sheriff—let only him out of the cell—to scrub the floor till the whole place stinks of lye soap instead of like a ten-year outhouse. Addison and me, we'll go down to the doctor's office to check on Maurice. Then I'll send the doc to tend to … the mayor."

Reedley looked up at the saloon balcony. The women were gone, Addison noted, but a man hustled inside the doorway.

Eunice and Otto Vogelsang ran up to the jail.

"How's Maurice?" the wagon master said.

"Doc's looking at him," from Eunice.

The wagon master told them to watch for two men from the saloon. According to Reverend Redmond, they were part of the mayor's crew of criminals. "We'll deal with them when I get back from the doctor's," Reedley said.

Addison followed Reedley toward the east end of town. The buildings, for the most part, were the same. Roofed over boardwalks in front. Dirt alleys between. *Clump, clump, clump, clump.* Two silent strides. Then more clomping.

"Addison." Reedley had slowed to let him catch up. "If you ever have to kill a man again, and you do not get that ugly taste in your mouth, throw your gun away and never touch another one. Understand?"

He thought about it. They clomped over another boardwalk. He understood, in a way, but couldn't say so. Instead, Addison nodded.

8.

At the doctor's office, they found Maurice lying on a cot. He had two broken ribs.

The Vogelsang boy and Eunice's brother stood beside the door. She sat on a chair by the opposite wall.

Reedley introduced himself and Addison to the doc.

Doctor Federson stood next to a table with Droopy Moustache sprawled atop it. "Dawson." He pointed to him. "He sent me a dozen beat-up-bad patients over this past year. Now he got his *own* jaw busted." He smiled. "About time somebody gave him a dose of his own medicine."

Federson, it appeared, wanted the wagon master to appreciate his joke. Reedley wanted to know about his son.

"I'm worried the busted end of his rib could poke into his lung. He needs to rest up for two, three weeks."

"I'll stay here with him." Eunice sat with her legs pressed together. She blushed when her eyes touched Addison's; then, she looked at her hands on her lap.

"We'll worry about that later." The wagon master turned to the Doc. "Can Dawson be moved to the jail?"

"Not yet. I have to rig up some kind of brace to hold those broken bones in place so they can set. Be a while."

"Another thing," Reedley said. "Fellow named Wesley Thompson is gut shot back at the jail."

"Our mayor. By virtue of his gang of gunmen. Live by the sword, die by sword. Applies even to mayors, I guess. I'll get my bag."

"We'll walk with you. Your preacher told us to watch for a couple of men in the saloon."

Reedley told the two young men to watch Dawson. "Watch him close. His kind is treacherous as a rattlesnake with the rattles pulled off. He tries something, don't hit him with your guns. Shoot him. When Doc says he can be moved, take him to the jail and lock him up."

Eunice had a long rifle leaned beside her. And a pistol in a holster. Addison hadn't noticed the belt gun. He'd focused on—

"Addison." Reedley said. "Why aren't you armed?"

Addison couldn't rustle up words for an answer.

"How we come through this afternoon with none of us even scratched, excepting my boy, well, the Good Lord been looking after us. Day ain't over, though."

Reedley instructed Eunice to take her brother's powder horn and bullet pouch and walk toward the jail on the other side of the street. "We'll walk this side. Watch ahead and behind us. We'll watch your back. Understand what I want you to do?"

She nodded and hustled with a rustling of skirt. Or was it skirts? It was like each leg wore its own.

With a start, Addison looked away from the girl's apparel. *Funny. It never occurred to me to think there are women legs beneath a dress. In pants, the legs are there, sure, but the woman looked half ways to being a man. But that split skirt thing—*

The wagon master stepped onto the boardwalk, studied the street, and spent a long moment studying what Addison thought to be the upper story of the saloon. He signaled, and they started walking toward the jail. As they stepped onto the space between Doc's building and the next one, Addison spotted Preacher Redmond walk out of the alley next to the saloon and into the street. A stream of men and women followed him. The wagon master and Eunice stopped.

Redmond stood in the street as his crowd—about twenty, half men, half women—assembled behind him. He gripped his suspenders over his chest and stepped forward. A young follower jumped ahead and held a batwing open, and the entire posse filed in behind the preacher.

"Judas!" Reedley, after a look at the upstairs window of the saloon, thrust his long rifle into Addison's hands.

The wagon master ran across the street, angling for the saloon.

Eunice hiked up her skirt and took a step forward, realized she was only helping one leg move more freely, dropped the skirt and took her long rifle in both hands, and hurried to keep up. Addison turned from watching her to check behind them. "Let's go, Doc. Stick close."

At the sheriff's office, Doc went inside.

Addison stayed on the boardwalk. Across the street, a man wearing a star on his shirt stood beside the saloon door. Reedley and Eunice waited opposite him. The man with the star, he resembled Wes Thompson. Same build, same sandy hair, same neat mustache.

From inside the saloon, the posse shoved a man out through the batwings. Reedley checked the man for weapons as a double barrel and a pistol were handed out to … the new sheriff?

Federson stepped through the jail door. "Wes Thompson's dead. I'm going back to my office."

Addison said, "Wait. I want to make sure that posse gets the other one."

Across the street, two of the posse held the arms of their final quarry as Reedley checked him and pulled two derringers and a boot knife from him. Then the new sheriff and the wagon master prodded the gambler and saloon manager across the street. Preacher Redmond led his holy posse through the alley beside the saloon and toward Second Street.

Doc looked at Addison, and he nodded his permission for him to return to his office. The notion he was doing something wrong ordering grown men around niggled at him…like Eunice's split skirt niggled uneasiness in him.

He stepped aside as the gambler and saloon manager marched inside, past the boots of the three corpses, and into the cell. Royal Howard locked the door on them.

The new sheriff was also a Thompson, Lester, younger brother to Wesley, older than the former sheriff, Chester.

The citizens of Thompson Township had appointed a Governance Committee, a judge, and a new sheriff. Lester said he told the Governance Committee he was the last man who should wear the star. They told him nobody else was capable of doing so, and they pinned the star to his shirt.

Up close, he was clearly Wesley's brother. Both were an inch or so above average height, slender, had sandy hair and neatly trimmed mustaches. Lester bore a ruddy, weathered look, while Wesley's appearance was indoor pallor, which didn't change much at his death.

The new sheriff asked Reedley to guard the prisoners for a while longer. He needed to get the bodies taken care of and had another matter to address. The wagon master agreed, and the lawman departed.

Royal Howard handed a pistol to Addison. "I loaded it for you."

"Is that Dawson's pistol?"

"It's yours," Reedley said and handed Addison an across-the-shoulder holster. "I wear this kind because I find it easier to draw my pistol when I'm seated, either on a saddle or a chair. Remember the trouble Sheriff Chester had trying to pull his pistol on you? Try this. Try a hip holster. See what suits."

Addison slipped the strap over his shoulder and started to holster his new pistol.

"Son, if someone loads your weapon for you, always check it before you stow it." Reedley took the pistol. "Five cylinders loaded. Grease gobbed over the chambers to keep the powder dry. Hammer over an empty chamber." He returned the gun.

The wagon master turned to Royal. "Go back to the wagons. Tell everyone we'll celebrate the Sabbath with Preacher Redmond's congregation tomorrow. Sunday, wagons roll at first light. And two of Redmond's families are coming with us. Get with them. Check their wagons and animals. Make sure they don't try to load too much."

Royal departed on his mission, and Eunice returned to the doctor's office on hers.

Reedley led the way onto the boardwalk.

A wagon pulled up in front of the sheriff's office with two men on the driver's bench. They were to pick up the bodies. The two climbed down, entered the jail, and returned carrying one of the mayor's henchmen. Reedley and Addison lugged the dead mayor out and arranged him next to the first corpse.

"Mr. Reedley, do I, um, do I need to worry about the new sheriff? Since I shot his brother."

The two men hoisted the last body into place. One of them said, "I'll answer that. Les Thompson disagreed with his brother over just about everything Wesley did. Wesley wouldn't listen to him, and one Thompson brother couldn't shoot the other. Once things settle down a bit, Les'll probably thank you."

The speaker climbed up and turned. "And I thank you for bringing your wagons to our town. Before you got here, some of us were considering pulling up stakes. But now we're getting our town back." He clucked the team into motion and turned it to head east.

The wagon master sat on a chair in front of the sheriff's office. His scout did, too.

Addison watched the body wagon turn left and an alley swallow it. Past the alley, the main street turned into the road that climbed the hill to the stump field beyond the crest. And farther east, home. At least, last week, it had been home. He'd dreamed of marrying Lizbeth. Pa refused to allow that, and he thought his life was ruined.

But here he still lived, he still breathed. Those three in the wagon, he'd stopped their breathing. He'd taken away their lives. "Thank God, always," Ma'd said.

What do I thank him for, Ma? That I didn't have to kill four?

A buggy approached from the west, swung around, and pulled up in front of the saloon. The sheriff pushed open a batwing and held it. Four women, dressed like ladies, filed out, and the buggy driver helped them board. A Negro man and boy carried out a large trunk and stashed it behind the second seat.

One of the women picked up the reins and said, "Giddup!" The horse started walking. She grabbed the buggy whip, snapped it, and the animal kicked it up to a trot.

Les Thompson crossed the street and entered his jail. Addison and Reedley peered in from the doorway. Chester, the former sheriff, and the man who'd sat on the cot during the shooting stood against the sidewall. His name was Hiram. The saloon manager and the gambler sat on the cot. The new sheriff drew his gun, cocked it, unlocked the cell door, swung it open, and pointed his weapon at the two on the cot. "Chester and Hiram. Walk out. Now."

They walked out, and the cell door slammed behind them.

"I talked to the Judge," Les Thompson told his releasees. "You are not being charged, but you both are on probation. Hiram, you are going to run my farm. Two months from now, assuming you behave yourself, I will ask you if you want to continue as my foreman. If you don't want to, fine. In the meantime, Chester, you are Hiram's hired hand."

"But I'm your brother."

"Chester, when you act like you're *my* brother and not Wesley's, I will treat you as such. Hiram, Preacher Redmond will hold a funeral service for … the deceased. Preacher Redmond says they're not criminals now." Les shook his head. "I should have thought about Wes myself, but I guess I'm not the man our preacher is. When that's done, take my brother to my farm and bury him next to my father and both his wives."

Addison figured Hiram was about his own age.

Hiram nodded and headed for the door. He waved a *come on* to Chester. The thirty-something followed the boy.

Addison watched the two of them cross the street. He thought of pointing his pistol at the man on the cot, Hiram, when the mayor's henchman tried to escape. He didn't know why he didn't shoot him. He was not glad, rather, relieved that he hadn't.

Hiram, he'd learned, had been born and raised on a farm in Indiana. In 1850, his father went west hoping to find gold before it was all gone, leaving his mother and him to run their eighty acres. They received one letter from him a year after he left and nothing more. A couple of months ago, his mother died. Hiram decided to go to California because there was nothing to hold him in Indiana. On his journey, he stopped in Thompson Township, bought a bath, and decided to spend the evening in the saloon. At the Faro table, he caught the dealer using a rigged dealer box. Dawson saw him get the drop on the gambler, was impressed with his gun skill, and offered him a job. Hiram had worked for Dawson a couple of weeks and was ready to pull up stakes. He didn't care for Dawson or the way he did business. But then the Abolitionists' wagon train came to town.

And I almost shot a good man.

Reedley walked out and stood on the boardwalk. Addison and Les Thompson followed. They watched Hiram and Chester walk side-by-side across the street as they headed for the alley running alongside the saloon and leading to the church on Second Street.

Reedley said, "I just had the notion that Hiram and Chester both started out normal tall, but the hand of God came out of heaven and squashed Chester's height to width."

The new sheriff barked a single syllable laugh. "This town hasn't had much to chuckle about for some time now. We need a bit of practice. Now we may get the chance. Thanks, Mr. Reedley. And you, too, Mr. Freeman."

Nobody had ever called Addison "mister" before.

Opposite them, a man propped a ladder against the building, climbed it, and began painting over "Saloon."

"It's going to be the new town hall." Les glanced at Reedley. "Can you hold the fort here a bit more? I'd like to attend the funeral service."

The church bell started ringing. The sheriff set off toward it.

Reedley sat.

Addison mused, "Maybe I should go—"

"No!"

Addison sat. "Mr. Reedley, you're sticking as close to me as a cow sticks to a calf when the wolves are howling nearby."

"Perhaps I am."

"How come?"

"It hasn't hit you yet."

"I puked."

"It hasn't hit you yet. Not like it's going to. Sometime today, maybe tonight, it'll come out of nowhere, and it'll be like a horse kicking you in the belly."

Reedley had killed a man, or men. Addison didn't have to ask to know. "Pa will take a switch to me. For killing those men. That's what I've been thinking about."

"You want him to? Sounded that way."

That drove every word Addison had in his mouth down his throat. He looked to his left past the wagon master. The ladies' buggy was out of sight. A light fog of orange-tinged dust hung in the air below the low sun. Inside his head, thoughts buzzed like bees around a just bumped hive. Not one of those thoughts seemed ready to light and give him a notion of what he was to do with himself. Then one did.

"No. I don't want him to switch me."

The wagon master smiled, leaned his chair against the wall, and slid his hat over his eyes.

The sound of a horse coming hard brought them to their feet. At the edge of town, where Tan Suit Wesley Thompson had stood, the rider slowed his mount to a trot. It was Oscar Wilson. Reedley had sent him, along with the wagon master's oldest son, Robert, back to Found Church to obtain a wagon of provisions.

Oscar's horse was lathered, and as it neared, he heard the animal blowing hard. It was close to collapsing.

Oscar Wilson stopped the horse in the middle of the street between the saloon and sheriff's office. The animal hung its head. Addison expected the beast to keel over. The man hopped down, and he almost fell. His legs steadied.

"Joshua," Oscar said. "Second Deacon Waverly. He isn't doing what Preacher Larrimer laid out. He is not selling our farms and coming to join us. He says he owns our places now. He pulled a pistol on Robert and me. Locked us in his smokehouse. But we got away."

"Where's Robert?"

Oscar hooked his thumb toward the east. "His horse give out. Back there coupla' miles. By this field of stumps."

"Is Robert all right?" Reedley said.

"Yes, sir. He told me to ride on. He thought we was close to catchin' up."

"Son of a bitch!" The wagon master glanced at Addison. "There's times when even the God-fearing-est man runs into something where won't nothing do but cussing."

Addison wondered if Job ever got to that point. No way to tell. If he did, they sure wouldn't have written those words in the Good Book.

9.

Addison jerked awake. From the east, dawn whispered, *I'll be along directly.*

A few minutes back, Reedley had slowed his horse to a walk. Addison had followed suit and fallen asleep in the saddle. Now, the wagon master had stopped by the lane leading to Sylvan Waverly's house and barn, and Addison had had to grab the saddle horn to keep from tumbling to the ground.

"Stay awake," Reedley growled, then led them to beside Waverly's barn and handed Addison the reins of his two horses. The animals were spent. They'd pushed them hard all night, switching every few hours. Horses slept standing. Just then, Addison could have too. Just let the eyelids drop. They were so heavy.

Reedley crossed the lot to the house on foot and banged on the door. Even though he expected it, the sudden loud knocking on the second deacon's door spurred his heart to thumping.

Reedley banged again.

Outlaw nudged Addison's arm. "You want oats. Maybe we can get you some."

The lighting of a lamp inside the house drew his attention. Mrs. Waverly answered the door. In her nightgown. "Never expected you to be the one to come back," she said.

Reedley pulled his pistol and aimed it into the house. With his other arm, he shoved the woman aside. She stumbled and dropped the lamp. The lamp burst, and a puddle of flame spread at her feet. She screamed. Reedley's gun didn't waver. He said, "Drop the gun, Sylvan."

Fire hemmed the bottom of Mrs. Waverly's nightgown. She started lifting the gown, as if to pull it off over her head, but stopped and screamed again.

Addison ran across the lot and arrived at the doorway as Waverly placed a shotgun on the floor.

Reedley pushed the woman away from the puddle of fire and ripped the neck of her nightgown. He turned her around and pulled the garment off her and spread it over the flames on the floor. The cloth covered half the burning coal oil.

"Get bedding, Addison. Quick."

Addison hurried past the woman, picked up the dropped shotgun, and entered the bedroom. He ripped a quilt from the bed and threw it over the fire. The quilt smothered it and the light. In the darkness, his eyes retained a flare of orange and red for a moment.

"Light another lamp, Sylvan," Reedley said.

Addison wrinkled his nose at the smell of coal oil and scorched fabric. A match flared. The wire lifting lever of a lamp *screek*-ed. Enough light reached the door to reveal the quilt smoking. He grabbed it and threw it out onto the dirt. He turned around. Waverly hadn't moved. His wife stood by the kitchen table, wearing not a stitch of clothes, seeming to be unconcerned about that. She blew out the match before it burned her husband's fingers.

Reedley told her to sit, and he held the lamp and knelt in front of the nude woman and inspected her feet. "Gonna' be blisters, I expect."

"I've had worse," she said, displaying not a lick of concern over her state of undress. "Thank You, God. There wasn't much oil in that lamp."

For a moment, Addison thought he was dreaming. A bare-naked woman praying to God? Then Joshua Reedley knelt in front of the bare-naked wife of another man like he was going to propose to her. In the real world, how could such a thing be?

Sylvan stood rooted to the spot by the table and looked over his shoulder at the two of them. Sylvan, an unarmed statue, did not concern Addison. His eyes moved back to the woman and her pale smooth skin.

"Get your wife some clothes. Move, man!" the wagon master said.

Sylvan Waverly stood still, the look on his face like that of a steer about to slaughtered with a sledgehammer and knowing fighting it would be futile.

"I'll do it myself." She first looked at her husband with disgust, then at the floor, for broken glass probably, and entered the bedroom.

The bare back and buttocks of … Mrs. … Lizbeth's mother disappeared into the bedroom. A minute later, she stood in the doorway, wearing a fresh nightgown, mercifully. She glanced at Addison. He looked away.

"You rode all night?" she asked, and Reedley said they did.

"I'll fix you something to eat."

"Uh, Mrs.—"

"Hah!" from Mrs. Waverly.

To Addison, that syllable had sounded hard and bitter. Still, it might have been a laugh.

"I'm not going to put rat poison in your food, Joshua. I might put some in his, though." She glared at her husband. "Stupid! I told you to wait a couple of weeks. And I told you somebody would come back from the train."

"I didn't think they'd get here for two weeks." The second deacon had *it's not my fault* smeared over his face.

"Ma'am," Reedley said. "Let me tend to your feet."

"I do not need a *man* to pop my blisters and rub on ointment." She walked to the stove, opened the stoking door, and shook her head. "Men, how would you survive if you didn't have women to lead you around and tell you what to do and when to do it?" She stirred up the ashes. "First, clean up the broken glass by the door." She fed in tinder and kindling. "Then," she said. "Tend to your horses."

Addison bent to pick up shards. Reedley told Waverly to get a broom. When they finished the chore, the second deacon wanted to get dressed. Reedley pushed him out the door as he was, in his nightshirt.

"Oh, Addison." Mrs. Waverley put the top on the coffee pot. "I saw you naked, too. Course it was eighteen years ago."

He turned and bolted out the door.

Lantern light glowed from inside the barn. He shivered as the night air chilled the sweat under his shirt.

He found Reedley cinching a saddle to Waverly's riding horse. Addison was to ride to all the farms and notify them that there was a meeting in the church for all men and boys over twelve.

"Get some of the young men, like Norm Niedlinger, to help notifying folks. Meeting time is half-hour after sunup. Go to your... to your old place last. Lizbeth and her husband, Orson Seiling, live there now. Don't shoot him. Unless you have to.

"First, ask Mrs. Waverly to give you something to eat. But don't dawdle."

At the house, he knocked on the door and entered. He was pleased with himself when he looked at her and didn't blush. She gave him a cup of coffee and a ham sandwich—a substantial one.

"Thank you, Ma'am."

She smiled at him and sighed.

As he mounted with the sandwich in his hand, he thought about her sigh. He wondered if it had been a what-might-have-been sigh for him and Lizbeth. Maybe it was for herself and her husband, and what they might have had if Sylvan hadn't been stupid and jumped the gun.

He bit off a chunk of sandwich, chewed, and gigged his horse into a canter. Swallowing the mouthful, he was about to bite off another when he thought about rousting Lizbeth and Orson from the bed they shared.

"Son of a bitch," he said, threw the sandwich away, and smacked the reins across the animal's haunch. It kicked up a gallop.

*****

Addison lit and placed lanterns along the sides of Found Grace Church. He found comfort in the familiar chore as if that simple task had brought him home again. Those few minutes, however, had ticked away almighty fast.

When he touched the match to the last wick, it seemed to throw light on the fact home was not what it had been. Neither was Found Grace Church. Nor was he the same. He had a pistol in a holster under his left arm. He wore it in a holy place. That pistol had … no. *He* had killed three men.

Killed three men.

It was as if his mind refused to put that *I* in front of the thought. Some spiritual force wanted that "I" to be there and make of it a proper sentence. But he, or his mind, pushed back and tried to keep that one letter so heaped with condemnation at bay.

Something pushed it, though. An angel, a messenger of the Lord, or a henchman of the devil?

Pa! Pa was saying, *YOU killed three men!*

A hand rested on his shoulder, and he flinched. Reedley.

"Son, a fox in the field eats rabbits and mice. We bless him for that. A fox in the henhouse has to be killed." The wagon master patted his shoulder. "Go stand in the back. Off to the side."

Reedley walked up the side aisle and stood by Sylvan Waverly, who sat on the deacon's chair, his arms bound to the armrests. He wore his nightshirt stuffed into pants. His chin rested on his chest.

A wagon rumbled onto the lot outside. Addison walked to the rear to stand in a corner.

The life of a fox and the life of a man. Was Reedley saying they weigh the same?

They didn't weigh the same.

He'd come to respect the wagon master. When he spoke, it was like hearing Larrimer preach. Sort of. In Larrimer's sermons, he, at times, could almost see the ladder to heaven that appeared to Jacob. Reedley's words, however, contained not *how to get to heaven;* they contained *how to get along on earth. The right way.*

Boots clumped on the small porch, and he stood up straight.

Axel Bosley took one step into the center aisle from the vestibule. His head snapped left. His eyes, Addison was sure, registered the pistol. Axel faced forward, stood for a moment, then he nodded. To Joshua, he thought. Not Waverly, who still had his eyes cast down.

Hooves, trace chains, planks rattling on crossbeams of wagon beds, all announced the arrival of the remaining stay-behinds.

Eleven men, and eighteen sons, filed in and occupied the first three pews. All of them were there: Axel Bosley to Thad Tamber. Except Orson Seiling. Lizbeth's husband was in the bride's dressing room. Addison fetched him. His hands were tied together behind him. A bandana ran under his nose and ended in a knot behind his head. Addison shoved him down the aisle and parked him in the fourth pew on the deacon side. He untied the bandana, pulled out the rag that had been stuffed into his mouth, and dropped it to the floor.

Joshua Reedley swept his eyes over the men. "Anybody side with Waverly?"

Orson Seiling stood. "I do."

Everyone turned to look at Orson. Except his father. Rudy Seiling, Addison noted, stared straight ahead.

Reedley smiled a little. "Orson Seiling. Anyone else?"

"Why you asking?" Marvin Dinwiddie, in the second pew, said.

"I want to know how many people I have to hang before I can go back to the crusade."

That plopped a heavy hunk of silence into the place.

After a moment, Orson Seiling said, "Pa?"

Mr. Seiling, in the pew in front of him, didn't turn around. "You made your bed, Boy."

Reedley faced the second deacon. "You have a choice. Come with us to Kansas and vote to abolish slavery, or you can hang right here. Which'll it be?"

Waverly raised his head. "You're not going to let him get away with this!" His eyes scanned the rows of seated men, looking at them, including Addison, for help, for pity, for salvation.

No one in the congregation responded to the plea.

"Three seconds to decide. One, two—"

"Kansas! I'll go to Kansas."

Reedley pulled a folded paper from an inside pocket of his coat and held it up. "This is a letter from Preacher Larrimer." He stepped down from the platform and handed the letter to Axel Bosley in the first row. "Read it out loud, please."

Bosley rose and faced the pews.

> To Whom it may concern
> Joshua Reedley has been appointed Wagon Master during our crusade and pilgrimage to Kansas. All in Found Church are subordinate to him, including myself, and including the members of our congregation still in Illinois.

"Preacher Larrimer signed it. It's his signature."

Reedley took the letter back and held it up. "Anybody want to argue with this? If you do, let's hear it now."

"Were you really going to hang Waverly?" Bosley said.

"I laid it out that I would."

"Nobody's siding with Waverly," Thad Tamber said. "Most of us were not happy with the direction he was taking us, but we didn't have the guts to stand up to him. And Preacher had appointed him deacon."

"He's no longer deacon," Reedley said. "We need a new one, someone we can trust to carry out the crusade Preacher Larrimer set us on. Who's the best man for the job? Anyone want to put forward a name?"

A buzz of mumbled voices rose, only to be squashed by the sound of wagons, a number of them, entering the lot. Reedley nodded to Addison. He pulled his pistol and went to see who had come.

He opened the rear door to find women, the wives and mothers of the males seated inside, climbing down from buggies. They crowded together and then a line peeled away and marched toward the door. "Women. It's the women." Then he retreated to Orson Seiling's pew and pushed him farther into it.

Reedley said, "Addison, put your gun away."

He'd forgotten he had it in his hand. At Lizbeth's house that morning, he'd forgotten to put it in his hand. Orson answered the knock on the door yawning and with tousled hair and holding a shotgun with the stock resting on the floor. When he saw Addison, he pulled the gun up and put it to his shoulder, but he'd forgotten to cock the hammers. Addison drew his pistol, and the double clicks of cocking froze Lizbeth's husband, and his eyes grew big.

In the church, all the men faced the rear. Addison, after holstering his weapon, did too.

The ladies filed in and took position, one at the end of each pew, seven, eight of them. Mrs. Waverly and Lizbeth entered and stood to either side of the door.

Lizbeth. When Addison looked at her, he saw not her, but *them* together. That thought hit him harder than his pa's refusal to let him marry her. It was like she'd been ruined. Forever ruined. He shook his head to get her out of there.

Her mother wore a dress buttoned up to her neck. Bare feet peeked out from under the lacy hem. The feet were red.

Agatha Janson and Loraine Rand marched through the door and down the aisle side-by-side. All the women wore bonnets except Agatha. Addison remembered her as having long black hair. Now her hair was cut short as his own. Agatha stopped between the first row of pews. Lorraine walked up to the deacon's podium and moved Joshua Reedley aside.

Addison knew Lorraine was in her thirties. Attractive. Brown hair. A ready smile, soft-spoken. But that Saturday morning, her face wore Preacher Larrimer's stern glower as she, as the preacher so often did, scanned the congregation for any spiritual whiff of sin.

Lorraine Rand's husband stood up in the second pew. "What in heaven's name are you doing, woman?"

Agatha Janson struck quick as a snake. "Omar Rand. Shut! Up! And sit down."

Omar sat and turned and looked at Eric Janson seated in the row behind him. Eric shook his head.

Lorraine rapped her knuckles on the deacon's podium. "Gentlemen. After Joshua gathered you men up, Agatha got us ladies together. We discussed Preacher Larrimer's crusade. We talked about where Sylvan Waverly would lead us. Preacher Larrimer thought Sylvan was good and righteous man. We all did. But Sylvan looked on the farms abandoned by half of our congregation and saw, not the means to further Found Church's holy pilgrimage. No. He saw the means for personal enrichment. Tomorrow, Sunday, he would have stood up here and read from the Book and told us he had a vision. 'God told him,' he would say, 'that Found Church's true mission was to stay where we are and preserve our island of pure righteousness in a sinful world.' We know this because Adele Waverly told us this is what he intended to say."

Lorraine pointed at the bound second deacon. "This wolf in sheep's clothing would have turned the house of Lord into a house to worship Satan and his deadly sins."

"We decided two things. Sylvan Waverly is no longer our deacon, and Agatha is our spiritual leader."

Lorraine stepped back, and Agatha strode up and took position behind the podium.

Agatha Janson cast a pretty darned fierce gaze, Addison thought, over the men in their pews. She looked as at home at the speaker's place as Preacher Larrimer did.

"Our first order of business, ladies and gentlemen," Agatha said, "is to re-consecrate this building to the worship of God in heaven and our souls to the reception of His grace."

"Huh! A woman can't be a deacon."

Everyone turned to stare at Orson Seiling.

"Orson, and the rest of you," Reedley said, "I will tell you the male deacons of Found Church have been a sore disappointment to our congregation and our crusade."

Addison's face flushed warm.

"Agatha is not our deacon," Reedley said, "She is our Judge Deborah. Just like for the Israelites. She is here to save us from the sin in our midst and to lead us to the new promised land. Judge Deborah." Reedley nodded to her.

"Joshua," Judge Deborah Agatha said, "take a seat."

Reedley entered the pew behind Addison.

The Deborah Judge directed Adele Waverly and Lizbeth Seiling to carry a backless bench forward and to place it before the step at the front of church. She explained the bench was their penitents' pew. "Joshua Reedley and Addison Freeman. You will hand over your pistols to Lorraine." Reedley handed over his, Addison gave his. "Come forward. Sit on the pew facing the congregation. Confess to God Almighty and to the congregation that you defiled the sanctity of the house of the Lord by bringing weapons inside. Ask for forgiveness."

"This is stupid," Orson Seiling said. "A woman can't be a preacher."

His mother walked across the aisle, slapped him, and returned to her place next to the fifth pew from the front.

10.

Addison sat on the penance pew as Reedley confessed his sin and asked for forgiveness. Agatha the Ruth invited the congregation to lift a united prayer to Father God in heaven that He hear brother Joshua's prayer and restore grace to his soul.

After a pause, every eye in front of Addison lay communal conscience on him. It hung on his shoulders like a winter coat. He took a breath, expelled it, then followed the simple script the wagon master had used. He finished and looked down at the floor.

"Father God in heaven," Agatha the Ruth began.

"Another thing. Yesterday, I killed three men." He rose, aimed his gaze down the center aisle lined with standing women, and he walked to and sat in the pew behind Orson Seiling.

Agatha the Ruth frowned. "You asked for forgiveness for bringing a gun into church but not for killing?"

Reedley stood. "Agatha the Ruth, in your penance pew, I see the wisdom of Solomon. I have been wagon master for only a few days. And I confess to the Almighty, and to all of you, I never needed anything as much as that moment I spent sitting here."

He thanked the woman behind the podium. "I'm not sure Addison knows how to answer your question. I do."

Addison asked himself, when you kill a man, or three, how in blue blazes do you talk about it? Or think about it? Or deal with it? Other than running away from it. All the things that happened since he'd pulled that trigger and cocked the gun and … squeezed, he hadn't pulled. He'd squeezed. And cocked and squeezed and cocked and squeezed. And three men were dead. Gut shot Wesley Thompson took a while and some agony to die.

"Thou shalt not kill," Reedley said. "We butcher all manner of God's creatures, and we eat them. We dig up potatoes. What have we done? We've killed animals and plants. Someone intends to shoot you, and you kill them first. Are you guilty of sin?

"Are you guilty?"

Addison flinched.

"There is a time for every purpose under heaven. You must feed your family. You must save your life when another would take it." Delivered softly, forcing Addison to focus his attention to pick up the words. "You are not guilty of sin.

"And neither is Addison a sinner. If he had not shot those men, he, and Royal Howard, and others of us would be dead. If he had not shot them, Preacher Larrimer's crusade would have died in a place called Thompson Township. A hard day's ride from here, and Thompson Township is many days of travel from where we need to go."

He raked his eyes across the congregation, just as the preacher did.

"We left here on Tuesday. We were innocent. As innocent as the Children's Crusade hundreds of years ago. Those children believed with all their hearts and souls that their holy purpose would see them to a blessed end. Their hopes were dashed. But Addison saved our hopes from dashing onto the stones of disappointment. And failure.

"To bring our crusade to a holy conclusion, we will have to become warriors. We have to be prepared to fight our way to our destination."

That was a pill to swallow.

Carrying the weight of three lives into eternity concerned him. Now the wagon master was saying he'd have more lives … deaths to carry.

"The other thing I will tell you is that Addison doesn't want to be forgiven for killing those men."

How did he know that?

"When you kill a man, sometimes you sin. Other times not. But sin or no sin, a death at your hands," the wagon master glanced at his own, "rides heavy."

So many times in that church, he had listened to Preacher Larrimer say words that laid out the path to salvation and how to avoid the one to damnation. That Sunday, Reedley preached another, *How in blue blazes do I live with myself on earth,* sermon.

He felt eyes on him.

Lizbeth. She stood at the end of the penance pew. Her eyes poured longing and eternal loss into his own. He could not bear it, rose, and walked out of church.

Outside, he found the sun above the horizon and put on his hat and stuck the Navy Colt in its holster. Outside, he found It easier to breathe.

From inside, the wagon master's voice carried across the lot. Agatha the Ruth said a prayer. Reedley said another. He didn't pay attention as he crossed the packed dirt lot to where a handful of saddle horses grazed in the shade of elm trees. Outlaw looked at him, bobbed its head, and returned to eating.

As he approached the animals, he began speaking slow and soft and low.

"You're thinking I'm going to pull you away. So, you're eating faster. Not for a while yet." He patted the chestnut on the shoulder. His stomach grumbled. "I had a sandwich, but I threw it away. Move over a bit. I'm hungry enough to eat grass, too."

"Addison!"

A steady stream of young men and women filed out of the church past the wagon master. Reedley gestured, "hurry it up."

Addison trotted across the lot.

Reedley nodded to those climbing into wagons and buggies. "They are going to roust up the supplies we need. Get with the Niedlinger boy, Simon. He's going with us. You and him pick two sound teams and a wagon in good shape. Find four saddle mounts. We'll leave the ones we rode."

"Not Outlaw."

Reedley glared at him. He stared back.

"Son." The wagon master put a hand on his shoulder. "Orson Seiling is going, too. Not much chance the penance pew can straighten him out." He grinned. "I told his mother you could."

"Me? I'm not straight my own self."

"You'll handle it. Now, I have more things to discuss with Agatha the Ruth. And you have chores to do. Enough dawdling here."

Reedley walked back inside.

He headed across the lot to tell Outlaw he was done eating. His stomach reminded him it hadn't started eating. "Yeah, yeah." He kicked a potato-sized rock out of his way.

*****

A few minutes before noon, the wagon with supplies for the crusaders entered the church lot. Reedley hustled his traveling companions into beginning the journey. Simon Niedlinger drove. Addison climbed atop the load, lay down on the sack of corn stalks mattress and was asleep with his head still on the way to the pillow.

A hand on his shoulder shook him out of slumber. Dry-mouthed, fuzzy-headed. His left arm tingled as it came back to life, and tingling and ache dragged the rest of his body into function.

They'd stopped at a creek. He walked upstream of the animals, and he drank and splashed water on his face.

Reedley told Addison to get them moving again. "My turn for shuteye. Wake me before dark."

The wagon master climbed up and under the tarp covering his single wagon train. The corn stalks rustled. A sigh issued forth from within.

He stood on the bank, his boots sunk an inch into the mud, water dripping from his face onto his shirt.

They'd parked the wagon on grass beside the road. Four draft and three saddle horses drank and swished their tails at flies. It was curious. The animals were doing two things at once. He couldn't do one. Outlaw, at the stream, and Orson Seiling and Norman Niedlinger by the wagon tongue, stared at him and waited.

He ran his fingers through his hair and put on his hat. "Um, hitch the team."

Norman wanted to know which team.

"The fresh team. Which horses were you riding?"

Orson laughed. "Those wearing saddles."

Ridicule at the hands of Lizbeth's husband woke him.

When they set out, Norman drove. The spare team and three saddle broncs were tied to the rear, as was Orson, by a rope around his waist. Orson's hands were tied in front of him, and his bottom lip was split and fat on one side. A bandana tied under his nose hid it and gagged him, so Reedley could sleep.

They splashed through the ford, and Norman snapped the reins. The team stepped into a canter. Addison rode behind. Orson surprised him. He kept up longer than he'd expected. Then he stumbled, and the wagon dragged him.

Norman stopped. They untied Orson, dragged him up to the team, and hoisted him onto the back of the right horse, just as the sheriff had been when the crusade entered Thompson Township.

"You best hold on," Addison told him. "You fall off, and either the wagon will run over you or the horses will trample you."

Orson hung on. They made good time. Reedley had said they should make Thompson Township before sunup. "With luck."

They passed through a town. Orson, sitting where he was, caused a stir. Men, women, and children looked, pointed, and laughed. One of them wore a sheriff star on his shirt pocket. He rubbed his chin as he studied the spectacle. Addison tipped his hat to the lawman and rode on. The sheriff squared his hat and pushed through the batwing doors of the saloon behind him.

Next to the saloon doorway, two men, late twenties, Addison thought, leaned chairs against the wall. As the wagon passed, the other townspeople went about their business. The chair-sitters, however, continued to study them. At the edge of town, he turned in the saddle. They were standing now, still staring. Sure as shooting, they were thinking about something other than the curiosity of Orson sitting bound and gagged on a draft horse.

Maybe they think to rob us. They'd figure they only had kids to deal with and stupid kids at that. Would they wait till dark? The sun was sitting on the horizon. There'd be a moon, but they might want some daylight to do their business.

A mile from the town, the road sliced through woods. Addison had Norman pull up and told him of his suspicions.

"We should wake Reedley," Norman said.

"Let him sleep. Just be ready to grab a shotgun. And don't worry so much about them coming from behind. Watch out front. There might be a way for them to get ahead of us."

"What about Orson? We going to leave him where he is?"

"Nope," Addison replied. "Help me."

They pulled him off the horse, bound his arms to his sides, tied his legs together, and stashed him under the driver bench.

"We should wake Reedley."

"Listen, Norman. What do you hear?"

He cocked his head. "Nothing."

"The bugs."

"Well, yeah. Them."

"The day animals and birds have gone to roost. The night creatures haven't yet left theirs. Anybody after us?"

"No."

They harnessed the spare team, and Addison told Norman to trot them. Addison stayed behind. When the wagon noise receded, he listened for riders. Nothing. Astride again, he ran his bronc, but not full out, and continued until he caught up to the wagon. Then he stopped again, ground hitched the animal, and walked a few paces to distance himself from its blowing. He listened.

Woods still walled the road, but ahead in the dusk, a way off, a lantern glowed in a window. Light from the just set sun still smeared the horizon. Behind him, a few stars had started taking over. Along with the new moon. Bug noises. An owl. Something skittered over dried leaves in the forest. After returning to the horse, he leaned against the animal's shoulder. It adjusted its stance.

"You hear or smell anything?" Addison whispered to the horse.

After a moment, he mounted and cantered up to the wagon and stopped it.

Norman had his hat off. There was enough light to see he was worried. Addison switched to Outlaw and sent the wagon on its way again.

Addison waited on the road for the rattle and jangle to pull away.

Outlaw bobbed his head. Riders. The wall of trees to both sides made the road a corridor of blackness. Addison pulled his mount a few yards into the trees and whispered, "Now when those horses pass by, if they whicker to you, don't you answer them. Nooo. You stand here real quiet."

It hit him then, what Norman had said. They should have awakened Reedley. He did not know for certain they only had to face two men. Others could have gotten around them. Others could be coming from that town. He could handle those he'd seen. What if there's four?

Stupid!

Too late now.

He stepped to the edge of the woods and saw them. Hatted black shoulder silhouettes floating on a sea of ink. He stepped back to Outlaw and rested his hand on its neck. The horse shivered. "Hooo now."

After the riders cantered past, Addison swung up and walked the bronc onto the grass alongside the road. "Go."

Outlaw launched into a full-out run. The grass muffled the hooves some, and the two men didn't hear him until the last moment. Both of them turned as he came even with the rider on the left. He smacked the man across the face with his Navy Colt, and he fell over the rump and off his mount.

Addison aimed his pistol at the other. "Rein up." The man did. "Step down and raise 'em."

Addison pulled a pistol from the man's belt. He stuck it in the saddlebag on Outlaw. He wasn't about to stick the thing in his pants without being able to ensure the hammer sat on an empty chamber.

"You robbin' us?"

"Sit down," Addison said. "Take your boots off. Do it."

"Stealin' a man's boots is low."

Next, Addison had the man strip off his pants, which shut him up for a minute. With his knife, he slashed strips of cloth from a leg. He sat the man against a tree and twisted a strip into a cord and tied the man's hands together. As he worked, the first fellow moaned. Then he dragged him to an adjacent tree and bound him, too.

"You cain't leave us like this," the one not bleeding from his mouth said.

But he did leave them, both bootless and disarmed and whining and moaning. He led their horses a mile down the road and tied the reins to saplings and dropped the boots there, too.

Outlaw overtook the wagon.

After he stopped the wagon, Norman said, "We should wake Reedley. He said before dark. It's good and dark."

"Let him sleep," Addison replied. "I'm wide awake. I'm going on ahead. Maybe I can find us some water."

"Outlaw." The horse launched into a canter and pulled ahead of the at-a-walk team.

His face smiled without him thinking about it or why. What he did think about was concentrating on his side-of-the-eye vision. The wagon master had told him, "Some animals see better at night than a man does in daylight. At night, a man staring straight ahead is blind. If you can make yourself use the sides of your eyeballs, you'll see things."

Reedley was right about that, as he was about most things.

"Your eyes work better than a man's at night, right?" He patted Outlaw's neck. "Your nose and ears, too. Horses sleep standing up. Can you sleep while you're running? Well, don't doze off on me now."

The horse's gait change roused Addison. He scanned all around, then scanned again with side-of-the-eyeball vision. Nothing. "What is it, Outlaw?" He cocked his head and heard night insects. He sniffed. Water? Water. He smelled it. It was time for water.

"Judas!" The realization hit that he'd fallen asleep, and he didn't know for how long.

The wagon could be miles behind them. It could have been waylaid. He looked up at the moon. Telling time by the sun was one thing. He had experience with that. He was about to turn around and find Norman and Reedley, but he had another thought. Water first, then find them.

The water was a lead and silver rivulet at the bottom of a gulley.

A wooden bridge spanned it. Off to the right of the road, the slope of the side of the gulley eased. They'd be able to get down for a drink.

They drank, and Addison led the horse back up to the road. As he was about to mount, Outlaw's ears twitched. He cocked his head. After a moment, he heard it, too. A wagon.

"If Reedley asks if I did anything stupid, don't tell him."

Outlaw snorted.

The wagon arrived with the wagon master astride a saddle bronc. Reedley had some questions.

"Why didn't you wake me before dark, like I said to? Do you have any idea where we are?"

Norman answered that. He gave the name of the last town they passed through and how many minutes ago.

"Where'd you get that Dragoon pistol in the saddle holster hanging from the horn?"

"I found it," Addison said.

Reedley took off his hat and looked up at the moon, then at Addison.

"Boy. It is possible for a man to grow wiser and stupider at the very same time." The wagon master put his hat back on. "Go button the trapdoor on Orson's long johns. He can't do it with his hands tied in front. Then load him on the wagon. Norman and me'll hitch the team."

When they were ready, Addison drove. Norman slept on the bed. Orson sat on the bench beside him. Reedley had taken the gag off him.

"You say a single word," Addison said, "and I'll put the gag back on you." He clucked the team into motion. The wheels set up a thunder crossing the bridge.

11.

A moon would have been nice. One was up there beyond the overcast. Hour after hour, rumbling down the dark road, unable to see beyond the horses' ears much of the time, thinking the beasts might take them over a cliff. At least that would end the endless night.

Addison's head buzzed. His eyes ached, and his mouth tasted like he'd swallowed a slug of nice cold milk that had gone bad. His stomach thought that might have happened too. *It would be nice if the bench stuck a splinter in my butt.* A sharp pain to replace, for an instant, the monotony of the all-over dull ache. The wagon slowed. He snapped the reins. "You aggravating animals." He'd taken to thinking of them as the Contrary Team. "I've a mind to stop and cut one of Pa's willow switches. Step it up now."

Unless he flicked the reins every few minutes and his voice conveyed irritation and held the promise of unpleasant consequences, the Contrary Team slowed. Which annoyed him. But it also kept him awake. At least a part of him awake.

He had never been so weary, never experienced such a long, endless night. Most of his brain and body were not asleep, but they refused to function unless something prodded them. His brain and body were like the Contrary Team. That thought rattled around in the core of wakefulness in the center of his half dormant brain. Then the memory of the night he'd changed his middle name to Job appeared.

Lizbeth. And Lizbeth's husband sitting next to him on the driver's bench. It wouldn't do to fall asleep with Orson there, ready to take his pistol if he nodded off. He wouldn't survive a second encounter with him and a gun in his hand.

Thank You, God.

What day was it? Figuring that out was work. Too much work. Time no longer meant what it did. Some days ago, Joshua Reedley whanged horseshoes together and turned the traveling half of Found Grace Church from disorganized rabble to a crusade. The crusade made as many miles that morning as they did in two of the previous days. They arrived in Thompson Township, and after killing three men, he and Reedley rode all night and returned home. Sylvan Waverly had betrayed Preacher Larrimer and Found Grace, and Lizbeth had gotten herself married. Reedley appointed Agatha the Deborah Judge as spiritual leader of the Illinois part of the congregation. And the wagon master, Addison, Orson, and Norman departed to rejoin the wagon train. It felt like a lifetime.

"Sylvan Waverly was stupid." Orson's first words since they set out. "I was stupider to listen to him."

That didn't sound like Orson. It sounded sincere. Trusting him, though, was a ways off yet. From inside the wagon, Norman snorted, and the corn stalks rustled in the makeshift mattress.

Addison snapped the reins. "Hey-up, you worthless flea-bags. We get to Thompson Township, guess which team ain't getting no oats." Ma would light into him for his trashy talk, but it was the appropriate way to talk to the Contrary Team. He snapped the reins over the left animal. "You. I'm calling you Sylvan." The reins popped on the back of the other. "Your name is Judas." He snapped the reins harder, and he cussed the team without using cuss words.

"We runnin' from somebody?" Norman said.

"Nope," Orson said. "Go back to sleep."

"We ain't runnin' away. Then why're you running the horses?"

"Addison thought they was dawdling. Go back to sleep."

The corn stalks rustled. The team slowed to a trot. Addison allowed it.

"Waverly had some of us watching the wagon train," Orson said. "I was watching Friday morning when Reedley rousted you all up and got you moving before sunup. I hustled back and told Waverly what happened. He thought we didn't have anything to worry about anymore. He married Lizbeth and me that afternoon."

He worked the reins. Waverly and Judas held to a trot.

"My dad told me I was stupid to listen to the second deacon. But I saw the most beautiful girl in the world as my wife. I saw me owning my own farm. I thought I knew better."

Orson was two years older. In school, he'd picked on kids littler than him. If he lost at pitching horseshoes, he'd pull a boy's pants down, or something else to make the smaller one cry. Now Addison was taller and heavier and had, in fact, picked on him a few hours ago. But Orson remained stuck in his head as a tyrant.

"Lizbeth and me—"

"Shut up, Orson. Or so help me, God. I will gag you and tie you behind the wagon and drag you the rest of way. Shut. Up."

The team busted into a run again.

Addison's anger fizzled out like a falling star. He was too tired to judge … Lizbeth's husband. He was too tired for anything but the thought of getting to Thompson Township before sunup.

Later, it could have been a short time or a long time, Orson elbowed Addison's ribs. "You see him?"

"Who?"

"At the top of the rise, left side of the road."

Addison made out the shadow form of rider and a horse.

"Reedley?"

The rider didn't turn around. The wagon made a racket. "Probably." Addison drew and cocked his Colt. In case it wasn't the wagon master.

He reined the team beside him, beside Reedley, and looked down on Thompson Township. A fire burned on the far side of the village. The blaze outlined the steepled church. Iron whanging on iron noise whispered across the mile to them.

"Royal Howard," Reedley said and gigged his bronc into a canter.

Orson said, "You kin have 'er. She sure as hell doesn't want me."

Addison shoved him hard, and he tumbled off the seat and onto the roadbed.

"*Giddyup,* you sons a bitches."

Sylvan and Judas galloped past the wagon master. Addison ran the team down the hill and over the mile to the edge of town. There he reined them in and stopped them in front of the saloon.

Reedley rode up next to him, and Orson Seiling slipped off the back of the horse.

"We can't have you throwing away our voters," the wagon master said. "I told Mrs. Seiling you would straighten her son out. Don't make me a liar."

Addison said he wouldn't.

"No time to dawdle." Reedley rode off. He wanted Otto Vogelsang to inspect the recklessly driven wagon.

Addison ordered Norman and Orson to water the horses in the trough behind the saloon. They said, "Yes, sir," as one. In front of the jail, a lantern hung from a post holding up the roof. In its light, he spotted Lester Thompson, the new sheriff, watching him. Addison crossed the street.

"Sheriff, I took your brother's horse. I'd like to buy it from you if you'll sell."

"We're square."

"Uh, you know, Sheriff, I'm the one—"

"We're square." Sheriff Lester stuck out his hand, and they shook. "Your friend, Maurice, wanted to come say goodbye. Doc says his bones is beginning to heal, but he should stay in bed another couple of days. Maybe you'd like to call on him."

Lamps lit the ground floor room in the doctor's place. Eunice sat in a chair beside the bed. Maurice lay propped on pillows.

Addison removed his hat. "Miss Eunice."

She smiled and dropped her eyes to her hands on her lap. A regular dress. She wore a regular dress, not a split-up-the-middle one.

He didn't know what to say to his friend. No words came to Maurice, either, for once. The wiseacre looked cat-got-your-tongue bashful.

"We're getting married," Eunice said.

Addison looked from Eunice to Maurice and back to her. Her chin lifted an inch, and her lips scrunched together.

"Not for a couple of weeks," the patient said. "Doc says I need to be healed up good, first."

Eunice blushed.

Joshua Reedley walked in. He congratulated his son and bride-to-be and told them he'd be back in the summer to form up the remainder of Found Church into a wagon train. "If you're of a mind to, Addison, you can come with me. Or if you want to stay in Kansas, you can see Mr. and Mrs. Maurice Reedley in the fall."

Addison shook hands with Maurice, nodded to Eunice, and followed the wagon master out the door.

"I want to get me back to Reverend Redmond's church for the morning prayer because I need it?"

"Every man-jack of us needs it, Addison," Reedley said. "And many of us need it more than you do. Once you deal with shooting those men, you'll understand. After the preachers say the prayer, you and Orson sleep in the wagon. Norman will drive."

"I thought I'd sleep in Pa's wagon."

Reedley shook his head as he mounted. "Do as I said."

Addison hesitated, then he grabbed the horn and pulled himself up and followed the wagon master to the church lot. The two preachers stood in an empty wagon. Preacher Redmond prayed for a minute and asked the Lord to bless the Found Church Holy Crusade. Preacher Larrimer prayed for another minute and thanked the Lord for the blessing of Thompson Township and the holy citizens residing there.

"On to Kansas," Reedley said and looked at the glow in the eastern sky. "Right on time."

As the crusaders hustled to their wagons, Addison noted that all the married women wore Eunice skirts. And it was funny. So many women wearing that kind of dress, it was no longer unseemly, no longer wrong.

He was too tired to ponder the right and wrong of things and crawled into the back of the provisions wagon. Orson was already asleep.

"Norman, give us an easy ride now."

"Sure. I'll give you a gentle ride. Just like—"

Addison did not hear the rest of what Norman said.

12.

His eyes opened. Something was wrong. Light out. Why would his mother let him sleep so late? "Ma?"

"Yes, Addison dear." Norman's girl voice. Annoying. "Should I empty your chamber pot or cook you breakfast?"

Orson, on the other side of the wagon bed, snorted and sat up. "We should change Norman to Norma and get him a Eunice skirt."

Waking to Norman's sissy voice was one thing. Orson's presumption he was a natural partner to banter, like a friend, that stepped beyond annoyance.

Addison sat up. "Why'd we stop?"

The silly grin on Norman's face dissolved. "Uh, it's close to noon. Time to water and graze the animals."

"Then why in blue blazes are you sitting there?"

"Norman, why are you just sitting there?" Royal Howard's voice, also beyond annoyed, came from the other side of the canvas cover. "We pull out in an hour. Get to it."

Royal had stopped at a stream with half the wagons on one side, half on the other. Their wagon was with the still-to-cross half.

Norman led the team. Orson took Outlaw and the other bronc to the creek. Addison inspected the wheels, tongue, and cross tree. Then he untied Contrary Team and walked them toward the stream. Off to his right, at a distance, he noticed a bridge. Not much of a bridge, but the stream wasn't much more than a ditch. Why didn't Royal lead them across the bridge? The road there paralleled the one they were on.

Judas stopped. His ears stood up. Waverly whinnied and pulled against the lead rope.

Addison dug in his heels. "Whoa now. What is it? You smell a bear? Don't you worry. A bear shows up here; we'll shoot him so full of lead, won't be one chunk of meat to him without a bullet in it. Don't you worry about a bear. Noooo."

The team calmed some, and they started toward the stream again when the ground trembled. Waverly reared, jerked the lead rope out of his hand, and tore off east down the road. Addison wrapped his arms around Judas's neck and pulled his head down to keep him from running off, too. The animal spun around, and Addison hung on, though he was no more than a straw-filled scarecrow to the spooked animal.

Reedley rode up and dropped a loop over the panicked horse's neck and wound his lariat around the saddle horn. Addison let go of the animal's neck.

"Royal," Reedley hollered. "Too many kids with the stock. Get men out there."

At the stream and in the meadow, mostly boys and girls tended the animals. Royal shouted and ran out onto the meadow with a number of men on his heels. The wagon master ordered Addison to chase down the runaway.

Woo woo. An ungodly roar of a beast escaped from hell came from the east. A column of thick black smoke rose above the trees from that direction.

"It's a railroad train," Reedley said. "Those blasted engineers love to blow their whistle and frighten animals."

Downstream of their road, the black engine rumbled onto the bridge and blew its whistle again. At the stream, cows and horses jerked heads upwards and backed away from the water. From the middle of the meadow, a bronc raced for the road dragging a boy on a rope.

"Let go," Reedley hollered.

The kid hung on. Otto Vogelsang ran to get in front of the horse and waved his arms. The animal pulled up and reared. Otto stepped aside as the hooves came back to earth, and he grabbed the bronc's reins and jerked it to a stop.

"Addison, catch that runaway fore it gets back to Thompson Township," Reedley ordered again.

Addison took the reins of the frightened animal from Otto and spoke to the beast. Vogelsang walked back and helped the boy to his feet. The straps of the boy's overalls had torn loose. He'd lost a boot and the overalls were bunched atop the one remaining.

Vogelsang pulled the youngster to his feet, looked at the wagon master, and grinned. "A *mensch,* this one, no?"

Addison vaulted onto the saddle and set off after Waverly.

*****

Addison stopped next to the wagon with Waverly on a lead. "Give him a drink and put him in harness," he said to Norman.

"I thought we should hook up the other team again, seeing's how that one run its fool self out."

"Nope. Contrary Team's taking another turn. Give Waverly a drink and hook them up."

"There's blood on the rope," Norman said.

Reedley was close by and came over. "Rope burn. Your shootin' hand, too." He led Addison to the next wagon behind. It belonged to one of the families from Thompson Township.

Theodore and Leah Welch had two boys and a girl.

Theodore, a tad shorter than Addison, outweighed him by more than a tad. He told Reedley, "Yep, my girl Mariah helped Doc Federson time to time." He checked the rope burn. "She tended things like this when Doc was out of town."

Mariah, when called by her father, walked out from behind their wagon. About fifteen, Addison thought. She wore a Eunice skirt. Her hair was sandy brown and, in a ponytail, sticking out the rear of a brimmed bonnet. She was … chesty.

"Let me see," she said and took his hand.

Their eyes met, and he quickly dropped his gaze to study the dirt.

She smelled of lilacs. Her fingers on the back of his hand disturbed him, stirred him. He felt his Adam's apple bob.

She climbed onto the wagon.

Addison turned around. Orson stood holding the lead ropes to the two broncs, and he stared at Mariah, who bent over the bench as she searched for things to treat his injury.

"Orson, Saddle Outlaw for me."

Orson grinned and nodded but continued to appreciate the view.

"Now."

"Yes, sir."

Mariah climbed down. She poured liquid from a bottle over the trail of raw meat across his palm. He sucked in air and alcohol fumes.

"Hold this." She gave him a jar, fingered a gob of white salve out of it, rubbed it over his wound, and wrapped a strip of cloth around his hand and knotted it. "When we stop for the night, come see me."

Her tone of voice disturbed him as much as her eyes and her touch. He nodded and walked away.

Reedley waited for him next to Judas, already in harness. Norman swung Sylvan into position on his side of the tongue.

The wagon master handed another shoulder holster to Addison. "Sure hoped I'd have more time to teach you things, but hoping don't get it done. Wear the gun under your right arm. Practice drawing, cocking, and dry firing the pistol with your left hand. Practice and practice and practice.

"Get mounted. You're riding with me."

Addison walked to the rear of the wagon. A blanket, but no saddle, lay across Outlaw's back. Orson stood behind Outlaw, looked up, and spoke to Maria,h who sat and smiled at him from the opening in the canvas cover at the rear.

Addison took his hat off, shook his head, put the hat back on, and kicked Orson in the butt. Addison didn't care whether the aggravating guy was mad or chagrinned. He picked up the saddle, being careful of his palm, and hefted it onto Outlaw's back. After buckling the cinch strap, he looked up. She was gone.

Orson stood beside the wagon. When he stared at Mariah's—when he stared at Mariah, you could see what he was thinking. No, in a way, he was like Pa. A person couldn't tell what he was thinking. Addison liked him better when he was openly hostile. "Help Norman."

"Yes, sir."

There was no sass in the voice, no respect either. It rode the line smack dab in the middle of the two.

"Ready?" the wagon master said.

"Yes, sir." Addison mounted.

They passed Norman and Orson hitching and checking the harness.

"Do I need to say who's in charge here?" Addison said.

Norman's expression said he was searching for an answer and not having any luck.

Orson knew. "No, sir."

They rode to the stream, splashed through, and cantered past Royal Howard and the lead wagon. After several minutes, Reedley slowed his horse to a walk. Outlaw knew to slow as well.

Woods walled both sides of the road. They clopped side-by-side. The still air sat damp and heavy on the land. A woodpecker's rat-a-tat-tat hammered over the steady buzz of insects.

"You set Pa to driving the wagon?"

The wagon master nodded. "Practice, I told you."

Addison took a deep breath and let it out. Pa would take it as another shaming. Sure as shooting, he'd cut a willow switch. That would come later though.

He pulled his Navy Colt with his bandaged hand and settled the handle against his scraped raw palm. The handle mashed the fibers of the bandage into the wound, and he winced, but if he had to, he could—would—fire the pistol.

Holstering the Navy, he gripped the Pocket Colt from the other holster with his left, made sure he gripped it firmly, so he wouldn't drop it, and drew it. After cocking it and aiming it at a tree alongside the road, he squeezed the trigger. Jerked it is what he'd done. Several times, he repeated the drill, his motions slow and controlled, intent on familiarizing his awkward hand with a new function.

The forest gave way to cleared fields adorned with occasional houses, barns, sheds, haystacks, corncribs. Off in the distance, Addison saw columns of smoke and the shapes of buildings fuzzy in haze and by distance.

"Urbana," Reedley said. "Tried something different this morning. Preacher Larrimer and your mother rode with me into Urbana. We went to the first church we come to, and our preacher talked to theirs. Their preacher talked to the town marshal, and we decided it 'd be best to skirt the town on this side. That'll keep us away from railroad tracks. Wouldn't do to have a train whistle spook our cows or spare horses and have them stampede."

Ahead and far off, a line of dark gray clouds stretched from southeast to northwest. Addison sniffed the air. "Rain tomorrow, I'm thinking, Mr. Reedley. We know what's ahead of us in terms of rivers and creeks? What we passed so far, we've forded easy. But a good rain would have made a difference at some of them."

"I'd a bet money you'd a dropped the pistol at least once with that left-hand draw."

Addison stopped practicing. "Would you have kicked me in the butt if I did?"

"Not as hard as you kicked Orson. I need you to be able to sit a saddle."

"Scouting?"

The wagon master nodded. "Not short range, though. Preacher Larrimer and your ma will do that for us. I need you to ride on ahead of us and scout the streams and rivers and figure ways for us to cross. First, though, you need to learn your left hand to shoot good as the right."

13.

The wagon shook. Addison woke. A black man-shape filled the oval opening in the canvas cover at the rear. He grabbed his pistol. His hand hurt. That didn't matter. He cocked the pistol.

Lightning flashed and lit Orson's big-eyed, open-mouthed face for a blink.

"What in blue blazes were you doing?" Addison removed his finger from the trigger.

"I, uh … Latrine. I had to use the latrine."

"You know the rule. Middle of the night, knock on the side of the wagon."

Everybody had guns. Most of the crusaders were not familiar with them. "Yet," Reedley had said. "Easy to spook someone in the dark. We can't be shootin' each other. Especially not a person of votin' age. So, listen up. This is a rule. You get up in the night, for whatever reason; when you come back, before you climb in or under the wagon, you rap on the sideboard. It's a rule."

A blast of thunder slapped the earth. Addison flinched. "Judas. I came close to shooting you, Orson. You know the rule."

"I didn't want to wake you. You haven't had much sleep."

"Worry about observing the wagon master's rules. I'll worry about my sleep."

Distant thunder rumbled and grumbled.

"You still pointing that gun at me?"

"Yes, I am."

Addison didn't know if he was angry at Orson or at himself. He also didn't know how close he'd come to shooting Lizbeth's husband. It had been a near thing, though. Reedley's words back in Thompson Township came to him. "If you ever have to kill a man again, and you do not taste vinegar in your mouth, throw your gun away."

Even though he hadn't shot another man, he tasted vinegar, and, still, he thought about throwing his guns away.

Outside, horseshoes whanged. Both Royal Howard and Joshua Reedley were hollering. "Hop to it. Hitch the teams." "Round up the animals."

Addison un-cocked the Navy. He pulled on his pants and boots and climbed out. Several of the crusaders had lanterns lit. He lit one of theirs.

Mrs. Larrimer was building the coffee fire. Orson, with his cup in hand, headed there, but Addison stopped him. "Horses and cows first." That, too, was a rule. Orson set Addison's teeth to grinding. By the time they reached Kansas, he figured his teeth would be plumb worn away.

Norman, who'd been on night watch, led the sociable team into place. Orson, after being told to, helped with the harnessing.

Reedley and Howard moved through the travelers haranguing and urging haste. "Ever job is lots more unpleasant in the rain. Hop to it."

Over their clothes, most of the men wore a saddle-roll-ground-cloth with a slit in the middle for the head to fit through. The wagon master's wife and some of the women had sewn reinforcing strips around the slits, turning the slits into buttonholes, in effect. The modified ground cloths were like small tents. "*Tentlings*," the women called their creation.

"The main purpose of the *tentling*," Reedley said, "is to keep the powder in your pistol dry."

Many of the women also wore the modified ground cover. All of them wore pants. "Pants will be easier to dry out than dresses and petticoats," Mrs. Larrimer told them last night.

As the crusaders prepared to pull out, Reedley assigned his son Robert the task of riding behind the train. Robert was to guard against any robbers who might have taken note of the bunch of religious people parading through Urbana and figured the "turn-the-other-cheek" pilgrims would be easy pickings.

"You remember, Addison," the wagon master said, "when you let me sleep and took on two robbers by yourself? When you grew wiser and stupider at the same time."

Orson snickered.

In the dim light from the scattered lanterns, no one would see him blush. "Orson," Addison said. "I owe you a kick in the butt. I'll pay it to you before we bed down."

Royal Howard ordered Otto Vogelsang to place his wagon last. If anyone in front of him got into trouble on the road, which was sure to turn muddy and troublesome after the rain started, Otto was the best man to deal with it.

Reedley assigned the oldest Vogelsang boy, Hermann, the task of rounding up axes and rope and loading them onto Contrary Team. As soon as the morning prayer was finished, the wagon master, Hermann, Orson, and Addison would ride ahead.

Addison sat Outlaw with Orson on another saddle bronc next to him. Teams were hitched with animals lashed onto the rear. Most of the crusaders were in their wagons or astride, except a few men and a few children. There was always a straggler or two.

Not a breath of breeze stirred, and the night animals and bugs did not disturb the silence riding heavy on the air like humidity. A horse snorted. Trace chains jangled when a draft animal shifted weight from one foot to the other.

"Morning prayer!" Then Larrimer boomed praise and supplication into the heavy blackness. For a precise minute, Addison thought. The crusaders tacked on a robust, "Amen."

"On to Kansas!" the wagon master said, and it was as if his voice ripped open heaven and God dumped a god-sized bucket of water on them. Gusts of wind, too, arrived and swirled and drove rain sideways.

"Try to keep it dry," Mariah'd told him when she bandaged his wound that morning.

A sudden gust bunched Addison's *tentling* under his chin, but he got his right hand under it, pulled it down, and tucked it under his arms before the downpour started. The wind tried to rip his hat off, but he held onto the front of the brim. With his knees, he guided Outlaw along the right side of Sylvan. Orson had a lead rope on him.

The rain doused the coffee fire. As lanterns blinked out, Reedley started his bronc down the road.

"Move out, Orson," Addison shouted.

"Can't see nothin'."

With his left hand, Addison grabbed Waverly's cheek strap and pulled him into motion. Hermann did the same with Judas. "This makes two butt-kicks, Orson." He shouted over the wind.

Once he'd gotten the wagon in line with the others, Addison pushed Outlaw through the blackness with raindrops stinging his face. He caught up to Reedley just as he passed the lead wagon. A gust tore his hat off. In an instant, cold water flooded through the neck hole and wetted the front and back of his shirt. As he got his hat back on, the wind ceased and the rain fell straight down. Reedley's form was as distinct as a ghost of black against a wall of darkness.

"Hermann," Addison called. "Glad you're with us?"

"I *vish* I *vasn't*."

"Wishin' won't get us to Kansas," Reedley hollered.

That was the end of the talking. When they passed through forest, rain on the leaves made one sound and another distinct sound when the foliage shed a secondary rain onto the ground. Hooves *splop, splop, splopped.*

Like a clock. Splop, splop instead of tick, tock. Addison found comfort in the realization time was passing. Slowly, but passing. When he concentrated on using peripheral vision, he could see better. He always had to remind himself of that. He wondered if it would ever become second nature.

The road out of Urbana led south. He checked the sky to the east. No sign of sunrise. Only darkness. But the new rivulet of cold water down his spine bit as brutal as the seat in the outhouse when there was snow on the ground.

He couldn't remember how long it had been since he checked behind them. He couldn't remember if he had checked even once since he called

Hermann. As he turned, a fresh trickle of cold soaked his shirt and crept under his butt, which had been dry. Now his right hand and armpits, where his holsters hung, were the only parts of him not wet and cold.

Exposure to rain and cold was not a new experience, but Addison's previous times were to accomplish a specific purpose. Ride through a storm to get to his church chores on a Sunday morning. Load hay on a wagon and cover it with a tarp before a downpour started. Completing the task had always been a seeable time ahead, and seeing the end of the discomfort, or the misery, made it endurable. Now, though, the deluge splatted on his hat and shoulders as if it could go on for forty days and forty nights.

This part of Illinois was flat, or almost so. No hills high enough to save a person from a Biblical flood.

The wagon master would not be happy with him. He worried over personal discomfort rather than be concerned for the wagon train. His thoughts meandered through fanciful notions typical of a ten-year old boy rather than a wagon train scout. *Vigilance*, he told himself.

Reedley rode fifteen yards ahead. Addison figured he could see perhaps three times that far. Dark forest walled the road. Slender Orson sat hunched forward on his saddle as did the broad-shouldered, hulking Vogelsang boy. The horses, Sylvan and Judas, plodded along, heads bobbing. Not so full of mischief now.

Addison guided Outlaw onto the narrow strip of grass alongside the roadbed. He wasn't sure Vogelsang even noticed him. Asleep maybe.

"Why you stop?" Hermann said.

"Check behind us."

"Bah. Who else be out in dis vedder?"

Hermann, leading Judas, plodded past. Addison recalled when Orson crawled into the rear of the wagon that morning and came close to getting himself shot. Addison had considered throwing away his guns. Shaking the water off his left hand, he reached up under the *tentling* and touched the butt of his Pocket Colt.

"What do you think, Outlaw? Would throwing my guns away be wise or stupid? 'Throw away those weapons from Satan!' That's what Pa'd say."

Outlaw tossed his head.

"Another instance of wise and stupid at the same time, Outlaw, that what you think? Heck of a thing to hold a man's life and his death in your hand."

Addison could no longer hear Reedley and the others. He cocked his head and sought sounds separate from the rain, sounds of someone following them. He rested his bandaged hand on his Navy Colt.

"Huh. I guess that answers Hermann's question."

He heard no signs of pursuit nor wagons, and he trotted Outlaw to catch up.

Minutes later, with visibility much improved, he topped a gentle rise and found Reedley, and the others, halfway down the slope, dismounted. At the edge of what appeared to be a pond. The road ran into the pond and, fifty yards across mud-brown water climbed out of it.

Reedley explained what he thought they faced. The road they followed crossed a small stream at the bottom of the slope. Off to the left, the small creek emptied into a larger one. Because of the heavy rain, the larger one spilled out of its banks and backed up the small stream in front of them.

"I'm hoping that means there won't be much current. I'm going to see if it's shallow enough to walk our horses through. Hermann, you follow me but don't' go beyond the edge of the trees there." Reedley pointed to the right.

On the far side of the pond, the water had also climbed up into the trees. "Mr. Reedley," Addison said. "I think it might be deep in the middle."

"Might be. Do you know how to swim, Addison?"

"Yes, sir."

The wagon master asked Hermann.

"I swim."

"Orson?"

"Uh—"

Reedley grinned. "I'm taking an end of the rope across. I'll tie it to a tree on the other side. When I come back, I'll teach you how to swim."

"Don't Worry, Orson," Hermann said. "Learn to swim is easy. My papa tell me remember *tree tings*. Kick legs. Paddle arms. Don't drink *duh wasser*."

Reedley left his guns with Addison and started his mount into the swollen stream. Halfway to the opposite shore, the horse had to swim. Not far.

On the other side, the wagon master secured a rope to a sycamore up the bank and returned.

"The water's still rising," Reedley said. "Orson, your swimming lesson has to wait. We'll have to float the wagons across."

"We're going to build a raft?" Orson said.

"You'll see." Reedley took Hermann and set him to work on felling a large oak. He told Orson to chop down two trees as thick as a man's thigh.

Orson felled the first one and started on the second as Addison trimmed the branches from the first with a hatchet wielded in his left hand.

The oak fell with a crash, loud in the stillness, in the mist and spitting rain.

Reedley put Orson to work on trimming the oak and Hermann on felling another large tree. "Addison, swim through the stream to the other side. Take your shirt off, hold it and your pistols above your head. Keep them dry. On the other side, scout the road for twenty minutes. Then come back to the creek. You'll be cold and wet. Never mind that. Keep a sharp lookout. When you get back, roust up wood for a fire in that clearing."

Addison held his pistol belts and shirt in his right hand and kept his left free to hold onto the saddle horn. Outlaw swam the deep part calmly. On the other side, Addison put his shirt back on under his tentling and buckled his shoulder holsters. Then he dumped his boots and wrung out his socks, using a corner of the tentling to keep his right-hand bandage dry, mostly.

Addison emerged from forest on both sides of the road to forest on his left side and farms to the right. Some of the farmhouses and barns were close to the road, some set back. Five minutes into the ride, Reedley was proved right. He shivered. Back at the creek, as he worked, he'd stayed warm. Now, sitting still, chill caught up to him and sucked strength and energy from him. He squeezed his arms to his torso and scrunched his head down as if to huddle the outlying parts of his body into a bundle to hold onto remaining warmth.

Stay alert, Reedley'd said.

"Eyes and ears," Addison said, "the rest of me is lollygagging—as the O'Riley brothers would say—but you can't."

Talking helped, but he had to remind himself to shut up now and then so the ears could contribute.

The rain ceased, the clouds parted, and a ray of sunshine kissed the sodden earth.

While it rained, walking Outlaw seemed the proper way to proceed. Now, a trot would do.

Traffic had packed the roadbed a few inches deeper than the bordering soil. If he avoided puddles, Outlaw's hooves didn't sink in much. The horse seemed happy to trot. Sixteen wagons and the extra horses and cows, though, would churn the roadbed to swamp.

To the right, across a field planted with corn, a house stood next to what would become a substantial barn. He reined up. At present, the structure consisted only of the frames of a long wall and one end. Stacks of lumber lay between the house and barn.

Addison checked his watch. Fifteen minutes. He looked back the way he'd come. Then he rode down the lane to the farmhouse.

*****

Back at the flooded road, Addison saw that the wagons were still lined up. Royal Howard and Otto Vogelsang had a crew of men working around the first wagon. Logs were lashed lengthwise under its bed. On top of and perpendicular to those logs, other logs, extended a yard beyond the wheels on each side of the wagon. These cross members would fit into notches chopped into the tops of the large tree trunks. The large tree trunks would float the wagon across the stream.

Ropes were tied from the harness on Judas to the front crossbeam. Hermann led the horse down the road and towed the wagon across the stream. When the wheels touched bottom, four men untied the front crossbeam and Judas towed the wagon out of the floats and up the rise. Another crew of four men hooked a team to the wagon and drove it to the meadow. Someone already had a fire going there. Sylvan, the draft horse, guided by the deposed first deacon, pulled the log float arrangement back across the stream.

The second wagon was moved into position, the team was unhitched and swum across to the other side. The float was tied to the next wagon bed. Royal Howard and Otto Vogelsang had every man in the crusade engaged in the effort.

Reedley crossed the stream on his mount. "What took you so long?"

Addison looked him in the eye. "Fifteen minutes from here, there's a farm with a barn under construction. I told the farmer we'd help him put up his barn tomorrow."

"Why'd you do that?"

"The roads are going to be a soggy mess. We will wear out the horses making a third of the miles we can on a dry road. Day after tomorrow, the roads will be in better shape, and the horses will be in good shape, too. If we help the farmer with his barn. He and his wife will feed us if we help. Three of his neighbors offered their barns for women and children to use to dry out. I thought it was a good idea."

Their horses were pointed in opposite directions. Reedley leaned over and clapped Addison's shoulder. "Boy," the wagon master shook his head. "Scout," he said. "Take Otto Vogelsang with you to that barn needs building. Show it to him. Tell him to figure out what we can get done tomorrow."

Preacher Larrimer crossed the stream riding the next wagon. Once across, he climbed down next to Reedley. "Every boy six and older has had a swimming lesson. The girls now get their lesson."

Larrimer looked up at Addison. "I overheard what you said. It's a good thing to help people in need. It will be a good thing for the second wagon train to have islands of friendship along the way."

The preacher relieved one of the men on that side of the stream. "The women have coffee going and laid out food. Get some and hustle back so another can eat, too."

14.

The east glowed. The west brooded black. Addison stood in predawn gloom on the halfway point between night and day. The framed front and back walls rose out of the dark toward the gathering brightness and blue in the sky like the remnants of an abandoned, decaying farmhouse.

He turned around. Lantern light glowed from the bottom floor windows of Mr. Papenheim's grand two-story residence. Breakfast fires lit up the middle of the huddled wagons. This morning it wasn't Joshua Reedley's or Royal Howard's voice haranguing the crusaders to hustle. This morning Otto Vogelsang's deep bass drummed urgency into his *vorkers.*

With the sky brightening by the moment, Otto herded his crew toward the barn. From the big house, a smaller group shadow men headed toward the construction project. It was impossible to tell if they were white or colored.

Yesterday, when Addison had stopped to talk to the farmer about possibly helping him put up his barn, he had found Mr. Papenheim and some Negro men at work on framing the building. He had also noted several smaller houses in a row behind the main house and against the forest.

Addison, astride Outlaw, nodded at the carpenters. "Your slaves, Mr. Papenheim?"

Papenheim was Addison's height. But slender. Light hair and

moustache. Blue eyes ablaze with cold fire as he looked up. There was something proud, and almost, but not quite, arrogant in the man's demeanor. He wore a pistol in a shoulder holster, plus four muskets leaned against a stack of lumber close by.

"These are free men. They have papers. I will not own another person."

Addison asked permission to step down. Papenheim nodded.

The farmer said he paid the men a wage and provided houses for their families. The scout explained the Found Grace Church Holy Crusade. On behalf of the wagon train, Addison had made a deal with the farmer. Yesterday.

Today, Otto's team of twenty met Papenheim's modest one. They spoke German. Then Otto said, "Okay den, *Herr von* Papenheim. We make three teams. Two frame the other sides. One builds roof trusses. You split your men among the teams. That all right with you, sir?"

Huh. Otto called the farmer *von* Papenheim. And he called him *sir.*

"Jawohl, Herr Vogelsang. With your permission, I work on roof trusses, although someone will have to show me what to do," Papenheim said.

"Joshua Freeman, you teach."

A sliver of sun fire peeked above the edge of the earth.

"Sunup!" Otto hollered. "Get to vork."

"Young Freeman," Otto pointed at him. "You stand there watching. Get to vork, or I have Orson kick the seata' your britches!"

Orson sauntered up to him.

Royal Howard drove a nail into a wall frame. *Bang, bang, bang.* Three solid blows to drive the nail. Other hammers added their percussion to the cacophony.

"Maybe I should just kick Addison now, Otto," Orson shouted.

"Maybe, Orson, you should get to *vork,* or I kick you in the britches."

Addison held a nail and wall frame board in place and gripped his hammer with his left hand. He tap, tap, tapped the nail, and bent it. His left hand had learned to draw a pistol, but it required additional education to drive a nail.

"Bend the next one, you know what I gotta' do," Orson said.

Trying to inspire discipline, maturity, and responsible behavior in Lizbeth's husband reminded Addison of three-year-old Rufus Tamber back at Found Church. A willful, mischievous chunk of a boy. Tell him, "No!" and he'd look you right in the eye and do what you'd forbidden him to do. His mother and father spanked him for such infractions, but the boy never cried.

Addison extracted the nail, straightened it, and, concentrating intently, tapped it in. He drove the second with more confidence. The third with more still. He looked up and found Orson smirking.

Father God in heaven, let this cup pass from me. But not my will.

Addison ordered Orson to cut boards to frame a window.

Orson stood and dropped his hammer in the mud. Addison jumped up, grabbed the hammer, and wiped it clean with the shirt of the aggravating—giant *three-year-old.*

Looking into Orson's eyes shoved a picture into his mind. Addison had been nine, maybe. He got a moment away from chores and climbed a tree in the back yard. Part way up, he encountered a large black bird sitting on a limb. The bird wasn't afraid of him and stared with flat dull eyes. Addison was sure the bird intended to peck out his eyeballs, and he hustled down the tree and tore his pants doing so, which earned him a switching. Orson's eyes were like that bird's. Flat and dark. They absorbed light but didn't shine any out at the world. That bird's eyes said: *I never ate an eyeball before. I'm going to try yours.*

"Orson," Addison said. "Saw boards for the window."

Eyes were supposed to be a window to the soul. Either Orson didn't have a soul, or he had the curtains drawn.

When the frames of the barn walls were up and braced, the crew broke for dinner—pork, potatoes, and sauerkraut.

"Eat," Otto Vogelsang instructed, "but no seconds. We have lots of vork to do, and we don't have time for you to be puking."

In the afternoon, one crew laid the floor of the hayloft, another hoisted and set the roof trusses, others nailed boards to the side frames.

At midafternoon, Reedley told Addison to saddle two horses. "Ride hard as far as you can go and return by sunset. Check the road conditions and the levels of any streams we'll have to cross tomorrow."

Addison returned with dusk settling and reported the road conditions were fair. "There're a few swampy spots where we'll have to cut brush and saplings to firm up the surface. A couple of streams to cross, but none more than belly deep on Outlaw, and they were receding."

"Good," Reedley said.

Addison nodded at the barn. Men on the tin roof tarred nails and seams. Others hung one-piece shutters over the windows with leather straps nailed to the tops. A crew worked at hinging the hayloft door.

"Good," Addison said.

"Otto worked us hard and smart," Reedley said.

"How'd Orson do?"

"I put him with Hermann Vogelsang. Talk to him at supper."

As the last of evening surrendered to night, Otto called a halt. "We eat supper. Do not take seconds. Udder vise, you puke and not sleep good. Vagon Master say we on to Kansas at first light."

During the day, Otto had been Barn Boss. With that job done, he passed leadership of the crusade back to the wagon master.

"Same as always," Reedley said. "At first light, the wagons roll. When the horseshoes ring, get up and don't dawdle. If you do, next morning I'll get you up earlier. To account for your sloth."

Addison got a plate and sat on a wagon tongue next to Hermann and Orson.

"Ach," Hermann said. "Orson. I sent him to fetch nails. He didn't come back. I find him talking with Mariah Welch. I spent more time watching him than getting my own work done."

It didn't appear to bother Orson to be discussed as if he were a horse or a dog.

Addison asked Hermann about the farm owner, Nicolas Papenheim, and about the *von*.

"Yah. That *von* means he was a count in Prussia. Papa says he was an army captain and ordered to arrest Catholics moving south to escape the Lutherans. Nicolas told his colonel they should let the Catholics go. They were no threat to anyone. Nicolas refused. He was arrested and sentenced to face a firing squad, but he escaped.

"His wife gathered what she could salvage, and they traveled to

Hamburg with a few servants. She booked passage to New York. From there, the Papenheims traveled here and bought land for a farm.

"Papa says back in Germany, being born into royalty tacks a von onto your name. But what Mr. Papenheim does here for the blackies, that earns him the *von* in America."

"He's got twenty niggers on the place," Orson said.

Addison jumped up and knocked Orson's tin plate from his hand. "We don't call colored people that name."

*****

The next morning, Reedley woke Addison well before horseshoe time and took him to the grand two-story farmhouse. In a large dining room, they found Mr. Papenheim seated at the head of a long table. Preacher Larrimer was to his right. Opposite Larrimer, sat Mrs. Papenheim. Three colored people occupied chairs on the hostess side: a woman, a young woman, and a young man.

Their host pointed to the chairs next to Larrimer. Addison sat across from the colored girl, about his age. The girl was attractive. Heat crept above his collar and warmed his face.

Mr. Papenheim introduced everyone at the table. His wife, Elise, Rose O'sharn, and Violet across from Addison. The young man next to Violet, Addison didn't remember his name.

As Larrimer said the blessing, Addison thought about Violet. Violets, he decided, were his favorite flower. He'd never had a favorite flower before.

At the "Amen," Mrs. Papenheim, Rose O'sharn, and Violet rose and trooped past the head of the table and into the kitchen. The young man across from Addison followed Violet with his eyes as if they were attached to her. A blade of jealousy stabbed him in the chest.

"Ahem." Reedley cleared his throat.

Addison looked at him, and the Wagon Master shook his head and glared at his scout.

In a few moments, the three returned carrying plates of food. An older man and woman, white haired, with white skin, carried plates also.

The host introduced Heinrich and Hulda. They had been born on the Papenheim estate in Germany and had worked for the family since they learned how to polish silver.

"Here, in America," Papenheim said, "I've tried to get them to eat with us, but Heinrich was appalled at the suggestion." To them, "Thank you."

Heinrich and Hulda bowed and departed.

"Mr. Freeman," Elise Papenheim said.

Addison had spent so much time studying the coloreds, he hadn't paid much attention to his hostess. Slender, her back straight as a board, dark hair shoulder length reflecting a splash of purple, complexion toned by the sun. Her face and her eyes smiled.

"Have you ever sat at table with Negroes before?"

"Uh, no, Ma'am. Until we started on our crusade, I only saw a colored person once before."

"Until we came to America, I saw perhaps a handful of *Negroes* in my life and never ate with them. Here, I," she glanced up at her husband, "*we* have the opportunity to do so."

The way she'd put emphasis on Negro, it could only have been a reprimand, a verbal switching.

"My Dear," the host said, "please take up your fork so we can eat our breakfast before it gets cold."

The hostess dipped her head, then raised her eyes again to her husband. The look she gave him was so like the one he dreamed and imagined Lizbeth would bestow on him. That dream lost on the day his middle name had become Job.

Elise Papenheim took up her utensils and speared a dainty sliver of potato.

Reedley picked up his knife and fork. Addison followed suit. Silverware clinked against plates.

Except for the col—Negroes—sitting opposite Addison. They watched the whites as if unsure of what to do, as if afraid of making a mistake. It was a fancy table, but Addison was hungry a lot, and only a little afraid of making a mistake. He sliced a bite of ham, dunked it in egg yolk, and forked it into his mouth.

"Mr. Freeman," Violet said, "please tell us about the first time you saw a colored person."

Addison swallowed the chunk of meat without chewing it. It went down hard. He swallowed a sip of scalding coffee. His eyes watered. Everyone at the table was looking at him. *She'd said colored?*

"Violet," Rose O'Sharn said, "Mr. Freeman has a long day in front of him. Let him eat."

Addison took a sip of water. "It's all right, Ma'am. I apologize for my manners. I don't mind saying it." His eyes glanced at Violet and bounced off her. "I was four or five. My father took me with him to the small town near our farm. A colored man—he cast a quick and fleeting glance at his hostess—was walking on a boardwalk. I pointed and said, 'Look, Pa.' He smacked my hand and said it was bad manners to point.

"When we got home, he told me, 'God created his children with many different skin colors. Yellow, brown, black. It doesn't mean any more than wearing a yellow shirt one day and black one the next. Does the color of your black shirt make you a different person than you were yesterday with a yellow shirt on?' He expected me to answer. I said, 'No, Pa.'"

"Then he gave you a switching, didn't he?" Preacher Larrimer said.

Addison nodded.

"White folks git switchins', too?" Violet shook her head.

The ... Negro boy next to Violet raised a finger to his lips. Worry scrunched his face into a frown. The way he looked at Violet twisted that blade of jealousy stuck in his chest.

"Violet!" Rose O'Sharn glowered. "Not one more word from you during breakfast."

"If I may, Mr. and Mrs. Papenheim?" Preacher Larrimer said.

The master of the house nodded.

"It seems both Negroes and whites have some things to learn about each other. Life has set us apart. We look different. When we meet, we cannot help ourselves. We stare at the strangeness of the other. But if we give ourselves the opportunity to study, without staring, we find that Addison's father is right. We are all God's children. And we are the same. The color of our skin does not make us different."

"Amen and eat," from the hostess.

At the end of breakfast, Preacher Larrimer married Violet and Ned. *Now I'll remember his name.*

*****

As they walked back to the wagons, Preacher Larrimer related what he'd learned about Nicolas Papenheim.

Addison asked, "Mr. Papenheim helps runaway slaves? And the purpose of breakfast this morning was to introduce us to six of them we'll take with us to Kansas?"

Three of the Negroes had been too shy to eat with the whites, but they'd come into the dining room to witness the marriage.

"Yes," Preacher Larrimer said. "He risks his fortune to help those who manage to escape bondage. His farm is a way station for the escapees. If they can make it this far, he helps them move farther on."

"There is real risk in what he does," Reedley said. "The law requires us to return runaway slaves to their masters."

"But," Addison said, "You agreed to take six of the coloreds with us. So, there is risk in what we do, too."

"Preacher Larrimer agreed. Without discussing it with me, the wagon master."

Larrimer said, "We put ourselves at risk when we embarked on this crusade, and every day, we've seen evidence that danger is all around us. Threats will assuredly dog us all the way to Kansas. New dangers await us there. But this is a holy endeavor. The Fugitive Slave Law is as wrong as slavery itself, but it was arrived at through a political compromise. For decades, the issue of slavery has bubbled and boiled among the people of this nation and threatened to tear it apart. The Fugitive Slave Law was given to the South as a way to preserve the Union. The dissolution of which was viewed as being a greater evil than condemning other men to the status of property."

"As wagon master, I argued against taking them. If we are caught harboring fugitives from the law, the entire crusade could very well end."

"But," Preacher cut in, "Mr. Reedley is the wagon master. It is up to him. I loaned Mr. Reedley a book by Thoreau. My arguments to bring the coloreds with us did not sway him, but Mr. Thoreau's essay 'Civil Disobedience' did."

"I agreed to take the six with us," Reedley said. "Then our sneaky preacher informed me that five of them were branded on the left shoulder. So, they will be easy to identify. A forged document proclaiming they have been freed will not amount to a hill of beans."

"Is Violet branded?" Addison said.

"No," Larrimer replied. "The three Smiths and the Jones couple are."

The Wagon Master humphed.

"Joshua," Larrimer said. "My subterfuge was reprehensible. I judged you would refuse to take them if you knew about the brand. But because of it, we had to take them. Those marks endanger Mr. Papenheim and the other Negroes on his property, and it would have prevented him doing future good works."

Reedley put a hand on Addison's shoulder. "Sometimes, a man needs a kick in the seat of the pants to see the way to doing the right thing."

"Yes," Preacher said. "But the devil also kicks people. That is why God created us with the power of discernment. It is a gift some men won't or don't know how to use. It is easier to just follow the crowd."

As they arrived at the wagons, horseshoes whanged. "Wake up, Crusaders." Royal Howard hollered as loud as Preacher Larrimer.

15.

At the morning gathering, Addison stood next to Orson. The Wagon Master occupied the driver's box of the Larrimer wagon. The six Negroes—Addison found himself preferring "colored" as it sounded better and further away from that other N word—lined up below him.

"These men and women are coming with us," Reedley announced. "They are," he pointed, "Athens Smith, his wife Retta, their son Ned, and he's married to Violet. Next is Willum Jones and his wife, Callie. They are freed men and women. Preacher has a copy of their papers.

"Slave hunters may be looking for runaways, and they take colored people back into slavery, whether they have papers or not. These hunters enlist the aid of local sheriffs. If we can, we'd like to avoid trouble. So, we're hiding the Smiths and the Joneses in our wagons for a couple of days. One to a wagon. Mrs. Larrimer will pick who will carry them.

"One last thing, if a slave hunter or a sheriff asks if we have colored people among our company, deny it. Lying about this particular issue is not a sin. Preacher will explain why.

"Preacher, please do so, say the prayer, and Royal, start us on to Kansas."

Reedley hopped down, mounted, and cantered off to get the wagons moving that overnighted at neighboring farms.

Larrimer explained the Fugitive Slave Law and repeated his opinion that the law was as wrong as slavery itself. In a confrontation with authorities, they would have to defend themselves as well as the Smiths and Joneses. In such a confrontation, they might have to kill. Lying was a much lesser evil.

He then raised his face and voice to heaven and prayed for the success of their cause, for the safety of them all but especially for the newest crusaders, and for the wisdom to find the straight and narrow way. "Amen!"

Addison noted spirited, zealous *Amens*. However, Solomon Adler and Mort Nielson didn't seal the prayer with their endorsement. They huddled next to each other, mumbling and staring at the coloreds. Solomon shook his head. Mort, with a grim frown, nodded.

Funny. On the first day of travel, Solomon had advocated throwing Mort off the wagon train because he slowed them down. Now they were best friends, drawn together by something other than intentions for the common good. He'd talk to Reedley about them.

"On to Kansas!" Royal hollered.

Women, wearing dresses, climbed up to driver benches, placed shotguns next to them, and moved their wagons into line. Addison's ma drove the lead wagon. She fell in behind Preacher Larrimer, mounted and wearing church clothes. His wife rode beside him. She wore a split skirt and held a double-barrel across the saddle behind the horn. Only children and Preacher Larrimer were not armed.

Reedley placed his son Robert, Sean O'Riley, and Adolph Freeman at the rear of the wagons. He instructed them to conceal themselves beside the road for thirty minutes. If they spotted riders following the train, Robert was to dispatch Deacon Freeman to ride hard and warn the Wagon Master. Then, after the riders passed their place of concealment, Robert and Sean were to fall in behind them. If no one passed in thirty minutes, they were to run their mounts, catch up to the train, and hide themselves again.

Addison rode with Orson and Alphonse Carlson. Reedley considered the Carlson boy to be almost as tough as his sister Eunice.

"Mount up," the scout instructed his partners.

The threesome cantered down Papenheim's lane and onto the road.

*****

That day, the wagon train made good time, and the crusaders encountered no one to whom they had to lie.

After supper, Addison sat cross-legged, sipping coffee. Reedley squatted next to him.

"The last town we passed through today, Preacher found out word of our Abolitionist Wagon Train arrived there before we did. Town people said there are slave hunters about looking for runaways from Mississippi. The O'Riley brothers will take turns and patrol around the edges of the camp all night with their dog. Tomorrow, I'm going to put strong men with Robert as rear guard."

To Addison, the Wagon Master as much as said, "Your pa ain't a strong one."

"I'm thinking," Reedley went on, "as scout, you need people you can count on. We should replace Orson"

Addison shook his head. "You promised his ma we'd straighten him out. Otherwise, I'd say kick him off the train. But we're stuck with him, and we have to know if we can count on him. He needs a test. Like the one we—I—got back in Thompson Township."

"I've seen you handle the Contrary Team. Orson isn't a horse. If we meet those slave hunters and they have a sheriff with them, it's going to be touchy. I could put Gallant Argyl with you and Alphonse."

"What did Preacher say? We face risks every day. If Orson gets me killed tomorrow, at least I'll be shut of the responsibility for him."

Wagon Master said, "Huh," and walked away.

That night, Norman Niedlinger slept in the wagon, Addison and Orson underneath.

Orson's ground cloth rustled. "That Violet. She's a good-looking girl."

"She's married," Addison said. "And so're you."

"I just wonder what it'd be like. Being with a colored girl."

"Shut up, Orson."

"You notice her husband, Ned? Fair skinned. Much lighter than his parents. His real daddy was a white man, I bet."

Addison packed as much warning onto, "Orson," as the name could carry.

"I bet you wonder about that Violet, don't you?"

Rage flared bright and red and hot like a suddenly appearing noon sun in a midnight sky. It blinded Addison's brain. He threw back the covers, crawled out from under the wagon, dragged Orson out by a leg, pulled him upright, and punched him in the face. And punched and punched. An animal growl penetrated his awareness. The sound came from Addison himself. He stayed his right fist in the cocked position and released the bunched handful of long johns.

Orson crumpled to the ground like a pile of underwear with no one inside.

Addison turned away from him.

And bumped into Reedley. "You want to rethink how we left our discussion?"

"No." Addison turned around again, grabbed up Orson like a sack of feathers, and tossed him under the wagon.

Addison crawled under and lay on his bedding. Chilly. Nothing on but long johns. He didn't care. Rather, it seemed right to suffer some.

Lizbeth. He'd loved her. Orson ruined that. He'd married her.

Violet. He'd been attracted to her. She married Ned. Still, Orson found a way to ruin his admiration for her.

Mariah Welch. She drew Addison like iron filings to a magnet. She wasn't married, but the way she looked at Orson didn't make any difference to her he was married to someone else.

Every woman he was interested in, Orson turned it sour. That thought slithered out of his head and down into his belly where it roiled around like half a dozen snakes wrestling with each other.

I should've shot him that night he came back to wagon and didn't knock.

No, Addison.

This sounded like a voice coming from outside himself.

You did the right thing. If you'd shot him, you would
have thrown your guns away.

I should've let him shoot me when I woke Lizbeth and him in our house.

No, Addison. God did not give you the gift of life so
you could just throw it away at the least bit of trouble.

At some point, he grew tired of wallowing in misery. And of arguing
with himself and losing every debate. His mind awoke, sort of, or came
back from where it had been.

Orson, the most aggravating person on the wagon train.

He knew he'd get to me with the way he talked about Violet and Ned.

He thought Orson wasn't smart enough to figure that out. Rather,
it was some innate sense he had and probably wasn't aware of. Like
breathing.

A violent shiver shook Addison. Orson, too, lay atop his bedding.

Addison shook him awake. He moaned. "Get under the covers.
Healthy, you're darned near worthless. You get sick; you sure will be."

Moaning. Bedding rustled. More moaning. Blessed silence.

Addison pulled his covers around him and rolled onto his side. Then
he decided he didn't want his back to Orson and turned the other way.

*****

Aside from dried mud ruts, the roads were good. The streams ran clear
and shallow. An hour short of noon, Addison stopped next to a grassy
meadow near water.

Orson caught up to him. His shotgun rested across the saddle.
Under his right eye, a purple bruise. Left lower lip bulged to twice
normal thickness. He hacked and spat. Spittle dribbled down his chin.
With the back of his hand, he wiped it away. Then he raised his eyes.

Addison looked for hate or fear or something in those eyes. But
they showed nothing, like a mirror that swallowed your image instead
of showing it to you. He willed his own eyes to show nothing as well,
but he doubted his were any good at it.

"It's a shame," Orson said. "You just got the bandage off your right
hand, and now the knuckles are all skinned up."

Addison drew a pistol with his right and pointed it at the meadow, away from Orson. "Works good." He holstered it.

Then he whipped out the other pistol with his left and pointed it at the forest behind Orson. "This one works even better."

Addison turned as Ambrose reined up next to them.

"Ambrose," Addison said. "Wagon train should be here in an hour. Ride back and tell them about this place for the nooning. Push your bronc hard, get a fresh mount, and meet us back here."

Ambrose set off.

"Like we did this morning," Addison said. "You ride down the right side of the road and lag behind. At a trot. I'll run ahead, stop, and listen. If we see riders coming at us, I'll pull up. You come even with me and cock a barrel. Then we wait and see what they do."

From Orson, no acknowledgement, no reaction.

"You understand what I want you to do? Say it. Yes or no."

Orson nodded.

Giant three-year-old.

Addison considered his nasty-minded, childish companion, seething with unrepentant anger over having been punished the night before, with a shotgun behind him. Earlier, he'd had Ambrose behind Orson. That had been some comfort. But it was time to find out if he could trust Lizbeth's husband with no one behind him. He also considered repeating the other contingencies he covered earlier that morning: like riders coming out of the woods after Addison rode past them and got between, or behind them both. Instead, he said, "Outlaw," and the horse bolted into a run. A minute into it, he glanced behind. Huh! Orson bobbed along, doing what he was supposed to do. After fifteen minutes, Addison reined up, climbed down, left Outlaw ground hitched, and walked half a dozen paces on the grass between the edge of the road and the forest. He listened.

Quiet. Outlaw's pounding hooves had shut off the bird and bug noises, but now they started up again. Tentative at first, but then with the enthusiasm of the women conversing while cleaning Found Church. Blue sky. Sun high. *Tat, tat, tat.* Woodpecker. A sudden crashing in forest drove his left hand to his pistol, but he didn't pull it. The noise had come from high up. A squirrel probably dropped the remnant of his lunch.

Time to head back to the mid-day-rest-the-animals spot.

Outlaw lifted his head and stared down the road. His ears twitched forward.

Two hundred yards ahead, the road cut to the left. Tall oaks and maples hid what was coming. He walked back to Outlaw.

Orson pulled up next to him. "We headin' back?"

"Quiet," Addison said.

"What for?"

"Ssssst!"

Two horses rounded the bend.

Men rode double on one and led the other. The one being led gimped on a foreleg.

Addison said, "Move to the side of the road. Cock a barrel."

Wonder of wonders. Orson did as told.

About a hundred yards from Addison, the double-mounted and the lame plodded along. Not a hurry in the world.

The front rider was thick-chested. His floppy hat sat low on his forehead. Behind Rider peered over one sloped shoulder.

Addison ducked under Outlaw's neck to be next to his long gun scabbard.

Behind Rider slid off the rear of the good horse. He was skinny, about half of the man he'd been behind. Skinny pulled a long gun from the scabbard on Gimpy Horse and moved to Orson's side of the road. The lame horse limped along, shielding Skinny from Addison.

Addison pulled his rifle. "Orson. Move into the trees. Now." They were at fifty yards and coming on steady.

"Hold on," Front Rider hollered. "We's the law. Y'all stay where we kin see ya. Put your rifle down and your hands up."

Orson hadn't moved. Now it was too late.

Behind Rider's rifle barked.

The head of Orson's horse jerked up, then the animal dropped. Orson's shotgun fired, and the charge chewed up dirt in the middle of the road.

Front Rider pulled a pistol from a saddle holster. Addison raised his rifle and fired. Front Rider tumbled backwards out of the saddle.

Addison dropped the rifle and ran across the road to where he had a clean shot. Behind Rider was reloading.

Orson howled, "Ow, oh, my leg's busted. Ow. Help me." His leg was pinned under the animal. No time for that.

Addison kept his eyes on Behind Rider and drew his pistol with his right hand. He could draw faster with his left, but the right shot straighter. Range, long for a pistol shot. No help for that, though. He two-hand gripped the pistol and aimed as Behind Rider cocked the rifle. Addison fired. The man went down. Gut shot.

Now two men yowled.

Addison ran and took the rifle, a pistol, and a belt knife from Gut Shot. The man had his teeth clenched, his eyes squeezed shut, his hands over his belly, and he moaned.

Addison checked on the other downed man. Dead, shot between the eyes.

The man's horse shied away. Addison spoke to her, told her he'd get her a bag of oats. After calming her, he secured a rope to the horn of Orson's saddle and to one on Front Rider's mare. Addison led the mare and hoisted Orson's dead horse enough so Orson could pull his leg free.

Behind Rider kept moaning. Orson continued to yowl.

Addison pulled the boot off and checked Orson's leg and foot.

"Orson. Your leg is not broken. Stop hollering."

He hollered on. Addison grabbed his arm and jerked him to his feet.

Fear. In Orson's eyes and on his face.

"That man by the lame horse," Orson said. "I saw him raise his rifle and aim at me, but I froze. I couldn't move. I just sat there and waited for the bullet."

"It'll go better next time."

Orson shuddered.

"Orson. Ride back to the wagon train. Tell the Wagon Master what happened. Tell him I need men to butcher your horse for supper and others with shovels. Now say it back to me."

Orson just looked at him. Addison repeated the message. Orson got it that time; then he set off on Front Rider's horse.

Addison walked back to Behind Rider and sat on the grass next to him. The man's gray face was covered with a week's worth of stubbled whisker. He looked like a man too sick to get out of bed.

"I'm Rafe," he said in a voice as weak as he appeared to be. "Pardner's Yance. We come up from Mississippi hunting five slaves runned away from Masta Holcomb's plantation. Masta Holcomb want the young girl the baddest, the one with light skin. He pay good money for dat one. The men, he pay money for dem, too, if'n we brung them back. The older wimmens. Shoot 'em, he said. Be too hard for us to herd five of 'em back."

Rafe seemed to want to talk. "We rounded the bend in the road. Yance says, 'It's two boys. They got two good horses.' We was also busted. Yance says you probly don't got no money, but maybe you got something we kin sell. Guess you wasn't no boys."

Rafe's breath *phooed* out.

Rafe and Yancy. They needed shooting every bit as much as Wes Thompson and his henchmen. Addison didn't remember their names but wished he did.

He spat vinegary spit on the road and dragged Yancy over next to Rafe.

16.

After supper, Addison took Orson away from the wagons and demonstrated how to hold and shoot a pistol. He explained at length about squeezing the trigger and not jerking the weapon. "Now, dry fire it at that tree."

"I know how to shoot a pistol. Wagon Master taught me with the others back at Thompson Township. Let me load it and shoot a bullet."

"Show me you can *squeeze* the trigger, not jerk it. Then we'll talk about using bullets. Point it at that tree and squeeze. Don't pull. Show me."

He cocked. He grumbled. He extended his arm and jerked the trigger.

"If the gun had been loaded," Addison said. "The safest place to be was in front of the tree. Everything around it was in danger."

"Kin ya learn me to shoot, Mist' Addison?"

Ned Smith. Addison hadn't heard him approach.

A colored person with a gun? That was a stranger notion than eating with them at Mr. Papenheim's. But after eating with them, the notion didn't feel strange anymore.

"Sure, Ned. I'll teach you how to shoot, and you teach me how to sneak up on people without making a sound, all right?"

"Yassuh."

"Besides learning how to shoot, you also have to learn how to speak properly."

"Yassuh, Mist' Addison."

"First thing. Don't call me mister. Just say my name."

"Mist' Addison. I tink bout it powerful hard, but my tongue, it be too scairt to not say mistah."

"All right, Ned. As your hand learns how to shoot a pistol, we'll teach your tongue how to talk."

Addison had unloaded the slave hunters' pistols but hadn't cleaned and reloaded them. He handed one to Ned. Orson already had the other. He placed his students side-by-side in front of the target tree and repeated his squeeze, don't-pull-the-trigger spiel. Then he had them practice firing while he watched the barrels of their weapons.

Addison noted the annoyance on Orson's face. He either didn't like Ned hogging some of the attention, or maybe he was afraid Ned might outdo him.

Since Orson had come close to being shot, fear had uncovered his soul. He hadn't had enough fear in his life. Ned, on the other hand, had too much of it.

Above them, not-to-be-denied stars started shouldering evening from the sky as the shooters *click, clicked* away.

"Enough for today. Tomorrow we'll load the guns," Addison said.

Something crashed through the brush toward them from the direction of the wagons. "Addison. Addison," a child's voice called.

"Over here."

Oscar Wilson's son walked up. "Your pa wants to see you."

Addison thanked him, told Orson and Ned to clean the pistols but not load them.

*****

Pa, or Ma, had pulled three chairs from the load and placed them next to the wagon tongue. There was light from the fire in the middle of the wagons. Pa indicated Addison should sit opposite him and turned to Ma and said, "Coffee."

"I'll get it," Addison said.

"Sit, boy." To Ma, "Coffee."

"Do as your father says." She rose to fetch.

Addison took the chair.

His father sat as he did on his deacon chair back in Found Church. Straight, stiff, and staring without looking at anything or anyone. He waited for Ma to bring the coffee. That's how Pa would plan such a session: Offer coffee; Ma would fetch two cups and hand them to the men; They'd sip; and then Pa would say what he wanted to say. Addison almost smiled. It played out just as he imagined.

Before the Holy Crusade began, he'd never have noticed any of this. If Pa wanted to talk to him, Pa said sit, and he'd have sat with his mind empty until Pa poured something into it.

Addison thanked his Ma. Pa didn't.

Pa sipped. "Drink your coffee."

Addison held the tin cup and looked at his father. He had no hostile intent, no rebellion in his heart, but he did want Pa to know that his son wasn't a little kid anymore. He glanced at his mother. During the day, when the Wagon Master ruled, Ma had a role to play, often with Mrs. Larrimer. A role out of character with the Ma he knew from back home. But here, in the evening, it was as if Pa put her back in her place.

He returned his gaze to his father. "Say what you want to say, Pa."

His father's jaw muscles worked as he ground his teeth. Addison smiled. It was as if he saw himself grinding his teeth over how Orson vexed him.

"Boy. You killed two more men today, and you sit there smiling like it was of no more consequence than swatting a mosquito. You are not going to be scout anymore. I'm going to Preacher Larrimer tonight. And you are marrying Mariah Welch. I'll ask Preacher to stop the train an hour early tomorrow for your wedding. First, though, fetch a switch. Mortifying your flesh may save your soul from eternal mortification in the fires of hell."

Addison sipped and looked at his cup. It was half full. "It's real good coffee, Ma, but I've had enough." He poured it out between him and Pa.

"Pa. I am scout until Mr. Reedley says I'm not. And I'm not marrying Mariah."

"You'll do as I say, Boy. I spoke with Theodore Welch. He and I agreed. You will marry Mariah."

"I will not marry her. I've seen her look at me. She doesn't want me. I'll not marry any woman who doesn't want me as much as I want her."

"Foolishness. That's why fathers must make these decisions. Young peoples' heads are too filled with foolishness to know what's good for them. Fetch a switch."

"No, Pa. I won't. And if you come after me with one, I'll take it away from you and whip you with it."

Addison stood, and his father flinched and raised his hands in front of his face.

"Son!"

Addison looked at Ma. "I'm not going to hit him. Unless he comes after me with a switch." He smiled. "Thanks again for the coffee. I'll wash the cup and bring it back." He turned. "Give me your cup, Pa, so I can wash it."

After waiting a moment, the son took it away from the father.

*****

The next morning, Addison stood at the rear of the morning gathering. Orson sidled up next to him, and then Ned and Violet Smith did too. Violet whispered, "Mister Addison, teach me to shoot." Before he could respond, the Wagon Master announced how far they'd traveled the day before.

"Mid-afternoon," the Wagon Master said, "We should come to the town of Broughton. From there, we pick up a road heading southwest toward St. Louis. To get into Missouri, though, we will have to cross the Mississippi. Some call it the mighty Mississippi. Fortunately, we have The Almighty on our side. And we will need His help to cross."

Reedley went on to say that the next morning he would send Royal Howard and David McTavish ahead. Royal was to scout the best way to cross the Mississippi. McTavish was to visit Boatman's Bank in St. Louis and deposit the Crusade's funds so they could draw on their account when they got to Kansas. Much safer than carrying cash.

"One more thing," the Wagon Master said. "Last night, Adolph Freeman—"

Before, Reedley had always called his father Deacon Freeman.

"Adolph Freeman thought he'd sinned for raising his son to be a killer instead of a God-fearing man. Adolph punished himself by whipping his legs bloody with a switch. Adolph judged his son by the standards of our sheltered community at Found Church. There, guns and violence could not touch us. Here, on the road to Kansas, we cannot escape them. The son did not sin. The father did.

"He rendered himself useless and made himself a burden, a hindrance to our crusade. We will tend him. Because he can vote when we get to our destination. But Adolph Freeman is no longer our deacon. When we get to Kansas, it will be up to Preacher Larrimer whether to reinstate him or not.

"Preacher, will you say the prayer please?"

After the prayer, and after, "On to Kansas!" Addison said, "Ned, this evening after supper, bring Mrs. Smith along with you for shooting."

"You can call me Violet."

"I'll call you Mrs. Smith. And you all best get to your wagons."

Before they could depart, the Wagon Master stopped them. "Ned and Violet, you two drive Mr. Freeman's Wagon and take care of him. Addison, you and Orson git to scoutin'."

Addison and Violet responded with, "Yes, sir." Ned with his version of agreement and Orson with sullen silence.

Addison grabbed Orson's arm and propelled him in the direction of their horses.

After they mounted, they joined Preacher Larrimer, Mrs. Argyl, and Mrs. Freeman, who had their horses in a walk ahead of the lead wagon. Reedley wanted the crusader wives to take turns riding with the preacher on his visits to towns ahead of the train passing through.

As Addison sidled alongside, the preacher turned to him. "My son, you can ask God for more than your daily bread, you know."

Addison tipped his hat to the man of God, made a *"tsk tsk,"* sound, and Outlaw stepped into a canter.

Addison didn't look around to see if Orson followed.

God, besides not liking to have to kill people, I'd rather not have to hurt Orson and have to carry that, too. If that's okay with You.

He reined his mount onto the grass along the side the road. The grass muffled Outlaw's hooves. Behind him, the creaking, rattling, and clopping crusade fell behind. Orson, still on the hard-packed road, was where he should be. He could tell without looking.

Thanks, God.

*****

The sheriff of Broughton was for the South, against the North, and especially against abolitionists. That's what a preacher from a small town two wagon-train hours from the large city had told Larrimer. He and his two shotgun female sidekicks of the day, along with Addison and Orson, rode hard to reach the town well before the crusade arrived. At the sheriff's office, the preacher and the women went in.

Watching through the door, Addison saw the sheriff take his feet off his desk and jump up, with outrage burning bright across his face. That's when the women cocked the hammers on their shotguns.

The sheriff raised his hands. "Whoa up, now. I *heerd* about what you did up in Thompson's Corner. Kilt the sheriff and his deputies."

"We didn't enter that town looking for trouble," Larrimer said. "All we wanted to do was to pass through peacefully, but the mayor and the sheriff and their henchmen wouldn't let that happen. Everyone we killed was in self-defense. Now, all we want to do here is pass through. If no one bothers us, we will bother no one."

"Preacher," Addison said through the door. "Half a dozen armed men heading this way."

"Well, Sheriff," Larrimer said. "What's it to be? Allow us to pass through your town peacefully, so no one gets hurt, or we shoot our way. If it's shooting, the women here will blow your head off first. It's up to you."

"I don't wanna' be *kilt* by no wimmen."

Preacher led the sheriff onto the boardwalk and stood beside him, the women right behind.

Larrimer: "Now would be a good time, sheriff."

The sheriff held up a hand. "You men stop. We're gonna' let these people pass."

The guy in front of the mob started, "But you said—"

"Shut up, Ozzie."

Larrimer said, "Sheriff, tell Ozzie to get your horse and bring it here."

An hour later, the sheriff and Preacher Larrimer rode side-by-side ahead of the crusade's train of wagons through the town. To the right side of the street, clumps of men wearing rough clothes and sidearms and carrying long guns occupied the boardwalks. A row of men, women, and children in Sunday-go-to-church stood on the other side.

In the wagon train, the women sang "Amazing Grace." Those in church clothes added their enthusiastic voices to the hymn.

The Holy Crusade passed through town in the middle of the main street, halfway between the two factions.

Just prior to the wagons entering between the first buildings along Main Street, Reedley stopped Addison. "We'll wait here."

Why? Shouldn't they be in front? Wasn't that where the danger was greatest? He kept those questions to himself, though.

The Crusade overnighted well clear of Broughton. At evening prayer, Preacher Larrimer confessed what he'd done in the town, that he had felt some attraction to the power he'd exercised over the sheriff, and he prayed, "Our Father, Who art in heaven, forgive my trespasses, and help me forgive those who would trespass against us."

Addison reflected, *If Pa'd been leading this crusade, we'd have been done for back in Thompson's Corner.* And if it'd been anyone but Preacher Larrimer leading them through Broughton, they might have made it but would have lost their souls doing so.

After the evening prayer, "Amen," Reedley asked David McTavish to read out the names of the men standing watch that night. Addison and Orson caught the one just before sun-up. As the praying meeting was breaking up, Reedley walked up to Addison. "You figgered it out?"

Addison was pretty sure he meant, *Why did I walk down the boardwalk on the good guy side of town?*

Addison didn't know the answer. But then, suddenly, he did.

Everybody was watching the bad guy side. "Easy for a wolf in sheep's clothing to slip in among the flock."

"You just figured it out, didn't you?"

Addison felt his face shape a … probably a sheepish look.

"Least you figgered it," the wagon master said.

17.

The road leading toward St. Louis was wider—wagons going in opposite directions could pass without one of them pulling onto the grass—and more heavily traveled than the ones the crusaders had encountered thus far. Half the men in buggies and farm wagons tipped their hats. The women and the other men stared, some with curiosity, some with hostility. A few of the children waved.

Also, more farms clustered around the towns they passed through. To Addison, it was the opposite of the country they'd traveled through to that point. Before it had been miles and miles of wilderness interspersed with isolated towns. Since leaving Broughton, it had been miles and miles of cleared land interspersed with brief pockets of forest bordering the road.

The second night after passing Broughton, Larrimer, with his shotgun ladies advance party, encountered a Preacher Deaver in the sizable town of Greenville. Preacher Deaver invited the crusade to overnight in the lot around his church, and his congregation treated Larrimer's to supper and an evening prayer service.

During supper, Deaver introduced Mel Detweiler and Jarvis Lindell to Preacher Larrimer. The two young men wanted to join the crusade. Larrimer and his wife sat on chairs next to their wagon.

Larrimer asked the two their ages.

"I'm twenty," Detweiler said, and he hooked a thumb at Lindell. "Twenty-one."

Larrimer turned to Deaver. "They workers or wastrels?"

"They work hard, are of sound constitution, and have strong moral backbones. Jarvis is engaged to my daughter."

Reedley sat on the wagon tongue behind his preacher. He stood. "We've had to fight our way across most of Illinois to this point. And Illinois is a free state. It'll be tougher crossing slave-state Missouri. That give you any pause?"

"No, sir," Detweiler said. "I … we know what we're in for."

"Mel left the congregation last spring," Deaver said. "He was going to California. See if there was any gold left. Tell them what happened."

"Made it to Kansas City," Mel said. "The farther I got into Missouri, the rougher it got. The men became rougher, and so did I. I didn't like what I was becoming. I came back."

"Can you shoot?" Reedley said.

Detweiler nodded.

"Long gun?"

"And handgun."

"How about you, Mr. Lindell? Can you shoot?" Mrs. Larrimer did the asking this time.

Jarvis rubbed his chin, as if the woman's words had slapped him.

"All the women, fifteen and over, can handle pistols and muskets," Mrs. Larrimer said.

Preacher Larrimer stood and placed his plate on his chair. "I do not carry arms, but I know how to use them and will if required to defend our crusade. We have passed through towns where the appearance of our armed women has deterred some who might consider us weak, turn-the-other-cheek Christians. If it had been our choice, we would fight the abomination of slavery only with the ballot box."

"But," Reedley said, "there are those who would stop us with bullets. We've had to fight back with bullets. We've had to kill men to protect ourselves and our crusade. You need to understand what you are signing on for. Do you? Understand? And do you still wish to join us?"

"Thou shalt not kill. There is a time for every purpose under heaven," Larrimer said. "We pray every day for the power to discern the proper time to ignore a commandment. So, young men, answer the wagon master's questions, please."

"I understand," Mel said. "And I do want to join you. We both do."

Addison sat on the ground, leaned against a rear wheel of Larrimer's wagon, and ate from the plate on his lap. He looked up to see all the eyes of those at the front of the wagon turn toward Jarvis Lindell.

"What about those coloreds you have with you?" Jarvis said. "Are they your slaves?"

"They are freed men and women," Preacher Larrimer said. "We keep them hidden in the wagons during the day. Less threat to them and the crusade."

A pistol popped from the edge of the church lot behind them.

"Shooting practice," Reedley informed the startled newcomers. "Mr. Lindell, you don't seem even lukewarm to the idea of joining us. Mr. Detweiler, come with me. I want to see you shoot."

The Wagon Master and Mel walked toward the sound of gunfire.

Preacher Deaver asked Larrimer to reconsider taking Jarvis. Part of the young man's hesitation was he didn't want to leave his fiancée.

"It's up to the wagon master," Larrimer said. "But, half of our congregation is still back in the northeast corner of Illinois. Once we have established ourselves in Kansas, the wagon master will return and bring the rest of them to join us. That second half of our congregation may pass through here in a couple of months. Maybe Jarvis will have made up his mind by that time."

"I want to go with you now," Jarvis said.

Both preachers turned as if astonished to find the man they'd been talking about right next to them, though he had been there through the whole conversation.

"Addison," Larrimer said. "Take Mr. Lindell to shooting practice and see if Wagon Master will agree to take him with us."

Addison shoveled in the last forkful of stew, stood, and chewed as he walked toward the front of the wagon. He swallowed, and holding his empty plate, introduced himself and extended his arm. Jarvis was fair-haired, fair complected, his own height, but skinny. He looked at the proffered hand for a moment, then shook it.

As soon as Jarvis released his hand, Addison set off for the shooting. Behind him, Jarvis said, "Uh—"

Addison pictured Jarvis behind him, wiping his hand on the trousers of his Sunday clothes.

When Addison cleared the wagons and those still eating or cleaning up, Jarvis caught up to him. "Can I ask you a question?"

"Shoot."

"Um, can we stop? Please."

Addison stopped abruptly, catching Jarvis by surprise.

"Are you mad at me, Mr. Freeman?"

Addison was mad. Mad that Jarvis was so delicate. The women on the crusade were tougher than him. Mad too because: *That's how I was three weeks ago. Except you're engaged to the woman you want to marry.* "I'm not mad. Yet. You wanted to ask a question. Ask."

"If I go with you, will I have to kill men, too?"

Addison shook his head, then looked off to where Reedley had one of the women from the crusade shoot at a tree. "Look there. If you go with us, everyone has to be prepared to defend the crusade. Since we started on this journey, we have had to fight our way through towns and fight off outlaws who wanted to steal from us. We've had to kill some of them. If you can't kill someone who would do us harm, then you should stay here."

"What's it like to kill someone?"

"During the actual killing, there isn't time for it to be like anything. Things happen fast, and you have to act fast or you are dead and the man facing you is left alive to harm the crusade. After the killing, I wind up with a taste in my mouth like I bit the head off a match and washed it down with vinegar. Any more questions, cause time's a wastin'?"

Addison set off again. And he was mad again. Before the crusade started, he was like Jarvis. Filled with love and hope, and he didn't wish to harm any of God's creatures except those he needed to kill so his family could eat.

But look at you now, Addison J. Freeman.

*****

Jarvis' father, it turned out, owned the general store in Greenville. "Mr. Reedley," the elder Lindell said, "My son knows how to run a store. I propose you take him and have him set up a store for you in your new Kansas community."

Great! We ain't even outa Illinois, but already we got the Jarvis Lindell General Store in New Found Grace, Kansas: Addison pictured Maurice the Wiseacre saying that. He hadn't thought of his friend for a long time. Maurice, and the Addison John he used to be before he became Addison Job, seemed to have nothing to do with determining the kind of man he'd become. It was as if he'd been born and grew up since the wagon train began its journey.

That night at before-supper services, Deaver's community took up a collection for the crusade and provided a wagon and provisions for Lindell and Detweiler.

At supper, served in Preacher Deaver's meeting house, he offered to ride ahead of the crusade with Larrimer and smooth the way through the rest of Illinois. Reedley agreed, but since the two preachers would be working farther ahead of the wagons than before, farther from help if they needed it, Reedley insisted that Larrimer carry a handgun in a shoulder holster under his coat.

Deaver also recommended the crusade cross the Mississippi at Alton. The town had a strong abolitionist core of citizens.

"But," Deaver said, "make no mistake about Alton. Some years back, a man printed a pro-abolition newspaper. He was unarmed when he was gunned down. The killer was captured but found innocent of murder at his trial. If fifty-one percent of Alton is pro-abolition, forty-nine percent is pro-slavery."

Addison and Orson sat at a table with the Reedleys, Larrimers, Howards, and Deavers. They were about finished eating when Mr. Lindell approached the table and asked if he could join them.

"Orson," Addison said, "Give him your place and help those gathering plates."

Orson did as told without a grumble or sullen look. *Progress?* Addison wondered.

Mr. Lindell took the vacated place and set a mug of coffee on the table. "I'm sending some money with Jarvis. I'll have him deposit it with Boatman's Bank in St. Louis. Then as he needs the money to set up the new store, he can write a draft on that account. I know drafts on Boatman's are honored farther west than Kansas."

"You may want to consider doing that too." Deaver looked from Larrimer to Reedley and back to Larrimer. "When we get to Alton, I will talk with Reverend Mittelmann there about raising money for your crusade. What we collect could then be deposited in your bank account."

"Riverboats do have accidents, and, out west, there is no shortage of lawless bands of men who'd rob from pro-slavery and abolitionists alike," Lindell said.

"Sounds like a good idea," Reedley said. "Preacher?"

Larrimer nodded.

"I planned to send an advance party," Reedley said. "Couple of wagons only, on a riverboat ahead of us as we cross Missouri. They would find and buy suitable land for us."

Joshua Reedley glanced at Larrimer, then the Wagon Master said, "That's what we'll do. We'll set up an account with Boatman's, and we'll send the three wagons to St. Louis. They can cross there and buy riverboat passage to just east of Fort Leavenworth. The wagons, yours, Royal, the O'Riley brothers, and Jarvis Lindell. Plus, I'll pick some of our young men to go with you."

"One more thing," Mr. Lindell said. "You might want to consider shipping your cows on the riverboat, too. That'd make your trip across Missouri easier."

The Wagon Master humphed.

*****

The next morning, Larrimer welcomed the new crusaders, Jarvis, Mel, and Cecille Deaver. Cecille would ride on the Larrimer wagon. Mrs. Larrimer would serve as her chaperone until the couple was married in Kansas. Then the preacher boomed out, "The Lord helps those who help themselves, and praise be to God, sometimes He helps when you aren't even smart enough to ask for it. He sent us our wagon master. And now, He's blessed us with your help, Reverend Deaver."

"On to Kansas!" the Wagon Master hollered.

When the crusade departed Greenville, Jarvis drove the wagon. Detweiler and Orson rode scout with Addison. That night, Addison added Mel Detweiler into the wagon master's notebook as a crusader to be counted on.

The next morning, Reedley had Jarvis ride scout with Addison. "See if you can get a handle on Mr. Lindell while we have a reasonably peaceful setting to work in."

Also that morning, Reedley sent his son Robert and David McTavish ahead, with the preachers, to Alton, Illinois. There they were to determine how the crusade would cross the Mississippi.

Addison thought Reedley, uncharacteristically, changed plans frequently that day. Was crossing the Mississippi that big a deal?

*****

Robert Reedley and Preacher Deaver rejoined the wagon train just after it stopped for the night. They wasted no time in reporting to the wagon master.

Preacher Deaver said, "The pastor of Our Savior Church in Alton, Reverend Mittelman, learned that a group of anti-abolitionists intends to ambush us."

"Did the reverend know how many, or where, or when?"

"He only knew they were coming, Pa," Robert Reedley said.

The Wagon Master saw Addison watching the exchange. Come along; he motioned to his scout. Then he told his son to fetch Royal Howard and asked the preacher to walk with him to the road they were following.

The wagons had been bunched on the de-stumped half of a grassy field, the trees of which had been felled a few years before. At the edge of the road, Reedley looked southwest toward Alton.

Royal Howard hustled to join them.

"Preacher," the wagon master said, "This the only road from here to Alton?"

"A couple of miles ahead, a small road cuts off to the right, goes to a small town called Milltown, named for the sawmill there. From Milltown, the road rejoins this one, probably halfway to Alton."

Addison watched the wagon master step into the road and take a couple of strides toward Alton. He removed his hat and wiped his brow with the sleeve of his shirt. Then he just stood there, staring ahead, holding his hat.

The air was heavy, warm, and still. Even standing in the shade of the trees to the west, sweat trickled down Addison's back.

Royal Howard joined them with Robert Reedley in trail.

Josh Reedley turned and stepped back to where Preacher Deaver and rest of them waited.

"This is what we're going to do," Josh Reedley said. "Royal, mount guards around the wagons and the animals. Make it two persons to a post. Everyone goes everywhere armed. Even if it's to the latrine. And, watch over Preacher Deaver."

The wagon master put his hat back on. "Robert, resaddle our horses. You and me will scout the main road to Alton. Addison, pick someone to go with you and scout that cutoff road to Milltown."

"I'll take Mel Detweiller." Addison started toward the wagons.

"Wait," the wagon master said. "Take a light-colored spare shirt or some long hunk of light-colored cloth. Full moon tonight. If you find the ambushers and return to the wagons to report it, wave that shirt and call out your name as you get within rifle range of the wagons. Wouldn't want you to get shot before you report what you found."

Addison humphed.

*****

Addison and Mel passed Milltown. A general store, a blacksmith shop, and six small houses snuggled close together. Lamplight showed through curtains of most of the houses. As their horses' hooves clop clopped, the lamps started blinking out, and pretty soon, the houses were as dark as the other two buildings.

About a half-hour past Milltown, Outlaw stopped. Its ears twitched forward.

Addison looked around. They were passing an area where forest had been cleared from both sides of the road. *No cover.*

"Preacher Deaver said we might encounter wagons, but if we met riders, it'd probably be ambushers."

"Quiet," Addison fussed.

Two riders approaching. Walking their mounts side-by-side.

Addison sat Outlaw on the left side of the road. Mel stopped on the right side.

"Pull your long gun," Addison said, "and drop behind me ten yards."

Addison started Outlaw walking forward hugging the left side of the road. As they neared, the moon turned those approaching from shadow into solid men and beasts.

When the riders got to within fifty yards, Addison stopped Outlaw. The riders kept walking their mounts forward, still side-by-side. At about twenty yards, the one to Addison's right stopped so that he was screened by the other, who continued walking his horse forward.

Suddenly, Detweiller's long gun boomed. Near Rider couldn't screen Far Rider tumble backward out of the saddle. Near Rider reached for his belt gun, but Addison whipped out his Colt Pocket Gun and cocked it. "I wouldn't."

Near Rider froze with his hand on the butt of his pistol.

"Take your hand off your gun and raise 'em. Real slow."

The guy was thinking about drawing.

"Think of your pard lying in the dirt looking up at the sky with eyes that don't see nothing no more. Look at him." The guy looked. "Last time I'm sayin'. Slow and easy. Hand off that pistol and raise 'em."

Detweiler was approaching, but Addison kept his eyes on Near Rider. He was trying to work himself up to drawing. Addison didn't want to have to kill him. He fired and nicked Near Rider's ear.

"Ow, goddamn." Near Rider raised a hand to his ear.

Addison gigged Outlaw, and he shouldered into Near Rider's mount.

Addison grabbed the man's belt gun, shoved him out of the saddle, and hopped down.

Detweiler got to the man first. "Stay there." He pulled Near Rider's boots off and found a sheath knife in one. After sticking the knife in his belt, he tossed the boots into the low brush.

"Hey."

"Any more a you pro-slavery shitheads coming this way?" Detweiler said.

"Ain't telling you *Abolitionists* nothin'," Near Rider sneered.

Detweiler kicked him in the ribs.

After the howling ceased, Detweiler repeated his question.

Near Rider was doubled up and moaning. He still didn't answer.

"Tie Ain't Dead Yet up and get him on his horse. Then hoist the other one across his saddle. Ride back toward the train until you come to the first stand of trees past Milltown. Hide there until I come back, or you hear shooting. If you do, plug this guy and hightail it back to the wagons and warn them."

"Ain't nobody comin," Ain't Dead Yet said. "By this road."

"Okay, Mel. If you do hear shooting from ahead, that means this one lied. Gut shoot him; then ride back and warn the wagons."

After Mel headed back the way they'd come, Addison walked Outlaw on the grass beside the road so he could hear riders approaching. When he saw stars burn through the diminishing glow in the west, he turned around and galloped back the way he'd come. He found Detweiler in a copse, just adequate to hide in in the dark. No riders approached during the night.

From off to the west, a flurry of distant and steady gunshots erupted. It lasted about as long as it took a man empty a pistol firing steady. Then, the last shots echoed away, and it was as if a heavy, dew-wet blanket of silence settled over the land.

"Wonder how many a you shitheads just bought it," Not Dead Yet said, his sneer resurrected on faith in his righteousness. "Guess that's it. Whatever a yore pards ain't shot dead will git hung dead come sunup."

"Now there's an idea, Mel. Hangin'. A good way to shut him up."

"You do that, and you'll be sorry. When the gang catches you, they'll hang you and cut you down and hang you again. One time we hung a nigger-lover six times before he croaked."

Addison shot a straight hard jab and felt the crunch of bone from Not Dead Yet's Nose. Not Dead flopped onto the ground, moaned, and rocked side to side with both hands over his face.

Addison walked away a couple of paces and listened, but he heard nothing.

Mel walked up and listened, too. "You think Reedley found them, got some men from the train, and ambushed the ambushers?"

"Please, Lord God of heaven and earth."

"What are we going to do with Not Dead Yet?" Mel said.

"I'm taking him back to the wagon train along with the one we shot. You stay here. You hear riders coming, mount up, and ride back and warn us."

Mel huffed out a breath. Of relief, probably.

"It's one thing to kill in the heat of a fight, but altogether another thing when coolly looking back and shooting a man for something he did even a few minutes ago." Mel, Addison thought, had seen some ugly things as he traveled west, but he hadn't killed anyone. Before this morning.

Mel hacked and spat. Probably that vinegar taste.

18.

A bit before sunup, Addison, along with Dead and Aint Dead Yet, heard the horseshoes whanging as they neared the wagons. Addison started waving his spare shirt and hollering his name.

"Come ahead," a voice hollered back. It sounded like Robert Reedley.

Addison leading two horses, rode up and found Robert Reedley sitting on stump in grassy field fifty yards from the wagons. Jarvis Lindell was with. Both of them held long guns.

"What happened this morning?" Addison said.

"Yeah, but you first," Robert responded.

Addison told his story.

"The Wagon Master," the son said, "and me scouted along this road. Found the ambushers camped out a few miles from here. Close to two dozen of them. They were drinking and laughing. Having a merry old time. We come back here and gathered up most of the men and returned to the ambush camp. We left Jarvis here with the horses and snuck close on foot. By the time we got there, the ambushers were asleep. Snoring like to knock leaves from the trees. Their lookout was asleep, too. We just walked right into the camp and woke them up. A couple of them pulled pistols, and we started shooting them. Half of them wound up kilt or wounded. We got the others tied up."

From inside the group of wagons came, "On to Kansas."

After two hours, the wagon train stopped next to the would-be ambusher's camp. Reedley wanted men, women, and gun-bearing youngsters, those twelve and older, to view the bodies. To see what they faced on their crusade, not even half completed yet.

Prisoners were set to work digging seven graves, including the one Mel had shot. Larrimer invited Preacher Deaver to say prayers at the graves. After the services, Deaver suggested he and the wagon master ride ahead and report what happened to the sheriff in Alton.

*****

Preacher Deaver had informed the crusaders that Alton was a sizeable town, that fishing and a rock quarry provided employment for a large number of men. The town was prohibitionist, but as they'd found out last night, a number of pro-slavery young men resided in the environs of the riverside city.

Gallant Argyl and Addison rode in front of the first wagon with two shotgun-bearing women astride saddle broncs behind them. As the wagon train neared Alton, Josh Reedley, Preacher Deaver, and two other men rode out to meet them. A mile outside of town, Gallant stopped the train as the greeting party approached. One of the men was Reverend Mittelmann, pastor of the largest church in Alton. The other was Sheriff Kerby.

As soon as Deaver introduced the lawman, all eyes shifted to him.

For his part, Kerby's eyes danced over the wagon train lead party, and the lead wagons like a hummingbird in a patch so filled with flowers the bird couldn't decide which blossom looked like it held the tastiest nectar.

"Understand you ran into some trouble last night," the sheriff said.

"Some of your citizenry ran into trouble, Sheriff." Gallant had exaggerated his Scottish brogue. "We had to kill seven of them."

"Had to?"

"Had to."

"You know who the leader of the bunch is?"

"Fellow named Buster Wiggins," Reedley cut in. "Leastwise, that's what a couple of the gang told us. Buster said he wasn't."

Kerby shook his head. "Oh, Buster would have been the ringleader, all right. How many you got and where you got 'em?"

"Fifteen. Six wounded in wagons. The others tied up and herded up in the middle of the train," Reedley said.

The sheriff nodded. "Here's what's gonna' happen. Reverend will lead you to his church. There's a place to graze your animals and set up camp. As soon as you arrive at the church, bring the prisoners to the gathering house next to the church. Judge Wiggins—"

"Wiggins?" Reedley said.

"Yep. Buster's uncle. But you needn't fret none. He'll be tougher on Buster than on the others."

The trial of the fifteen concluded in time for supper. Fourteen of the gang were sentenced to a month of labor in the quarry cutting stone to cobble Second Street in Alton, Main Street having already been cobbled. Buster received two months labor, and all of them were to wear leg irons for the length of their sentences and live in shacks at the quarry. One of the prisoners would serve as cook for all of them, which according to Sheriff Kerby, most prisoners considered that to be the severest part of their imprisonment. The wounded were awarded deferred sentences, which they would serve as soon as they healed.

*****

As soon as the trial concluded, the women of Reverend Mittelmann's church converted the meeting house from a courthouse to a supper house with the tables and chairs rearranged to serve as such. Each family from the reverend's congregation brought a cast-iron stew pot filled enough to feed fifteen. The first to eat were the prisoners. They were served tin plates outside and sitting on the ground, unbound but guarded by a sheriff's deputy and men from the crusade and from the reverend's flock.

After eating at the tables inside, the young men and women of the crusade washed plates and utensils for the second and third seatings. As soon as the after-meal cleanup was completed, Reverend Mittlemann conducted a Thanksgiving service outside with crusaders and parishioners arrayed around him. He thanked, "Father God, Lord of heaven and earth," that He brought Found Grace Church's holy crusade to visit them in Alton. He asked the Lord to help the wagon train across the mightiest of rivers, and that it, "please God," would be the greatest obstacle they would face between now and when they began the work of turning the future state of Kansas into the promised land.

Addison thought the reverend's voice was rich and full of smooth golden phrases that made the world, the men, the bugs, and beasts hush up and listen to the captivating words delivered as a spoken song without accompaniment. Then Preacher Larrimer, his voice one of power and brute force, thanked the Lord of All for His continued presence on their journey, that everywhere they encountered opposition, He provided what the crusade needed to overcome it, to be able to continue His holy work to abolish the loathsome sin of slavery, "The abomination of slavery, that would eat at and rot the core of the nation the founders sought to establish.

"And thank You, Lord, for bringing us to these God-fearing people here on the bank of this great river. They are a holy oasis in our journey through the desert. They are an example of what we hope, with Your grace and with Your aid, to establish in Kansas Territory."

*****

After the service, while most of the two congregations prepared for bed, the two preachers met in the meeting house with the Wagon Master, Royal Howard, Gallant Argyl, Addison, and a man from Alton named Rudolph Potts.

"Rudolph," Reverend Mittelmann said, "Is sixty-six years old, still strong as an ox and sharp as a tack. I tell you this because if I didn't, he would tell you and commit yet another sin of pride."

The Reverend turned to Reedley. "You asked if there was someone here who had experience with riverboats on the Missouri. And that's Rudolph. He has established businesses in several of the major river towns between here and St. Joseph. He ships supplies to his general stores on the boats every day of the week."

"Excepting the Sabbath, Reverend," Potts proudly, Addison thought, proclaimed.

Reedley informed Mr. Potts of his intention to send a small advance party by riverboat ahead of the wagon train.

Potts grabbed a handful of his grizzled-black beard as if he was thinking of pulling his chin off. "Have you heard of the Massachusetts Emigrant Aid Society?"

Reedley and Larrimer shook their heads.

"The Society was formed to sponsor and provide financial assistance to northeasterners to emigrate to Kansas for the same purpose as your Holy Crusade, Preacher Larrimer. Besides the Massachusetts one, there are other such societies. But this is the one I know most about."

Potts faced Mittelmann. "Reverend, perhaps we should ask the farms around Alton to host the wagons of the crusade for a couple of days. I can travel to St. Louis and speak with the Emigrant Society people. They maintain an office there. Perhaps I can work out an accommodation with them." Turning again, "Mr. Reedley, Preacher Larrimer, there is a possibility the Emigrant Society would fund riverboat passage for your entire crusade. There is a fairly steady procession of one and two riverboat groups coming down the Ohio River to St. Louis, and from there shifting to boats plying the Missouri River to the border with Kansas. it will save you considerable time. It there is a group of easterners due soon, they quite possibly would be happy to have you with them. You see, a lot of pro-slavery Missourians have *emigrated,* or invaded, Kansas and have established a significant pro-slavery presence just inside the border. There'd be safety in numbers. And if funding is an issue, I would help out with that."

Rudolph Potts might be a proud man, Emerson thought, but he was definitely generous.

*****

Rudolph Potts led Preacher Larrimer, the wagon master, and Addison along the Illinois side of the Mississippi to St. Louis. Once they arrived at the city, Potts would introduce them to the people at the Emigrant

Aid Society Office. Perhaps, the Aid Society would help the crusaders arrange for, and pay for, passage on riverboats to northwestern Missouri.

The Emigrant Aid Society was delighted to assist Preacher Larrimer's crusade. It just so happened that one riverboat was immediately available. It would be hired to transport half of the crusade through Missouri to the border with Kansas. The second half would not be more than a week behind.

Two days later, the Found Grace wagon train arrived opposite St. Louis, ferried across the Mississippi, and loaded aboard the boat. Otto Vogelsang organized the men into teams. They removed the loads, wheels, and tongues from the wagons and stacked the beds atop each other. This made room for the crusaders' gear and animals. This boat would travel up the Missouri River with another Emigrant Aid Society boat filled with New Englanders bound for Kansas also. The New Englanders intended to disembark at St. Joseph. Reedley intended to leave the river near Leavenworth.

The Emigrant Aid Society provided Mr. Foster Wente to serve as a guide. He'd made the journey up the Missouri a half-dozen times. He explained It would take the small flotilla three or four, or maybe five days to reach northwestern Missouri, depending on river conditions and whether or not the riverboat captains would travel at night. There would be stops for the boats to take on wood and water for the boilers, but barring mishaps, there'd be no stops for any other purpose.

"Mishaps?" Joshua Reedley said. "What kind of mishaps might we run into?"

"Riverboats run into things. Like sandbars and logs. Boilers explode."

"These mishaps happen often?" Reedley said.

Foster Wente shook his head. "Not often. But they do happen. Only once to an Emigrant Aid Society Boat. Two years ago. We were just getting started. Since then, we've learned who we can trust in hiring boats and who we can't."

While the boats were being loaded, Joshua Reedley came up with a new plan for the advance party. He, his son Robert, Addison, and Mel Detweiler would board another riverboat, one departing immediately.

This advance party would arrive at the Kansas border a day, or two, or three ahead of the other boat.

Meanwhile, Royal Howard would be in charge of the first boatload of crusaders.

19.

Reedley and his traveling companions stood on the riverbank holding the reins to their mounts and scanning the length of the boat. Up close, Addison thought the boat looked big. Smokestacks on either side belched steady streams of smoke. Two narrow bridges from shore to vessel provided the means to board. Over the one closest to the paddle wheel, a steady stream of men lugged sacks and wheeled large barrels on dollies. A stream of men, women, and children paraded across the other bridge. A lot of people were boarding. With that in mind, the boat didn't look big enough to hold that many people, plus their already loaded horses and wagons.

"Addison," Reedley said. "Remember Thompson Township? How I said I'd hoped I'd have time to talk to you and Maurice about what we might encounter later in our journey? Turned out there was no time for warning. Except for you refusing to ride on into that town, we'd have ridden into an ambush. I should have instructed you from the git-go. As it turned out, your instinct saved us."

The wagon master explained they'd be aboard for several days. None of the passengers would have any work to do. Most men will look for someone to talk to. Jawing, drinking, playing card games for money, those were about the only ways to pass the time. Probably half the people aboard will be pro-slavery. Now, same as before, we want to avoid trouble if at all possible. Men will come up to you and say, 'Where're you bound?'"

"Before you answer, hesitate awhile, maybe look off somewhere, let it get uncomfortable, then say, 'West,'" Reedley said. "Then the fellow is likely to ask, 'Kansas, Santa Fe, or all the way to Oregon or California?' Again, hesitate before answering. Then say, 'California.' He might ask, 'Hunting gold?' This one, just shrug. Maybe the guy will take the hint and try to find someone more talkative."

Reedley also mentioned beer and whiskey. Mel Detweiler had experience with booze. The wagon master didn't mention whether he and his son Robert had such experience, but Addison figured he did, or he wouldn't be able to speak so authoritatively about it.

"While we're on the boat," Reedley cautioned, "steer clear of booze. Booze loosens a man's tongue, and that could be dangerous."

That was okay with Addison. If he drank spirits, Pa would switch him bloody. Or try to. On the other hand, Preacher Larrimer had pounded the notion that *licker* was liquid evil so deeply within him, if he did allow himself to drink, maybe he'd let Pa beat him.

"We're going to be in a room with two beds. We'll take turns sleeping on the floor." The wagon master shook his head. "Wish we had more time before I threw you into this."

Then leading his mount to the back-of-the-boat bridge, he crossed it with the others in trail. Once on board, with the horses tied in stalls, and Robert watching the animals, Reedley found a Negro room steward who led the three to their cabin. After the steward departed, Reedley remarked, "The steward's a freed man and is safe aboard the boat. Ashore, anywhere along the river, and even into Kansas, to many men, a freed colored person is nothing more than a runaway slave."

Addison had no trouble understanding that Negroes traveling with the wagon train, being runaways with forged papers, were in danger, but even properly freed colored people were in danger too?

The steward had given Reedley two keys to the cabin, and he gave one to Addison.

The wagon master said, "During our trip upriver, we'll try to minimize the times when any one of us is alone." They filed out of the cabin and into a passageway with a steady stream of people moving in both directions. Reedley led them back to the main deck, to where

Robert had stayed with the horses, and he told Mel Detweiler to stay there, too. "When we pull away from the riverbank, they'll toot the whistle. Might take two of you to calm the animals." Then he and Addison climbed up to the top deck to watch the departure.

Two decks above the main, they found the railing packed with men, women, and a few children. Reedley invited Addison to look forward and aft. "What do you see?" he said.

"The river, the riverbank all filled with people, wagons, and horses."

"The boat's level," the wagon master said. "When a boat leaves a town, people always jam the side to watch. We're level. That means the crew has moved cargo to the other side to keep the boat from tipping toward shore."

Addison humphed, Reedley smiled at him, and stopped behind a man and woman they could both see over. A young girl, maybe seven, and a young boy, maybe five, and both in Sunday go-to-church clothes, pushed on their parents' legs to get to the railing, but the man and woman were both intent on waving to people on the wharf.

Reedley got down on a knee and asked the girl if she'd like to see. She nodded and he picked her up. The little boy stretched his arms up, too, and Addison picked him up.

The boat whistle blew, and the girl screamed.

The woman at the rail spun around. A horrified look flashed over her bonnet-rimmed face, replaced in an instant by indignation. "Put! My! Daughter! Down! This instant!"

The whistle blew again: *Toot, toot, toot, toot, toot.* The girl grabbed Reedley around the neck.

The woman's mouth dropped open. Even in the charged situation, Addison noted that she was beautiful. Pale complected, blonde hair in curls, blue eyes, sparkling now with outrage. "Jared." A frown wrinkled her smooth brow. "Do something."

The girl said, "Mother—"

"Hush, Penelope," the woman snapped.

The man, of slight build and an I-spend-my-time-indoors complexion huffed himself up. "Unhand my daughter!"

Addison glanced at Reedley. In one way, the wagon master was just like his used-to-be-a-deacon pa. You couldn't tell what either man was thinking by what was on their faces. Reedley stood there a moment, eyes locked on the irate father's. Then the father noticed Addison, and the man's eyes darted from one to the other. "Put my children down."

Reedley lowered the girl to the deck. Addison followed suit, and as he stood up again, Reedley said, "If I had children like these, I'd have had my eye on them in the midst of the commotion of getting underway."

"Outrageous! First you have the audacity to touch my children, and then you insult my wife!"

"I wasn't insulting your wife," Reedley said.

Addison didn't have any trouble reading what the irate father was thinking. It had taken the man a moment to realize he'd been insulted. He pulled the glove off his left hand, stepped forward, and started swinging the glove at Reedley's face. The wagon master caught the man's wrist and twisted it. The man grimaced, and fear showed plain and clear on his face.

Reedley stepped closer to the man. "I can see you'd prefer to die like a gentleman, but if you try to hit me again, I will break your arm and throw you over the side. You might want to think on how it'd be to die that way."

"I asked the man to pick me up," the little girl, looking up to her mother, said.

"You folks are making a commotion." The speaker wore a short-brimmed cap and rough clothes. "I need you to stop, or I'll have you taken to your cabins and kept there."

"Who are you?" the father demanded.

"First mate of the *Belle of St. Joseph*."

"Ah! Arrest these two men and throw them off the boat."

"A little late for that, Sir." First mate nodded toward the shore. The stern of the boat was well clear of the shore. The stern paddle wheel began to thresh the water, and the power in the wheel vibrated through the deck under Addison's feet.

"I demand to see the captain. Immediately," the father said.

"The captain ain't seeing nobody just now," the mate replied. "He's concerned with getting the boat out and onto the river safely. Now, stop the commotion, or I will have you taken to your cabin. What's it to be?"

"Sir," Reedley said to the first mate, "We wasn't looking to start a ruckus. We'll go."

"Your name, Sir?"

"Joshua Reedley."

"So, Mr. Reedley, come with me, please."

"Where to?"

"Why," the mate smiled sweetly, "to see the captain, Sir. And bring your companion."

"Jared!"

"Hush," Jared snapped at his wife. He grabbed his son by the arm and stomped off toward the stern. The woman and their daughter followed.

The mate started forward. The passengers lining the rail were all watching the parties to the commotion, not the shore.

"Sorry for the disturbance, folks," the mate said, and after a few paces, repeated his apology, and repeated it, and repeated it, until he came to a door into a space at the forward-most part of the boat structure. He opened it with a key, entered, and motioned *come in* to Reedley and Addison.

The mate closed the door behind them. Addison found himself in a large room extending from one side of the boat to the other. Windows made up half the front wall, affording a grand view of the river and shore. A man stood behind a wheel festooned with handgrips, as if the wheelwright forgot to end the spokes of a wagon wheel at the rim.

Three men stood in front of the wheel man. Two were of Reedley's height and build. And age. The third was an inch or two shorter and more slender. And younger. One of the older said, "Ease your rudder to right fifteen."

"Ease my rudder to right fifteen," the wheelman repeated and turned the wheel as he stared at an indicator dial in front of him.

The mate, close to Reedley, whispered, "That wheel is called the helm. The helm is connected by ropes to a rudder located on the stern of the hull, underneath the paddlewheel. An indicator needle in front of the helmsman tells him the position of the rudder."

"Starboard lookout, report." The same man demanded.

A crewman on the right side of the room looked aft and said, "Clear to starboard close by, Captain. One vessel downstream a thousand yards and closing slow."

"Engine ahead standard," the captain said.

The crewman next to the helmsman moved a lever mounted to a pedestal in front of him. A bell jangled. Addison felt the silent vibration through the deck ease a bit.

"Running a riverboat, Mr. Reedley," Addison said, "It's sort of like running a wagon train, isn't it?'

"One big difference," the wagon master said, "When the captain gives an order, the crewmen listen to him without a moment's hesitation."

Addison caught the small smile that wrinkled the mate's face. He said, "Come," and led them forward and introduced them to the captain.

The mate said, "I brought these passengers to you, Sir, because they had an unfortunate run-in with Jared 3rd and his wife."

The captain's hair and beard were grizzled black. His eyes were like Preacher Larrimer's. They held the power to shrivel Goliath to a whimpering David who forgot his sling.

The captain took in a deep breath, huffed it out, turned, and walked to the side of the room where a chair sat atop a one-step high platform. He took his seat, like Larrimer used to take his in Found Church.

The mate herded Reedley and Addison to beside the captain's throne, maybe, Addison mused.

"Saw the whole thing, Cap'n," the first mate said and related the entire incident.

"Mr. Reedley," the Captain said, "Would you, and your"—the Captain's eyes scanned Addison down and up again— "companion do me the honor of dining with me at midday?"

"The honor, Sir," Reedley tipped his hat, "would be ours."

The captain nodded and turned to look out his windows, as clear a dismissal as any spoken one could have been.

The first mate led them out the door on the right side, and he explained the large room they'd just departed was called the pilot house. The older man who'd been standing beside the captain was a pilot, a man experienced and knowledgeable about navigating a paddle wheeler safely around sandbars and obstacles in waters around St. Louis and into the mouth of the Missouri River, up to the town of St. Charles. There the pilot would boat ashore, and the captain and the crew would drive upriver.

"I'm Symonds." The first mate stuck out his hand, and Reedley shook it. "I have to be about my business. Midday meal with the captain will be on the deck above us. Pleasure to meet you, Mr. Reedley, Mr. Freeman." He touched his forehead, spun on his heel, and headed aft.

"On boats and ships," Mr. Reedley explained, "stairs are called ladders. This isn't the right side, it's the starboard. The other's the port." He pointed forward, "Stem or bow. Backend is the stern. Used to be, boats had a paddle wheel on each side. You still see those. But most of the new boats working the Missouri have stern paddle wheels. That's cause a number of the sidewheelers hit snags or ice that wrecked the wheel. That happens, your boat is a canoe way too big to paddle. Putting it in the back protects it."

"How is it you know so much about boats?" Addison said.

The wagon master leaned his elbows on the railing and looked ahead to where the front end of the boat, the bow, shouldered waves of water aside, like a big man shoving his way through a crowd of people. Addison also leaned on the railing.

After a long pause, Reedley said, "I rode a boat when I was your age. Boats didn't go far upriver then. Couple of years later, a few boats went up pretty far. I worked on one coming back down to St. Louis."

Near the wooded shore slipping past, an eagle dove out of the sky, leveled just above the water, snatched a fish with its talons and, with a furious flapping of wings, climbed again with supper dangling and writhing below it.

"When I see something like that, Addison, I am just gob smacked over how God made creatures able to come out of a dive at just the right level above the water to snatch a fish and keep right on flying."

Addison watched the eagle and thought, *Holy smokes!* And even though he'd never heard the word *gob smacked* before, he was sure it meant *surprised as all get out.* And he was surprised as all get out to hear the wagon master talk about the eagle the way he had. He'd made the bird's feat seem amazing, holy even. Preacher Larrimer saying something like that wouldn't have been surprising, but Mr. Reedley? Back at Found Church, Addison had him pegged as quiet, wouldn't open his mouth to holler, "Help!" if his life depended on it. His middle son Maurice had a cruder way of talking about his taciturnity. Addison humphed. *Don't ge*t much call for that word.

It had been a surprise—a gob smacking one at that—to watch Joshua Reedley assume the role of wagon master. One moment he was Joshua wouldn't-say-a-peep Reedley: the next, he was Moses' Joshua tumbling down the walls of Jericho with a voice as deep and powerful as Larrimer's.

*****

It was a day for gob smacks. Who was at the captain's table with Reedley and him? None other than that uppity Jared. With his wife and two kids. And another older fellow. As Reedley, with Addison trailing, approached the table, the captain and the older man stood.

The older man growled, "Son."

Uppity Jared's chair scraped against the floor as he pushed back and rose also. His cheeks were sucked in as if he'd just bitten into an apple he expected to be sweet but was sour. Uppity stared at the older man. He and the captain stared back. Reedley just stood there waiting. He didn't appear to be uncomfortable, but Addison did.

"Son!" This time the older man's—Uppity Jared's father apparently—growl was packed with … impatience, and maybe menace.

Addison noted Jared's wife with her eyes cast down onto the plate in front of her. Her cheeks bloomed a bright crimson. The young girl smiled at Reedley and the boy acted happy to see Addison.

Uppity cleared his throat and faced Reedley. "Please, Sir, accept my apology for my behavior this morning. I see now that you were trying to be nice to my children. I should have known that, but, unfortunately, I did not." Jared stuck his hand out. "Please accept my apology."

Reedley shook. "Sir, we were strangers to you. I should have asked your permission before touching your children. I accept your apology. Please accept mine."

The older man nodded, appearing satisfied.

Uppity Jared started to take his seat.

Again, the older man chastised, "Son. We are at the captain's table. We do not sit until he does."

It turned out the older man was Jared Edgewood 2nd. He owned the *Belle of St. Joseph* as well as fourteen other river boats. Uppity was Jared 3rd, and his son was The Fourth. The children's mother was Winifred, and the daughter, Penelope.

Addison glanced around the dining room. Eight tables accommodated up to ten people each. A general happy, excited buzz of conversation filled the room, or cabin, as the captain called it. The same invisible cloud of excitement and joy of adventure hovered over their own table. Despite Jared 3rd and his wife sulking. The captain and Jared 2nd were enjoying the day, the opportunity to sit together and share a meal. To Addison, the captain and owner were much like Preacher Larrimer and Wagon Master Reedley. Aboard the boat, the man who owned the vessel and employed the captain deferred to him.

The children were well-mannered. They didn't butt in when the grownups were speaking, but in lulls, both jumped in with snippets of reports on their experiences to their grandfather. He obviously doted on them.

Wine was served with the meal. Winifred, the children's mother, didn't touch her drink or her lunch. Next to her, her uppity husband swilled his wine and two refills while he picked at his food. A waiter approached the table to refill 3rd's glass, but the elder Edgewood waved him away. Jared 3rd slumped, like a kid in school made to sit in the corner.

Reedley did not touch his wine. Addison didn't either until the wagon master invited him to. "Sip it," Reedley said. "Hold the sip in your mouth and let it sit on your tongue a moment, so you get all the flavor out of it, then swallow."

Addison did as instructed, then took a second sip. Reedley watched. As did the others. Addison placed his glass on the table and inched it away from his plate. Reedley smiled.

Over coffee at the end of the meal, Jared 4th, across from Addison, said, "You know what we get to do this afternoon?"

"What do you get to do?" Addison said.

"All of us get to move to steerage. Right Grandpa?"

The elder Edgewood grinned and nodded.

Winifred stood and left abruptly. The men didn't have time to get to their feet.

"Young Jared, Penelope," the elder said, "say goodbye to Mr. Reedley and Mr. Freeman." They goodbye-d and smiled. "Son, take the children and wait for me in the lounge."

"Mr. Reedley, I'm going to ask you to vacate your room and move to cabins on this level. One of the crew will help you move."

Fifteen minutes later, a crewman opened the door to their new cabin. And then Addison got the biggest gob smack of the day.

20.

Addison, Mel Detweiller, the wagon master and his son Robert got their own cabins on the top level next to the captain. Reedley, with Addison in tow, tracked down the first mate and asked him why they had been given such luxurious accommodations.

First Mate smiled. "Jared Edgewood, the Second. Ain't many like him."

The original Jared, the mate related, brought his wife and ten-year-old son to New Orleans in 1810 to establish a riverboat construction business. During the War of 1812, Mr. Edgewood was challenged to a duel, during which the two parties killed each other. Mrs. Edgewood took over the business and put her son, Jared 2nd to work in the boatyard making sure he learned every aspect of the business.

"By the time Jared 2nd was twenty-five, riverboat travel on the Mississippi had expanded. So had Edgewood Enterprises. Ever way there was to make money on the river, he and his ma had a piece of it.

"But Jared 3rd turned out different."

They were standing at the rail of the deck above the main, and the mate looked out toward the shore sliding past. "Jared 2nd left his son to run the New Orleans businesses while he set up new ones in St. Louis and St. Joseph.

"Jared 3rd got tangled up with *high society* folks. He took a high faluting wife, built a big house for her, and stopped payin' attention to the business. The yard foreman took advantage and began diverting earnings into his own pocket. The Second picked up on it pretty quick, went to New Orleans, sold the business there and his son's house, and brought his wayward son and family with him. Right now, they are on the way to St. Joseph. Pa Edgewood gonna keep his thumb on his boy till he learns to run a business the right way."

Reedley humphed.

"Then," the mate said, "I told the captain how Jared the third treated you when you were trying to be nice to the children. The captain told Mr. Edgewood, and he decided he couldn't wait to begin teaching his son. Jared 3rd should never again treat a customer the way he treated you two." First Mate glanced at Reedley. "The elder had his son and grandson move into the steerage class men's bunkroom. His daughter-in-law and granddaughter moved to the women's bunkroom." A smile broke through the mate's face hair. "She, the daughter-in-law, was fit to be tied. 'I will *not* stay in steerage,' she said. 'Fine,' the elder said. 'Boat captains have authority to marry people. They can also divorce them. If you don't go to steerage, you will be put ashore at our next stop with divorce papers and thirty silver dollars in your purse, and you will not take my grandchildren with you.' She's in steerage now."

Joshua Reedley humphed.

"That's it?" First Mate said. "After the whole story, you give me a *humph?*"

Addison laughed. "Well, sir, you just have to learn about Mr. Reedley's humphs. That one meant, 'That was one heck of a story, and that elder Mr. Edgewood, he's one heck of a guy.'"

"So, young Mr. Addison, you saying your Mr. Reedley is a man of few words, but he's one heck of humph-er?"

"Yep … uh, yep, sir," Addison replied.

*****

The boat stopped at Jefferson City, Glasgow, and Kansas City. The next day they'd arrive at Leavenworth, Kansas. Reedley and his party planned to debark there. Before the crusaders left Alton, the Emigrant Aid Society had advised against disembarking south of Leavenworth.

Pro-slavery advocates flooded that area. A few were farmers, but the majority considered themselves soldiers in the fight for the soul of Kansas. Calling themselves Regulators or Guerillas or States Righters, bands formed around charismatic leaders and earned their living raiding settlements of Free-soilers. Many of these raids earned the title of *Massacre of* ....

The Free-soilers had their own militant forces. John Brown attracted a number of followers, and he led his band in the Pottawatomie Massacre, which was a retaliation for a Regulator raid on Lawrence. Other armed conflicts went down as the Battle of Black Jack and the Battle of Osawatomie. Newspapers called the territory "Bloody Kansas," for good reasons.

The night before they disembarked, Reedley gathered Addison and the other two in the salon of the owner's suite. He told them, "The closer we get to Kansas, the more I hear about what we're walking into with our crusade. Seems like deciding free state or slave will be done with bullets, not ballots. We are marching into the middle of a war. If it comes to shooting, there can be no hesitation on our part in pulling our guns and firing."

Someone knocked on the door, then Mr. Edgewood pulled it open and said, "Mind if I join you?"

Reedley stood. The others followed suit. "Of course, sir."

Edgewood dragged a chair from the dining table to their circle. They made room for him.

"Sorry for interrupting," Edgewood said. "But I just learned something you should hear."

The elder Jared sat, and his gaze stepped around the circle, looking each man in the eye. "I just learned my son is a treacherous snake, and he shames me something fierce.

"My son blames you, Mr. Reedley, for his humiliation, being sent to live in steerage, which of course was my doing and not yours. My son paid two of the crewmen onboard to get word to the State's Righters near Leavenworth that your wagon train will arrive shortly. Fortunately, the crew of the Belle of St. Joseph is loyal to Captain Wilson, and one of them reported what my boy wanted him to do."

"If the crewman hadn't gone to the captain, we'd have run into an ambush," Reedley said.

Edgewood nodded, then said, "My recommendation is to get word to the boats following with the rest of your group to put off disembarking until Atchison, and I can help you with that. That will put Fort Leavenworth between you and the southern sympathizers. From there, you'll get your wagon train on a safer start to the last leg of your journey."

Atchison was an interesting town, according to Mr. Edgewood. The place had been established just a few years back and named after a Missouri senator named Atchison. The senator was pro-slavery, pro-states' rights. He wanted a town created which would support that notion. The first newspaper in Atchison was just that, pro-slavery, but then a man with the opposite philosophy bought the paper.

"And, so," Edgewood said, "Atchison was created to be a bastion of slavery, but by the start of this year, it had become home to free-soil supporters, including a band of Jayhawkers. Note, Mr. Reedley, I did not say that now it is home to *only* free-soil sentiment."

"Mr. Edgewood," Reedley said, "I want to thank you for your generosity. You've been more than kind to us."

"I have enjoyed meeting you and hearing about your enterprise. I wish you luck with that." Edgewood paused and looked earnestly at the wagon master. "Might I have a word with you in private?"

Robert Reedley and Mel Detweiler stood up. Addison was the last to realize the three of them had been dismissed.

In the passageway outside the lounge, Addison said, "Wonder what he wants?"

Robert grinned. "Was I a betting man, I'd lay money on Mr. Edgewood asking my pa for some payback for his *generosity.*"

Addison humphed, and Robert and Mel laughed at him. Addison blushed, and the two laughed harder.

*****

As the Belle of St. Joseph neared Atchison, Addison remembered Mr. Edgewood saying:

"Approaching a river town, I always think two things. Ah. A pleasant dose of civilization in the wilderness. And, what a shame to spoil the unspoiled wilderness God created."

Reedley had remarked, "These towns are just like people. Possible to be good and just as possible to be bad."

It was clear the second Jared and the wagon master enjoyed talking together. Maybe it was because Reedley had spent a stint working on a riverboat in his youth. Mostly, though, Addison thought, *their eyes see things that others can't, that I wish mine could.*

Addison and Mel Detweiler saddled the horses on the main deck while Reedley and his son went to say goodbye to Mr. Edgewood. The wagon master wanted to be among the first passengers to debark in Atchison.

On the west edge of town, he'd learned, there was a lot used by wagon trains assembling for their trip along the Oregon Trail. A number of people would be leaving the Belle for just that purpose. None of them had wagons or the wherewithal to make the journey west. So, they'd squat there while they outfitted. When a boat docked, space in the staging area went fast.

The town charged rent, which encouraged the travelers to not tarry. Another inducement to not tarry was Norb Bass, who managed the staging area and kept the peace.

Bass, according to what Mr. Edgewood told Reedley, didn't care to argue. At the hint of opposition, he drew his pistols and had proved himself ready and eager to use them. There were a few graves next to the staging lot. Some were for infants and women who died in childbirth. Death from consumption and other ailments filled a few more, and a handful of wooden crosses marked a would-be Oregoner who'd argued with Bass. Josh Reedley said the graveyard next to the lot was a behave-yourself signpost.

The boat lurched and paddlewheels on the boat reversed. They were getting close to shore. Addison was snugging the cinch strap on Outlaw when Reedley and his son approached along with the second and third Jareds, the latter's wife, and a Negro couple right behind them.

The elder approached Addison and stuck out his hand. Addison wiped his hand on his pants and consummated the proffered shake.

"A pleasure to have met you, young Mr. Freeman. Godspeed."

After also greeting Mel, Mr. Edgewood walked away.

Addison faced the wagon master and frowned.

"They're going with us," Reedley said. "I'll explain tonight. Now let's get in line to get off the boat. The crew will have freight wagons ready to back onto the boat to offload cargo, and they could trap us on here for an hour. We need to move."

Reedley took the reins to his and his son's mount and led them to where crewmen were winching the gangway over to the dock. Robert herded the Edgewood and Negro couples ahead him.

Addison and Mel walked their horses side-by-side in trail.

"Why would Reedley want to bring those folks along?" Mel whispered. "Plain to see this Jared hates us. His wife does too. And the darkies? Even in Kansas, the men won't be able to vote. We already have a handful of 'em on the other boats."

"He said he'd explain tonight," Addison replied, although he agreed with Mel.

Don't we have enough people we already have to keep an eye on? Mr. Waverly, Orson. The next name came up out of the back of his mind grudgingly. *Pa.*

*****

The wagon master sent his son and Addison to the staging lot outside the west end of Atchison to rent space for three wagons. Joshua Reedley and Mel took the Edgewoods and the coloreds, Samson and April, to get outfitted for the rest of their journey.

A rail fence ringed the staging lot. Addison followed Robert Reedley through the open gate. Wagons filled half the lot, all parked nose to tail and huddled against the fence they'd just come through. None of the wagons had draft animals hitched. Across the lot, beyond the fence on the far side, was an extensive pasture accommodating a large herd of grazing animals.

A man stepped into Robert's path from behind the first wagon to the right, and he held up his hand. Robert reined up. The man lowered his hand.

"You from the *Belle of St. Joe?*" The lean, broad-shouldered six-footer wore a pistol on each hip in two crisscrossed holster belts. Addison stopped Outlaw to the side and a little behind Robert.

"Yes, sir, we are," Robert replied.

"You joining the Holder wagon train?"

"No, sir. We're with another outfit."

"The lot's full. The rest of it's spoke for."

"Uh—" From Robert.

"Are you Norb Bass?" Addison cut in.

The six-footer, clearly annoyed, switched his attention.

"I told you, boy. The lot's full."

"So, you're *not* Norb Bass." Addison rousted up a tiny smile, like he was confident, but his heart pounded. If he had to pull his pistol, he hoped he wouldn't drop it.

The man on the ground squared off against him. If it came to shooting, Addison would draw with his left hand. It was better located to deal with the positioning. The decision settled Addison's agitation.

Another man wearing a sidearm stepped out from behind the wagon and stood beside Two Gun. A third gunman appeared opposite him.

Addison whipped out his pistol, cocked it, and aimed at Two Gun's head. "Stop!" Addison barked.

Two Gun's henchmen held their hands out to the side near their pistols.

Two Gun grinned under his soup-strainer. "You two is dead ducks."

"You won't live to see it," Addison said. "Robert, aim for his heart. I'll get him between his eyes."

The outside corners of Two Gun's smile snuck under his mustache.

"Now, then, let's settle down a bit, Mister," Addison said. "Nobody needs to die here. Just tell us where we can find Norb Bass."

Outlaw's ears flicked up. The click of a gun being cocked came from behind Addison. A man growled, "He's right. Nobody needs to die here. Son. Let the hammer down on your pistol, nice and easy like, then put it away."

Two more men appeared in the lane leading from the gate through the parked wagons. Each of them carried a double barrel.

Slow and deliberate, Addison holstered his weapon, then he turned in the saddle. "Mr. Bass? I hope."

The man behind him held a double-barrel as well. The end of a holster showed beneath the edge of the man's unbuttoned dark brown coat.

Mr. Shotgun nodded. "Norb Bass. Pleased to make your acquaintance."

"Addison Freeman, Mr. Bass. My partner, Robert. We wanted to see you about renting space on your lot."

"Always happy to see new customers," Bass said. "See the house on the far side of the lot. Ride on over there. I'll be along shortly. I need a word with friendly Mr. Holden here."

21.

Addison and Robert Reedley found a sign, black letters on a white-washed board nailed to a post next to the hitching rail in front of the one-room shack. The sign read:

Rules

Behave your damned self
Don't leave no damned mess

Chop your own damned wood

Behave your damned self

Norb Bass ambled toward them with the shotgun on his left shoulder. He stopped a couple of paces from Addison. "Shoulda made another rule: Don't make me have to cross the lot lessen my saddled horse is tied to the hitching rail."

"You might need two more signs to hold that one, Mr. Bass," Addison said.

Bass stared hard at Addison. "Don't sass me, boy. That's another rule."

"We'll abide by your rules, Mr. Bass." Addison didn't look away from the man's frosty glower. "Probably."

"Ain't no prob'ly here!"

"Mr. Bass, our wagon train traveled across Illinois and now Missouri. Several places the law we encountered protected outlaws, not law-abiders. So, I said probably." Bass was about to jump in, and Addison held up his hand. "Now I think I know what you contend with on your staging lot. Folks come and go, and most of them are pushy. They kind of have to be if they hope to make Oregon, or California. But you can't have every wagon train comes in here make their own rules. Lotta your customers would wind up shooting each other. Those outfitter businesses on the edge of town would lose their customers, too."

Bass took off his flat-brimmed black hat and smacked his leg with it. "I could use another deputy. Pay's decent. You get a bunk in the shack there behind you. I supply the grub, lead, and gunpowder."

"Thank you, sir, but I got a job."

*****

Addison would have been happy to get up and start the cooking fire, but last night, Reedley told him and Mel to stay in their sleeping rolls under one of the new wagons until called. Then he said the elder Wedgewood had convinced him to take his son and daughter-in-law as well as the freed colored couple.

"Why'd you agree to that?" Addison said.

Reedley looked across the fire at his scout. "I agreed to take them."

Addison mopped stew gravy with the edge of his biscuit.

Now, this morning, Robert Reedley showed Jared 3rd and the colored man, Samson, how to build a fire pit, how to get wood from the pile at one end of the staging lot, how to get the fire going, and how to saw and chop logs into kindling to replace what they'd taken. Mr. Reedley showed the women, Winifred and the colored woman, April, how to slice and fry bacon and potatoes and eggs.

The night before, at supper, the wagon master showed the women how to cook whatever-you-got stew in an iron kettle. It was clear the women were very used to being waited on. Samson and April had been servants to Jared 3rd and Penelope. Cook slaves did the cooking, and it was clear both the freed coloreds thought freedom had shoved them onto a step lower on the social ladder.

Winifred had been hot enough to have started the fire without a match. The wagon master told her, "You don't pay attention, you ruin the stew, we'll throw it out, and I'll fix a new potful, but you won't get any. You'll go hungry. And you'll keep going hungry until you start pulling your own load. If you starve to death before you get to that, no big deal to me at all. Right now, you are worse than useless. You are a burden."

Addison's opinion of Jared 3rd and his wife went lower. The Edgewoods didn't appear to miss their son and daughter the least little bit. They were totally consumed with outrage and humiliation and loss of status, to which, clearly, they thought they were entitled.

Samson and April, it seemed, were consumed by fear. They'd been comfortable with their previous positions as personal servants. They were above the ordinary house slaves. Being a house slave seemed better than what they had now, living like outdoor animals. They were free, but freedom had ripped away the thing of most value to them. Freedom ruined them, and it was frightening.

Last night, as Addison crawled into his sleeping roll beneath a wagon, he recalled that Saturday—it seemed like ten years ago—when he'd asked Pa if he could marry Lizbeth, and how the denial destroyed his world. The memory scoured up sympathy for Samson and April. They did not know how to live with freedom any more than he'd known how to live without Lizbeth. He even found a bit of sympathy for Jared 3rd and Winifred, but that burned out like a shooting star.

Now, this morning, Addison watched the wagon master spend as much time counseling April to, "Let Winifred do it," as he did showing her how to fix breakfast.

Enough lying in bed.

Addison climbed out of his bedding and rolled it up. Mel Detweiler did the same, and then they walked to the row of six outhouses in the corner of the lot by the woodpile.

*****

After breakfast, Addison and Mel rode west along a spur of the Oregon Trail. They were to scout out the way ahead for the wagon train, once it assembled.

The Trail cut through miles of neat, orderly farms. The land appeared to be rich and fertile. But not hospitable. Farms were fenced, and lanes leading off the road to farmhouses were roped or chained off. Some of the lanes had a sign posted: No Trailers.

After what Addison figured would be six hours of wagon train travel, the one-snuggled-against-the-next-one farms started giving way to larger and larger intervals between the houses and barns and cleared land. Patches of prairie dotted with stands of trees became the norm.

According to Norb Bass, once they passed the inhospitable farms, they'd have to pass through a stretch of dangerous prairie.

"Addison, Mel," the wagon master told them the night before, "Norb Bass is known as the head Jayhawker in this area. The pro-slavery folks steer clear of him for some distance out of Atchison, but about twenty-five miles from town, expect to encounter guerillas. That's what they call themselves. Generally, these guerillas travel in packs, and they are looking for Free-staters. If they believe you're bound for California or Oregon, they might let you go, but they're quick to shoot or, if a tree is close by, hang those they suspect of being abolitionists. I wouldn't send you, but I need to know about grass and water for the animals."

The last thing Reedley gave them before they left the staging lot that morning, besides, "Be careful," was binoculars.

During the morning and afternoon, Addison stopped frequently to glass the road ahead and behind. He and Mel studied the horizon for signs of dust. All they had encountered was a few farm wagons on the way to Atchison.

Late in the afternoon, Addison stopped. Ahead, a half-mile or so, an extensive stretch of woods snuggled against the north side of the two-rut road. It looked peaceful enough. Quiet, too. Outlaw's tail swished flies. A gentle breeze riffled over the knee-high grass like a hand over the back of collie.

He pulled out his binoculars and studied the woods. He studied until it felt as if the eyepieces were about to suck the eyeballs out of his face. Lowering the glasses, he blinked to get his vision working straight again. Then he sniffed.

"Smell that?"

"Smell what?"

"A just put-out campfire."

Mel, too, glassed the woods.

"Rats!" Addison said.

"What?"

"Sun's right in our face. It flashed off the glass when you were looking. Would have off mine too. There's men in those woods. I feel them. And even if they were half asleep, they know we're here."

Addison turned around. "We'll set up camp by the stream we just crossed."

"We should head back."

"I want to find out who's in those woods."

"Norb Bass said we run into folks out here, most likely it'll be bushwhackers, guerillas, or raiders, not Jayhawkers or Red Legs."

The latter two were Free-staters.

"We should go back."

"Mel, if they come out of the woods after us, we got a half mile head start on them. We'll set up camp and watch. It's all prairie around us. They won't be able to sneak up on us."

Mel grumbled a cuss word.

Throughout the day, they'd collected kindling whenever they passed a wooded area and bundled it in Addison's bedroll. Both of them trailed a spare horse. Reedley wanted them to change mounts every few hours. If they had to run from guerillas, they could run on rested horses.

Addison returned to the stream and noticed a low spot south of the road. It would afford some protection if they got into a fight. They moved into the depression, and Addison unpacked the kindling.

"You starting a fire?" Mel said.

"They know we're here."

Mel mumbled something, then tended the horses. Addison skinned the rabbits he'd shot, got a fire going, stuck the rabbits on a stick, and roasted them.

As they ate, they kept their eyes on the woods. Addison watched Outlaw. Every once in a while, the horse would abruptly raise its head from the grass and stare at the woods for a time; then, it would go back to grazing.

While they drank coffee, Addison said, "We'll have just a sliver of moon tonight. Not much more than starlight. Those guys might try to Injun up on us."

"We should head back and tell the wagon master what we found here."

Addison poured the last of the coffee into Mel's cup. "I expect there's at least half a dozen in that bunch of trees." He shook his head. "Right now, the extra horses complicate things."

"Didn't you hear what I said? We've got to go back."

Addison stood, without answering, and took the coffee pot to the stream to rinse it out. When he returned, he said, "Here's what we're going to do. We'll wait for it to get dark. Then you head back to Atchison with the two extra horses."

"What're you gonna' do?"

"We, Outlaw and me, we'll wait and see if the ambushers come after you. If they do, we'll ambush them."

"We? There's just you. Outlaw can't shoot no gun."

"I wasn't saying **we** is Outlaw and me. The **we** I meant was me and my three pistols."

"This is crazy. We should stick—"

"Hush!" Addison held up his hand and cocked his head to the side. "Wagons."

"A number of them. You figger they're in cahoots with the ambushers?"

"If it was riders, maybe. Wagons, less likely. Get the horses ready."

Addison hustled back to the stream, filled the coffee pot again, and doused the fire. Mel saddled one of the spare horses, then Outlaw as Addison stowed the gear.

Mel stood holding the reins as Addison lay on the side of the depression, with a pistol in each hand, and watched the wagons approach. The wagons were dark shadow silhouettes against the deepening dusk. He wouldn't see them without the racket they made, telling his eyes where to look. As they got closer, though, detail emerged from the dusk.

The lead wagon stopped opposite the depression. The driver stood and hollered, "Jibway Jim."

"Here!" came from behind Addison. He spun around. Some twenty yards past Mel, a man shadow stood in the knee-high grass.

Mel said, "They won't be able to sneak up on us," in a snotty schoolyard sass.

"You boys is from Josh Reedley's wagon train," the lead wagon driver said in a Preacher Larrimer voice. "You'd be Addison Freeman, not so? Come up to the road. We'll talk."

As Addison and Mel, with Jibway Jim right behind them, approached the lead wagon, the driver took off his hat. "Ziggy Holstetler." Shiny bald on top, a goodly crop of face hair, broad shoulders.

Hostetler ran freight from Atchison to a settlement of Free-staters two days farther west. The men in the woods worked for him. There were a number of good ambush spots along the road going west. Sometimes bushwhacking slave-staters set up to waylay anything heading west. If a wagon train was made up of abolitionists, they'd be shot or hung. Men, women, and children. It was kinder to shoot the women and children than to leave them in the wilderness on their own.

"Least, that's how they see it," Ziggy said. "So, it's best if I send men ahead to occupy those ambush spots first, or to have my scouts warn me what's waitin'."

Jibway Jim scouted for Hostetler. He'd been a kid when his parents brought him west along the Trail of Death as the Ojibwe were relocated to Kansas some twenty years ago.

Ziggy paused his recitation and looked at the Indian. "Any trouble in front of us?"

"Yes. Half day." Jibway held up both hands with the fingers spread.

"Ten men?"

Jibway grunted.

"Boys, I think," Jibway said. "Like—" He nodded toward Addison and Mel. "Boys. They laugh. They talk. They drink *whick skee.*"

"They got pistols, though, don't they," Ziggy stated.

Jibway grunted.

*****

Mel, with the spare horses, rode back to Atchison to report to Reedley. Addison stayed with Jibway Jim and scouted ahead of the wagons.

Hostetler pushed on through the night until he arrived at a stream where Addison waited. The hideout of the whiskey-drinking boys was about two miles farther.

From that spot, Jibway Jim had proceeded on foot south of the road. Hostetler's men, the one's in the trees who had spooked Addison into stopping, proceeded north of the road toward the boy ambush spot.

Addison had wanted to go with Jibway.

"You stay. White man make noise."

So, Addison stayed, and waited. His annoyance at being left behind did not make the time pass quickly.

By the time the wagons arrived, the sun was up, though Addison couldn't see it because of the band of haze sitting on the eastern horizon.

Ziggy stopped his mules next to Addison. "You hear anything?"

"Not a peep."

The other wagons pulled up and formed two rows.

"Comes to fightin'," Ziggy said to Addison, "these wagons make us a fort. Meantime, you mind startin' us a fire. Time we et."

One of the drivers cooked while the others tended the mules. Once the animals had been watered and were grazing, Ziggy took his tin plate heaped with potatoes, bacon and eggs and sat on the driver's bench to eat. He forked in a mouthful, started chewing, then stood up. "Jibway and the others. They're coming. With prisoners."

Off to the west, a little less than a mile, a passel of men on horseback walked their mounts toward them.

Addison was the last, and next, in line to get food. "I'll go help them."

"They got it handled," Ziggy mumbled through a mouthful, which he swallowed and chased with a sip of coffee. "Eat. They git here, we take over, and they git grub."

Addison sat on a wagon tongue and ate. He was on his second cup of coffee when the group arrived at the parked wagons. Jibway Jim and four others herded eight young men, mounted, with their hands tied in front of them.

Ziggy belched. "Jibway, you said ten."

"Two of 'ems buried back there in the trees. Jim done 'em with his knife," Zeb Pendergast, one of Hostetler's men, said.

Zeb had been introduced to Addison the night before as a member of Norb Bass's band of Red Legs. According to him, being a Red Leg earned a man more money than being a freight hauler.

Addison left his plate and tin cup on the ground and helped pull the prisoners from their horses and line them up by Ziggy's wagon as Jibway Jim led the horses away and tied the reins to the rear of the wagon.

Jibway returned to the front of the wagon. "I hear them talk. They get five dollars for scalp. Buy heap more whick skee."

A double-barrel shotgun lay across Ziggy's lap as he sat on his bench. "One at a time," he said.

One of the drivers grabbed the arm of the first prisoner in line and pushed him to stand next to the wagon. The driver stepped back.

The young prisoner, Addison figured, was his own age. Sand-colored hair. Hat hanging from a cord around his neck. Shoulders and arms looked like they were used to working.

"That what you was gonna do? Shoot us and scalp us?" Ziggy said.

"Ain't tellin' you nothin'," Sandy Hair said.

"Maybe so," Ziggy cocked a hammer. "I got two other things I want to know. First is your name. Second, I want your promise you will never take up arms against Free-staters as long as you live. Which if you don't tell me what I want to hear, ain't gonna' be long."

"Ain't tellin'—"

Wham!

The kid flew back with his face all blown to chopped meat.

Judas Priest! Addison hadn't expected that at all. *Ziggy just shot that kid.*

"Next," Ziggy said.

The next prisoner said his name and gave his promise, and said, "Yes, sir. We … we was gonna' shoot you and scalp you. We thought it'd be easy. But, I won't never come back out here agin. I promise."

Ziggy wrote the name in a ledger. "I'm giving you parole. Got your name in here. Your name will be passed around. You bust your parole and come back here, you will be hung."

"Next."

The next young man also gave his name and promise, but Ziggy wanted to know one more thing. "Names of guerilla fighters you know."

The kid shook his head. Addison saw him struggling with what to do. The kid turned and looked at his dead and bloody and faceless companion; then, he turned forward again. Grim, defiant determination written hard on his face.

Ziggy shot him, too.

Addison thought he should do something. Stop this cold slaughter of boys, but he couldn't make his mouth work. And he wasn't about to pull his gun in the middle of Ziggy's men. He'd get his own head blown off.

The rest of the prisoners gave their names, gave their promise, and gave up names of the guerilla fighters they knew.

All the names went into his ledger; then Ziggy ordered the six remaining prisoners to bury their friends, after which he allowed the six to depart on three horses, with three pistols, no extra lead or powder, and no breakfast.

Zeb Pendergast said, "Seven horses, guns, gear. Not a bad payday."

Ziggy said, "Young Addison, you prob'ly think I deserve to be shot for killin' those boys. But think on this. Those boys woulda killed all of us for a bottle a whiskey. Still, I offered them a chance to live. With parole. But I needed their word they wouldn't come after us agin. They wouldn't give it. Now that's the kinda world you and your wagon train is comin' into. If you can't stomach what I done, maybe the lot of you ought to turn right around and go back to Illinois. Out here, the meek don't inherit nothin'. They git scalped."

22.

When the wagons started west again, Addison rode on the driver bench next to Hostetler. Ziggy explained they were headed for a Free State settlement called Potts' Trading Post. It was located on the far side of the Delaware River and north and a little west of Lawrence.

"Potts," Addison said. "Same man owns Potts General Store back in Atchison?"

"Yep. I work for him."

According to Ziggy, the trading post was a thriving business. It sold to folks traveling the Oregon Trail. "Far enough from Atchison for the pilgrims to wake up to the fact they got a rough way ahead of them. Last chance to stock up on what they're gonna need.

"Plus, there's a Potawatomie res northwest of the post. They trade there as well. I'm pretty much on the road all the time. I make a trip out here with wagons carting as much as they can carry. Then I leave the wagons and the mules to be sold to the pilgrims, and I hustle back to Atchison to bring another wagon train of supplies out here."

Around the trading post, Ziggy explained, a dozen free-stater families had settled a year ago. A blacksmith, a gunsmith, some men work a sawmill, and a couple of farmers.

"Folks on our wagon train are all farmers," Addison said.

"Just what's needed." Ziggy spit a stream of tobacco juice. "They's plenty of farmland between the trading post and that res."

They arrived at Potts' Trading Post late in the afternoon the next day.

Word spread quickly through the settlement that Addison was a scout for a free stater wagon train forming up in Atchison. The community put on a dinner. Everyone wanted to speak with Addison.

After the dinner, Addison told Ziggy he would stay at the post a day to scout out the farmland available for squatting.

"Boy, you don't wanna do that," Ziggy said. "You'd be easy pickings for a pack of slave-state guerillas. The next bunch you meet up with ain't gonna be no snot-nosed schoolboys."

"Thanks for the advice, Mr. H. But we're going to have thirty-five, maybe forty families to settle. I need to see if this place can handle all of us."

"You ain't gonna' listen then?"

"Oh, yes, sir. I listen to every word you say."

"Then you go and do what I damn well told you to not do."

"Pretty much. Sir."

*****

Hostetler asked Jibway if he'd stay with the pilgrim. "See if you kin keep 'im from gittin' his fool self killed." Jibway nodded his assent.

The next morning, Hostetler, his wagon drivers, and his posse, he called them, set out to return to Atchison. The gunsmith and manager of the trading post, Aaron Zerjav, showed Addison and Jibway Jim the land available for squatting north along the Delaware River and to the west. Just after noon, the party arrived back at the trading post. Zerjav invited the party to eat before they headed east.

Jibway shook his head. "We go now."

Addison noted how the Indian pushed his horse for a time, then allowed it to walk a spell, to catch its breath, sort of, and pushed it into a canter again. About three hours from the trading post, Jim stopped them next to a stream, a trickle of water, but water, and with grass, and a clump of saplings snuggled against the trickle.

Jim pulled a flimsy saddle from his bay, rubbed it down, and led it to the stream. As the animal drank, he gathered wood from the stand of trees and quickly got a fire going with sparks he struck with the back of his knife blade on a piece of flint from his pocket. Then he led his horse to the grass, hobbled it, and returned to the fire. There he quickly skinned the two rabbits he'd killed earlier with arrows and spitted them on sticks to hang over the fire. With supper cooking, he walked out to the grass where his horse grazed and lay down. He appeared to fall asleep instantly.

Addison walked over to study Jibway's saddle. Not much to it. A thin leather pad for across the horse's back. Straps attached to stirrups sewn to the leather pad. He lifted it. Couple of pounds, maybe. His own probably close to twenty pounds.

He and Mel hung a scabbard for a long gun from their saddles. Jibway had his muzzle loader, with a cord tied to it, across his back along with the powder horn and bullet pouch. Also, across his back, he had a bow and a quiver. White men, it seemed, put as much load on their horses as they could. The Indian, however, put as much of it on himself as he could. White men also seemed to need to drag along a lot more gear and provisions, which the Indian got along without: coffee pot, skillet, flour, salt, side-meat, extra clothes. Jibway did have a rolled ground cloth lashed to the flimsy saddle.

*****

At mid-morning, Addison and Jibway Jim arrived back at the wagon train staging lot at Atchison. They found the first boatload of Holy Crusader wagons arrayed on the back side of the lot, away from the road.

Jibway headed for Norb Bass's shack. Addison asked Mel to take care of Outlaw as he joined Joshua Reedley, Royal Howard, Preacher Larrimer, and Ziggy Hostetler sitting on the ground in a circle, talking and drinking coffee.

Reedley stood, shook hands with Addison, then studied his scout. "Ziggy was telling us you got the makings of a half ways decent scout. And where'd you get the bow slung across your back? Did that Indian you rode in with make it for you?"

"No, sir. I made the bow. But Jibway Jim showed me how."

"Abbie," Reedley called to his wife by the cooking fire. "Bring Addison a cup of coffee, please?"

Reedley gestured for Addison to sit. He sat.

"Good to see you, again, son," Larrimer said. "Good to be getting our crusade back together also. We've been on separate boats less than a week, but it feels like a lot longer."

"But the boats got us across Missouri in a couple of days," Royal Howard said. "Took us a month to cross Illinois."

"We had a lot to learn about crusading," Larrimer said. "Hopefully, you'll make better time with the rest of our congregation."

Reedley looked at Addison. "In the morning, we'll leave the staging camp and join Mr. Hostetler and his supply wagons. According to him, along the Delaware River would be a good place to set up New Found Grace Church. Preacher Larrimer agrees."

Royal Howard said, "You and I, Addison, will return to the stay-behinds, wagon-train them up, and bring them to Preacher's new church."

Reedley nodded. "We've found out that you could cut straight west across Illinois and pick up riverboats at Hannibal."

"Another couple of months," Preacher Larrimer said, "Found Grace Church, God willing, will be together again in Kansas."

Addison sipped from his tin cup. "Can I tell you what I found at Pott's trading post?" He didn't wait for an assent or a nod. "A man named Aaron Zerjav runs the trading post. He showed me around the country. Plenty of good land to support forty families.

"Here's the other thing he told me. The fight between free state and slave state is being fought right there, in that area, from Lawrence, Kansas, north to Potts. There's a town called Prairietown between Lawrence and the trading post. Lawrence is hard free state. Prairietown, and the sheriff there, are hard slave state. Found Grace Church could shift the balance from where it is now, sort of even, to all the way to free state.

"One more thing. From what Mr. Hostetler and Mr. Zerjav told me, we have to expect to fight. The slave staters won't let us move in there without trying to stomp us out. And it won't be a handful of them come after us. It'll be a small army."

Addison stopped talking, and a barrel of silence dumped over the men. Every eye around the circle aimed at him.

From behind the seated circle came, "Boy done growed up some, ain't he now?" Norb Bass leaned against Reedley's wagon. He spat a squirt of chaw juice and smiled.

Addison was relieved to get all those eyes off him. A crow cawed.

Reedley humphed, got up, went to the fire, and returned with the coffee pot and a cup for Norb Bass. He said, "We need us a new plan," and poured the coffee.

By lunch, they'd agreed to a new plan.

Joshua and Abigail Reedley would return to Found Grace Church and get the second wagon train formed and headed west. With a bunch of women running the Illinois community for over a month, having Abigail Reedley along was considered prudent. Robert Reedley would drive the family wagon. Mel Detweiler would accompany the wagon master and serve as scout during the trip across Illinois.

Royal Howard was appointed wagon master for the string of wagons to depart in the morning. At first light. Addison and Orson Seiling would scout for them. Otto Vogelsang and his family would stay in the staging lot to get the wagons of the second boat of crusaders reassembled. Otto and the families from the second boat would travel west in company with Ziggy Hostetler and his next trip to Potts Trading Post.

*****

Royal Howard, Addison thought, was as good a horseshoe whanger as Reedley. As far as providing motivation for a first-light departure, he took a lesson from former deacon Freeman. Royal used a switch to pop across a slow-moving man's, woman's, or child's backside. He'd warned the wagon train the night before. "It's been a week getting onto the boat, traveling on the boat, and getting off the boat. I know it doesn't take anywhere near that amount of time for a passel of people to lose discipline. Y'all listen up now. We will pull out at first light."

And they did. All the wagons filed out of the staging lot and snuggled onto the end of Hostetler's four freight wagons. In all, this half of the first half of the Holy Crusade now consisted of twelve wagons, the original number leaving Found Grace Church. When they started on their journey, each wagon carried a voter. Now they had a couple of supply wagons and a couple of wagons for the colored people. Still, they had more voters than when they started. The last one through the gate was Otto Vogelsang. Instead of following the wagons though, he waved to Orson and Addison and turned left for the river. The boat bringing the rest of the crusaders was expected to tie up at, "Just about now," Otto said.

After Otto passed through the gate, Addison noticed the Oregoners' wagon master, Holden, leaning against a wagon. He had his weight on one leg, the other angled across, and the toe of the boot resting on the dirt. His arms were crossed. The brim of his hat hid his face in shadow, but the man gave off a sense of threat so strong Addison thought he ought to just shoot the guy right there.

Shoot him.

A month ago, he separated people into *From Found Grace Church* and *Not from Found Grace Church*. Now he separated them in *Needs to be Shot* and *Doesn't need to be Shot*. He recalled the first three he'd needed to shoot. Back in Thompson Township. The mayor. Tan Suit. He remembered seeing him, just before the attempted jail break. The mayor had been alert, watchful. He'd been waiting for an opportunity to pounce.

Addison hadn't thought of that incident in that way before. He wondered if he hadn't noticed the mayor and how he acted, would he have been able to shoot Tan Suit's henchmen?

"You fall asleep?" Orson said.

"Sort of," Addison replied.

"Well, maybe we ought to sort of catch up to the others and sort of do our scouting business."

Orson having to remind me *of my duty!*

Addison humphed, reined his horse around, and said, "Outlaw," and the animal galloped to catch his rider up to his duty.

Near the center of the train, Addison passed the wagons of the Edgewoods and the two coloreds, Samson and April. April drove their team and seemed to be doing the job well. Penelope Edgewood, however, held the reins. Hermann, the oldest Vogelsang boy, sat between the couple, speaking continuously. There was a hint of exasperation in Hermann's voice.

"Thing is," Hermann said, "A horse is a dumb animal, but the horse doesn't know he is, and he sure doesn't like to be treated that way."

Addison continued and recalled: *A chain is as strong as the weakest link.* He hoped a train wasn't as strong as the weakest wagon.

Royal Howard rode between the first crusade wagon and the last freight hauler. Addison told him his observation of Holden back at the staging yard.

"I spoke with Norb Bass last night," Royal said. "He doesn't much care for Holden. The man needs constant reminders about the rules in the staging lot. And Norb thinks he spies for the pro-slavery folks."

Shouting, from a couple of wagons back turned Addison in the saddle. Royal pulled to the side and stopped his horse. The Welch wagon had created the disturbance, or rather, Mr. Welch had.

"This … Orson keeps coming round to pester Mariah. Orson is married. I told him to stay away, but he keeps coming back. It's not right."

"I'll talk to the Preacher." Royal switched his eyes to Orson. "Stay clear of Miss Mariah, hear?"

Orson didn't answer.

Addison sidled his horse between the wagon master and Orson and grabbed the reins from Orson. "Outlaw." Outlaw launched into a run. Addison glanced behind. Orson had managed to hang onto the saddle horn.

*****

Just after sunset, Hostetler fired his pistol into the air and turned to the right. Every wagon behind him turned right as well. Even-numbered wagons turned a larger angle to the right. Addison, Orson, and Royal Howard watched the evolution.

When he was well clear of the road, Hostetler stopped his wagon. Odd-numbered wagons stopped behind Hostetler such that their teams were sheltered by the wagon in front of them. The even-numbered wagons turned to form a circle with the sides squished in, and their teams also protected by the wagon in front of them.

"Slicker'n snot," Orson enthused. "When Hostetler explained this, I didn't understand what he wanted done. Then he passed around the drawing he made."

"What did you think of how we did?" Royal asked Addison.

"Pretty slow. It looked like everybody was intent on doing it right, forming the squished in circle properly. If bullets were flying, getting it done quickly would be just as important as forming the circle properly."

"Yep," Royal said, "when the wagons stopped, everybody piled out and took up positions under the wagons with their weapons pointed out. They did that smartly. Tomorrow, we'll practice this at noon and the night-time stops."

"A day or two after that, we'll be there," Orson said. "Then we'll start building houses and never have to fort up our wagons again."

"Young Mr. Orson, one thing all of us need to learn is that knowing how to fort up is a skill we are going to need for a long time to come. When we start setting up farms, how are we going to protect each other? The answer to that is going to be a lot harder than forming a circle of wagons. Think on that, why don't you, and not are you doing work that might not be needed."

That night, after the animals had been cared for, and before supper, Preacher Larrimer said the same thing to the crusaders. "Once we arrive at our destination, our fight is not over. We may have to defend ourselves for a long time. For years, even. Though, please Almighty God in heaven, let it not be so, but in all things, Thy will be done."

23.

The Oregon Trail, a raw dirt road, sliced through knee-high prairie grass. Addison and Orson scouted a hundred yards north of the road while Jibway Jim was somewhere south. Addison couldn't see him. Sometimes Jim tethered his horse in a stand of trees and scouted on foot. The man could run all day and half the night and not even be breathing hard.

Outlaw's ears stood up. Addison stopped him. He heard it then. A horse coming from the west. Coming fast. In front of them, a ways off, the road hooked right around a stand of trees. Addison hopped down and pulled Outlaw down to lie on its side.

"Orson!" Addison hissed. "Get your horse down."

Orson dismounted.

"Why in blue blazes do I have to tell you everything to do? You saw what I did. You should have followed suit immediately. Now shut up."

"I didn't say nothing."

Addison emitted a soft *sheesh,* then he jerked his mind away from Orson the aggravator and laid down next to Outlaw and peeked over the animal's head.

A rider rounded the corner by the stand of trees. He pushed his mount hard, running it full out. Addison turned around, half expecting Orson to be standing and waving at the guy. But he wasn't. He lay behind his horse. The horse was fidgety, though. Addison said, "Outlaw," and he crawled over to Orson's horse.

"There now." He spoke soft and drew the words out. "No need to fret, *noooo*. Just lie still. That's it. No need to worry. *Noooooo*."

On the road, the hatless rider raced past.

"Just a little longer," Addison cooed to Orson's horse. "We have to listen. To see if anyone's chasing that guy."

"No chase." Jibway Jim rose from the grass.

"God damned Injun," Orson said. "Like to peed my pants. I hate the way he sneaks up on a person."

"Pay attention then," Addison said.

"What? Are you saying you knew Jibway was coming through the grass?"

Addison said, "Outlaw," and the horse rose to its feet. "I did. Outlaw heard or smelled something. I looked and saw the grass moving different from the way the wind was blowing it. But then I heard the rider coming."

Orson coaxed his mount to stand.

Jibway strode through the grass toward them. "You make Indian. One day." He nodded toward Addison. "Him," he nodded at Orson, then shook his head.

"That rider," Addison said, looking at Jibway, "I'm thinking he's probably from the trading post. He's probably here to warn the wagon train we got trouble ahead." Addison rubbed his chin. "The wagons can make it to here if they push it. Then, we can make the Delaware River by nightfall tomorrow. That right, Jibway?"

The Indian grunted.

"Then, I'll send Orson back to the train to tell them to push to make it here by nightfall. You and I, Jibway, we'll hold down that thicket of trees ahead. In case the *trouble* that rider came to warn about might think those trees would make a good ambush spot."

*****

Just west of the stand of trees, a small stream cut across the Oregon Trail. Hostetler and Royal Howard agreed they should stop there for the night. As supper was being prepared, Hostetler, Royal, Addison,

Jibway, and the rider from Pott's Trading Post, Nathan Goodfellow, sat on the ground and talked about the next day.

Hostetler confirmed that the wagons would arrive at the Delaware River late afternoon the next day.

"River current's sprightly, like it is of a spring," Goodfellow said. "But there's a raft can haul a wagon and team."

"Most times, I swim a couple of saddle broncs across to pull the raft over with a tow rope," Hostetler said. "Last time we wuz here, the river lowed it."

"Delaware's feisty," Goodfellow said. "She ain't nasty mean."

"Now then," Royal Howard said, "what do we know about the ambushers? How many of them? Where are they coming from? How will they attack us?"

Nathan Goodfellow ran a weekly supply wagon down to the town of Prairietown. Most of the citizens there were pro-slavery, but a few free-staters lived there as well. The free-staters told him about a raid the pro-slavers were planning. They planned to hit the Abolitionist wagon train as it crossed the Delaware. Get part of the train across, a wagon on the raft in mid-river, then they'd attack.

"That's how I'd do it," Hostetler said.

Royal Howard laid out a plan as to how to use the man- and woman-power they had to protect against attack. "Anybody got a better idea?" No one did. Then he asked Jibway Jim if he liked the plan. JIbway grunted.

Royal said, "What do you think, Addison? Did that sound like a Joshua Reedley humph?"

Addison laughed, then thought that was probably the last laugh he'd feel like for a day or so.

*****

Jibway wanted one man with him, but Hostetler and Royal Howard insisted he take three. The Indian could pick them. He picked Addison first.

Jibway and his party ate, slept three hours, then started west toward the Delaware River.

Atop Outlaw, Addison sat a Jibway saddle. And like the Indian, he had musket, bow, quiver, shot pouch, and powder horn on straps across his back.

The foursome set off with the horses at a trot. After about a half hour, Addison figured, Jibway kicked his horse into a run, and the others stayed with him.

"Start horse slow run. Horse think this hard work. Then run horse fast. Show fast run hard work. Horse think slow run not hard work." Jibway had told Addison that a day prior. To the Indian, a trot was a slow run.

Overhead, a moonless star-filled sky, with some points of light so close together their glows touched, and behind the ones he could see, Addison knew, he just knew, there were other dimmer stars hiding behind their brighter neighbors. Countless as the sands on the seashore.

Addison! They were riding to keep an enemy from harming them, to kill them before they could kill members of the crusade. He was pretty sure Jibway would not let his mind wander from the task at hand.

They stopped at a stream to water the horses. By holding his watch just so, he could see it had been four hours since they left the wagons. Jibway watered his horse, led it to grass, then, with the reins wrapped around his wrist, he fell asleep. Addison imitated the Indian, and came awake when Jibway did. The other two, Jibway kicked their feet to rouse them.

"Damn. Just got to sleep," one said.

"You want go back? Go."

Jibway didn't wait for an answer. He grabbed a handful of mane, swung up, and set off again, with Addison right behind him. By cocking his head to the side, he could hear the other two tagging along.

When Jibway stopped them, dawn was working itself up to break loose the day.

"Get light. We walk beside horse now. We look like animal, not man on horse." Then he led them away from the road to the south. To the west, Addison could make out a dark band, a wall rising out of the forever flat prairie and hiding the horizon. Trees along the Delaware. He recalled the first time he'd seen those trees after crossing miles of prairie without seeing anything grow taller than the knee-grass. He'd mused Kansas sure wasn't Illinois or Missouri. There it seemed as if trees decided where they would grow and grass had to move aside. Here grass decided where trees could grow. Actually, rivers decided, but he'd enjoyed playing with the idea that there was a place where grass could decide. He'd thought it was sort of like David and Goliath of the plant world.

Addison!

He admonished himself to get his mind occupied with what was important here. Which was scouting. For an enemy. Bent on killing him, on killing members of the Holy Crusade. He shook his head, acknowledging he had that weakness. If he was with Jibway Jim or Joshua Reedley, he ceded leadership to the other men. Totally.

He put his mind to work. His mind put his eyes, ears, and nose to work. And the other sense as well. After he worked those senses for a bit, he consciously shut them down, and put touch, feel to work. Jibway had told him, "Spirit of man," and here he tapped his chest with a fist, "*feel* spirit of another man close by." Though, Addison wasn't completely sure he wasn't deluding himself, he tried to put *touch* to work.

Jibway led them through the grass and every once in a while, he'd stop them—and Addison thought—it was to let his senses work with minimal interfering noise from his companions. This time when they stopped, he did what the Indian did, he listened, looked, sniffed, and felt.

What he *felt* surprised him. He *felt* the two men behind him. Addison had attached himself as second in line behind Jibway Jim. When he was closer to the Indian, he felt as if he learned from him better than if he was in the rear. But now the men behind him, it was as if his spirit could feel the other two scouts and nothing beyond them. When Jibway started forward again, he stayed still until the other men passed him by.

Now, someone is guarding our rear.

Addison couldn't see the sun yet, though it was light enough for it to be up. Haze or mist hovered above those trees along the river, hiding the sun. *For another couple of minutes.*

Jibway stopped and raised his hand, cocked his head, then he pulled his horse down. The other two men and Addison pulled their mounts down to lie in the grass as well.

Addison heard a horse—no, more than one coming from the east. Coming fast. Two riders, it turned out, whipping their mounts with the reins.

When the riders were well to the west, Jibway and his horse stood. He gestured the men to huddle around him. He said, in a whisper, "You stay here, and you stay here," pointing to first one, then the other of Hostetler's men.

"Why you want us to stay and not him?" The speaker hooked a thumb toward Addison.

"You no Indian." Jibway pointed to Addison. "He half-way Indian."

The deadly sin of pride bloomed in Addison's head, as did a picture of Pa wielding a switch. "Pride," in-his-head Pa said, and struck a blow across his back, "Goeth," and he winced and gritted his teeth against the pain.

Jibway brought Addison back to here and now as he explained that, originally six men had ridden from the west until they found the wagon train. Then two of them, in the middle of the night, headed back to report they'd made contact with the wagon train. Now two more riders headed west to report the wagons were moving again.

Hostetler and Royal Howard planned to have the wagons arrive at the river in late afternoon or evening, to overnight on the east side, and to commence ferrying wagons across at sunup. They figured the pro-slavers would attack after a couple of wagons had gotten to the west bank. They also expected the ferry to be in midstream when the attack started. They expected a large band of bushwhackers on both sides of the river.

Jibway looked at one, then the other of Hostetler's men. "When sun there," he pointed straight up, "Last two scouts ride by." He pointed to the south of them. "You stay here. Make no fire. Riders come," he swept his arm from the east to the west, "you hide here. He pointed to the sky again, this time to late afternoon. "Sun there, bushwhackers come." His arm swept from south to a bit north of them. "They hide until time to attack wagons. You stay here. Quiet, not too close. Until middle of night. Then you move closer."

"You know this for a fact?" one of the men asked.

"It is what I would do," Jibway said.

"What're you and this half Indian gonna do?" the other man wanted to know.

"We get behind bushwhackers on other side of river."

The first speaker grinned. "We're gonna bushwhack the bushwhackers."

Jibway positioned Addison off to his left; then he led them farther south, walking beside their horses. At about ten o'clock, Jibway stopped and said. "I sleep now." He pointed straight up. "Sun there, you sleep."

"You want me to wake you?"

Jibway grunted, and at noon, he woke himself before Addison could.

By the time Jibway woke him, it was late afternoon. As they ate jerked meat and biscuits, Jibway held up his hands, palms open, fingers spread. Then he closed the fingers and spread them again.

"Twenty riders?"

Jibway grunted; then his fingers said twenty again, and he pointed west.

"And twenty more on the other side of the river?"

Jibway grunted. Then, "Now I sleep. Till sundown."

"You want me to wake—" Addison chopped off the tail of the question.

Jibway slept and woke and led them to the river as dusk oozed over Kansas.

At the Delaware, Jibway lashed together a small raft, tied his and Addison's weapons atop it. The Indian led his horse into the water, grabbed a handful of mane, and the horse swam the man and the raft across.

Addison held onto the edge of the flimsy saddle, and Outlaw followed the other animal.

On the other side of the river, Jibway stopped in waist-deep water.

He stood still, his head cocked like a robin listening for a bug in the grass. Addison stopped in chest-high water, and he, too, listened, sniffed, and felt for bushwhackers nearby.

After a moment of listening, Jibway left his horse standing in the water, pulled the raft to him, and placed it on the bank; then, he walked the horse onto the bank.

The band of trees snuggled up against the Delaware was about the same width on the west bank as it had been on the east. Once they cleared the trees, Jibway mounted and led Addison, the horses at a walk, along a hardpacked dirt road.

At midnight, Jibway stopped and acted like a robin again. For a moment. Then he dismounted and led them away from the road, heading roughly northwest, out into the prairie grass.

After some time, Addison noted a faint glow well off into the distance. Potts Trading Post, he thought. Jibway stopped them. He signed *I sleep*, and laid down, with his weapons still slung across his back. Addison stood next to Outlaw as the animal munched grass. He listened, sniffed. Leaving his mount grazing a few yards from Jibway, Addison walked toward the river for a few minutes. Then he stopped facing the band of trees, stark dark against the lesser dark of night, and he felt them. Out there in the dark, deadly, yet at the same time, vulnerable. He knew they were there. They didn't know he was here. He could—

But then he doubted. The bushwhackers were out there, but he knew it to be fact because Jibway had told him they were there.

A chill, like the icy breath of a monster, slithered over the back of his neck. *Someone's behind me.* He ducked, drew his pistol, and spun around. Outlaw stood like a statue, looking at him.

24.

Addison woke in panic and tried to pull the hand off his mouth. The dark outline of the big man hovering over him hissed.

Judas priest Jibway!

Addison sucked in a big breath and let it out. Quietly. His heart coasted down from hammering like Reedley whanging the wake-up horseshoes. Above stars, no moon. This was one of the times of the month when you saw the moon during the day. One more deep breath, one more exhale, and he sat up and pulled on his boots. When he got to his feet, Jibway grabbed his upper arm and studied him for a moment, then the Indian grunted and let go of his arm.

Outlaw had been saddled.

Jibway set off toward the river leading his horse. After a couple of paces, he stopped, turned, and pointed to where he wanted Addison. The Indian wanted Addison and Outlaw to walk behind him; then he set off again, walking at a good clip.

After a time, the horse in front of him dropped a trail of biscuits. He led Outlaw to the side. Jibway stopped, dropped the reins, walked behind his animal, and walked through the manure. Then he grabbed Addison by the arm and had him step on a few biscuits. The Indian pointed to the river; then, he tapped Addison's nose.

Huh! Some white men claimed to be able to smell an Indian from a mile away. They were closer than a mile to the river. Smelling like horse manure was okay for sneaking up on bushwhackers, but it sure as shooting wouldn't have been good for courting—

Woman! Why can't you leave me alone?

Heck of a time for her to decide to haunt him. He shook his head to clear it of Lizbeth. Jibway was hobbling his horse. Addison hobbled Outlaw. When that was done, the Indian set off again, walking bent over, with a good bit of his torso hidden by the prairie grass.

They reached the dirt road skirting the edge of the trees along the Delaware. Jibway stopped. Addison sniffed and smelled the remnants of last night's fire. He also smelled horse manure coming from the trees, not from his boots. Then he heard a hoof stomp. Like a horse shaking off annoying bugs his tail hadn't been able to brush off. Later in the year, during the time of cicadas, that's all he'd hear.

Jibway held up his fist with two fingers extended. He pointed in front of him and tapped himself on the chest. Then he pointed to Addison's right, and then he pointed at Addison.

Jibway pulled his belt knife.

Oh Sweet Jesus! Yesterday Jibway had shown him how to sneak up behind a man, put a hand over his mouth, and cut his throat. At the time, it had been an exercise, learning how to become half an Indian. At the time, he was sure he'd never be able to actually do it. But here he was, in the middle of the night, near Found Church's promised land, with enemies in front of him intent on murdering the crusaders.

Jibway pointed again in the direction of Addison's target, then he crawled across the road and into the brush and trees. The Indian didn't make a sound.

*****

Addison crawled on his hands and knees across the dirt road. A memory gnawed, like a dog on a bone, at the edge of his mind. That memory played in his head, and it was as if he were outside himself, watching a guy named Addison shoot a pig, slit its throat, and catch the blood in a basin for making blood sausage. Prior to that, he'd liked blood sausage, but since then, he'd never eaten another bite of the stuff. Pa'd had him kill other pigs and butcher them in the same way, and he'd gotten used to it. A little. But every time he'd sliced open a pig's throat, he'd felt a knife slice his own. Now he was about to sneak through the brush and kill a man that blood sausage way. The handle of the knife clutched in his fist, and it was as if he was aware of that knife and not one other thing.

Throw the knife away!

Sometimes silent screams are louder than out-loud ones.

Judas Priest, Addison!

Jibway was counting on him to take care of the second man. Rising to his feet, he entered the waist-high brush. He made as much noise, it seemed in the pitch blackness, as ringing the church bell on Sunday mornings. Stopping, standing still, he listened. The sound of breathing, a sort of *phew* sound, came to him. Regularly spaced, soft.

Addison cocked his head to the side, looked with the sides of his eyes. It wasn't pitch black there in the trees, just almost pitch black. He couldn't see his target, a sleeping sentry, but he knew where the man was. He could feel him. As he moved forward, brush scraped his clothes. Feeling with a moccasin-ed foot before putting weight on it, he felt twigs that he'd have snapped if he'd worn his boots. He didn't move through the brush as quietly as an Indian, but he was quieter than a white man.

Addison broke out of the waist-high brush and stopped. It took time for him to build a picture of what his eyes were seeing. A tree. A man slouched and leaned against it. *Phew,* p*ause, p*hew: asleep alright. The man's chin rested on his chest. A hat obscured the head. And the throat.

This wasn't how he and Jibway had practiced sneaking up on a man from behind, clamping a hand over the man's mouth and drawing the knife across the throat. One, two, three. Over and done.

Addison stood up straight, walked toward the man with no effort to be quiet. He knocked the man's hat off, kicked his foot, and whispered, "Get up."

The man against the tree started and pushed himself up and said, "I ... I just closed my eyes a minute."

Addison clamped his hand over the man's mouth, forced him back against the tree trunk, and slashed the knife across the throat. Warm, sticky fluid sprayed over Addison's knife hand and his face. He smelled the blood. He caught the sagging body and lowered it to the ground.

Addison sensed someone behind him. He crouched and spun around, the knife in his right hand. Drawing a pistol with his left, he cocked it.

Jibway.

It was noticeably lighter under the trees. *God damn.* I might have shot the Indian.

Addison huffed out a big breath, eased the hammer down, and holstered the pistol.

Jibway held up his hand, with two fingers raised out of his fist.

"Hey, Fred, George," a voice came through the night. From the direction of the voice, Addison saw the glow of fire. "We find you asleep, we're supposed to kick your ass, then make you walk home."

Another man laughed, then said, "Where the hell are you guys?"

Jibway started toward the voices, hunched over, moving fast rather than quiet. Addison was right behind him.

"George, goddammit, wake—"

The other voice: "Oh, Jesus, goddamn!"

The two men were looking down at the body of the sentry.

Jibway sprang from the brush going for the man to the left. Addison lunged at the other. This time, it worked just like they practiced. From behind, clamp a hand over the target's mouth, jerk him tight against your chest, slash the knife across the throat, cutting deep.

Addison let his victim slide to the ground.

Jibway pointed toward the fire glow and started walking in that direction. He had his pistol drawn. Addison drew his and followed.

Voices of two men came to them.

"So after we ambush those pilgrims, we shoot them all and scalp them? Right?"

"Yep."

"And the sheriff pays us five bucks for each scalp?"

"Women and kids, five bucks for theirs, too?"

"Yep."

Jibway and Addison hunkered in the brush watching the men saddle horses. The animals were tethered to a rope strung between trees like a hitching post.

Jibway started down the row of broncs not saddled yet. One of the animals whickered and jerked back against the rope.

"Who's there?"

The other man laughed. "Probly jist a damned raccoon."

Jibway passed the first saddler and moved to the second. He had his back to the hitching rope. Jibway killed him as Addison dispatched the other. Then Jibway moved down the rope cutting reins as he went. Addison did the same. They cut the reins of the horses at a second hitching rope as well.

After all the animals had been cut free, Jibway took a set of the reins and slashed the straps across the rump of a bronc. It tore off through the brush heading north, toward the ambushers' camp. Jibway drew his pistol and fired twice in the air, and the horses stampeded after the first runaway.

Jibway ran after the animals. Addison followed him but couldn't keep up. From ahead came shouts, a scream, which was suddenly cut off, and another which went on and on. Running full out in the pre-sunrise gloom in the trees, a shadow rose out of the brush and grabbed Addison's arm and jerked him to a stop. *The dark shadow of death!* Fear flooded Addison, froze him. *I will fear no evil—*

The dark shadow hissed. *Jibway!*

The Indian pulled Addison down into the brush and whispered, "We wait."

Addison knelt on a knee next to the dark shadow. When he'd been jerked to a stop, he'd resigned himself to death. And it was as if he'd gotten halfway there, and now he was trying to come back. To the land of the living.

From the camp, a voice shouted, "Git them horses."

Another said, "We best hunker down. Gunshots set off that stampede. Somebody's behind us."

Jibway rose and started firing a pistol. Fire a shot. Cock and fire, cock and fire.

Jibway dropped the pistol and drew another. "You shoot."

The Indian started firing again. Addison rose, pulled his pistol, and started shooting at the milling figures with a fire behind them, exposing them, making of them easy targets. Addison fired, and his target dropped. He fired again, missed again, then knocked another down.

From the north a wave of gunfire erupted.

Jibway dropped his pistol, pulled another from his belt, and said, "Run."

He headed back toward where they'd left their horses.

*****

At noon, Addison and Jibway joined Royal Howard and Hostetler at a camp they'd set up on the east bank of the river. Wagons were being rafted across the Delaware. That job was about half done, it appeared. A couple of Hostetler's posse guarded a dozen men huddled, hands tied behind them and sitting on the dirt. Another of Hostetler's posse knelt and spoke to one of the bound prisoners. After speaking a bit, the kneeler wrote in a notebook and moved to another. Addison knew what that was about. Entries were being made in Hostetler's book of those captured and paroled.

Royal had started his own ledger book of parolees. He'd had the women of the wagon train copy Hostetler's.

Jibway reported what he and Addison had done and seen to Hostetler and Royal Howard. The scalps clearly upset Royal. He expressed the opinion that some of the killed ambushers should be scalped, and the scalps taken to the sheriff, but Preacher Larrimer intervened.

"Found Grace Church's Holy Crusade would not be allowed to slide into such depraved behavior." The preacher's voice brooked no opposition. "There is a moral boundary, beyond which our church will not go. Scalping these men, no matter their evil intent when they were still alive, is at that boundary."

Royal took his hat off. "I apologize, Preacher. I got caught up in … in—"

"In a lust for killing," the preacher finished for him.

Addison felt like he shouldn't be there listening to that conversation. But he didn't want to leave either.

Larrimer placed his hands on Royal's shoulders. "You are a courageous, just, honest man. If this lust for killing can catch up a man like you, this is a message from Our Father in heaven. We must guard against it as we wage war against the wickedness of the devil. Tonight, we will hold a penance service at the place of our new home."

"Preacher, your message has touched my soul. I should have known enough to guard against that deadly sin, but I needed your help to see it. As to tonight, myself, and all our able men have something we have to do. It will lessen the chance that violence will visit us again. We will pay a call on that sheriff who offered reward money for our scalps, and I will offer him the choice of parole on his word that he will not wage violence against us again. If you want, you can ride with us. Then, we can have the penance service tomorrow afternoon."

Preacher Larrimer thought about it and finally nodded assent.

That's when the vinegar taste crawled up out of his belly and sat on his tongue. He'd killed those men by the river, with a knife, and with the blood of one them spraying him, and he hadn't tasted the vinegar. He'd come to believe that the vinegar taste saved his soul after violating the "Thou shalt not." Someday he'd have to tell Mr. Howard how it saved his soul to hear him talk with the preacher.

Then it got busy. The prisoners were split into two groups. One group, under armed supervision, dug graves for those ambushed ambushers on the east bank of the river. The other did the same on the west bank. Once the bodies were laid in the graves, Preacher Larrimer prayed over the departed. Then the graves were filled in, and the gravediggers were allowed to depart on foot and unarmed. Except for one man. He would lead Royal, and his men, to the sheriff's house.

*****

By four that afternoon, the Holy Crusade wagons were circled up a couple of miles north of the trading post. Hostetler and his posse, including Jibway Jim, departed for Atchison. The crusaders ate an early supper. Royal left the O'Riley brothers in charge of security at the wagons. The women would be armed, and they would stand watches through the night while the O'Riley brothers alternated between sleep and patrolling around the camp perimeter with their dog.

With an hour of sunlight left, Royal, with the rest of the able men, and the captured bushwhacker as guide, headed south to visit the sheriff. Preacher stayed behind.

Addison told Royal how Jibway got miles out his mount, and the deputy wagon master thought it was as good a way to go as any he'd heard about.

A well-used dirt road led south from the trading post to the town of Prairietown. The sheriff owned a farm north of town.

"Take us maybe four hours," the guide opined. "Took us near seven yesterday."

With Addison and the guide riding ahead, Royal pushed the horses. After the sun set, Addison grew uneasy, worried over riding into an ambush, but they arrived at a point, about a half-mile from the sheriff's farm, according to their guide, about three hours and forty-five minutes after setting out. They'd passed no farms alongside the road. No occupied farms. They had seen a good dozen burned-down houses and barns though.

Royal stopped his band and sent Addison and the guide on ahead to scout the place.

Keeping Ambrose, the guide, in front of him, the two rode until the guide stopped and pointed to a lane leading off to the left. The lights of Prairietown glowed a hole in the night to the south. The lane cut through a stand of trees, and lights showed through the foliage.

"Don't shout a warning," Addison said.

"I done give my word," Ambrose replied.

"Give it again."

"I ain't gonna holler."

Addison had them dismount and lead their horses down the lane.

Trees gave way to a view of a large two-story house with lamplit windows on both floors. Six saddle horses were tied to hitching posts in front of the house.

They returned to Royal, and Addison reported what he'd seen.

25.

Two windows looked into a large dining room on one end of the ground floor. Seven men sat around the table. Most of them smoked cigars. All of them had whiskey glasses in front of them, and the bottle roamed up and down the table. Royal Howard tiptoed across the porch to keep his boots from announcing his presence to those inside. His gang stood huddled close together, pistols drawn.

"Addison, you and Orson go around back," Royal whispered. "Go through the kitchen and wait outside that closed door into the dining room till you hear us. Then you pull the door open and cover them from that side. I'll give you two minutes."

Orson held Ambrose, their guide, by the upper arm.

"Fishboch, you watch Ambrose," Royal said.

With Orson on his heels, Addison hustled around the house to the rear. There was a solid door into the house. A path from the door led to two outhouses. The back door wasn't locked. Addison drew his pistol and pushed the door open. A Negro man with white hair and a woman with grey stood at a counter washing and drying dishes. A young Negro woman was carrying a stack of plates across the floor. She stopped and gaped at the pistols pointing at her.

"Go on," Addison said. "Put the dishes down on the counter there."

"Go on, girl," White Hair said.

She moved then and did as ordered.

"You folks keep quiet, and we won't hurt you," Addison said. To Orson, "Keep an eye on 'em."

Addison was about to exit the kitchen when he noticed Orson leering at the young woman. "Orson," he started and was cut off by the sound of windows breaking and Royal's shout, "Don't nobody move."

Addison tore open the kitchen door, crossed a hallway, and opened another door. He looked across a table and locked eyes with a startled David McTavish staring into the room through a broken window. McTavish swung his pistol and aimed it at Addison, and Addison saw recognition flash over his face. Relief at not getting shot flooded Addison, but then someone did fire at him, and the bullet whizzed by his ear and tore splinters from the door. Addison dropped flat on the floor, shielded by the table from those outside, and then a general firing commenced.

Addison could see three men on his side of the table. They all had pistols in their hands. The one nearest to him aimed at Addison, but Addison fired first. The man beside the one he shot was aiming at someone in a window and Addison shot him. Those outside fired and fired.

Royal Howard hollered, "Cease firing. Cease firing, goddammit!"

Addison's ears rang. Gunsmoke filled the room as thick as morning fog above a river. He raised his empty left hand, not wanting to get shot by his own people, and pushed himself up onto his knees when a bullet smacked into the door jamb just above his head. From behind and above.

A woman stood at the top of a flight of stairs holding a smoking pistol in two hands.

"Ma'am," Addison said, "Put the gun down."

She cocked and aimed it. Addison jumped back into the dining room as a bullet again smacked into the door jamb. That's when Orson shot the woman. She fell to the floor, and her pistol tumbled and thumped down the stairs.

*****

Royal Howard kept Albert Fishboch and Ambrose with him in the dining room, sent two men to check the upper story, and the others to search the barn and other outbuildings. Then he dealt with his scout.

"You shoulda hollered before jerking open that door," Royal said.

By jerking open the door to the dining room, Addison had precipitated the killing of five men around the sheriff's dining room table and the wounding of the sheriff and one other. Not to mention the sheriff's wife. Not to mention Addison had almost gotten his own fool self shot.

Addison held his hat in his hand. "Sorry, Mr. Howard." Then he held it in two hands.

"It's me should be sorry," Royal said. "I put too much stock in how you took to scouting in the outdoors. Shoulda' seen it. Fighting indoors takes a different kind of thinking.

"You jerked that door open and Oscar Wilson thought you were another of the sheriff's men and cut loose at you. That started the sheriff and his men into pulling their weapons. That got our guys firing through the windows. A wonder they ain't all dead."

The sheriff had a shoulder wound and a crease in his scalp above his left ear. The other had been shot in the chest. He wheezed and bubbled bright red blood-tinged spit between his lips.

The sheriff wouldn't answer Royal's questions. Chest Wound couldn't.

From upstairs, a girl screamed. Boots clumped down the stairs outside the dining room.

"Let those children go." The colored woman, Addison thought. "Lizzy, Georgy, come here."

Hermann Vogelsang herded the gray-haired woman, carrying a girl, maybe eight, into the dining room. The white-haired man came next holding the hand of a boy, maybe ten. Solomon Adler came in last.

"Get those kids out of here," Royal ordered.

"Take them to the kitchen," Addison said. "Uh, if that's okay?"

It was okay, and Hermann herded the party back into the hallway.

"Mama!" the little girl cried.

"Don't look, child." Gray Hair.

Two young colored men were found locked in a shed, but no others were discovered.

Royal had two of his men carry the dead woman out onto the porch while others hauled the five dead men from the dining room. Royal tried again to get the sheriff to speak, but he refused.

Addison could almost see possible courses of action wrestling for domination in Royal's head. He grabbed the feet of one of the dead men, helped carry him out, and lined him up next to the others onto the front porch. When he came back inside Royal ordered him to: "Take Hermann and that guide and ride into town. Bring the mayor and a doctor back with you. Hogtie them and throw them in a wagon if you have to. Get going."

The doctor came willingly. The mayor came unwillingly, barefoot and in an ankle-length nightshirt.

After they returned, Hermann led the doctor into the dining room. Addison dragged the mayor off his horse and plopped him in a chair at the end of the table, opposite to where the wagon master sat.

The doctor knelt and looked at Chest Wound lying on the floor. The doc shook his head, got up, and walked around the table. He felt the sheriff's upper arm. Almost as one, the sheriff and the doctor grimaced.

"Bone's shattered. Arm has to come off," the doctor said.

The sheriff had had defiance chiseled onto his face until then. Defeat took its place and he slumped back in the chair. Addison was about to turn away when he noticed the sheriff look up at Royal. The defiance was back, and so was a blazing hot hatred.

"I'll do the surgery in the kitchen," the doctor said.

"Go with him, Hermann. Have the colored folks take the kids to bed."

The sheriff had his back to a busted-out window, and Addison stood across from him. The sheriff reached for something under the table with his good right hand. Addison reached for his pistol. Royal was looking at the doctor and Hermann. From under the table came the sound of a pistol cocking.

"Royal," Addison shouted, as he drew, cocked, and aimed.

A pistol cracked as the wagon master threw himself aside and off the chair.

Addison fired, striking the sheriff in the head. He slid off the chair. Addison hurried around to the head of the table. Royal was up on an elbow staring at the sheriff. The sheriff's dead fisheyes stared back, his face, now just that of a man devoid of defiance, hate, and defeat. All that, Addison thought, drained out of the man along with the blood and life puddling behind his head.

Albert Fishboch brought the two young Negroes they'd found locked in slave quarters. He told them to cart the sheriff out onto the porch.

"No," Royal said. "They are to have nothing to do with any of this. Addison, you and Albert take him out."

Addison re-entered the dining room. Royal still occupied the head of the table. The doctor sat next to him to one side. The mayor sat opposite him.

"Mr. Howard, I will take the sheriff's children with me as well as the two house Negroes."

"Two?" Addison said. "There were three."

"There is young woman housekeeper. I didn't see her," the doctor replied.

Orson. Addison hadn't seen him for a while.

Addison started heading for the door into the hallway, but Royal stopped him, and asked where he was going.

Royal sent Solomon Adler to look for Orson.

Then the doctor asked if someone could hitch a team to a wagon so he could take the children to town and get them to bed and away from where all the killing took place. Royal sent two men to do that.

Then Royal sent the white-haired Negro to fetch paper, pen, and ink.

While Royal related what had happened up north, Addison was to write down what was said. The sheriff had sent thirty-five men to ambush the Found Grace wagon train. Scouts from the wagon train had located the ambushers and ambushed them. Fifteen of the ambushers had been killed, and the others were paroled. Before being paroled however, they had been questioned. The parolees had confessed that the sheriff had told them to kill everyone, men, women, and children. After slaughtering them, the ambushers were to scalp the dead. The sheriff would pay five dollars for each scalp. Plus, the ambushers could keep the horses and anything else they found of value belonging to the wagon train.

It had been Royal Howard's intention to capture the sheriff and take him to the US Army fort at Leavenworth. At this, Royal stared at Addison, who had no trouble interpreting the look: *Don't say different.* Addison went back to writing. When he finished, Royal had the mayor sign the document, acknowledging he'd been told what had happened at the Delaware River crossing north of there.

Royal also wrote letters saying that the sheriff's two slave fieldhands had been granted their freedom. The mayor at first refused to sign the letters, but Royal growled that he better sign, and he did.

Royal stood up from the table, stretched his back as Solomon Adler walked into the dining room. "Did we find Orson?"

"Nope. We looked in barn and all the outbuildings. We also couldn't find the brindle mare he was riding."

One of the crusaders reported the buggy was ready to take the doc and the rest of them to town.

Hermann Vogelsang herded the old Negro couple and the two children into the dining room.

"Where's the young woman?" Addison said. "When we entered the kitchen from in back, there was a young Negro woman with these two."

"Yes, sir. That be our daughter Lurleen," White Hair said. "She went away with that Massa Orson. He gonna set her free. That what he said."

Royal's eyes touched on Addison's, then looked away and out one of the busted-out windows.

Then he turned back to the Negro man. "You and your lady want to be free, too?"

"No, suh. Who be looking after these *chilruns*? An we don' know nuthin' bout being free."

Royal nodded. "Might I have your name, sir?"

White Hair took that "sir" like a slap. But then he recovered. "I'se Cicero. This is Coretta. She be my wife."

"Mr. Cicero, Mrs. Coretta, a privilege to meet you both. With the doc here, you might be the only honorable people in this town," Royal said.

Adison saw the young girl in Mrs. Coretta's arms clinging tightly to the woman's neck. The boy stood next to Cicero, holding his hand. The boy's eyes were red, but he was done crying. Now he looked around the room. Memorizing faces?

The doctor led the mayor and the sheriff's slaves and children outside and loaded them all into the buggy waiting for them. As they crossed the porch, they all looked at the line of bodies, which now were covered with blankets.

As soon as the buggy drove away, Royal pulled the blankets from the corpses, wadded them up and tossed them in a pile in front of the porch. The sheriff had been scalped. His good right hand rested on his belly grasping his swath of top hair.

"Didn't want the kids to see that," Royal said, "But when the folks come from town to take care of these. Them, I want to see it."

As they rode out of the sheriff's lane, Addison turned in the saddle and looked back at the house. Lanterns burned inside upstairs and downstairs windows. Addison's final glimpse of the scene appeared cheerful, welcoming.

26.

Addison trailed the crusaders as they headed north. He listened for sounds of pursuit. And ground his teeth over Orson. Let him near a good-looking woman, and he forgot about everything else that was going on. Even the fact that he, Orson, was part of an armed posse invading the home of a sheriff, an officer of the law. Never mind the fact that the sheriff used the law to cover his efforts to stop the crusaders by massacring women and children. The crusaders were new to the territory, and they were taking on the law of the land. What they were doing was beyond dangerous. Every member of the posse man needed to count on every man who rode with them.

And where was Orson? Off cavorting with a comely young woman.

And why did women find him attractive? Something drew them, even though it was obvious. As soon as a *new* pretty face showed up, there he went panting after her and forgetting about the ones who had so recently held his attention. Couldn't those women see how shallow, how insincere, how fickle, how—

Hail Mary, full of grace,
Then look at Orson, Lord, he ain't got any.

Outlaw stopped. His ears stood up. Off to the right, something crashed through the brush making enough noise to wake the dead. Addison's heart hammered, and he jerked his pistol from his holster and almost dropped it.

Outlaw started forward again.

A night animal foraging for supper. Probably a raccoon.

Addison reined up and listened. Normal night noises, bugs, an owl, frogs.

Silent stars above and a big harvest moon peeking above the trees. No hint of pursuit. He said, "Outlaw," and the horse started walking forward. Addison made a *tsk, tsk* sound and the animal kicked it up to a trot.

Addison confessed to Father God in heaven that he was a sinful man, that if he ever deserved a switching, it was that very night, because he had committed so many sins. He whispered, "Sorry, God, with Your help, I will try to do better. Now, please excuse me, I have to get back to work."

*****

Once he got his sins properly confessed, and himself properly remorseful, Addison performed his rear-guard duties well, staying behind Royal Howard and the others by thirty minutes. When he could see Pott's Trading Post in the moonlight, Addison turned Outlaw around, backtracked south a couple of miles, and setup a cold camp in the grassland side of the road to Prairietown. On the river side, brush and trees crowded right up to the road. If someone came, he and Outlaw would duck into the trees, or if a large party approached, Addison would hightail it back to the wagon train and roust everyone out of bed.

Through the night and early morning, no one came from the south. At sunrise, Hermann Vogelsang and Orson rode south to take over watching for trouble from the south.

"What in Sam Hill is he doing here?" Addison demanded of Hermann.

"Now, now. Just listen, vill you?" Hermann said. "Orson was in the kitchen with the three Negroes. They told him the girl, Lurleen, every time the sheriff had those men to his house, they ate and drank and talked. Then the sheriff give Lurleen to the men, and they take her to the barn. That Cicero, he asked Orson to get his daughter out of there. Orson told the man there wouldn't be any trouble from the sheriff. 'You going to kill him?' Cicero asked. Orson told him we wanted the sheriff alive. Cicero said if the sheriff stayed alive, he would bring trouble to Lurleen. 'Please take her away,' Cicero begged. Orson did."

Addison had been puffed up with rage and outrage over Orson abandoning his post for his own vulgar, lurid, and obscene purposes. Now, it all drained out of him, and he looked at his fists and unclenched them. He'd been so ready to pound his fists into the soulless face until Orson was beat to a bloody mess.

I've become Pa. Pa was so ready with his switches. Addison was so ready with his fists. Still, Orson had said he wondered what it would be like to have a colored girl.

Addison said, "You didn't do anything to the girl, Lurlene?"

"I didn't."

"Still, you shouldn't—"

"I shouldn't have abandoned my post in the kitchen," Orson said. "Royal already told me. That sheriff could have had other men on his farm, and they could have come in through the kitchen, and we'd have wound up with some of us of getting shot."

Addison looked up at Orson atop the saddle of his mount. Orson, the bane of his existence, till now. Had the aggravating fellow turned the corner? That seemed a stretch.

"Well," Addison said. "It's not like you were the only one made a mistake down there in Prairietown."

"Royal told me that, too."

The words, gilded over with the smirk, almost got Orson jerked off his horse. It was the thought Addison had had earlier about being like ready-with-a-switch Pa that saved both of them.

*****

The men who'd raided Prairietown were told to sleep until noon. After three hours of sleep, Addison rose and found Royal Howard, Preacher Larrimer, and Otto Vogelsang at work on a table drawing a map of the area. The location of the church was plotted at the southern end of a large swath of territory. A cluster of houses had been drawn around the church. "Brotherton" had been penciled in above them.

Royal Howard explained. Preacher Larrimer had said all men were God's children, thus, they were all brothers. "Your mother, Addison, suggested the name Brotherton. One of the women said that brother and sister should be in the name. 'How about Brothsterton?' she suggested. But your mother said women could generally work out how to get along. Men, however, could stand to have the reminder. And Preacher Larrimer said, "Amen."

More of the raiders from the night before awakened and joined those around the table. The map had been carved up into rectangles. Each rectangle represented a farm assigned to a specific family. The men wanted to know where their farms were.

The preacher explained that the plots of land had been assigned by drawing names from a hat. He went on to explain that for the immediate future, family homes would be built close together around the church. Security, and the necessity to protect themselves from pro-slave staters would be a fact of life for, perhaps, years to come. In addition, large communal barns would be built near the edge of the area laid out for housing. Individual homes and outbuildings located on each farm would be vulnerable. Farmers would ride out to their places in the morning, work the land and return to Brotherton before sundown.

The Negro families would be assigned farms as well. Theirs were all closest to the church.

At noon, Royal Howard whanged the horseshoes. When everyone had assembled, Royal climbed up onto Preacher Larrimer's wagon and faced the crusaders. "This is a hostile and hate-filled land. We will have to be vigilant. Our raid on Prairietown is bound to generate a wish for vengeance and an attack on us here. They will attempt to wipe us out, just like those bushwhackers intended by the crossing of the Delaware River. Thus, we will assign two young men, or two young women, to a watch station near the crossing of the river. Another two will guard the road from Prairietown. One person can sleep, but one must always, always be awake. One of the reasons we were able to surprise the bushwhackers is because the sentries they posted fell asleep."

Royal paused and scanned the upturned faces. "Those sleeping sentries had their throats cut."

Other security measures were discussed, and Preacher Larrimer said a prayer of thanksgiving for safe arrival at their new home, Brotherton. When the "amen" rang out, he said, "Our first order of business here in Brotherton will be to build New Found Grace Church. And we will work that task from horseshoe time till the sun goes down. Men and women will also plant their winter wheat and oats. Now let's eat. Then we get to work."

*****

Addison and Orson had the 4 p.m. to midnight station on the road to Prairietown. Prior to eating, they conducted practice with guns for youngsters over twelve and Negroes. Orson, Addison saw, had grown proficient with weapons, and young people paid attention to his instruction on safety and firing. He was also impressed with Ned Smith's prowess with both hand and long guns.

After wrapping up the practice, Addison found Royal Howard and Preacher Larrimer at a table under an awning slung from the side of a wagon. He asked to join them, and the preacher nodded assent.

"Ned Smith has gotten quite good with guns," Addison pointed out. "How about if we have him instruct the other Negroes?"

"Ah, Addison," Larrimer said. "An elegant *sounding* solution. But we will have Ned instruct our **white** young men and women. You pick a couple of our men to instruct the Negroes."

*****

Addison and Orson rode south to take over the guard station along the way to Prairietown. They started out as they normally did—Addison in front by twenty yards and riding the left side of the road. Orson took the opposite side. A few minutes after they passed the trading post, Orson pulled up next to Addison.

Addison was about to chide him when Orson said, "You want to know, don't you?"

"Know what?"

"Whether I found out what it's like to be with a colored woman."

"Orson, get back in position."

"With the guard station manned south of here, I figure we're safe."

"What if a group from the south snuck up on our sentries and killed them, like we did to the bushwhackers who thought to ambush us? Here in Kansas, we are not safe, and if you act like we are, we are in even more danger."

"Oh," Orson said. "I never thought of it that way." He stopped his mount to let Addison pull ahead again. "But I didn't. I didn't lie with that colored girl."

Addison didn't particularly care to hear Orson talk. He especially did not like to hear him talk about being with women. But it was good to know he hadn't taken that young woman away from the sheriff's house just for that purpose. And Addison had been convinced Orson had done just that. All of them on the raid thought that.

Still, when the shooting had started in the sheriff's dining room, and the young woman had run out the back door, Orson should have gone to support Addison confronting the men with the sheriff. Instead, he'd gone after the girl. She had been terrified the sheriff's men would win the gunfight, and if they did, she knew what she'd be in for.

Orson had made a mistake, but then, Addison had made mistakes that night, too. Even Royal Howard had. But, making allowances for Orson required some new thinking. Addison had thought he knew everything he needed to know about the onery … kid. Now, it seemed Orson might be maturing.

*****

After turning over their guard post at midnight, Addison and Orson rode side-by-side back to the crusader's circled-up wagons. Through the entire ride, Orson didn't say anything. Until they passed the trading post.

"Addison, I'm sorry about Lizbeth. Ma told me I shouldn't listen to Deacon Waverly. Pa said I best be careful and maybe not jump into that marriage without thinking on it some. Of course, I knew better. Sorry."

They passed one of the O'Riley brothers and the dog, and Addison said, "I'd like to be able to tell you, if I'd have been in that situation, I'd have listened to my ma and pa, but that'd be a plain out lie."

They rode on then until a female voice hollered, "Stop. Who are you?"

"Addison and Orson."

"Come on then."

As they passed the two sentries, Addison said, "Good evening, ladies."

"Good evening, my foot!" the one who hadn't issued the challenge said. "It's the middle of the dad-burned night."

Addison tipped his hat. He was surprised Orson hadn't popped off with something wise-acre-y. He thought about Maurice. Maurice would have said something to the gal with her feathers all ruffled and out of sorts.

Lord, it'll be good to have old Found Grace Church together again in New Found Grace.

At the circle of wagons, they dismounted, and Orson said he'd take care of the horses. Addison found Royal Howard and Preacher Larrimer sitting on chairs near a fire with coffee cups in their hands.

"Royal, it is commendable," Preacher said, "that you want to shoulder responsibility for the shooting and killing at the sheriff's place, but you should not deliver the statement of what happened to the army at Leavenworth. I am sure they will arrest you, put you on trial, and probably hang you for shooting an officer of the law. They will consider the statements from the paroled bushwhackers as contrived, as no evidence at all. You cannot go yourself."

"If I go, I will absorb their hatred, and you will be … more safe."

"We will not be more safe," Addison butt in. "They will see you reporting in person, Mr. Howard, as an admission of guilt. They will try you and hang you and visit retribution on us here. No one has to go and deliver the report in person. Send the report to Atchison and have it mailed from there to the commander of the post."

"I'll take the report." Adolph Freeman stepped closer to the fire. "Reinstate me as deacon, Preacher Larrimer. I have one suit of church clothes left. Let me take the letter."

It was decided then that reinstated deacon Freeman, would carry the report to the commanding officer of the fort at Leavenworth. He would be escorted by his son to the outskirts of the town, at which point, Addison would turn around and head back to New Found Grace. Deacon Freeman, after delivering the report, if he was not detained, would ride north to Atchison, and return to the crusade in company with Mr. Hostetler on one of his supply runs.

"Deacon," Larrimer said, "Do not sacrifice yourself needlessly on this mission. Deliver the report. Say we felt obligated to report what happened to duly constituted authority but admit no guilt. Return to us. Let this last guide your actions and your tongue."

"Yes, Preacher."

"Deacon," Addison said, "in the saddle prior to horseshoe time."

27.

As soon as they crossed the Delaware River, Addison's pa challenged his son's authority. He removed his shoulder holster and told Addison he would not wear a pistol.

"We went over this, Pa. You told Preacher Larrimer you'd wear the pistol and do your part to defend us if it comes to a fight."

"Yes, but the preacher himself told us that it is okay to lie to serve a higher purpose. I want to save your soul, and if I have to die … if we both have to die to do it, it is a small price to pay to avoid eternal damnation."

Addison stopped Outlaw, and Pa pulled up alongside. "Give me the pistol, Pa." Former Deacon Freeman did so. "Get off the horse, Pa."

"I will not."

Addison pushed him off the saddle, and he landed on the dusty roadbed.

"Pa, go back to the crusade. Go join the slave-staters. It doesn't matter."

Addison dismounted, went through his father's saddlebags, and removed the envelope with the report for the army. This he put in his own saddlebags. Then he stripped the heavy saddle off his father's horse and left it beside the road next to his father.

"Think about what you're doing, son." His pa sat on his butt; his skinny legs stretched out in front of him.

"You think about what you're doing, Pa. You are betraying Preacher

Larrimer. You're betraying the Holy Crusade. Slavery is an abomination. Remember saying that back at Found Grace Church that Sunday the Preacher launched the Holy Crusade. Your betrayal is an abomination."

Addison mounted, grabbed the reins to his pa's horse, and left the man and his saddle beside the road.

Instead of heading for Leavenworth, Addison headed for Atchison. The next day and halfway there, he met Jibway Jim scouting for Hostetler, who followed with a wagon train loaded with building materials for the crusaders. And tacked onto the rear of the freight wagons was the remainder of the early crusaders.

Addison told Jibway a party of riders, more than ten he estimated, had passed close to him last night.

"Hostetler." Jibway pointed east. "One, two hours. You tell."

Addison said he would. Then Jibway reached out his hand, and Addison touched his thumb, the one with the knife scar, to Jibway's the way they had when they became blood brothers after ambushing the bushwhackers. Then the two men nodded to each other and rode on.

A pa like Pa, and a brother like Jibway.

Your ways, Lord, are not my ways. Preacher Larrimer had said words to that effect often enough. He'd also preached on children honoring their father and mother. And of course, there'd been the "lying is the lesser of two evils" bit. And then Addison remembered how Preacher had prayed for help in finding the straight and narrow way. That, Addison decided, was a good prayer for a crusader, trying mightily to be holy, to keep handy.

An hour and a half later, he met Hostetler driving the lead of five freight wagons, and Addison told him about encountering the night riders and that he'd met and spoken with Jibway.

Behind the freight wagons, he found Gallant Argyl as wagon master of the remainder of the early crusade group. It was good to see Gallant and the others. It was good to think of them being together again. The early crusaders belonged together.

As Addison headed east, he tipped his hat and howdy-ed the crusaders as he passed them in their wagons and astride. Then he pushed on to Atchison. There he found Norb Bass and explained his mission.

Norb wrote Addison a letter of introduction to a sympathetic-to-free-soilers army captain at the fort, and he assigned one of his men, Lem, to ride with Addison to Leavenworth.

Lemuel, his proper name was, but, "Nobody calls me that. Even Ma." Lem had a regular cloud of black hair covering his face. "I git it trimmed once a year. Come Christmas." As they left Atchison, these tidbits of personal history dribbled out. They'd ride with Lem leading, just the way Addison liked to move down a road, one rider on the left side and ahead of the other on the right. But then, Lem would stop and wait and disclose, "I wuz scalped once. But only once." Then he took his hat off and showed the strip of raw-looking red flesh down the middle of his black hair. "Makes me part red skin, see?" Then Lem rode on.

The next time he stopped, he said, "Jibway Jim tole me I wuz lucky I got shot running away. Otherwise, the passel of Injuns that ambushed me and my pard would have cut my heart out and ate it. Since I run, though, I had no bravery in me. Being a coward doesn't stop an Injun taking your hair though."

By the time they arrived near the fort property on the north side of the town of Leavenworth, Addison had learned a lot about his traveling companion. One of the things he learned was that Lem was no coward, never mind his ready admitting to having been one. Lem wanted to camp the night and not spend money on a hotel and livery stable. He would spend his money filling his whiskey canteen before heading back to Atchison.

*****

When he was escorted in to see the commander of the fort, Addison was glad he had Norb Bass's friend with him. Otherwise, he was sure he would have been summarily slapped in prison. But the captain spoke up for him. "Were you with the gang of men who attacked the sheriff?" the commander asked.

The man kept his black, grizzled with gray, hair trimmed close. His mustache matched the hair. But once the commander's cold blue eyes locked onto Addison, he didn't notice much of anything else.

"No, sir. The posse left after I went to bed, and they returned before I got up."

That's what Royal Howard told him to say.

"But," Addison continued, "I was with the men who attacked the bushwhackers before they could ambush us."

"I didn't ask you that," the commander snapped.

"No, you didn't, sir. But I thought you ought to know that. There were two gangs of them. About twenty men in each. They were going to wait until our wagon train was half across the Delaware River, then attack. They were going to kill every man, woman, and child of us, scalp us, and the sheriff was going to pay them a bounty on each hank of hair they brought him."

The commander huffed himself up, like a rooster fluffing his feathers to make himself look bigger prior to a fight. "I have another report. It says you and your band of renegades attacked a peaceful party of men in the middle of the night, snuck up on them, and without provocation, shot and killed a number of these men."

"Our wagon train traveled across Illinois, and, during that time, we were attacked twice. We learned to put scouts out in front of the wagons. Our scouts found those bushwhackers hunkered down in the woods on both sides of the Delaware River. During the night, we put men behind both groups. We didn't shoot at them until they attacked our wagons the next morning. When the shooting was done, we found each man had a long gun and at least two pistols each. Some of them wore a special shirt with extra pockets sewed on the front. In these pockets, they carried extra loaded cylinders for their handguns. These bushwhackers came to do a powerful lot of shooting."

"You can't know that."

"I do know that, sir. The ones who didn't get killed told us, and then we paroled them. Their names are in that letter."

The commander hooked spectacles over his ears and looked at the letter. "Why didn't this Royal Howard come himself? Why'd he send a boy to a man's work?"

"Sir, my Pa and me set out to deliver this letter, but his horse threw him, and he was hurt some. He told me to ride on and get that letter to you. He said those low-life skulkers probably got word to you that we ambushed them. Pa was right?"

The commander smacked his hand atop his desk. "Boy, you got a right smart mouth on you. I've a mind to stick you in the stockade and send a troop to capture this Royal Howard and bring him back here."

Addison clamped his mouth shut lest it say something. Just then, anything he said would only make things worse.

The commander jumped to his feet. He wasn't very tall. In his fancy soldier suit, he reminded Addison of a banty rooster, thinking being atop a manure pile made him big.

"Captain," the commander said. "Get this sass-mouthed whelp out of my office, and if you ever bring anything like him in front of me again, I'll bust you to private and throw you in the stockade."

"Sorry, sir. It won't happen again, sir."

The captain grabbed Addison's arm and propelled him out of the office, through the reception area and front door, and off the boardwalk.

"Young Addison," the captain said, "if I was you, I'd skedaddle. The commander in there is right now thinking on how you made him look like a fool. Best you not tarry."

"Sorry for getting you in hot water, captain."

"Not to worry. I'll have to lick his boots the rest of today, but if nothing else ruffles his feathers, he'll be over it by tomorrow. He'll want everyone to forget how he got showed up by a sass-mouthed whelp."

Addison tipped his hat to the captain, reined Outlaw around, and made a *tsk, tsk* sound. Outlaw set off at a canter.

*****

When Addison crossed the Delaware River, he found Orson and Ned Smith manning the sentry post watching east.

"Welcome back, Mistah Addison," Ned said.

Addison wondered whose idea it was to put Ned out here with Orson.

"In case you're wondering," Orson said, "It was the two wagon masters and Preacher Larrimer decided to put me and Ned out here."

Addison humph-ed at Orson and tipped his hat to Ned.

"You be surprised, Mistah Addison," Ned said, "When you get to Brotherton, and you see what been done."

When he arrived, Addison found Brotherton consisted of a church just like the Found Grace building back in Illinois, except this one had a bell tower. No one was in the church. A new stone-walled meeting house stood next to the church. No one was inside it, either, but behind it sat the wagon lot. Funny, he mused. They'd started the crusade with a dozen wagons. Now, with the arrival of the second half of the original train, the number had grown to twice that many, and they were all arranged in rows of eight wagons each.

Mrs. Larrimer sat in a circle with three young women by their wagon at the rear of the church. They were peeling and quartering potatoes. And twittering, at least the young women were. One of the three was Mariah Welch. She noticed Addison approach and looked at him. Her face kind of smiled, as if to say, *Oh, Addison, it's good to see you.* But that washed away and left behind a look of … disappointment? Hurt?

Both, he decided. *But what did I do to hurt you?*

"Ah. Addison," Mrs. Larrimer said. "We weren't expecting you for a couple of days yet. I know my husband will want to talk to you, as will the row leaders."

"Row leaders?"

"Yes. Each row of wagons has a leader. Your mother is leader of this row. Royal Howard the next row, and Gallant Argyl the last one."

Addison noted a party of women preparing supper in the center of the other two rows of wagons as well.

"Laura," Mrs. Larrimer said to the McTavish girl. "Saddle a pony and find my husband and the row leaders. Tell them Addison is back. Hustle."

"Yessum," Laura's grin said she was not saddened to be leaving the potatoes.

"Mariah, you and Lainie keep after the potatoes, please."

"Come with me, Addison. There's something in the meeting house I want to show you."

She put her knife atop the bowl of unpeeled potatoes, wiped her hands on her apron, stood, smiled, and said, "Come along."

As they walked side-by-side, she said, "Everyone works every day except the Sabbath, of course. Otto Vogelsang's carpenters will be starting on a large barn in a few days. They are waiting for more building materials. Meanwhile, though, every able-bodied man and woman is plowing, planting, laying out farms, working in the sawmill, tending animals and children."

"Or standing south and east sentry duty," Addison said.

"Yes, that will continue as long as we can foresee. Royal Howard said we have to be prepared for a retaliation raid for busting up the pro-slavers ambush. It could come tomorrow, or three years from now. The only thing certain, he said, is it will come. And that's why we have our wagons huddled together here. It wouldn't be safe if we lived scattered on individual farms."

They were halfway to the meeting house. Mrs. Larrimer said, "I told you everybody works in the fields, but not Mariah. She is our healer and stays here, so we always know where to find her."

As they passed down the side of the meeting house, Addison pointed to a roofed-over wooden addition to the stone structure. "What's this?"

"That is Otto Vogelsang's idea, and the women love him for it. In the cold-weather months, we will cook inside. In the warm part of the year, we cook out here, and we won't have to get up so early to get the cooking done with time for the place to cool down before after-services supper." Mrs. Larrimer pulled open the door.

"So it's one chimney with an outside fireplace and an inside one?" Addison said.

"He's clever, Otto Vogelsang is."

Mrs. Larrimer led Addison into the attached kitchen.

"Addison, would you stir up a fire, please. I'll get the coffee pot ready. When the men, and your mother, get here, they'll want coffee as you talk."

Addison uncovered some glowing embers in the fireplace, got a tinder fire going, then added twigs and kindling. Mrs. Larrimer set the coffee pot on the grate over the fire and led him into the meeting house. Inside, Addison noted the door to the add-on kitchen was sturdy and rigged so a length of two-by-six could be used to prevent entry from the outside.

Three tables with benches along the long sides occupied a small portion of the floor space. "Making the rest of the tables is not a priority right now, according to Royal and Otto." She pointed to the end of one of the tables. "Let's sit here. I'll be able to hear the coffee pot gurgle."

They sat. "I've something to tell you about your father."

Mrs. Larrimer was sunken-cheeks thin. She always wore high-necked dresses as black as her husband's suits. Her dresses, though, were adorned with thin strips of lace around the neck and sleeve cuffs. When you looked at her brown eyes, they seemed to be the only thing worth noting. They brimmed with care, concern, love with no constraints, no questions asked. As a young schoolboy, he'd seen some of his schoolmates fall on the playground and scrape a knee, and even if their own mothers were nearby, they'd run to Mrs. Larrimer.

On the other hand, when the crusaders ambushed the bushwhackers at the Delaware River, he knew Mrs. Larrimer and his mother had been leaders for the women who defended the wagons while the men were ambushing the ambushers. Addison wondered what her eyes looked like when she was shooting at someone. For that matter, he wondered what his own eyes held when he was killing men.

Now, Mrs. Larrimer's eyes poured out, *You are not my child, but I am your mother.* "The afternoon of the day you and your father departed for Fort Leavenworth, he returned and denounced you to the Preacher. He wanted my husband to banish you from Found Grace church. You killed so many men that it turned you into a cold-blooded killer without compassion, remorse, or concern over the value of a human life. Furthermore, you were a willful, disobedient, disrespectful young man. He said you were no longer his son."

The coffee pot gurgled, and the preacher's wife went to pull the pot off the fire.

Addison looked at his hands atop the table. He wondered at how he was feeling about his pa's words. They didn't make bearing the weight of so many lives worse, as he thought they should. His pa was rigid, blinded by his own sense of self-righteousness. There was no reasoning with him. Like there'd been no point in trying to reason with the men in that jail in Thompson Township, with those slave hunters from Mississippi, with the bushwhackers. And his pa was not trustworthy enough to put him on a parole.

Mrs. Larrimer returned. "Our preacher chastised your father. He should have supported you, helped you carry the burden of the lives you were forced to take. Then my husband told your father he had one more chance with Found Grace church or *he* would be banished. He was to prove he was worthy of membership in the church by humble and obedient service to those members in good standing, "Which is everyone, except you, Adolph Freeman." He went on to say that your father would not be allocated a plot of land to farm, but that you would be, and that your father will work for you."

Mrs. Larrimer chuckled. "That one surprised you, didn't it? I've one more thing—"

But she was interrupted by the arrival of Preacher Larrimer, Royal Howard, Gallant Argyl, and ... Ma.

28.

Back at the start of the crusade, when Addison and Joshua Reedley had ridden back to the church to put Sylvan Waverly and the other half of the congregation to rights, it had been a surprise to see Agatha Jansen assume the role of spiritual leader, but she stepped up, took hold of the reins, and that quick it seemed right for her to be just that. It was easier to accept that than it had been accepting women in split skirts.

But now, here he was making his report to Preacher Larrimer and the three row leaders, and Ma was one of them. Except, she was Ma. That's all she was and had ever been. Pa was … had been deacon, and Ma lived in his shadow—had lived under his shadow. But she was row leader. Preacher Larrimer said so.

The preacher and row leaders sat on one side of a table, Addison on the other. They sipped coffee as Addison spoke. He talked, and when he finally took a sip, it was cold, and he wrinkled his nose at it. Mrs. Larrimer noticed and brought him a fresh cup.

Addison thanked her and wrapped up his report. "That army commander at the fort, I am pretty sure he is not on our side. And it was clear that the pro-slavery folks have ready access to him while we are a three-days ride away. And you, Mr. Howard, are the only name he knows. So far. Except mine, of course. But he thinks I'm just a kid. If he decides to come after anyone for killing the sheriff of Prairietown, he'll come after you."

Preacher looked at Royal Howard. "Tell Addison your new name."

Royal said, "Boyd Calloway."

Addison's mouth dropped open.

Preacher Larrimer sat broom handle straight on the bench, his hands in his lap, but then he brought his hands up and rested his arms on the table. "I wanted a name easy for the people to remember. We are building our new church on a foundation of lies, and I know we must get ourselves back to living the truth. I pray to God that Boyd Calloway is the last lie we need to tell. But for now, we have to protect Ro—Mr. Calloway. He put his name out there to draw the attention to himself to protect us. As it in my power to see right and justice in this matter, baptizing Mr. Howard with a new name is the right and proper thing for us to do."

"There is one more thing, Addison," Ma said.

"Would you like me to say it, Mrs. Freeman?" Gallant Argyl offered.

"Thank you, but no. It is for me to do." His mother looked at him. "We, the town council, allocated farms to the Negro families and located their plots in the center, near the church. We wanted them in the center to better protect them. We judged them to be the most vulnerable, most in need of protection. Solomon Adler and Mort Nielson objected to the coloreds owning property at all and them getting choice locations to boot. White folks, members of the original congregation should get those choice locations near church, they said.

"Preacher told those two that Negroes were people just like the rest of us, and 'they are more devout practitioners of the faith than some from our original congregation,' he said. Now, all of them were members of New Found Grace Church. Just like the rest of us, they can and do own property here."

Ma took a breath and let it out. "That should have been the end of it, but my husband, your father, got together with Solomon and Mort and convinced them to join him in wresting control of the community and church from Preacher and our Town Council. But the people rejected their proposal. To a man, woman, and child."

Ma looked at him. Addison saw a pained look on her face, like she had a toothache. "We convened the Town Council and decided the three traitors to our crusade would get one final chance to redeem themselves. None of them would be allocated property. Their wives would, however."

"Your mother," Preacher Larrimer said, "didn't want the property in her name. She asked us to put it in yours. She asked us to make your father subordinate to you, not to her."

Too much was coming at Addison too fast. He thought back to that Saturday night in the Spring when he asked Pa if he could marry Lizbeth, and Pa denied him everything he wanted. Now things he hadn't asked for were being dumped in his lap. Things he wasn't sure he wanted. Pa subordinate to him? How on earth did that make sense?

Addison rose and started walking toward the door into the attached kitchen.

"Addison." His mother's voice.

He kept walking.

"Let him go." Preacher.

He exited the gathering house and walked to the church. In the vestibule, he hung his guns on the hooks provided for that purpose, entered the church proper and sat on the last bench.

Back … in Illinois. He'd almost thought *home.* But this was now home. And he owned a farm. And Pa the Switcher was subordinate to him. He was afraid of that last one.

Make your father subordinate to you.

His next thought was he had to go out and cut a switch.

Addison looked up at the seven-foot-tall cross against the front wall.

Honor thy father. *Father God in heaven, forgive me.*

Thou shalt not kill. *Father God in heaven, forgive me.*

Thou shalt not bear false witness. *Father God in heaven, forgive me.*

Keep holy the Sabbath. *I don't even know what day of the week it is. Forgive me.*

Thou shalt not covet. *I still want Lizbeth so much it hurts. Forgive me.*

Behind him, the door to the church opened and closed again. Boots clumped and paused. Something heavy clunked onto the small table in the vestibule. More clumps, and Preacher Larrimer sat on the backless bench in front of him, facing him.

"You are listing your sins and asking God to forgive you."

The Preacher hadn't put it as a question.

"I do that three times a day, Addison, for I have led us all into this holy crusade. And the sins we have committed during our journey here, they rest on my soul, not on yours. And our purpose is holy, for we embarked on it to rid our nation of the abomination that is slavery, and to start that holy purpose here in Kansas. We did not commit any sin for our own gain, or for pleasure. We sinned because in the circumstances we found ourselves, it was better to sin than to let others stop our crusade. I know that in your heart, you see that. I also know you are afraid to believe it because it seems too self-serving."

Preacher smiled, reached out his long arm, and rested it on Addison's shoulder.

"People tend to look at us preachers like a sort of Moses. We go up holy mountains, get the word of God chiseled onto stone tablets, and bring them down again so the people know how to behave. Of course, there are those, like Solomon Adler and Mort Nielson—"

"And my Pa."

"Yes. Like your father, too. Thou shalt not kill becomes thou shalt kill, ever. It is easy to read that commandment with that ever tacked onto the end. But the Book also says, *There is a time for every purpose under heaven.*

"Jesus said the meek shall inherit the earth. Which means the earth will be given to the meek. I think Jesus would prefer that the proud and haughty who own the earth, will give it away of their own free will. But it may be that some have to wrest it away from the proud and haughty before it can be given to the meek."

The Preacher's dark brown eyes, normally hard and cold and hot at the same time, were suffused with warmth and softness. "You are a good and righteous man and blessed with much that we in Found Grace Church have come to rely on. God is merciful. If He can forgive a sinner like me, He will forgive you, my son."

"Yes, Preacher. Thank you."

*****

That night, supper waited till the men from the fields returned at sundown. That was also when Otto Vogelsang called a halt to the day's work on the new barn, located north of the third row of wagons. Addison told his Pa, "You and me—"

"You and I," Ma cut in. "You've been associating with some rough men, and you've picked up some of their speech. Speak properly and set an example for them."

Addison nodded. "You and I, Pa, will be doing the cooking and cleaning up." He looked at Ma. "If that's all right with you, Row Boss."

"We'll take turns," Ma said. "Addison you do breakfast. Adolph, lunch. I'll do supper."

"That way we get one decent meal a day," Addison said.

"Don't be a wiseacre, son."

Maurice the Wiseacre. It seemed like years since he'd seen his friend.

"Any word from Mr. Reedley?" Addison said.

Ma answered, and this felt strange. Before the Holy Crusade began, Addison sat quietly while Ma and Pa conversed about the weather, crops, the chickens, church, and neighbors. Addison glanced at Pa and wondered if that's how he had looked at the supper table, sort of hunched over his plate and looking at his food, or maybe just down, mindful of many speak-only-when-spoken-to switchings.

"Yes," Ma said. "He crossed the Mississippi River at Hannibal. An Emigrant Aid Society boat had stopped there for wood and water. Joshua sent a letter with them for Preacher Larrimer. He had made a fast crossing of Missouri and expected the same of Illinois, and if the Stay-behind Crusaders were prepared, and if the good fall weather held, and if God so willed, and if he didn't have to wait too long for Emigrant Aid Society boats at Hannibal, and if there was no boat trouble on the rivers, the Second Crusade would arrive here at New Found Grace Church before the end of October. He closed with, 'May God watch over you, and please pray for us.'"

Addison expected Pa to voice a prayer, but he continued to look down. Ma was looking at her son with a look that said, *Well. We're all waiting on you.*

Addison sat up straight. "Father God, Lord of heaven and earth, thank You for all the blessings You've bestowed on our crusade to get us to our new home. Please abide with our brother Mr. Reedley and the rest of our brothers and sisters as they travel to rejoin us. Please take care of Mr. Reedley's **Ifs**."

"Amen," Ma said.

Pa sat looking down.

"Adolph!" Ma said.

"Amen," he said, quiet as a mouse tiptoeing past a cat sleeping on a kitchen chair in front of the mousehole.

*****

As First Row Boss, Ma was responsible for ringing the church bell at horseshoe whanging time. She took Pa with her and had him yank on the rope. The bell was rung at noon also. It signaled *stop work, say the prayer, eat.* And it rang again a half-hour before sunset, summoning those working in the fields to return to Brotherton.

That morning, when the bell clanged sleep away from the crusaders, Addison was already up and frying bacon. Breakfast duty prevented him from attending the morning prayer service. That worried him. He figured he needed morning prayer service more than most of the other citizens of Brotherton, and he looked forward to settling into his new home, into this closer-knit community. Closer knit because of the dangers they'd faced and still faced further into the future than he could see. Breakfast duty held him outside his new home, Brotherton, kept him from being a brother to the other citizens of their town. Like he was doomed to be a scout, apart, alone, and on his own ... forever?

Which let Lizbeth through the door into his mind.

The smell of potatoes turning into charcoal roused him from his *Oh woe is me!*

"Foot," he mumbled. The people of Brotherton didn't have food to waste like that.

On the large butcher paper plan in the meeting house, the town of Brotherton was laid out with squares representing houses. Life in Kansas was to be very different from the one back in Illinois. Here there were individual farms, but the farms were run for the common good of the community. And there would be no houses on the farm plots. The farmers would live in the town of Brotherton. All the animals were held in corrals adjacent to Otto Vogelsang's barn. The layout of the town was intended to provide protection from attacks of pro-slavers. If the crusaders lived on their farms, they could be picked off one by one. The animals also had been deemed to need protection. Hearing some of the men who worked for the freight-wagon man Hostetler, when they went on Red-leg raids on pro-slaver farms, they always returned with plunder, including horses, cows, and chickens. So, in Brotherton, the farm animals were community property and kept in the center of the town north of row three.

Three rows of houses had been designated for the crusaders then in Kansas. Outside of town, 150-acre farm plots had been laid out as well. The farms adjacent to the town boundaries were vegetable and fruit farms.

On the Brotherton layout, Addison's farm—and there was a thought to make a man shake his head—was located at the far east end of row one. After breakfast, all three Freemans rode out to their acres, which were located at the far east end of row one and overlooking the flood plain of the Delaware River. For now, the farm would be run to grow crops to serve the community, but "Someday," Addison said, "after we've voted to keep the state free, we'll be able to build a house out here and live like we did in Illinois."

So, Addison asked Ma to pick a spot for the house. She did with a view of the river. Some of his acres were forest and would have to be cleared before they could grow crops, but there was enough clear prairie land to support fields of corn, oats, wheat, and hay. Addison drew out the plans of *his* farm and asked his father what he thought about "The layout of **our** farm?"

Pa shrugged and looked away as if he hadn't heard the emphasis denoting shared ownership.

"Fine," Addison said. "Gather firewood and make coffee, and we'll have lunch."

*****

The next day, after morning prayer, Royal Howard assigned Addison and his pa to the plowing crews along with Preacher Larrimer. The Brotherton community owned six plows. They had plowed fields on the farms starting at the center of the first three rows of plots and working outward. Addison was to plow the winter wheat and oat fields of the far west farm in row three.

When they were dismissed, Addison selected a team of draft horses and hitched it to a wagon. He ordered Pa to catch Outlaw and a saddle bronc for himself. They loaded a plow and a harrow on the wagon and headed west with Otto Vogelsang's men working on the roof of the barn.

Heading west, Addison followed a straight-line road wagon wheels had cut into the prairie, though the farther west they went, the less worn was the road. At their assigned workplace, they found the fields staked out with one marked for wheat and the other for oats. They unhitched the team, unloaded the plow and harrow, and Addison said, "I'll plow. While I cut a couple of furrows, you take the saddle broncs out into the grass and hobble them. Then you drag the harrow."

Addison had chosen the contrary team, and he picked Judas to pull the plow. Guiding him to the stake with the plow skidding on the surface, Addison turned the animal north. "Now get ready. When we set off, I'm going dig the plow into the dirt. You're going to have to work to pull it. Hey up."

Judas took a couple of steps and Addison dug the point of the plow into the dirt. And Judas stopped. "Hey up." The animal leaned into the harness and started cutting the first furrow into Albert Fishbock's farm. It was funny, Addison thought. Judas behaved himself like a good Found Grace draft animal. Pa did what he was told with a sullen, Orson-like *Well, if I have to* attitude.

After cutting three furrows up and down, Addison turned Judas over to his pa. Judas was behaving himself. Pa and Judas plowed while Addison and the other Contrary, Waverly, harrowed. It took three passes to bust up the clods properly, so the plowing stayed ahead of the harrowing.

If Addison hadn't been listening for the noon bell, he wouldn't have heard it whisper, *Pray. Eat dinner.* He heard the evening bell as he was hitching the saddle broncs to the wagon. "If you think this harness is bad, Outlaw, think of Judas and Waverly pulling the plow and harrow all day. If we go with the plow team again tomorrow, maybe you'd like a taste of that harness." Outlaw snorted. "I'll take that as this harness ain't—isn't so bad."

Funny, he thought, as he had a couple of times that day. Ma wasn't really there with them, but she was present to chide him on his rough speech. Pa was really there beside him on the driver bench, but he was farther away than northeastern Illinois.

That day, Otto Vogelsang finished work on the barn.

29.

The next day, Addison and Orson, and ten other men were assigned timber cutting duties. Four wagons and the lumberjacks headed northeast to a stand of timber that, once cleared, would be a farm one day.

When the wagons were loaded, Addison and Orson rode together on one of the wagons. Orson didn't say anything for most of the way back to Brotherton. Then, as they rattled and jounced over hard dried ruts, and Addison bit his tongue. Orson said, "Mariah's with child."

"What?" Addison reined the team.

From the wagon behind, Hermann Vogelsang hollered, "Vye you stop? No wheel fell off."

Addison turned around and considered pulling aside. Instead, he snapped the reins. If he'd allowed the other wagons to pass, he'd have beat Orson bloody and broken bones till his fists couldn't take anymore. But he'd committed to himself that he would no longer hit Orson to force him to shape up.

Orson. The guy just knew Addison's most sensitive spots, and he honed right in on them. Maurice the wiseacre, he might be annoying. But he had boundaries beyond which he would not go. Orson identified boundaries only so he could bust them. But the hitting on even an Orson had to stop. It had to stop, not because he didn't deserve to be beaten, rather because he wouldn't fight back. The most maddening thing about that thought was that Orson probably understood that was his best defense.

Lord, God, You rule heaven and earth. Help me rule my urge to beat the snot out of Orson.

"And you made her that way?" It was mostly a question.

Orson nodded.

The wagon bounced over more hard ruts. The axles and wheels were taking a beating as if they knew Orson deserved one, and they had to step up and take it for him.

"Who else knows?"

"No one. For now."

"God damn, Orson. Just god damn."

*****

That night after supper, Addison walked back to the row 2 wagons and looked up Mariah. He found her washing dishes in a kettle of soapy water. "Will you ... walk with me, Mariah? Please?"

"I have to finish here."

Fine, Addison thought and was about to spin on his heel and walk away. Mariah wasn't his problem in the first place.

The twelve-year-old McTavish girl piped up. "You go, Mariah. Take all the time you want." Then she raised a hand to cover her titter.

Addison wondered who blushed brightest, Mariah or himself.

"Fine," Mariah said.

"Thank you," Addison said.

The McTavish girl tittered again.

Mariah set off toward Vogelsang's barn. At a goodly clip.

"This is a problem you can't run away from."

Mariah stopped and spun around. "My father talked to yours about us getting married. Your father said you don't want me."

Addison came up to her, but not too close. "That's not what I said. I told my pa I had seen you look at ... another man and I'd seen you look at me. The way you looked at the other man, you cared for him. The way you looked at me, you didn't care for me at all. That's what I said. I didn't want a woman who didn't want me as much as I wanted her. I told him that too."

"Oh," she said.

It would have been much better to have this conversation in the daylight, so he could see her face. But daylight, in Brotherton, was for other things.

"Why did you want to talk to me?"

"I wanted to see if things had changed, if maybe now you could care for me. I … I was … I was attracted to you before I saw you look at that other man. I wanted to see if, maybe now, it could be different between us."

"Oh."

"Come," he said. "Let's walk to the barn."

They passed through the row-three wagons and away from the fires. There was a big harvest moon in the east, casting plenty of light on the path. The night air settled like cold hands on his shoulders. He took off his coat and draped it over her shoulders, and before he removed his hands, she reached up and her fingers touched his left hand. A static spark jumped into his hand where she touched. And he jerked the hand away.

He had things lined up to say to her, but he couldn't recall a single one.

"Addison, there's something I have to tell you."

"I know."

"You know?"

"Yes."

"Orson told you."

It wasn't a question, so he didn't say anything.

"And you still—" The night swallowed the rest of her question.

Approaching the barn, someone challenged them. "Who's there?"

"Addison and Mariah," she said at the same time as he said, "Mariah and Addison."

"Courtin'?" the male voiced asked.

"No," she said at the same time as he said, "Yes."

The barn sentry snickered.

Addison blushed; then, he led Mariah to the corral.

His horse whickered and trotted up to the fence. Addison rubbed the animal's forehead and said, "Sorry, Outlaw, I don't have a carrot for you. Next time, though, I'll bring you one."

Then he told Mariah how he'd come to own Outlaw. "I see the hand of God in how Outlaw and me … I came to be together. I wound up being a scout for our holy crusade wagon train. It was a job I knew not one single thing about. Any number of times, though, Outlaw has given me warning of danger. I think this is a holy crusade we are on, and it didn't end when we arrived here, but anyway, God put Outlaw and me together to serve the crusade."

Mariah reached up to touch Outlaw's head, and the horse jerked back.

"Speak to him," Addison said. "Soft and slow and easy."

She imitated his manner of speaking, and the horse allowed itself to be stroked.

"Wait. Did you bring me out here to see if your horse would approve of me?"

"I asked you out here to talk to you. And I wanted you to meet Outlaw. Like I said, I believe God put him and me together. And maybe He means for us, you and I, to be together, too."

"You pick a wife like you pick a horse!"

Outlaw snorted and walked away.

"Mariah. That's not it at all. Thinking about how Outlaw came into my life, I saw the hand of God in shaping how it happened. It opened my mind to consider you and me, to think about what put us together in this holy crusade. I think the hand of God is at work in this. Right now, I … I don't love you, but it's because you won't let me. I could love you. If you let me."

"You have an answer for everything, just like—"

"Orson."

She didn't answer. It hadn't been a question in the first place.

"Mariah, I *do* have an answer for everything. When I make myself be quiet and listen for the voice of God. I wish I could say I do that as often as I should, but that would be a lie. And I won't lie to you."

"This is not at all how I expected things to work out."

Sister, this sure as shooting isn't how I expected things to work out either. But his mouth had just enough sense to keep its lips pressed firmly together.

"Addison, I … I wish I could hear the voice of God, but right now, I hear a voice telling me I should be so thankful to you. Then, I hear another voice telling me I don't need that Addison's pity."

"There's no pity—"

"Shush."

He shushed, and they walked back to and through the wagons and entered the church, dark except for the one candle on the altar table. Addison led her to a last row bench, and they sat.

The walls and roof of the church, seemed to Addison to have sliced a segment from all of God's creation and isolated it for the New Found Grace people to see, to live in, to understand a little bit better than trying to take in the entirety of the creation all at once. He heard the voice of God. *Listen to her,* it said.

"Mariah, would you like me to leave you here?"

She grabbed his hand. "No." She squeezed it. Hard.

They sat together. Holding hands. For a time that was neither short nor long.

"Addison, forgive me?"

"Forgive you. How can I forgive a—"

"Sin against God. That's what you were going to say, isn't it? I will talk to Preacher Larrimer about that sin. But I also sinned against you, and I cannot live with you as your wife unless you forgive me. Will you? Forgive me, Addison J. Freeman?"

Addison John Freeman, killer of men, turned toward the adulteress, so their knees touched, and he could hold both her hands. There in God's house, he told her about Lizbeth and the night he became Addison Job Freeman. "I blamed Pa for keeping me from marrying her, but it was not God's plan for us to be together. It was His plan for you and me to be together. It is the easiest thing in the world for me to forgive you, Mariah. And I do. But I have more to tell you."

He told her about killing men, and how many of them he'd sent to face the final judgment. "You are a healer, a saver of lives, and I am a taker of lives. Can you live with such a man as me?"

*****

The following Saturday, the town of Brotherton stopped work at noon and assembled in New Found Grace Church at two to witness the marriage of Addison and Mariah. Following the service, the congregation presented the newlyweds with a well-provisioned wagon. Addison drove them to their farm. That night they sat on the driver bench with a single blanket around them and looked down on the moon-gilded silver Delaware River.

"With all my heart, I thought I wanted to marry Lizbeth. If we had wed, I do not know what our marriage would have been, but I do know, now, that I wouldn't have thought of it as Holy Matrimony. But that's what we have. A sacred union."

"Husband, since the night in church, I am finding new things to love about you every day. One of those is you can say in words things I only feel in my heart. I feel these things, but I know if I try to say them, my words will diminish what I'm thinking. But you say such a thing, and it shines even brighter than how I thought it. I love that about you, and I love you with all my heart, Husband."

"And I love you, Wife, with all of mine."

The next morning, as Addison washed the breakfast dishes and Mariah dried them, he said, "Wife, shall we walk around our farm? I'll show you where Ma thought the house should be, but you can pick where you'd like our house to be?"

"Mrs. Larrimer said we'd all be living in Brotherton for years to come."

"I think she's right. We don't even know when the state will vote yet. It could be years. But once we do vote and keep Kansas a state where no one can own a Ned or Violet Smith, I believe we will be able to live on our farms, as we did before. We have a dream for Ned and Violet, and we should have one for ourselves as well."

*****

The following week, Addison, Orson, and Jarvis Lindell drove two wagon loads of lumber to Prairietown. There Jarvis traded the lumber for crates of canned fruit and vegetables as well as fresh in-season garden produce. While Jarvis bartered lumber for the crusaders' nourishment, Addison visited Doctor Bennett. Addison hadn't learned his name the night he'd met him at the sheriff's house.

Dr. Bennett ran his practice on the ground floor of his two-story house. He and Mrs. Bennett were setting a broken forearm of a ten or maybe twelve-year-old boy. The tow-head bit on a strip of leather and his face was scrunched into a grimace. He was sweating though it was cool in the room. The boy's mother, probably, sat on a chair wringing a hanky to death. The Bennetts finished wrapping splints into place, and the Mrs. knotted a sling around the patient's neck.

Doc said to the waiting woman, "Now make sure to keep him quiet and resting. Gotta give those bones a chance to join together."

"Cain't I have him at least gather eggs?"

"Not for a couple of days. Bring him back tomorrow afternoon. I'll see how the arm is doing, and maybe he can gather eggs. If he's careful at first. Then, if he's careful, maybe other things. Maybe he'll be a one-armed cow milker. But these first couple of days, keep him quiet. Hear?"

"Okay, Doctor." Mrs. Bennett handed the boy over to his mother, and she put a protective arm around him. As they left the house, Addison heard the mother mumble, "Some boys'll do anything to git outta work."

The door closed on the two, and Doc Bennett stared at Addison. "Ah. That night at the sheriff's house."

"Yes, sir. I was there. I'm Addison Freeman."

"What can I do for you, Mr. Freeman?"

Addison explained about his wife Mariah having some medical knowledge, but she would like the opportunity to learn more. "Could she come down and work with you for a day or two?"

The doc rubbed his chin whiskers. "I could use some help here, and Mama would be free to join the ladies in town for quilting and other women doings. She'd appreciate an opportunity to do that. But I'd need to see how much she knows, and she'd have to stay for a week."

"A week!"

"I see," Doc said. "You're newlyweds."

Which set Mrs. Bennett to smiling and Addison to blushing. And sweating like the kid with the broken arm.

30.

The wagons returned from Prairietown to Brotherton late. The next morning, prior to morning prayer, Royal Howard announced there were some changes that had to be made. Hostetler had arrived the day before with wagons of provisions for the trading post. And news.

Norb Bass had learned the army at Fort Leavenworth intended to send a patrol to Brotherton, take Royal Howard into custody, and put him on trial for the murder of the Prairietown sheriff.

"From this point on," no longer Royal but now Boyd Calloway said, "We decided Molly only has to change her last name." Boyd swept his eyes over the assembly. "Hostetler gave me a letter from Norb Bass. In it, he said Holden, the wagon master of the Oregoners, wanted to stay in the assembly yard until he rounded up ten more wagons, but Norb wanted him gone. An argument followed, Holden pulled a pistol, and Norb shot him. Dead. Norb offered me the job of wagon master. The Oregon-or-bust wagon train should arrive tomorrow, with Norb serving as interim wagon master. He says he hopes I will take over and get those twenty wagons of pilgrims to their destination. I'm going to accept the job. When the army gets here, tell them I heard they were coming and fled north into Indian country with my wife."

Boyd looked at Molly again. "I suggested she stay here and work the Calloway farm. But she said, 'Whither thou goest—"

"One last thing, we agreed that Gallant Argyl will be town boss of

Brotherton, and we've assigned Laurie McTavish and Velda Vogelsang as bosses of rows two and three. Gallant."

Boyd stepped away from the deacon podium.

Gallant took his place. "We've altered the plot map in the meeting house. Royal Howard has been scratched out, and Boyd Calloway entered. We'll tell the army that the wagon train arrived here after an unfortunate accident took the life of their wagon master, and although Boyd Calloway wanted to leave the train and join our community, he offered to guide the train to Oregon, and we promised to hold the Royal Howard farm for him."

Preacher Larrimer, standing at his podium to the congregation's right, said, "Go with God Boyd and Molly Calloway. Know that we at New Found Grace Church are profoundly grateful for all you've done for our crusade and that we will pray for you each and every day until you return to us. Tell them the rest of it, Gallant."

"This was also in the letter from Norb Bass. Provisional capital towns had attempted to establish themselves from Prairietown to Leavenworth. Right now, it seems to be Leavenworth, but the sheriff in Prairietown had been a major driving force in what passes for an interim Kansas legislature. He had bullied several in the assembly to where, fearing for their lives, they were ready to declare the state pro slavery, but his death has taken the wind out their sails for the moment. Thank God, and Royal Howard, for that reprieve."

Preacher Larrimer took over again. "Father God, Who art in heaven, this morning we abolition-ed our brother and sister Royal and Molly Howard—"

Did he mean to say abolished? Addison looked across Mariah to Ma. *Or was that Preacher Larrimer's idea of a joke?* He was sure the incredulous look on her face meant she was thinking the same thing. In all the years she had known the preacher, never once had she heard the man make a joke.

Mariah squeezed Addison's hand, and she nodded toward the preacher.

Pay attention to the prayer. Yes, Dear.

*****

That day, Gallant assigned Addison to work on Otto Vogelsang's house building team. The Brotherton community had decided to erect houses for the Negro members first. A single abode had been completed the day before in row three. Today Otto had two teams working on additional structures in the same row. All of the domiciles would be built to the same plan. A major kitchen and living area, a master bedroom, and a girl's and a boy's bedroom.

The O'Riley brothers asked for a modification: two master bedrooms instead of the current plan.

"Ach," Otto said. "Ve got lots of houses to build before da snow comes. I make exception for you, everbody want exception. No exceptions."

Gallant Argyl said, "Otto's the boss of building houses."

Hermann Vogelsang had Addison and another man dig a root cellar and then help lay a stone foundation. At the end of the day, blisters adorned Addison's hands, and muscles he'd forgotten he had ached like the first time Pa had taken him to work in the fields. But that night, he felt good having put in a good day's work and to come home to a wife and to eat supper with her and lie beside her in their wagon. Fall evenings, Addison thought, were made for a husband and a wife. They settled in with their arms around each other and shared bodily warmth.

The next morning, after prayer, Addison went to work framing the house for Ned and Violet Smith. In the afternoon, he worked nailing the thick, musket-ball-stopping planks to the lower level of the structure. When all the houses were done, each structure would serve as a small fort sited close enough together, so they offered mutual support against an attack. Otto, Addison thought, was a heck of a builder.

Also, that afternoon, the Oregon wagon train arrived at the trading post. The wagon master, Boyd Calloway, asked Otto if his son Hermann could help him assess the twenty wagons in the train. Were any in need of axel grease, new wheels, or outright replacement before they set off on their journey?

"Once we start," Boyd said, "I want to make as many miles as we can before the snow flies."

"Addison," Otto said. "Keep verking. You not help anyone by listening to us talk."

The next morning, horseshoe whanging woke Addison, followed shortly by the church bell clanging.

After a quick breakfast, Addison and Mariah went to say goodbye to Boyd and Molly Calloway.

"Wish you well, wagon master," Addison said. The two men shook hands and Molly and Mariah hugged.

"Wish you were scouting for us," Boyd said.

"He does, too," Mariah said. "But I won't let him."

"Funny, isn't it Addison," Boyd said. "It's a man's world, and then you get married."

"Women allow men that bit of self-delusion," Molly said, and she hugged Mariah again. "And we wish for you God's greatest blessings in great abundance."

"Excuse me for interrupting."

Addison turned and found Pa standing there, hat in hand. "I'd like to go with you, Wagon Master. If you will have me, I could lead your prayer services."

Boyd frowned. "It's up to Addison. That's how things stand here. What do you say, son?"

"If he can be of help to you, sure, he can go."

Boyd said, "Adolph Freeman, wagon master Joshua Reedley said you were no longer a deacon. Addison says you can go. If Preacher and Gallant say you can go, we will welcome you. And maybe I will reinstate you to deacon. Ask the preacher and the town boss and let me know what they say. It's time for morning prayer."

Preacher Larrimer led the minute-long prayer for the Oregoners and the people of Brotherton. Then Boyd hollered, "On to Oregon."

And the first wagon rolled. Adolph Freeman drove the last wagon in the train. Number twenty-one loaded with extra provisions purchased from the trading post, now managed jointly by Jarvis Lindell and Aaron Zerjav.

As the wagons trundled away with the brightening horizon at their back, Addison, with Mariah next to him, said, "Ma. You okay with him going? I should have asked you before I said he could go."

"It's all right, son. There may be salvation for your pa on the trail to Oregon. I sure didn't see any of that for him here."

Horseshoes whanged.

"Ve got houses to build," Otto Vogelsang hollered.

"Ve got fields to plow," Gallant hollered in a voice stew of exaggerated German and irrepressible Scottish accents.

*****

Addison built roof trusses that day.

The next morning, after morning prayer, two wagons filled with lumber departed for Prairietown. Riding with the wagons were, David McTavish and his wife, Addison and Mariah, Orson, and Jarvis Lindell and his wife Cecille. They'd been married on the riverboat from St. Louis, and Preacher Larrimer blessed their union in New Found Grace Church.

Jarvis intended to speak with the owner of the general store in Prairietown and propose that they combine their requirements for supplies from the east. Cecille was interested in learning the store business, and Jarvis intended to ask the store manager in Prairietown to let her work for him for a week. She was a blonde, seventeen-year-old with lively blue eyes that, it seemed to Addison, drank in everything around her.

Gallant Argyl sent McTavish and his wife to accompany the wagons to Prairietown. Mrs. McT and her husband would travel on to Lawrence. There, McTavish would call on the sheriff and the mayor and tell them about Brotherton.

Addison was a member of the party to get him away from the crusader settlement during the army visit. Mariah would spend a week training with Doc Bennett while Addison accompanied the McTs to Lawrence.

And Orson was to serve where he was needed.

When the party departed Brotherton, Addison drove the lead wagon with Mariah beside him. Orson rode ahead of them a hundred yards.

Addison watched his erstwhile aggravator. *Funny.* There were times when he'd been ready to shoot the guy. But here he was with Mariah beside him. As Wife. And he owed that to Orson.

"Husband, I can feel you lifting heavy thoughts around. And I see you staring bullets at Orson."

"Already you read my mind."

"No. I don't know what you are thinking. I just know you are."

"I was thinking God works in mysterious ways." He turned to look at her, and sight of her face framed by her bonnet melted everything inside his ribs. "Every time I look at you, Wife, it is as if I fall in love with you brand new and fresh. And I love you even more than I did the last time."

"I thought you might be jealous."

"Oh, in one little, tiny corner of my mind, there is a bit of that, but mostly, I am grateful, and amazed that we are together. How is it I deserve such a blessing?"

Mariah laughed.

"What?"

"I was just remembering Mama telling me to be wary of the smooth-talking boys. 'Run away from them,' she said. But one of the things I love about you is your way with words." She squeezed his arm. "You smooth-talking boy, you."

After they arrived in Prairietown, Addison took Mariah to meet Doctor Bennett and arranged for her to stay with him for a week. Jarvis called on the owner of the general store. Cecille would stay with the owner of the store and his wife.

Addison, Jarvis, the McTavishes, and Orson pressed on to Lawrence, where they took three rooms in the hotel. Jarvis wanted to propose a partnership with the owner of the general store in Lawrence like the one he'd agreed to in Prairietown.

*****

It was one thing to sleep next to a guy under or in a wagon, Addison thought, but another thing to sleep in the same bed with him. Maybe if he'd had a brother. But he hadn't, didn't have one.

Another thing made sleeping with Orson uncomfortable. Addison had barely spoken a word to him since Orson announced, "Mariah is having a baby." Addison didn't want to talk to Orson about that situation. It happened. An adjustment was made. A person moved on.

Because Orson got Mariah pregnant, Mariah's life, and that of her baby, plus Orson's life, and most importantly, Lizbeth's life would have been ruined if it got out. Addison had no idea what Preacher Larrimer would have done. He might kick Orson and Mariah out of the church, make them leave Brotherton. For something like this, and *this* was beyond coveting another man's wife! Of one thing, he was sure. The Penance Pew would not do for this sin.

And then, wonder of wonders. He'd gone to Mariah and asked her to marry him, to save all those lives, especially Lizbeth's, and … he remembered the moment. She'd been pushing back at his effort to convince her, and then she stopped fighting it. She accepted her situation, and she accepted him. And a magic thing happened to Addison. He went back to that morning when he noticed Mariah as a desirable woman. The feelings he'd felt for her at that time seeped into him again, and he desired her again, but fresh and new as if there hadn't been that first time.

And he thought about how many of the fathers of Found Grace Church arranged their children's marriages. The parties to these unions, as far as he could tell, learned to love each other. Their sacrament, Mariah's and his, of matrimony had also been arranged by Father God in heaven. How else on God's green and Kansas' flat earth, could it have come to pass that Addison would love Mariah, with child, and by another man, and find it to be the greatest blessing of his life. And more, once he saw it as a blessing, he understood how much his soul needed and longed for that very blessing.

Another blessing. Being apart from his wife for a day or two, he could really see the magnitude of the blessing Mariah was to him.

"Thank you."

"You're thanking me?" Orson said.

Crap. Addison had meant his thank you for God, and he hadn't meant to say it aloud.

"I wanted to thank you," Orson said, "but I just couldn't come up with the way to say it. None of the words I came up with seemed anywhere close to good enough."

"Just say one word, Orson. Thanks. Say that one word."

"Uh," was what he managed.

"Say the word, Orson."

"Thanks."

"Do you feel it, Orson? Like a great load has been lifted from your soul? That's what I feel."

"Yeah. Like a headache you had so long you forgot you had it, and then you suddenly realize it's gone."

"A reasonable way to put it. And Orson."

"Yeah."

"We don't ever have to talk about this again."

"You mean like it never happened."

"Not like that at all. It did happen. In a few weeks, Mariah said the baby will begin to show. Many of the people will figure she ... and I *canoodeled* before the sacrament. Something sure as shooting happened all right. And the folks can think what they want. You thanked me, and I thanked you. We both had something to be thankful for. Now we let it lie. And we move on. We already said all that needs saying. From now on, we don't talk about it anymore. Ever."

Orson humphed.

"Were you trying to sound like the wagon master?"

"No. I was trying to sound like *YOU,* trying to sound like the wagon master."

You're a piece of wor—"

Addison stopped. He knew he would not get the last word in on Orson. He rolled onto his side, his back to the Aggravator and didn't say goodnight. Orson did, though.

Addison hoped to high heaven he wouldn't reach across the bed in the middle of night looking for an are-we-really-married reassurance bed-hug.

31.

The law in Lawrence was not called sheriff. Marshal Eustice Crabtree joined the McTavishes in the hotel dining room for breakfast.

Crabtree was a mite under six feet. Once Addison realized some of the man's bulk across the chest was due to a pistol in a shoulder holster slung under each arm, he figured the lawman was close to skinny. He stood straight as a rake handle. He dressed fancy. Flat brimmed black hat, long suit coat, over a white shirt with a ribbon tie knotted into a bow, black trousers, over shiny black boots. His complexion was sun-browned. As the marshal approached the table, David McTavish rose and gestured Addison and Orson to their feet.

When McTavish introduced him to his wife, Crabtree's eyes smiled more than his face did. Then, Addison was introduced, and the warmth in the lawman's eyes evaporated. Those brown eyes grew hard and cold as they measured. Measured, assessed, judged. They shook hands.

The same thing happened with Orson.

After they were all seated, a waitress appeared and poured coffee into cups on saucers.

"Menus on the chalkboard there." She hooked a thumb over her shoulder.

Mrs. McTavish ordered one egg. The men all ordered substantial meals. When the orders came, Mr. McTavish cut off a piece of ham and shared it and a half piece of bread with his wife. It was quiet then, save for the clink of silverware on plates, as if the men's stomachs needed to be convinced food was on the table before the mouths would be enabled to speak.

Crabtree chewed, swallowed, dabbed his lips with his napkin, swiped the napkin over his mustache, and sipped coffee. "So, Mr. McTavish. You all filed for incorporation of Brotherton into the county?"

"No, sir. Not yet. Not quite sure how we do that."

"After we finish breakfast, I'll take you to meet our town lawyer. He can advise you. And I wouldn't dawdle. The sheriff in Prairietown is expected to be replaced any day now. And I'd bet a flapjack against a hundred dollars, the new sheriff will be pro-slavery just like the last one."

The marshal went on to explain that the state had struggled with setting up a state government, where to set it up, and who would be representatives to this legislative body. "Right now," he said, "Leavenworth acts like it's the center of power. The Army is there, and everybody recognizes the Army. The deceased sheriff killed a free-stater spokesman in a duel outside of Leavenworth, and he intimidated the other free-staters. A vote was scheduled for the week after he was killed. If he hadn't been killed, the second half of your Holy Crusade would have arrived in the slave state of Kansas.

"Now, the men who would govern us are about equally split on the issue of free versus slave state. All they are able to do is talk themselves red in the face. Neither side will bend."

The marshal sipped his coffee and brushed the bottom of his mustache with a finger. "Pro-slavers will view Brotherton as tipping the scales from favoring them to not favoring them. It is imperative that you get your settlement incorporated as a town, and that you maintain a posture of vigilance and readiness to fight. You all, whether you want to be or not, are in a war."

*****

The McTavish party stopped in Prairietown to rest the horses. The others ate while Addison went to see Mariah.

Main Street, Second Street, and The Other Street comprised

Prairietown. Doc Bennett's house was on second. Addison and Mariah walked south down Second Street,

"Mariah, last night, away from you felt like a hundred years. I mean, we've only been married a handful of days, but, in a way, it seems like my whole life."

"Oh, Addison, your idea, that I come and work with Doctor Bennett, it was … wonderful. I learned so much from him."

Addison winced. He wanted her to have missed him as much as he had missed her. "Some of Doc Bennett's men patients didn't want 'No woman doctorin' on them.' Doc said, 'If you want doctoring, Mariah will do it and I'll watch. Otherwise, ride to Lawrence.' Well, it was funny. They wanted to cuss but couldn't in front of a woman. So, they mumbled, and I tended to them. I learned so much yesterday and this morning."

"Well then, you can come back with us now."

"Silly. The doctor expects me for five more days."

They reached the end of the houses and cut east across a no-name connecting street, and headed back up The Other Street.

"Addison, I miss you, too, but—"

He stopped, took her in his arms, and kissed her with an entire lonely night's worth of denied passion.

After a moment, she put a hand on his chest and pushed gently, and he let her go.

"One of us, Husband, needs to maintain a sense of decency here."

They started walking again.

"Wife."

"Yes, Husband."

"I understand why Adam couldn't stop himself from eating the apple."

She squeezed his arm.

It took all his will power to keep from kissing the heck out of her right there in the middle of the street.

"Faith, hope, and love," he said. "I also understand why the greatest of them is love."

*****

Addison threw himself into building houses when told to build and threw himself into plowing and planting when told to plow. He hoped the work would take his mind off how much he missed Mariah. It didn't work. During the day he ached for her. He called the hours of darkness Job nights.

But even Job nights came to an end. The blessed morning arrived when he could ride to Prairietown and retrieve Wife. However, before it was over, the morning turned into Job morning instead of blessed.

The morning prayer had become a fifteen-minute affair. Thanking and praising God for bringing the crusaders safely to Kansas required more time than had been the case with the *Please God Get Us There* prayer chopped short by "On to Kansas!"

After the *looong* prayer, town boss Gallant Argyl had words to say. "Ziggy Hostetler, as you know, arrived yesterday with supplies for the trading post. Plus, one wagon load for the general store in Prairietown. Today, Jared Edgewood will drive the wagon there."

Jared 3rd? Addison hadn't thought about him since they disembarked in Atchison.

The party headed for Prairietown would include a load of lumber. And Winifred Edgewood. She'd ride in the wagon with her husband. Once they arrived, she intended to ask Doctor Bennett if she could take Mariah's place as his assistant. Orson was also going. Addison Freeman was master of the two-wagon train.

Gallant concluded the morning business, and the members of New Found Grace Church, the citizens of Brotherton, filed out of the house of worship and gathered in the lot. Those part of the wagon train climbed aboard or mounted, and then everyone turned toward Addison.

Oh. They expected ON TO PRAIRIETOWN or some such.

"It's durned near sunup. Hey up the teams fore the deadly sin of sloth catches us."

Mounted and holding the reins to Outlaw, Orson rolled his eyes.

Heat rose over Addison's face. *Next time he'd just say Go.* He started walking toward his horse when Violet Smith grabbed his arm.

"You ain't gonna fergit to ask that Doc Bennett 'bout me, Mist' Addison?"

"I won't forget on one condition. You have to say my name without the mister in front."

"Uh … Addison, you be asking that Doc fer me?"

"I'll ask him, Mrs. Smith."

"How come I be Mrs., but you cain't be Mistah?"

"I've explained it to you a number of times."

"Still don't make no sense, though."

"Uh, Addison," Orson said, "we're wasting a lot of daylight."

The wagon master jerked the reins from the Aggravator and slapped his horse on the haunch, and his mount shot forward. Scouting ahead, that was Orson's job.

Jarvis Lindell drove the second wagon. Addison told him to hold up and tied Outlaw to the rear; then, he climbed up onto the bench to sit beside the driver.

Jarvis' face wore a smirky smile.

"What?" Addison demanded. Though he was sure of what was going on. That day back in Illinois, just short of Alton, when he had looked down his nose at Jarvis. Jarvis finally got to snicker at wagon master Addison Freeman.

Jarvis hey up-ped the team and shrugged. He settled his team enough in trail to allow the light westerly breeze to ease the dust rising behind wagon one to the side.

"Do you know what's come over Jared 3rd and his wife?"

"Some. From Cecille. Which she got from Winifred."

Orson was no longer in sight. He'd ridden hard to get well in front of the wagons; then, he'd stop and wait and listen before running ahead again.

"According to Cecille, Winifred and Jared were shocked by the ambush at the Delaware River. That those men would have killed and scalped women and children changed their minds. Seeing Violet and Ned Smith firing pistols at the bushwhackers also affected them. They had never heard slavery called an abomination before, but they believed Preacher Larrimer after that night along the river.

"And I've seen Jared working right alongside the colored men both building in town and plowing fields. He does his share."

Jarvis was driving Contrary Team. He snapped the reins. "Hey up, you lazy flea bags. I'd shoot you and eat you for supper, but you're too damned lazy to taste good. Hey up."

"I don't call them contrary anymore," Addison said. "They're good, strong horses. They just don't like to feel like they are doing all the work while the lazy driver sits on his backside and dozes."

"Well, they're still contrary to me. One other thing Winifred told the women. When her father-in-law made them ride in steerage on the *Belle of St. Joseph,* she was so mad at Jared 2nd. But after the ambush, she began to appreciate the lesson she wasn't going to learn any other way."

"Huh. Almost as amazing as what happened with—"

"Orson? You were going to say Orson, right?"

"Stop the wagon. Time I got to guarding our rear."

*****

In Prairietown, Addison pushed to get the lumber unloaded quickly and head back to Brotherton with Mariah. Doc Bennett wanted them to eat before they left. Mrs. Bennett wanted to feed them. Mariah overruled Addison, so they ate together.

Doc Bennett was happy to have another assistant in the person of Winifred Edgewood. Mrs. Bennett was even happier. She would be able to continue her reentry into female society.

Supper was served in the gathering hall next to the church. Four tables of town and church people attended with their guests scattered among the tables. Addison and Mariah sat at the table with the mayor. Once grace was said, and everyone had begun eating, the mayor said, "Mr. Freeman, please convey to your compatriots up at Pott's Trading Post, we appreciate the service you all have rendered in delivering merchandise to our general store. Before, many of the wagons from Kansas City got waylaid by bandits. Some of us surmised that our former sheriff was more interested in those bandits being fed than he was in our own citizens getting what they, we, needed."

The mayor forked mashed potatoes and gravy in his mouth, swiped both sides of his mustache with his napkin, and swallowed. "We received word that a new sheriff has been appointed. Name of Malichi. Pro-slavery, but we are hoping he's not so zealous in his commitment to that … cause as his predecessor. At any rate, the more reliable flow of supplies via the trading post has earned you some free-stater support among the citizenry here. We expect the sheriff will be mindful of the concerns of the people who appointed him, but we pray he will also bear in mind the concerns of the people he lives among."

*****

With the plowing and planting chores completed, including those fields assigned to the second half of the Holy Crusade, work on the houses in Brotherton proceeded at a rapid pace. Hermann Vogelsang oversaw crews of cellar diggers and foundation layers while his father supervised the carpenters.

When he and Mariah returned from Prairietown, Addison found his house completed at the east end of row one, which had been named Main Street. That night, his ma insisted on sleeping in the wagon.

"But there's two bedrooms, Ma."

"Your first night in *your* new house with a new wife, I'll sleep in the wagon."

"Mrs. Freeman," Mariah said. "You sleep in the house. We'll take the wagon."

"You'll do no such thing. You and your husband will sleep in your house. Now, I'm the Boss of Main Street, and I have spoken."

Later, Husband and Wife lay with their arms around each other, Mariah said, "We were rather noisy."

"You mean Ma knew we'd be?"

"Yes."

Addison rolled onto his back. "Ma and Pa like you and me?"

"How did you think you and your sister came to be born?"

"Storks brought us."

"Silly. Your Ma and Pa loved each other."

"Loved?"

"Your ma told me about when your sister died. Your father was convinced they'd done something to offend God. He was sure he hadn't done anything, so he blamed your mother."

Judas priest!

Pa. Understanding him some better didn't make it any easier to accept the way he was. And how could he think it was his job to judge Ma?

"Husband." She squeezed his hand. "Come back to me."

He squeezed back. "Father God, Who art in heaven."

"Hallowed be Thy holy name," she said.

And they alternated lines of the prayer until they amen-ed together.

Then she pulled him to her, and they were so very tender with each other.

And fairly quiet.

After Mariah fell asleep, Addison slipped out of bed, pulled on pants and boots, slipped out the back door, and crossed the yard.

"Approaching the wagon, Ma," he said.

"Come," she said. "What's wrong?"

"Nothing, Ma. Not one single solitary thing across all of flat Kansas. I just wanted to say goodnight."

"Goodnight, Son."

"Ma. Tomorrow night you sleep in the house."

"Goodnight, Son.

32.

The first of October arrived with frost on the morning. Work on houses for the second half of the crusaders proceeded with considerable Vogelsang urgency. Construction on first, second, and third streets had been completed. The dwellings on Fourth Street were well underway, with a modification to the original plan. Provisions for a blacksmith and a wood working buildings were incorporated. Colored men would operate both.

Mariah had begun keeping a journal of developments in Brotherton. The first entry:

> September 6. Brotherton incorporation papers submitted to county seat at Prairietown. Gallant Argyl named first mayor. David McTavish named town marshal with deputy marshal Addison Freeman.

Other entries detailed the weekly arrivals of supply wagons from Atchison and of trips made by citizens of Brotherton, including Mariah Freeman's and Winifred Edgewood's weeks of work with Doctor Bennett in Prairietown.

> September 20. Jarvis Lindell and Jared Edgewood 3rd establish a partnership, J&J Enterprises. J&J Enterprises formed business arrangements with merchants in

Prairietown and Lawrence for the reliable delivery of supplies. Wagons from Atchison now arrived at Potts Trading Post every other day vice weekly. Construction of houses on First, Second, and Third Streets complete. Otto Vogelsang agrees to allow some of the unmarried young men to work for J&J Enterprises, delivering supplies to Prairietown and Lawrence.

September 21. Preacher Larrimer absolves Solomon Adler and Mort Nielson of sins against the community. They will no longer be required to sit on the Penance Pew to attend church services.

September 22. Violet Smith departs for a week of service with Doctor Bennett. September 23. Ojibway Jim asked to join the Brotherton community and New Found Grace Church. Ojibway Jim welcomed.

September 24, Ojibway Jim offers to buy Maybell, one of the Negroes from Mr. Von Papenheim's farm in Illinois, for his wife. He will pay four horses for her. Deputy Marshal Addison Freeman ordered to explain to the newest citizen that in Brotherton, people were not sold. "Not even wife?" Ojibway asked. "Especially not a wife," deputy Freeman told him. "White people strange," Ojibway remarked.

September 25. Jared 3rd and Winifred Edgewood depart to visit their children residing with their grandfather in St. Joseph. Winifred will then travel to St. Louis to attend university for medical training.

September 30. Ojibway Jim and Maybell marry. Preacher Larrimer declares that now the town truly deserves its

name. O. Jim gives mayor four horses. "It right thing
for me to do," he declared.

October 1. A message from Joshua Reedley arrives via
Ziggy Hostetler that the second half of the Holy Crusade
would arrive in Brotherton near the end of the month.

October 2. Violet Smith returns from stay with Doctor
Bennett. She carries messages from mayor of Prairietown
and marshal of Lawrence. Both messages indicated the
pro-slave staters knew the rest of the party settled around
Pott's Trading Post were due to arrive later this month.
They will have to attack the settlement and burn it out
before the second half arrives. Whether Sheriff Malachi
will have a hand in the anticipated attack is unknown.

*****

Deputy Marshal Addison Freeman won two arguments with Marshal
David McTavish. Jibway Jim should be appointed deputy marshal. He
was. The town's two deputy marshals should scout for possible pro-
slavery invaders. McTavish wanted to send twenty men looking for the
bushwhackers.

"Marshal," Addison said, "we don't know when they'll come or by
what route. Twenty men are most of the fighting age men in Brotherton.
If our scouting party misses them, they could attack and Brotherton
would not be able to defend itself."

"The women handled themselves at the Delaware River crossing
ambush."

"That was wagons huddled in a tight circle. Now we have a town
sprawled all over acres and acres. It'll take more defenders to protect
Brotherton."

"But we ambushed the ambushers at the Delaware."

"Because Jibway found where they were going to hunker down for
the night."

"And you and Jibway want to scout for them by yourselves?"

"I wouldn't say we want to, Marshal. I'd say we have to."

Jibway said, "We find." He hooked his thumb at Addison. "Him pretty good Injin."

The arguments took place after morning prayers concluded and most of the citizens had left the church. Addison and Jibway Jim and their wives stayed to talk to Gallant Argyl, David McTavish, and Preacher Larrimer.

"When will you leave?" Royal Howard said.

"Right away," Addison replied.

"You will not, Addison J. Freeman. You didn't tell me you were going to propose this … this—." Mariah had her hands on her hips. And she was mad.

*****

It was noon when Addison and Jibway crossed the Delaware River near the lookout position, still manned or womaned every day. Once over, they headed southeast, walking the horses side-by-side.

Jibway said, "Black woman with white woman ways. I no understand."

"White woman with white woman ways, I no understand," Addison said. "Better say man no understand woman ways."

Jibway looked at his fellow deputy. "Sometimes, Blood Brother, you not as dumb as you look."

"Sometimes, Blood Brother, I think you spend too much time among white people."

"I think we put women back in Brotherton now."

Jibway pushed the horses and Addison to eat miles. They rode their mounts hard for a time, then trotted on foot beside them for a time.

They doused the supper fire an hour before sundown, and they rode on again. During the night, they stopped twice for two hours, taking turns sleeping.

Late the next afternoon, they were trotting beside their horses when Jibway stopped and pointed ahead.

Addison stopped Outlaw next to him and said, "What?"

"Dust."

Once he knew to look for it, Addison saw it. A wide ribbon of faint brown against the hazy horizon.

Jibway led them north in the above the knees grass. He kept checking the dust cloud and finally decided they'd come far enough away from the track the bushwhackers were following. Talking to his horse, Jibway pulled it down to lie on its side. Addison followed suit and removed his hat, but he stayed low, trusting Jibway to be better at concealing himself as he watched the approach.

A good half hour had passed when Jibway pointed toward the approaching bushwhackers. Addison inched his head up. A lone rider was heading right for their position. The bushwhackers had scouts ahead of the party. Jibway pointed again. There, directly ahead of the main party, rode another rider. The main party was a sizeable gaggle. Addison started trying to estimate the number, but he switched his attention back to rider approaching their position.

Jibway lay across his mount's neck, holding his bow with an arrow nocked.

Addison pulled his own bow and an arrow from his quiver. "Still, Outlaw. Lay real still," he cooed. Lying on his back, he strung the bow, nocked an arrow, and rolled onto his belly, keeping his head low. Jibway would watch the rider approach and not be seen. He made his breaths go in and out slow and even, trying to control the juice gushing through his veins that shouted *DO SOMETHING*.

In the corner of his eye, Addison saw Jibway rise and let fly his arrow. The rider tumbled backward out of the saddle, and the Indian sprang forward, grabbed the reins of the horse, and began soothing it.

"Come," Jibway hissed. "You wear hat."

"Stay here now, Outlaw," and Addison glanced to his right, at the rider in distance directly in front of gaggle of invaders. The man's horse plodded straight ahead. Addison hustled to the fallen man and pulled his hat off and put it on. Jibway gestured for Addison to mount the scout's horse and ride ahead.

"You put Outlaw close. This side."

The side away from the rider to their left. At the distance separating them, he might not notice the extra horse. Unless he used binoculars.

Addison climbed into the saddle, got Outlaw into position, and started his mount walking. He checked on the man to his left. He still plodded along. Apparently, he hadn't noticed anything up there on the north flank.

The man Jibway had shot had two dragoon pistols slung from the saddle horn plus a long gun in a scabbard. Addison checked the loads of the dragoons. Satisfied, he re-holstered the big pistols. He was not satisfied with the dead man's hat, however. It was too big, and were it not for his ears, the thing would cover his eyes. Plus, the white hat was heavily sweat stained above the brim and felt oily on his forehead. But his own hat was black. He had it strung from the saddle horn with the pistols. He reached across Outlaw and pulled his own rifle. He trusted it. Rather he trusted it more. Trust was a thing of degrees, whether it had to do with trusting a man, or a woman, or a gun. Only after the trigger was pulled and the gun fired was it right to say it was right to trust.

Rider-to-the-left plodded along.

The sky was clear and Kansas blue. A gentle breeze fanned the tall grass, rippling it like the surface of a pond. The horses' hooves didn't make much noise. The prairie didn't either. Not like a forest alive with bird and bug noises and tree rats and scurrying ground beasts. Ahead, a hawk glided, dead silent, on stretched out wings, searching for supper.

Also ahead, Addison saw a line of small trees, probably a small stream, lined with saplings. If the gaggle behind him were a wagon train, it'd be a good place to rest and water the animals.

When he arrived at the stream, he dismounted and allowed the horses to drink while he went upstream a pace or two and refilled his canteen, drank and, relieved himself. Then he mounted and walked the dead man's horse through knee-deep water. He came out of the saplings, and more unadulterated prairie stretched before him. He checked to his left. Nothing.

Maybe rider-to-the-left was still watering his horse.

Addison had another thought and recrossed the stream and saw rider-to-the-left hightailing it back toward the gaggle. He'd finally figured out something had happened to his flank rider.

Jibway wanted to get behind the gaggle of invaders to count them. Did he have enough time for that? *Probably.* If so, he'd have ridden north a bit to get well clear of them, then race for Brotherton to warn them.

What will the invaders do?

Would they know about Jibway?

Maybe not. Jibway had left the man with an arrow in his chest and scalped. They could conclude that Addison was a lone Indian who'd ambushed the flank rider to steal his horse, then took his place looking for an opportunity to steal more.

If Reedley were leading the invaders, what would he do?

Reedley would want to know if his flank rider had been ambushed by a single Indian or if more of them were in the vicinity. He'd come himself with one other man he could count on.

The invaders will send their most experienced frontiersman with one other.

These two would most likely follow Addison's trail. They might ride hard either to the north or south of him and try to get around him. But that would take time. No. They would pick up his trail and follow it. They'd find the man Jibway had killed and scalped. They'd see sign that there'd been two Indians.

Jibway. What would his blood brother do?

He would expect men to come and see what happened to their flank rider. Jibway would head north for a bit, then cut east and get into position to count the invaders. Once he'd determined the size of the army, he'd hightail it back to Brotherton and warn them. He'd expect Addison to take care of himself.

Addison considered riding back to Brotherton. Even if he could arrive before Jibway, all he could tell them is: *They are coming.* Which they already knew. He decided to stay where he was, for the time being, watch for those hunting him and see if he could kill the invader's Joshua Reedley.

Addison kept the horses hidden in the trees, and he fashioned a spear from a sapling and gigged two frogs, skinned them, and started a small fire. After roasting the legs, he ate and doused the fire. Then he waited. Not long, though. Four men followed his trail. With his binoculars, he figured out which one was the enemy Joshua Reedley. He rode a big black, probably a hand taller than the other broncs. Just out of rifle range, Enemy Reedley stopped his mount, raised binoculars, and aimed the glasses right at where Addison hid.

Enemy Reedley lowered the glasses, pointed north and one of his men galloped in that direction. He sent another south. Enemy Reedley trailed the northbound man, while the fourth man trailed the southbound.

Addison wanted to kill Enemy Reedley, but taking him down when there'd be two of them? It'd be tough. He decided to go after the southbounders, hustled back to his horses, and pushed them hard just clear of the saplings. When he figured he'd gone far enough, he reined up, and leading the horses into the trees, left them there, crossed the stream with the two rifles. He could hear the two riders slow from a gallop.

At the edge of the trees, Addison parted the chest high brush and spotted both riders headed toward him. Southmost was to his right and well within rifle range. The other was a long shot. The other concern was Enemy Reedley. What was he doing? One thing for sure, using time to his advantage. Addison cocked the dead man's long gun and laid it on the ground at his feet. Then he took his own rifle, and steadying it against a sapling, aimed at the man to his left. He adjusted his aim up a tweak, took a breath, held it, and squeezed the trigger. Without waiting to see if he hit his target, he dropped his rifle and picked up the other one. Southmost rider was pulling his long gun from its scabbard. Addison aimed, fired, and the man tumbled out of the saddle.

Addison glanced back toward his original target. The man's horse was galloping back toward the enemy army. No sign of the man.

No time to dawdle either. He gathered up the rifles and hustled back to the horses, where he loaded his rifle and mounted Outlaw and set off northwest at a run. Glancing behind, he spotted the big black burst from the saplings and charge after him.

"Outlaw," he said, and the animal kicked up the pace.

Addison headed northwest, for Brotherton. Glancing behind him,

Enemy Reedley headed west, giving the pursuer an angle of advantage. He turned Outlaw toward Prairietown, taking away the angle. The big black was still closing. Addison's arm holding the reins to Dead Man's horse was straight behind him, slowing Outlaw. Addison considered dropping the reins to the other animal but was sure the black would still overtake them.

New plan.

Addison pulled his long gun, waited until the black closed to just inside rifle range, and said, "Whoa!"

Outlaw squatted on his hind legs and skidded to a stop. Addison jumped down and raised his rifle. He was breathing hard and had trouble holding the gun steady. Enemy Reedley was stopping his mount, too, but it was taking him longer. Addison lowered his weapon, took a big breath, huffed it out, raised the gun, aimed when Enemy Reedley fired. Addison dropped to the side and a bullet zipped by, close over his head.

Now while he's reloading.

Addison raised the gun again, steadied it, and started squeezing the trigger when his target fired again. Again, Addison ducked to the side and a bullet plowed into the grass where he'd been.

That guy sure reloads fast!

New plan.

Addison rolled to his right and stood up. There was Enemy Reedley switching his aim to right at him. Addison ducked as the man fired again. This time he stood up as soon as the bullet *thwipped* past. He exhaled, held his breath, aimed, and squeezed. Enemy Reedley was raising his rifle when he lurched backward, then fell. Addison reloaded, watching for the man to rise again. But he didn't.

Holding his long gun, Addison mounted Outlaw and looked for signs of Enemy Reedley. The big black stood still, ground hitched. The grass didn't move.

The fourth guy! Haven't seen him for a long time.

The immediate danger, though, was Enemy Reedley. He nudged Outlaw into motion and walked the animal toward the big black. There he found Enemy Reedley lying on his back, open, unblinking eyes staring at the blue Kansas sky as if he was sure going to miss seeing that.

Addison's bullet had struck the man in the throat.

Lucky! Then he had another thought. *Thank You, Father God, of heaven and earth! Even God of Bloody Kansas.*

"Addison." From behind him. He spun around, raising his Navy Colt.

Jibway stood there, his hands raised.

"Jesus!"

"No. I Jibway Jim."

Addison started laughing, the tension gushing out of him; then he remembered. "There was a fourth man."

"He with ancestors."

Enemy Reedley's long gun was a breech-loader.

"Ziggy Hostetler want buy this kind rifle."

"If more of the raiders have them, we'll have a fight on our hands at Brotherton."

"Maybe some of raiders have. But this is only one I see." Jibway held the rifle out to Addison. "You take. I take black horse."

His blood brother had asked a question. Addison nodded.

They returned to the sapling bordered stream and collected the horses and weapons of all their victims. "You ride Brotherton. Tell them raiders come." Jibway flashed all ten fingers eight times.

"Eighty men!"

Jibway flashed his fingers again. Indicating seventy this time. "Maybe this many when they get to Brotherton."

Addison led the string of captured horses roped in trail, and all carrying long guns and pistols and powder and shot. He headed northwest. His blood brother rode the big black north along the stream. The raiders, Addison knew, were due to lose more men.

33.

Mariah was mad at him.

"Why are you mad at me?" Addison said. "I was only gone two days. You were gone a whole week."

"But I was in Prairietown with Doctor Bennett. You and the Indian were out sneaking around in the brush, killing men who were trying to kill you."

"Mariah—"

"You brought back six horses. Six men were trying to kill you."

"Jibway—"

"He didn't kill all of them! I know that's not true."

"I wasn't going to say that. Jibway taught me a lot. Joshua Reedley taught me a lot. I am not helpless out there. But these people want to kill us. All of us, including you and Baby."

She cried then, and that was worse than her being mad. He lay there on his side of the bed staring at the ceiling, wanting her, aching for her. Second most, he ached for sleep. Two days with nothing but short naps holding the reins to Outlaw, expecting him to sense danger. Sleep, though, was out of the question. He ached for her so much, sleep could not happen. She was mad at him, so loving her could not happen. Addison Job Freeman. He was him again.

"Hold me," she said.

"Uh—"

"Men!" She rolled over against him. "Hold me."

He rolled onto his side and put his arm around her, and she pulled him close. Then she cried again, softly. Caressing her back, he spoke to her, like he did to Outlaw when he needed to quiet it.

Her crying stopped. He thought she'd fallen asleep, but she said, "Addison." And A. Job Freeman's patience and faith brought him a reward better than he could imagine.

*****

Jibway returned the next morning. He led a string of five horses, each with a long gun in a scabbard and saddlebags full of handguns, powder, and lead.

After an On-to-Kansas-length morning prayer, Gallant Argyl asked Jibway about the raiders. "According to you and Addison, they've lost ten men already. Have they turned back?"

"Not turn back. Four raiders sneak away. Head east. Chief catch another try leave. Chief shoot him." Jibway held up his hand with all the fingers splayed. "Till pistol empty. Chief big mad. He say burn Brotherton to ground. Kill us all. Then they ride north and kill Indians until they run out of bullets."

"How many of them?" Gallant said.

Jibway indicated seventy. "They split up. Half head north. Cross river there. Others head west."

"Can we ambush them when they cross the river?" Gallant said.

"Must hurry. They cross soon."

Gallant, David McTavish, Addison, and Jibway discussed how to use the limited man and woman power available. It was decided Addison would take eight crusaders south, figure out where the raiders would cross the Delaware, and ambush them. They were not to engage in a protracted gun battle, however. They should spring the ambush, inflict as much damage on the raiders as possible, then hightail it back to Brotherton.

Violet Smith piped up from her pew, "Ned and me. We go with Mistuh Addison."

Gallant had been naming men and young men to go with Jibway

Jim to ambush the north-bound raiders. He shook his head, but before he could open his mouth, Addison said, "I'll take the Smiths. One thing though. I'm going to assign one person to watch our horses when we set up the ambush. If I tell you, Violet, to watch horses, will you give me any sass?"

"No, suh, Mist' Addison. You tell me, I watch dem hosses good."

Addison and Jibway both had eight people assigned to them. David McTavish went with Jibway. He'd be in charge of the other young men and young women on the west bank of the river. Jibway planned to cross the Delaware and trail the raiders, sending smoke signals to mark their progress north.

Addison figured he'd set up his ambush halfway between Brotherton and Prairietown.

*****

From within the trees and brush along the river, Addison couldn't see the sun. It was low above the horizon. He figured the raiders to cross in the dark and arrive at Brotherton at maybe one in the morning.

Dust! He wouldn't have spotted the faint cloud without the binocs. The cloud was well south of their position.

Addison stood to see if he could see any activity on the riverbank ahead of the dust cloud.

"What is it?" Alphonse Carlson said.

"Sssst!"

Addison heard it, faint, but the sound of axes swam upriver.

Probably a raft to bring guns and powder across dry.

"Alphonse. Get the others to move out to the road, walk the horses, don't ride them. Move south of here a quarter-mile, then hunker down in the woods again. Just like we did here. Be quiet and be quick."

"Uh—"

"You got it, Alphonse?"

"Yeah. Quiet and quick."

"And be ready. They may have put scouts across. Move."

Addison picked up his breech loader and hustled toward the road.

Going through the brush would take too much time. Leaving his crew of pilgrims on their own—he hated that. But just then, it couldn't be helped. At the edge of the brush along the road, he checked up and down. Clear.

Alphonse was still forming up the crew. Addison started running south as fast as he could go.

Off to his right, the yellow-red disk kissed the horizon. Legs pumping, carrying the long gun in one hand and a pistol in the other. When the edge of the earth had eaten a clean slice off the molten cookie, he coasted to a stop. Checked behind him. Far enough. He stripped the leaves from a white oak branch and left his hat hanging from it. He breathed in and out. Slow. In and out. Stringing his long gun across his back, he hunkered over to eyes-just-above the belly-high scrub oak and headed for the river. Like Jibway taught him. Every few steps, he stopped, listened, then crept on.

The next time he stopped, he heard whispered voices. Indistinct. Directly ahead.

Judas Priest!

Alphonse. If he and the rest of them came crashing through the brush, it'd blow any chance for an ambush. Addison drew his bow from the quiver and strung it. He pulled three arrows; then he started forward again. The whispering continued so he didn't stop.

Addison could hear them clear.

"Seems like it's dark 'nuff. Why don't they come across?"

"Shut up, Bobby Joe."

"Wisht we could make a fire. Smoke'd keep the skeeters back some. Coffee'd be nice."

"No fire," third voice said.

Bobby Joe smacked his hand on the back of his neck. "Damned skeeters."

Addison had them all located. Bobby Joe stood by a tree. A rope had been tied to it as high as Bobby Joe's head. The rope led out into the river. Shut Up sat cross-legged to Bobby Joe's left staring across the water. Third Voice stood to the left, also staring across the river. He had his thumbs hooked in his gun belt. Him first.

The arrow struck Third Voice in the back. He let out a "Huh" and sank to his knees. Bobby Joe turned to look. Shut Up jumped up and jerked his pistol. The second arrow struck him in the chest with a muted thunk.

Bobby Joe spun around again and watched Shut Up fall over sideways. He started pulling a pistol.

"Was I you, Bobby Joe," Addison drawled. "I'd freeze like a baby bunny just had its nest uncovered."

He froze.

Behind him, Addison heard his gang—hopefully, his—cutting through the brush from the road.

Alphonse appeared first.

"I told you to be quiet," Addison said.

"We was."

Violet appeared next. "You want I should scalp em fer ya, Mist' Addison?"

Judas Priest!

Alphonse gathered the raiders' weapons and horses and tethered them with the crusaders'. He also took Bobby Joe with his hands tied behind him.

Then Addison laid out how to spring an ambush. "Nobody shoot until I do. And I'm telling you, I'm going to wait until they get real close. Then, after I shoot, you fire your rifles, empty one pistol Then, you run for your bronc and hightail it for the trading post.

"Don't think about being scared. Think about how scared those raiders are going to be, swimming their horses and holding a pistol above their head to keep the powder dry. Think about what those bastards want to do us, to our families. Set your hearts cold and shoot them between the eyes.

"And. Do *NOT* shoot until *I* fire *MY* gun."

Addison spread his gang out along the riverbank, just inside the trees.

The big old harvest moon climbed above the trees on the raider's side of the river. Men led horses down to and into the water. When the broncs started swimming, the raiders hung onto saddle horns and held their pistols above the water.

Addison counted thirty swimmers. And one on the raft, pulling it across with the rope strung from one bank to the other. Against all of them, he had eight counting himself, plus a horse holder. All of them had fought in the battle around the wagons at the Delaware crossing when they first came, but this was different. Would they stick? Would they do what he'd told them?

Addison watched the swimming horses and the raft plodding across. The horses were drifting downstream a bit with the current. Some of the raiders tried to correct their mounts, but most just let the animals head where they wanted. *Just get me across.* Addison imagined them thinking that.

He noticed what was happening. *Thank you, Father God in heaven.*

The current was dragging the whole line of raiders to the south. Now Addison's band would face the northern end of the enemy line of swimmers. Not the center of the line, which would give that northern bunch of raiders the opportunity to cut the crusaders off from Brotherton. The raft, though, kept coming right for Addison.

He restrung his bow and pulled all his arrows and stuck the points in the riverbank. The swimming horses were getting close. Addison notched an arrow and let fly at the man on the raft. Then he pulled an arrow and shot a man next to a horse directly in front of him. In quick succession, he fired the remaining arrows. Then he pulled his colt and fired into the face of a man in waist-high water.

That set off thunder and flashes to both sides of him. But no one fired more than three rounds. *Oh. Nobody left to shoot at.* He slashed the raft rope, turned, and headed for Outlaw when Violet crashed into him.

"Whoa. Where you going?"

"Down there. Ain nobody up here left to shoot at."

"No. Do what I said. Back to the trading post."

"My pistol ain't empty yet."

"Violet— Ned. Take her to her horse. Drag her if you have to."

He dragged her.

Addison ran down the bank a piece. Not far, just enough to make sure his gang had run for it. Then he ran for it.

Alphonse had waited for him. Addison took the reins, vaulted into the saddle, and hunkering low behind Outlaw's neck, he started him forward through the brush.

Outlaw busted clear of the woods and onto the moonlit road. South, all clear. North, thundering hooves and Broth—home. Addison reined Outlaw around and gave chase. He counted horse butts. All there. *Thank You, Father God in heaven.*

*****

Pott's Trading Post sat in the middle of a wide-open chunk of land with no cover for a hundred yards all around the structure. From there, it was a quarter mile to the church in Brotherton. Addison intended for his gang to spring the same kind of ambush as they had on the riverbank. This time, though, they'd have to open fire from a longer range. Each of his men, and women, would fire both their long guns. Then they'd skedaddle for town. But, hopefully, they could still cut down the number of raiders the town had to face.

Please, God, I know You already helped us tonight, but it would sure be nice if they didn't recover their raft with all their powder and guns.

He heard the hooves, like thunder whispering, *I'm a ways off yet, but I'm coming to get you.*

Violet and Ned Smith were to the left of the trading post and hunkered down with their rifles resting on crates.

"Violet," Addison said. "I need to know. When I say 'Skedaddle' are you going to cut out, or are you going to do what you darned well please?"

"She be listenin' to you, Mist' Addison."

"I need to hear her say it, Ned." To Violet, "You don't do what I say, you put us in danger. You see that?"

"I do wut you say."

Ned poked her in the back.

"Mistah Addison," she said.

"Get ready," he said.

As the raiders rode toward them, Addison figured them at about twenty. A big guy on big horse was in front. The leader? Addison aimed at him with the breech-loader and fired. The big guy tumbled back and over his horse's rump. Addison's band volleyed as he picked another target and knocked him from the saddle. Another volley. A raider horse's front legs collapsed and threw its rider forward, where he landed, bounced, and layout flat on his back. Not moving. Another horse screamed and reared, pitching his rider. The raiders started milling about. Some of them turned and headed south.

"Skedaddle!" Addison hollered. He started to rise from behind the crate he'd rested his weapons on when he noticed a man in the middle of the milling raiders. He was hollering at them. He shot one of the ones fleeing south in back. The leader. He had to be. Addison reloaded his breech loader, raised the rifle, aimed, and a bullet zipped over his head.

A raider, thundering down on him from the left. He had a pistol in each hand. *Pow, pow.*

Then Violet was beside him firing her pistol at the raider. Addison pushed Violet aside and drew his pistol as Ned fired and knocked the raider from the saddle.

Addison put his pistol atop the crate and picked up the breech loader again. The man was still trying to rally the raiders. Addison huffed out his breath, aimed, and fired.

The leader fell from his saddle. And it was as if the world stopped for an instant. Then it all kicked into motion again, and the raiders fled the field, heading south.

Violet got up, jammed her pistol in the holster. "Why you push me down?"

"I hollered skedaddle and you didn't. Still, I didn't want you to get shot."

"Well, I seed you stay after you holler, and I didn't want you to get shot neether."

Ned said, "I shoulda' lef' boffa' you git your fool selfs shot. You bust your own rule, Mist' Addison. Put us in danger."

"I did, Ned. Sorry. Thanks for pulling my bacon out of the fire."

*****

The gunfire had stilled, but left Addison's ears ringing. Through the ringing, he heard the cries and whimpering of wounded men. The big moon high overhead wasn't stingy with the light it dumped on earth. Three horses were down. More than a dozen dark lumps lay scattered across the open area before the trading post. At least a dozen bodies.

"Violet, ride back to Brotherton. Get ten men and women to come back and guard the trading post. Bring three wagons and—he almost said men—folks to butcher horses. Bring Mariah to tend the wounded raiders."

"Horse," Ned said. "Don' like eatin' no horse."

"Gonna' be what's for supper," Addison said.

In all, there were nine wounded and six dead on the field. Two of the wounded died before the sun came up. The dead were buried in a common grave at the far end of the trading post lot. One of the wounded, a nineteen-year-old named Billy with shoulder and leg wounds, identified the bodies. Their names were carved on the cross beams of wooden crosses which were planted in the mounded dirt.

One of the deceased was Jean Generette. He'd been the leader of the raiders. According to Billy, some of the raiders had been ready to quit and go home when they started losing men before they got halfway to Brotherton. Generette had shot two men who said they were quitting.

"After that," Billy said, "nobody talked about quitting, but some snuck away and went home. Generette was so mad he threatened to shoot another one of us for each man who deserted.

"After we swam across the river last night and y'all ambushed us, and we lost most of our guns and powder, we all wanted to quit. Generette shot another one a us. 'We got loaded pistols,' he said. 'And they's just church goin' farmers. They won't be able to ambush us again.' But y'all been ambushing us steady for days. Course, I didn't say that. I didn't want him to shoot me next."

By mid-morning, the burying had been completed, and the wounded had been tended as best Mariah and Violet could. Some of them had been shot in their arms and shoulders. They'd recover, but she wanted Doc Bennett in Prairietown to see them. They could sit a saddle. Billy, with his leg wound, would go in a wagon along with a guy named Titus. He'd been shot in the back, and his legs didn't work anymore.

As Addison helped Billy up into the wagon, he said, "I don't understand why ya all is being so nice to us. We come to kill you, and you bury our dead ones with a preacher prayin' over 'em. Us you patch up, and if we promise not to fight against you no more, you put our names in a book, and say after Doc looks at us, we kin go home. Yore preacher even said he'd give us this wagon to take Titus home."

"Billy, we won't go attacking you in your homes, but you come after us, and we'll fight. And if you keep your promise, you'll have no trouble from us."

"Ain't never goin' up agin you folks, ever—" Then Billy stared over Addison's shoulder and said, "Bobby Joe. Never figgered to see you agin."

Bobby Joe nodded toward Addison. "He snuck up on us and killed Abner and Zeph with arrows."

"Snuck up on ya." Billy said. "Cause you wuz tawkin'. Damned fool Bobby Joe tawks more by hisself than a passel wimmen quiltin'."

34.

David McTavish lost seventeen-year-old Mavis Fishbock from his gang. Their plan had been to do the same as Addison's team. Once they picked their ambush spot, keyed by Jibway's smoke signals, they'd hide in the brush along the river. Each of them had two long guns and two pistols. They would fire the rifles, empty one pistol, then hightail it back to Brotherton.

McTavish had his ambushers lie on the ground behind driftwood logs. Mavis had stuck to the plan through the firing of her two long guns. Then, at pistol firing time, she'd stood up.

"Most of the raiders swimming their horses never got a shot off," McTavish said. "But a couple did. One of them killed her." McTavish's head twitched and he *tsk*-ed. "By the time our pistols were fired out, the river was full of pandemonium. Horses and riders milling about, men hollering and splashing as they tried to get the horses turned around to swim back across and the horses all anxious to be done with the river and get ground under their hooves again. But we cut out like we planned and rode back to the edge of Brotherton and set up there with the others from town to meet any of the raiders still anxious to kill us."

Jibway arrived at midmorning to report that all the surviving raiders had fled south, many singles, a couple of pairs and threesomes. "Not many left," Jibway said. "Some drown. Not swim good. Some shot. I catch this one."

This one was Harlan Bellman. Twenty-six-years old. A farmer, he said. McTavish gave him the option of a hanging or a parole. In exchange for the names of others who been on the raid. Harlan did what he had to, to win his parole. He gave up seventeen names, two of which belonged to bodies they found. The rest had apparently washed down the river. He didn't know the others riding with the raiders. Generette had gathered them from western Missouri and eastern Kansas, where Harlan lived.

Harlan Bellman was released with one horse and one pistol and no extra powder or shot.

That afternoon, Gallant Argyl asked Addison if he was up for a ride to Prairietown. "If you need to sleep, I'll get someone else."

Addison saw Mariah watching him, frowning. She wanted him to say he was too tired to go. He looked away from her pleading, threatening, pleading eyes. Then he met them again and while looking at his wife, said, "I'll go, Mister Argyl."

Mariah acted like she'd been slapped and turned away and left the meeting house.

"Pick six to ride with us," Gallant said.

Addison asked Violet if she would ride in the wagon with the two wounded raiders. She said she would, but Mariah came back into the meeting house then and announced she would ride with the prisoners.

"Mariah—"

"I'm going," she said. And she did.

*****

As the sun was setting, they arrived in Prairietown and stopped outside Doctor Bennett's house. Mariah knocked on the door and explained about the wounded. While the wounded were lined up for the doctor to see, Gallant, Addison, and Ned Smith went to call on the new sheriff.

"The new sheriff," Doc Bennett said, "along with two deputies, lives in a house at the south end of Main Street."

After Gallant knocked on the door, a man pulled it open. Clean shaven, swarthy, long black hair hanging over his ears, with a napkin tucked into the collar of his mostly white shirt. And he wore a sidearm.

"Gallant Argyl, sheriff. I'm the mayor of Brotherton. Sorry to disturb your supper, but I have something I need to tell you about."

"Abolitionists!" the sheriff said.

From inside the house, chairs scraped on a wooden floor. Addison drew a pistol. Ned followed suit. Behind the sheriff two men appeared, also wearing tucked napkins but under bushy black beards.

The sheriff was staring hard at Ned. "Boy. I'm going to hang you. First, though, I'll cut off—"

Gallant grabbed the sheriff by the arm, yanked him out onto the porch, put his arm around the man's throat, and stuck a cocked pistol in his ear. "Sheriff, best you don't even twitch."

He didn't until Gallant shoved him into the front room and they got the sheriff and his men unarmed, divested of clothing down long johns and tied to chairs. One was called Derwood. He didn't wear underdrawers.

"I don like to be lookin' at that Derwood, Mistah Argyl."

"Go out on the porch and take over there. Send Addison in."

Gallant and Addison sat on chairs facing the sheriff and his henchmen.

"Sheriff. I came down here to talk, to see if there was a way we could live together in this piece of Kansas without trying to kill each other. I have to tell you; it's not looking like we can."

The sheriff glared.

Gallant smiled. "One of the things I could do is make you resign as sheriff, then, if you give me your word you will never again bear arms against us in Brotherton, I'd give you a parole and let you go with a horse and a pistol. Will you do that? Will you give me your word on it?"

More hostile and hate-filled glare.

"Well then, that leaves us with two choices. I can bring Ned back in here and have him shoot you. Then I'd put on your marker that you'd been shot by a colored man. Or I could hang you. Which would you prefer?"

"You ain't gonna' hang me neked, is you, Mister?" Derwood cut in.

Gallant looked at Derwood. His beard was short, so you could see his Adam's apple bob up and down.

"Sheriff," Gallant said. "Last time I'm asking. Can you figure a way to let us live in Brotherton without trying to kill us?"

"Mr. Argyl," Addison said. "These pro-slavers won't change. Let's stop wasting time. Hang him, I say."

"Let me shoot him, Mistah Argyl. I ain't shot me nobody since yestiddy."

"Get a rope, Addison."

"Wait," the sheriff said. Just goddamned wait."

Gallant and Ned slept in the sheriff's bed. He refused to sleep in the bed Derwood had occupied and slept on the floor. Derwood slept in the sheriff's spare long johns.

Addison sat in a chair for two hours, then woke Ned for his turn.

The next morning, the men from Brotherton, and those from the sheriff's office, met with the mayor of Prairietown in the church meeting hall.

The mayor told the sheriff the people in town benefited greatly from their relationship with Brotherton. They would not abide anyone interrupting the steady supply of goods for the general store, lumber, and tools that came since Brotherton was established.

"Neither will the people abide a return to the way things were under your predecessor. We expect you to protect all law-abiding citizens, free and slave stater alike."

It didn't take long for the sheriff to agree to the terms of his continued employment.

After Doc Bennett was finished with those wounded raiders he'd pronounced fit to travel, Gallant and the sheriff saw them off. Each had a horse and a pistol, but no spare powder or shot. Each had two days' worth of grub.

Billy, with his leg wound, would have to stay with Doc Bennett for a couple of weeks, maybe longer, before he'd be able to ride.

The other wounded, Titus, Doc said he'd never walk again.

Titus wished he'd have gotten shot proper. Killed. Mariah talked to him long into the night.

The next morning, Mariah announced that Titus would go back

to Brotherton with them. She would help him find work there. She would help him learn how to adjust to his … state.

Gallant was anxious to return home, and he left Ned and Addison to escort the wagon back.

At the start, Addison drove the wagon with Mariah beside him. She sat on the driver bench with some distance between them. He glanced at her. She stared straight ahead.

It seemed like she'd been mad at him for years. And here he was again, in the depths of despair because of a woman. He didn't even know what he'd done to make her mad. He sure didn't know what to say to her.

He felt eyes on him and spun around. Titus smiled at him from his corn husk mattress.

Addison faced forward again. *What did that funny grin mean?*

Doc had said Mariah sat with Titus all night.

He spun to the back again. "Titus. We have Ned watching out in front of us. Would it be okay if I spun you around so you could watch behind?"

His grin took over his face. "Sure."

He handed the reins to Mariah, crawled in back, and muscled Titus around.

"That all right?"

"Yes, sir."

"Addison."

He looked as if it took brain muscle to get the notion arranged in his head. "Addison. Feels kinda funny. Yesterday we was aimin' to kill each other."

"Yesterday, we had reasons to want to kill each other. Today I have no such reason."

"Me neither."

"Let's see if we can keep it that way."

He climbed back on the driver's bench. Mariah didn't hand him the reins.

Gonna' be a long ride back to Brotherton.

Mariah scooted next to him.

Or not.

She leaned close and whispered. "That was nice. To help Titus feel useful."

"Uh—"

That hadn't been what he'd been trying to do at all. That look on Titus' face, and she being mad at him. She'd sat with him all night. Maybe she had developed feelings for him. Maybe she was one of those didn't like to be with just one man.

Addison!

The voice of Joshua Reedley called him to get his mind on the business at hand. Just yesterday, this road was packed with dozens of pro-slavery men intent on wiping Brotherton from the face of the earth. And he was all worried about whether Mariah was mad at him. He needed to worry about one, or even more, of yesterday's raiders lurking in the brush beside the road. One, or even more, of the raiders had their horse wounded, and he, they, could have made it this far.

Addison.

The voice of Jibway agreeing with Reedley.

Mariah grabbed his arm and hugged it to her, causing the rein to jerk the team to veer right. He straightened the rig in the road again.

"Addison." She was looking at him with melt your heart eyes. "Please don't go where men are trying to kill you. For a little while. Please."

"You're not mad at me?"

"Of course, I'm mad at you. You scare the beejeebers out of me. When there's fighting, you're always in front."

That's when her tears started.

Addison freed his arm, got the reins in one hand, and put the arm around her. Her sobbing her heart out, it was the most wonderful sound he'd ever heard.

Oh! Father God in heaven, You mind putting one of Your angels to doing my watching for me for a spell? Please?

Mariah blew her nose into her hanky and snuggled closer. "If I lose you, it would kill me, too. And the baby."

"Your're gonna have a baby," Titus piped in. "That's wonderful. Uh, and you two need to talk, gist go right ahead. I cain't hardly hear at all."

35.

Otto Vogelsang built Titus a chair with buggy wheels on it. He called it a *klein vagon*. His son Hermann said it wasn't a small wagon, it was an *ein heiny* wagon.

Preacher and Mrs. Larrimer turned their house over to Titus and moved to one on Street Four. Addison's ma moved into their second bedroom.

Lurleen, the young colored girl Orson Seiling rescued from the sheriff in Prairietown, right before the sheriff got himself killed, tended Titus during the day. Two women stayed with him overnight, changing his diaper and cleaning him. Mariah visited Titus every day to check him for bed and chair sores.

A week later, Mariah showed up for her daily visit and Titus told her he and Lurleen were going to be married.

Titus smiled. "Didn't expect that did you?"

"No. No, I didn't."

"That night, at Doc Bennett's, I wanted y'all to let me die. I didn't want to live crippled, half a man. You told me most of what a man is, is in his heart and his head. Living without your legs not working, it's going to be hard, you said, but don't give up on it before you even try."

He looked down at his hands resting atop his dead lap. "'We'll help you,' you told me. He looked her in the eye. "I thought that was hogwash. Even if you wanted to help me, I was sure the rest of your folks here would want to hang me. But you prayed over me. I done no prayin' my own self in a lotta' years. When you wuz done, you said I should get some rest. You got some shuteye, but I tried that prayin' bizness while you slept. Just before you woke up, a voice in my head said, 'Ask them to take you with them to Brotherton.' Which I done soon as you woke."

"Lurleen?" Mariah said.

"She told me how that sheriff, the dead one, down in Prairietown had treated her. He'd have men to his house. They'd talk and eat and drink. Then he'd give Lurleen to his friends, and they'd take turns. Using her.

"Lurleen said she never wanted to be used again. Ever. Still, she thought it would be good to live with a man who couldn't. Use her. So she asked me to marry her."

Titus shook his head. "You folks. I don't think I'll ever understand you. How can anyone be so all-fired good? How can you even trust me?"

"St. Paul was transformed. You can be, too," Mariah said.

"I done been transformed. Two weeks ago, there was no way I'd ever think about marrying a colored girl. It could not happen, but today it can. I told Lurleen, if she wanted to marry me, I'd work hard to be the best crippled husband she ever had."

When Mariah told Addison that story as they lay in bed, she said, "Our Father Who art in heaven, please don't let Husband ever have reason to say that to me."

He said, "Amen," and then, "Wife." And he held her. And didn't use her. But she used him.

*****

Otto Vogelsang turned one of Titus' bedrooms into a gunsmith shop. Every day, Orville, the gunsmith from the trading post, spent a couple of hours teaching Titus the business. With all the captured weapons needing checking, there was plenty for two smiths to do.

Ned Smith and Violet and Jibway Jim and his wife shared a house on Fifth Street. Ned and Jibway attended Mort Nielson's farming school. As did Addison.

"I don't teach readin', writin' and rithmatic'," Mort said. "I teach plowin', plantin', and spreadin' cow poop."

The school was just for those three. The rest of the community's young men had learned by doing, but those three had been off on other missions for the community during plowing, planting, and spreading time.

Norb Bass visited Brotherton and spoke with Gallant Argyl and David McTavish. He was planning a Red Leg visit to some of the men in eastern Kansas he'd paroled. He intended to ask them if they were sticking to the terms they'd agreed to. Norb wanted Jibway to come along with him. They sent for Jibway. He agreed to accompany them but wanted his blood brother, *Addson*, to go also. They sent for him. He and Mariah came. Jibway asked. Addison looked at Mariah. To see if she was mad at him. He didn't think she was.

"Are you leaving from here or will you come home and collect your gear first?" And she walked out.

She was mad all right.

*****

Norb had seventeen Red Legs with him. They visited five isolated farms where the visits pretty much played out the same. A shotgun-toting parolee answered a pounding on the door to find an army in the lot between the barn and his house. The parolee laid the shotgun down in front of his bare feet and the hem of his nightshirt and raised his hands.

"You keeping to the terms of your parole?" Norb Bass wanted to know.

A couple said they were. The rest nodded.

"Best if you continue to do so," Norb said. Then he tipped his hat to the terrified woman behind the man and led his crew to the next farm.

Four days after departing, Addison and Jibway returned and reported to Gallant Argyl, David McTavish, and Preacher Larrimer.

Addison said, "Norb figures we ought to be safe through the winter. Come spring, he doesn't think the pro-slavers will be able to mount any kind of large expedition, like the last one. But there might be small raiding parties, and we need to be on the lookout for those.

"Norb plans to continue visiting parolees every month until the snow flies. Then he'll resume those visits in March or April, depending on the weather. Norb says 1859 should be an interesting year."

"Hah," McTavish said. "And 1858 wasn't?"

"Did Mr. Bass know if the state would vote next year?" Preacher said.

"No, sir," Addison said. "The pro-slavers were pushing to vote this year. They thought they'd prevail, but after the former sheriff of Prairietown was killed, the pro-slavers aren't feeling confident anymore. Now they're dragging their feet."

Gallant said, "So we keep our guard up. As long as we have to. We manage our farms and our town. Each day we are here, we are stronger." He looked at Larrimer, and the preacher nodded.

McTavish said, "We have a steady flow of information from the Jared 3rd and Jarvis enterprise. They have businesses, and an ear to the ground, in Lawrence, Prairietown, Atchison, and Fort Leavenworth. Still, most of our trouble brews up south of Kansas City. So, like you said, Gallant, we keep our guard up."

The Preacher proclaimed a prayer of thanksgiving for the safe return of two of their members.

Addison added a thanks of his own that he didn't have to kill anyone the last four days.

After the communal "Amen," Gallant said, "Oh, Addison, we got word Joshua Reedley, and the rest of Found Grace Church, will be here in the next day or two."

Lizbeth, he thought but said, "Be good to have us all together again."

"Amen," from Preacher.

"I hope Maurice is with them."

"Yes," Preacher said. "Having the Wiseacre with us through the winter, that'd be good."

As Addison left the meeting house, Mariah was leaving Titus' place. They both stopped and looked at each other, drinking each other in. Then she turned and strode off toward Main Street, which ran in front of the church. He thought she was going to their house. "Wait, Mariah."

But she didn't wait, and she wasn't going to their home. She entered the church and sat on a pew halfway to the front. Addison, not sure if she was mad at him again, entered the one behind him. Without turning around, she patted the place beside her. He moved beside her.

She said, "Our Father, Who art in heaven. Thank You for bringing this man, who is daily bread for my soul, back home to me safely." Her hands dropped onto her lap, and she bowed her head.

He wanted to touch her, to hold her, but they were in God's house. There was a time and place for everything. This was not the place for that.

"You're not mad at me?"

"Of course, I'm mad at you. When you are gone, I can't eat, I can't sleep. I just worry Jibway will come back and tell me you were killed. Or worse. Neither of you will come back, and we'll never know what happened to you."

Addison rose, walked to the front, and sat on the penance pew. "Wife. It hurts my heart that I hurt yours. I ask you to forgive me. I ask you to know and understand that I did not and do not, seek this, what to me now has become duty." And then he was flat out of words.

There were tears on her cheeks, and her eyes cut into the core of him, like the midday sun in August suddenly emerging from behind the clouds and melting everything inside him. He wasn't sure he had the strength to stand up. Just enough to speak.

"Our Father, Who are in heaven. Thank You for Wife. Every day she fills my heart with love and joy and faith and hope ... and all good things. Please help me stop— Please help me to hurt her less and less."

She wiped the tears with a hanky. "Husband."

"Yes, dear?"

"Can we go home now?"

"Yes, dear."

*****

Two days later, Joshua Reedley and the erstwhile stay-behinds arrived at the ferry across the Delaware. Besides the ferry, Otto Vogelsang had built three sets of wagon floats, like the ones they'd used to cross the swollen stream back in the early days of the crusade.

Otto supervised hooking floats to the wagons on the east bank, so Joshua Reedley swam his horse across. As he reached the west bank, Preacher Larrimer walked knee-deep into the river and embraced the wagon master.

"Preacher, forgive me. I didn't mean to get you wet."

"Ah, brother Joshua, this is a new baptism for me, and I didn't realize how much I needed one until I saw you."

When the preacher stepped back onto the riverbank, the muck sucked one of his boots off his foot. Addison went in and retrieved it.

Next, Gallant Argyl and David McTavish greeted Reedley with their boots muddy but not filled with water.

"The women have coffee and stew up there beside the road to the trading post," Gallant told the wagon master.

"I'd like to see the town, if you don't mind."

"McTavish," Gallant said, "Would you show him what Otto Vogelsang and his army of builders have created. And by the way, Joshua, David is the marshal of Brotherton."

Joshua Reedley tipped his hat. "Marshal."

"Aye," McTavish said and tipped his. "Shall we, wagon master?"

"Ah. We've arrived at our destination. No need for a wagon master any longer."

"Brother Joshua," Preacher Larrimer said. "We've fought off two attacks from pro-slavers since we came to this place. And we may be safe for the moment. But we will have need of you in the days ahead."

"I will be among your flock, Preacher. And if you, or the marshal, or the mayor, need me, I will come. But I'd like it to be as it was before we left Illinois. The only Reedley you heard about was my son Maurice, The Wiseacre."

"We will need your council, brother Joshua."

Reedley dipped his head, like a small bow, to the preacher.

Then the marshal and erstwhile wagon master rode back to town.

The wagons came across in bunches of three or four. On the west bank, a young man from Brotherton led his new neighbors to food and coffee. After the travelers had eaten, they were led to the gathering house. There they were shown their house of the layout map of their new town.

Addison stayed by the river crossing. He was anxious to see Maurice, and he also wanted to see Lizbeth and Orson reunited. The last three wagons to cross belonged to Agatha the Ruth and her husband, Maurice and his wife Eunice, and the Waverlys, including Lizbeth.

The regular ferry raft at the crossing carried the last of the travelers and the horses while the wagons were towed across. As the ferry neared the shore, Addison spotted Lizbeth standing next to Maurice and Eunice. Maurice spotted Addison and grinned and waved his hat. Addison waved back. Eunice grinned and waved. Lizbeth, a head shorter than Eunice, just stood and stared … at Orson? *Or me?*

Then Lizbeth stepped off the raft on the west bank of the Delaware River and ran, not to her husband Orson, but to Addison. And threw herself into his arms, almost knocking them over. She wrapped her arms around him tight. Addison could feel the sobs shaking her.

Addison thought of the night he had knocked on the door of his old house, but then the property of Orson and Lizbeth, and the door opened, he's seen not his heart's love, but he'd seen Orson's wife. He struggled to get over her, and at times, wondered if he ever would. Now, she clung to him as if her life depended on him.

He pried her loose and, gripping her arms, pushed her back. "Lizbeth. I'm married. We're going to have a baby."

*****

That afternoon, Preacher Larrimer, Agatha the Deborah Judge, Mayor Gallant Argyl, sheriff McTavish, and Joshua Reedley met in the meeting house for a half-hour. Then Lizbeth, Orson, and Addison and Mariah were summoned.

Agatha related that Lizbeth had appealed to her to set aside her marriage. Her father was not a real deacon, a man of God. Rather he was a greedy pawn of the devil. So, it hadn't been a real marriage in the first place. And her marriage was not consummated. On their wedding night, she could not bear to lie with the man her own father, deacon before being deposed, had joined her to in holy matrimony. Agatha had replied that Orson had to be heard before she would render a decision. Also, she intended to consult with Preacher Larrimer. But Lizbeth had made up her mind. She would not live with Orson. If Agatha and Preacher Larrimer would not free her from the false wedding her father put her into, she and Addison would leave the church. And go to Oregon. All that had occurred shortly after Reedley and Addison had returned and deposed Deacon Sylvan Waverly.

Preacher Larrimer invited Orson to speak. He confessed some of his sins, confessed the kind of man he'd been, that it had been right for Lizbeth to reject him. He had changed, he said. Thanks to Addison, but it was too late for him and Lizbeth. "I look at her, and she despises me just as much as she did on our wedding night. If she wants to be free of me, I have no claim on her."

Agatha asked Addison if he wanted to say something.

Holding Mariah's hand, he said, "I am so sorry, Lizbeth. If it had been my choice, I'd have chosen death rather than hurt you."

Lizbeth rose and looked into Addison's eyes, then she turned away and walked out. His heart felt like a piece of it had been ripped out.

Two days later, the last Oregon-bound wagon train of the year stopped at the trading post for a few hours. Lizbeth indentured herself to one of the families, despite her parents and most of the congregation trying to dissuade her.

Joshua Reedley said, "If you're set on going, wait until the spring. Wintering on the trail ain't no fun."

"I'm not going to have fun," she said.

At evening prayer service, Preacher Larrimer opened with a long appeal to the Almighty to watch over Sister Lizbeth on her journey into the wilderness.

Orson sat on the penance pew and confessed to the entire congregation how much he'd wronged her.

36.

I n January 1859, during a spell of reasonable weather, a band of five young pro-slavers tried to burn the church down. The sentries on the road to Prairietown heard them coming and alerted Brotherton. The cemetery south of the trading post sprouted new graves.

Gallant Argyl sent a letter report to the Army at Fort Leavenworth detailing the latest attack by pro-slavery elements. The Army sent a letter back to the mayor and the marshal inquiring whether Royal Howard had shown up. They replied he had not.

During that same respite from winter conditions, Jared 3rd and Jarvis sent a large wagon train from Atchison to resupply Brotherton, Prairietown, and Lawrence.

On March 31, Mariah delivered a baby girl. She and Addison discussed names, working first and middle names of their mothers. They could not settle the matter that night, however.

The next day, word reached the trading post that Lizbeth had died of consumption in the Oregoner's winter camp.

On April 2, Mariah and Addison had their daughter Lizbeth baptized.

At supper after the service, Agatha the Ruth brought the swaddled newborn back to Mariah. "Every female in the congregation has held her. Now she wants her mother." She handed over Lizbeth.

"Last year," Agatha said, "Preacher Larrimer launched us on a *holy* crusade. There have been times when I wondered if it would turn out to be holy or not. But now, seeing the two of you with your baby, it truly was, and is, holy."

Maurice said, "And it'll stay holy, Holy Addison, as long as you steer clear of the deadly sin of pride."

That was the first wise crack anyone had heard him spout since he rejoined the community. He and Eunice were expecting their own baby in November, which seemed to fan the embers of his enthusiasm back to former levels of irrepressible expression.

After Mariah nursed Lizbeth, Addison took the baby, changed her, and put her in the cradle. Then he came back to help Mama to bed.

"You act like I'm … like I need as much help as Titus."

"My ma said I shouldn't let you overdo it. She said the worse thing is for you to feel good enough to plow a field. So don't be plowing, hear?"

She leaned on his arm as they made their way to their room with the cradle at the foot of the bed. He helped her in and pulled the covers up to her chin, then he climbed in on his side. They held hands and thanked Father God in heaven for the blessings bestowed on them and the Holy Crusaders that day. They asked the Lord to receive Lizbeth into his tender care. "Amen."

"Daddy."

"Yes, Mama."

"Last year was filled with so much hardship, so much fighting. On my part, so much foolishness. So much sin."

"We don't have a penance pew in our marriage, Wife."

"I needed one just then. I was hoping 1859 would be so much better, but Lizbeth Waverly … Seiling. Her dying seemed so wasteful. It makes my soul feel empty."

"I feel that too. For Lizbeth surely, but it seemed to take so much for us to get the crusade to Brotherton. It's like I don't know how to live without being scout for Mr. Reedley."

Mama, Wife, Mariah squeezed his hand, and they lay together quietly, listening for the baby.

"I think the Lord will not give us anything to face that we can't handle this year." Papa, Husband, Addison said. And after a pause, "I wonder if the state will vote free or slave this year. I hope they wait a year so I can vote. That's what we came here to do. I'd like to be part of it."

"So would I." Thus spoke Mariah.

Which gob smacked Addison. *But then, of course women would want to vote.* He'd just never thought of it before.

"Tell you what, Wife. When I get to vote, I will ask you who or what to vote for. I'll vote for who you say. And please, God, someday enable Mariah to vote on her own, not have me cast it for her."

"I pray Lizbeth will be allowed to vote."

"Wife."

"Yes, Husband."

"I see the fingerprint of God on our child's middle name."

"Lizbeth Hope Freeman."

List of Kansas Bound Crusaders:

Preacher Larrimer   Deacon Adolph Freeman   Otto Vogelsang

Royal Howard   Oscar Wilson   Gallant Argyl

David McTavish   Delbert Carlson   Joshua Reedley

Albert Fishboch   Solomon Adler   Mortimer Nielson

Sean and Timothy O'Riley

Plus wives and children

Members of Found Grace Church to stay behind initially:

Axel Bosley   Ralph Niedlinger, Norman

Marvin Dinwiddie   Omar Rand, Loraine

Bert Eckle   Rudy Seiling. Orson

Henirich Grossman   Calvin Simmons

Zeke Isaacson   Thad Tamber

Eric Janson, Agatha   Sylvan Waverly, Adele